THE DUKE'S INDECENT PURCHASE

INDECENT DUKES

BOOK THREE

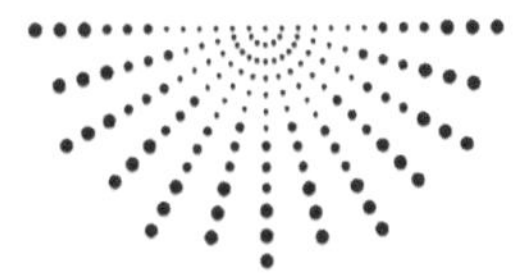

GOLDEN ANGEL

CONTENTS

PROLOGUE

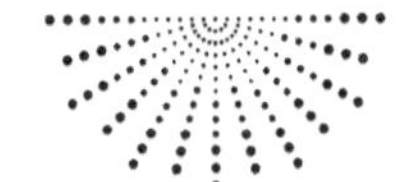

JOHANNA

"There's nothing I can do," Dr. Roberts said, shaking his head and packing his case on the nightstand next to Johanna's mother's bed.

Her mother lay pale and thin, her head turned away from the doctor, eyes closed, as if she had already given up. It made Johanna's throat clog, so she could not even respond to the doctor. His dark eyes were sharp in his wrinkled face.

"If you won't let me bleed her…"

Johanna closed her eyes, shaking her head, though she could not bring herself to speak yet.

"Absolutely not." Rose crossed her arms over her chest, glaring at the doctor and speaking for Johanna.

If not for her cousin Rose, Johanna would have been inclined to listen to the doctor, out of sheer desperation, but her mother had worked with Rose in the stillroom quite a bit. Johanna did not have the skills that either of them had; she tended to get her plants mixed up and certainly couldn't tell the difference between them once they were powdered. She trusted Rose fully, and Rose was saying no.

"She is already weak enough, and you want to make her weaker?"

The way Rose scoffed at the doctor bolstered Johanna's courage.

When Dr. Roberts looked at her, she shook her head again, this time more definitively.

Rolling his eyes, he closed his bag with a snap.

"Then there is nothing I can do here. Since you think you know so much better than I what to do, I'll leave you to it." He stalked out of her mother's bedroom, nose in the air, thoroughly offended.

Johanna doubted he would be back. Not that they had the money to pay him to return, anyway. Just this visit had cost them dearly, and they had completely run out of things to sell. Her neighbors, the Blackstones, had sent a package when her mother had fallen ill, but with a family of five to feed, they'd gone through it so quickly. There was nothing left. And her mother was dying.

Sinking down onto the chair beside her mother's bed, Johanna covered her face with her hands.

"It is alright, darling," her mother murmured, reaching out a skeletally thin hand to pat Johanna's side. "I did not want to be bled, anyway."

"But..." Johanna's voice hitched on a sob. She turned toward the bed, taking her mother's hand. Her fingers felt cool, despite the warmth of the air, and so frail that Johanna was afraid to squeeze them, worried she might accidentally break her mother's brittle bones.

Rose went to the other side of the bed, to the woman who had raised her as her own. Rose's mother had died in childbirth. The bastard of Johanna's mother's cousin, she'd been taken in by Johanna's family when Johanna was a small child, after Rose's father went exploring at sea and never returned. They'd been raised together as sisters, though they could not have looked more dissimilar.

Rose's brown skin came from her mother.

Johanna's pale countenance, which burned so easily in the sun, came from her father.

Rose had black curls and dark eyes, while Johanna's white-blonde hair was stick-straight, and her violet eyes looked oddly colorful on her otherwise light features.

They were both far too thin now due to the lack of food. Johanna was uncertain how the family would survive the upcoming winter. The spring and summer were difficult enough, despite the warmer weather and the ability to grow at least something in the garden. The last of their reserves had been used this past winter, and she did not see how they would be able to stockpile more. But she could not think about that right now. She had to focus on her mother, who she was worried would not survive until summer. Everything else would come after.

"You be good girls, and do not worry about me." A whisper of a smile curved her mother's lips. "I am tired now. I need to rest."

Resting was all her mother did lately. She was wasting away right before Johanna's eyes, and there was nothing Johanna could do. Tears burned as she swallowed the lump in her throat and nodded her head. She glanced at Rose, whose normally fully lips had flattened into a thin line.

They left the room together.

"What do you think?" Johanna asked in a low voice once they reached the hall. Her brother and sisters were several rooms over, playing some sort of game. She could hear their exclamations while they waited for Johanna and Rose to come tell them the news.

"I think she is over her illness," Rose said softly, meeting Johanna's gaze. The hall was dark, but for the lamp Rose held. They had to conserve their fuel as much as possible. "I think she is starving to death. And... Johanna... I think she is choosing to do so."

Johanna closed her eyes against the pain. She'd had the same suspicions, but she hadn't dared voice them aloud. Hadn't wanted to think that her mother would deliberately leave them.

Leave her.

"She thinks she is saving us," Rose said in a low voice, full of sorrow and anger. Not anger at Johanna's mother, but at the situation. "One less mouth to feed."

Johanna straightened, resolve stiffening her spine.

"I am not allowing that to happen," she said, and her words were a vow. "I will find some way."

The house party she had been invited to at Blackstone Manor, in hopes that she might land a husband, had not worked out. She'd been called away too quickly when her mother fell ill. But there must still be something she could do.

Johanna was the sister of an earl. An impoverished one, to be sure, but still an earl. Micah was only fifteen, too young to marry. He had the title, but not the responsibility. That lay within the hands of Mr. Jamieson Blash, her father's third cousin and their closest living relative on her father's side. He was Micah's guardian and was responsible for sending the funds for them to live. Funds that had grown increasingly smaller before vanishing entirely during the winter.

"I am going to London," she said with determination. "I am going to find Mr. Blash, and I am going to force him to help us."

"I am going with you," Rose said immediately.

"No." Johanna shook her head firmly. "You cannot. Someone needs to stay here with the children and mother in case… in case…"

She could not make herself say the words. The idea that her mother might pass while Johanna was away, attempting to save her, was too terrible to contemplate.

Rose let out a long, reluctant breath. After a moment, she nodded, though it was clear she did not like it.

"I will stay here," she said softly. "I will look after them. I'll ensure your mother eats."

"Good." Johanna nodded, letting out her own sigh of relief. "Good. Thank you."

Tears sprang to her eyes again as she and Rose hugged. The warmth of Rose's embrace helped bolster her, making her even more determined.

Somehow, Johanna would save them. Her mother. Rose. Her siblings.

Whatever the means, she would find a way.

CHAPTER ONE

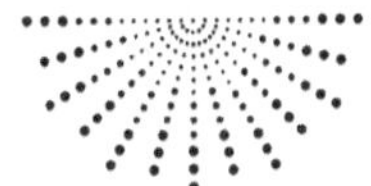

The air was rank. The thin dress she was wearing, the one she had arrived in London with, did nothing to help dispel the chill she felt. Or perhaps the chill was coming from within herself.

Neither of the two men beside her seemed to feel it.

She turned to Mr. Blash, her brother's guardian. Not much taller than her, he was thin with narrow shoulders, but he did not bother using padding. His dark eyes were set deep within his face and topped with dark-grey brows that matched the dark-grey hair on the top of his head, which paled to a lighter grey around his temples. As usual, he was not smiling, but there was an air of anticipation around him.

Johanna supposed there was one around her, too, though hers was more of dread.

"Mr. Blash..." Her voice trailed off as he turned to look at her. There was something about the manner with which he appraised her that had unnerved her from the moment she'd appeared in his London office. Though he'd put her up in a room in a boarding house not far from him for the past few nights while he got things in order— out of his own pocket from the money he made as a solicitor, as he kept reminding her—and all proprieties had been observed, he always looked at her in a way that made her feel like cattle. "Is this truly the only way?"

Even though she'd asked before, she felt the need to hear the answer again, to help steel her nerves.

Her virginity was apparently worth more than enough money to save her family. Johanna could scarcely believe it, yet when Mr. Blash had explained it, it seemed simple enough.

One night, which would ruin all her future prospects but save her family from starving to death. Save her mother from starving to death.

Quick. Simple. Easy.

That was how he'd made it sound.

Now, beside this stage that she was expected to go on in a few moments, adjacent to a room full of the rumbling voices of men— some of them rough, some of them smooth but cruel, some of them laughing—it did not seem so simple. Nor easy. Hopefully, though, it would be quick.

"I'm sorry, my dear, but it truly is," Mr. Blash said, putting his hand on her shoulder. His expression turned to one of sympathy, but his eyes remained hard and glittering in the dim light. "There is nothing else that will gather the money you need quickly enough if your mother's situation is as dire as you made it sound."

"It is." The feel of her mother's hand, nothing but skin and bones, flashed through her mind.

"Then this is the only way. One sale, and you will have enough money to buy food for everyone for the next year and pay me back what I have sent from my own income."

That had been another surprise, an unpleasant one. Apparently, the money they'd received from the estate had not been from the estate at all, but from Mr. Blash. He'd been using his own funds to support their coffers. And her mother was still starving to death.

One night.

She'd be ruined. She would never be able to marry, not within Society.

But it did not matter. It was hardly as though she could find a husband even before this. The Blackstone house party had been an unexpected chance, and she'd dashed that opportunity by rushing off to attend her mother's illness. She should have sent Rose home alone and stayed to try to snag a husband, but...

She'd been so afraid her mother was dying, while she was sleeping in a comfortable bed and eating delicious foods, the likes of which her family had not tasted in months. If she'd known then what she knew now... but she had not, and the choice had already been made.

Now, she was making a different choice.

If it saved her family, it would be worth it.

"It's time," Mr. O'Connell said, rubbing his hands together. If he'd been listening to Johanna and Mr. Blash's conversation, it did not show in his demeanor. He gestured to the woman beside him. "Come on, Penny."

He did not even look at Johanna as he strode out onto the stage. The other woman, who had been standing quietly with them, followed him mutely, giving Johanna a blank look before she did so. It was as if there was no life, no hope, left in her. Neither of which helped Johanna's nerves.

Closing her eyes, she gulped again, wishing she were anywhere but here.

Like at mother's bedside, watching her die?

No.

There were worse things than here.

She could do this.

"Good evening!" Mr. O'Connell greeted the audience. "Who is ready for our special auction this evening? A real, live virgin!"

The sound of cheers and jeers made Johanna's blood run cold, and she might have actually run despite everything, if not for Mr. Blash's hand gripping her shoulder, his fingers now digging in as if he knew she was thinking about it.

"She's a sweet one, alright." Mr. O'Connell chuckled. "A real lovely *lady*, if you get my meaning. The likes that we have not seen since the Tramp claimed his lady."

Johanna did not know what that meant, but the crowd must have understood because the men grew even louder. Her stomach turned over, and she thought she might spew. Thanks to Mr. Blash, there was actually something in there for her to vomit.

The remind of how recently she'd eaten steadied her.

She was doing this for her mother. For Rose. For Micah, Bridget, and Charlotte. So that they could have something in their stomachs, too.

"Come on out, sweetheart, let them get a look at you," Mr. O'Connell said.

Penny moved toward the side of the stage again, her expression dull as she reached out her hand to Johanna. Her heart was in her throat as she took the first step, then Mr. Blash's hand propelled her forward. He let go of her right before she reached Penny.

But she did not take the other woman's hand. She could not. Her hands were too tightly clenched at her own sides. Penny did not seem to care, her hand dropping back down as she stepped behind Johanna, as if guarding her from running away.

Head down, Johanna forced herself to the center of the stage. One step at a time, repeating the reasons she was doing this with each step.

For mother.

For Micah.

For Rose.

For Bridget.

For Charlotte.

The roaring of the men who were looking at her was even louder than the buzzing in her ears. When she reached Mr. O'Connell's side, she forced herself to look up at the crowd. The brightened area of the stage and the dimness of the rest of the room made it difficult to see very far, but those closest to the stage were visible.

Big men. Shouting. Jeering. Laughing. Staring at her with such expressions on their faces that she felt utterly faint, like she might fall over right then and there.

"Let us begin the auction! A real live virgin should be worth at least a hundred pounds, eh?"

A hundred pounds.

The starting amount resolved her. That would be fifty pounds for her and her family, because Mr. Blash had promised them half of whatever she made. He would split the other half with Mr. O'Connell. It was more than fair, they'd explained, since she would not be in a position to make nearly as much without their assistance.

And, indeed, Johanna could not imagine asking a man for a hundred pounds in exchange for her virginity.

But that was Mr. O'Connell's starting point, and men were already shouting out higher offers. More money.

I can do this.

I can do this.

Hearing the amounts being thrown around made her courage stronger.

One fifty.

One sixty.

One ninety.

Two hundred.

Up, up, up, the amounts went, the number of voices shouting them out quickly dwindling.

Five hundred pounds.

Johanna could have cried with relief.

At this rate, she was going to be able to feed her family for the next two years off of one night.

"Two thousand pounds."

The room fell utterly silent. Johanna's eyes widened in utter shock at the sudden jump in amount, from an entirely new voice she could swear was familiar, yet she had not heard bidding until now. How could someone here be familiar? Who could she possibly know?

She knew no one.

But that was not true, she realized as the silence had Mr. O'Connell calling out the final opportunity. The man who was making his way down through the room, who had bid two thousand pounds for her virginity, *was* familiar.

Dark hair that waved back from his forehead, dark eyes, broad shoulders in an impeccably tailored coat, he swaggered with all the confidence of a duke… because he was one. Johanna's mouth dropped open as she recognized the Duke of St. Albans, who she'd met at the Blackstone house party, though when she'd met him, he had been smiling. This was the first time she'd seen him without an affable expression on his face, and it made him appear rather imposing.

"Sold, to you, sir," Mr. O'Connell said, grinning and pointing at the duke. Clearly, he did not realize the gentleman's identity. Johanna stared at St. Albans, wondering if she was dreaming.

MATTHEW

Lady Johanna was staring at him as if she'd seen a ghost. Matthew supposed he could not blame her.

This was hardly his usual surrounds. He'd followed his friend Drake, the Duke of Ormonde, here, trying to figure out what he was up to, as this was not a place he would expect Drake to frequent, either. It was pure chance that he'd seen Lady Johanna and the virgin auction. But that was often what Matthew's life was like—ruled by chance and luck.

It was her good luck, as well as his.

Her family might have fallen on hard times, but that was no excuse for walking away once he'd seen her.

"Right this way, sir," the auctioneer said cheerfully, gesturing. "We'll take care of the paperwork and payment, then bring you to her room. Penny will take her there now and prepare her."

"No." His voice was hard, clipped, very unlike his usual tone. He sounded more like Drake at that moment. Reaching out, he took hold of Lady Johanna's hand and pulled her toward him, threading her arm through his. "She stays with me."

"I… ah…" The auctioneer blinked in surprise, apparently flummoxed. Then he shrugged his shoulders, as if to say there was no explaining the quirks of the aristocracy. It would hardly matter to him as long as he was paid. "Very well, then. This way, sir."

Lady Johanna walked beside Matthew, utterly silent, and appeared rather dazed. He could not blame her. This was hardly the kind of arena he would have expected to find *himself* in, much less a young lady of Society.

He had not planned to come here at all this evening.

But he and Christian, the Duke of Montagu, had been following Drake. The Duke of Ormonde had been skulking around recently, keeping his activities from his friends, and they'd seen a chance to find out what he was up to. Their group of friends were all dukes who had bonded when their fathers had died in a gunpowder explosion and the subsequent fire in the hunting lodge where they'd been staying.

At first deemed an accident, and still publicly thought to be one, they'd discovered it was no innocent mishap that had left eight dukes dead.

They'd come together, united by their grief (those who felt it) and the unexpected inheritances being thrust upon them. Matthew was one of those who did not grieve his father overly much, but he did want to know who had murdered the man. Especially to give his friends the peace and justice they desired.

Which was why he and Christian had been drawn to follow Drake and investigate his secret activities. Matthew did not believe Drake had anything to do with their fathers' deaths—Drake and his father had been quite close—but he was up to something.

A bawdy house such as this was hardly where Matthew had expected to find him, even if Drake was sowing his wild oats before his marriage.

Was Drake investigating the murders on his own? Had he found something that he did not want to share? Or was he truly going off the deep end in anticipation of his upcoming marriage to Lady Astrid? He claimed he was enjoying his last Season as a bachelor, but there were far more enjoyable brothels and houses of ill repute that would cater to a duke than this dismal place.

Matthew glanced over his shoulder to see if he could spot either of his friends before he disappeared behind the stage, but neither was in the room.

"Ah, Mr. Blash, you heard of our good fortune?" the auctioneer said, drawing Matthew's attention back to the matter at hand. There was another man waiting behind the stage, one who looked at Matthew, then paled. He might recognize Matthew as the Duke of St. Albans, but even if he did not know Matthew's exact title, he obviously recognized Matthew's standing.

From the other man's attire, Matthew guessed Mr. Blash was well-to-do gentry, connected, but a working man. A similar kind of assessment would tell Mr. Blash quite a bit about Matthew, just as it had the auctioneer. Not to mention the princely sum that he'd offered for Johanna.

But they did not know that he was not just purchasing her virginity; he was saving his bride.

He rubbed the pocket where his lucky coin was kept, the one he used to make all of his decisions. Including the decision to bid on Johanna. When he'd flipped it, he'd meant to ask if he should save her, but the question that had popped into his head was whether or not he should marry her. And the coin had indicated yes.

So, here he was, purchasing his soon-to-be bride's virginity.

The main goal was to remove her from this situation as quickly as possible, hopefully without anyone realizing who either of them were. She was highly recognizable, with her extremely pale hair and wide violet eyes, but the majority of the audience had been drinking heavily. Very few were of the *haut* ton, if any. And once she was cleaned up and properly attired, most would never guess she was the same young woman who had appeared on a bawdy house's auction stage.

They would assume it was just another young lady with similar coloring.

Because what duke would purchase his bride from a virgin auction?

Matthew barely managed to keep from smiling at the thought; his friends would all believe it. This was exactly the kind of situation his luck would put him in, but he always came out hale, hearty, and better off than he'd been before. Which would be true now.

His hunt for a bride was finally over.

He just had to pay for her, then make their escape. Surely, she'd be so grateful, she'd throw herself at the opportunity to marry him.

CHAPTER TWO

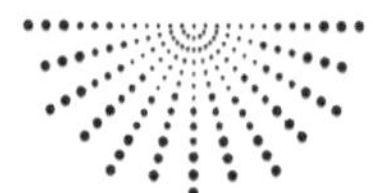

JOHANNA

With her hand on the Duke of St. Albans' arm, Johanna felt as if she was in a dream. She must have fainted before walking out onto the stage, and at any moment, she would awake to find that she still must go on.

But the dream did not end as St. Albans gave Mr. O'Connell a princely sum of money—an amount that could have been a respectable dowry. She only managed to stir when she realized that Mr. Blash had disappeared. She frowned, but she supposed he did not need to be there for this part. Mr. O'Connell could pass on his share later.

It was not until Mr. O'Connell turned away from her that she stirred.

"Half of that is mine," she said, starting out faint but her voice growing stronger as she spoke. "I need it for my family."

"Half of it is Blash's," Mr. O'Connell said without looking up. "What he shares with you is none of my business."

"But—"

"Do not worry," St. Albans said soothingly. "Whatever you need, I will provide."

"But—" she tried to protest again, but the duke was already steering her out of Mr. O'Connell's office. Despite several days' worth of regular meals, she did not have the strength to pull away from him or to turn them around.

"We need to get you out of here," he said in a low voice as he swept her into the hall. "It is not safe here."

Although she was uncertain what he meant, she did believe him. He sounded completely sincere, and she trusted him at least somewhat. He would not have been at the Blackstone house party, and she would not have been introduced to him if Lady Astrid had not thought him a suitable prospect for a husband.

Another man appeared at the end of the hall, also dark-haired, but his hair was shorter, his eyes lighter, and his complexion swarthier than St. Albans'. She recognized *him* immediately—Lady Astrid's betrothed, the Duke of Ormonde. What was he doing here? A moment later, another man turned the corner, who she also recognized from the house party as he'd been the only blond duke present, the Duke of Montagu. Even here, in their tawdry surroundings, next to two other exceedingly attractive dukes, his male beauty made him stand out. She'd heard the titters at the house party—the ladies called him the Adonis of the *ton*.

"Good, you've got her," Ormonde said shortly. "You and Christian get her out of here."

"And what are you doing?" St. Albans asked, but Ormonde had already turned on his heel and was striding off. St. Albans picked up his pace, pulling Johanna along with him to the juncture where Montagu waited with a grim set to his jaw. "Where is he going?" St. Albans questioned.

"I do not know, but he is not wrong about needing to get her out of here," Montagu said shortly. His gaze swept over her as if to ascertain she was unharmed, but then flicked away as if dismissing her once he knew she was hale. "There are already rumblings in the other room about who might have her after you're done with her."

A chill swept through Johanna as St. Albans cursed under his breath.

"We'll talk to Ormonde later," he announced. "How do we get out of here?"

"This way. My lady." Montagu smiled charmingly, bowed, then led the way, which was in the opposite direction from where Ormonde had disappeared.

Several turns, then they were out the door and into the night. Despite the warmth of the evening air, Johanna still felt chilled. Her mind was desperately trying to keep up with what was happening around her. She was physically safe now, but without the promised funds… but still in possession of her virtue and a duke who said he would take care of everything.

Did she dare trust that? What other choice did she have at this moment?

Both men pressed against her, one on either side. Guarding her, she realized, as they made their way down several streets before reaching the carriage waiting for them. She was grateful for their presence as the fog of London curled around the dark streets, creating foreboding shadows in every nook and cranny. Being on her own would have been terrifying.

St. Albans helped her into the carriage, then followed her into the enclosed space. It was not until Montagu had joined them and rapped his knuckles on the roof, causing it to lurch forward in response, that she shook herself free from the silent shock that had gripped her.

They might think they were rescuing her from a horrid situation, but she had been there for a reason, and she'd received no assurances from St. Albans other than the initial declaration. Why would he give her money for nothing? He must have been trying to get her out of there to save her reputation, but her reputation was worth less than nothing if she couldn't save her family.

"Wait! I need the money, my family—"

"I told you," St. Albans said, taking hold of her hand and squeezing it tightly. He sounded completely serious. "I will take care of it. All you have to do is agree to marry me."

Now she knew she was dreaming. The Duke of St. Albans had just proposed marriage to her. It did not sound like jest, but surely any moment, both men would explode into laughter. Except that, across from her, the Duke of Montagu's mouth had dropped open in utter shock, but he did not laugh, nor did he protest. St. Albans ignored him, keeping his gaze steady on her even as she stared back and forth between the two dukes in utter disbelief.

"Marry you?" Her voice squeaked. Montagu's reaction or not, she *had* to be dreaming.

"Yes. Marry me." The duke sounded completely serious. "Then my funds will be yours to spend as you please."

"I... You do not understand. My family..."

"Is very poor." He nodded, looking at her dress. "I can see that."

She felt color bloom in her cheeks. The dress had once been light blue, but now it was faded grey and tattered. She'd taken care of it the best she could since arriving in London, but she knew it was hardly the kind of garment a lady of the *ton* would willingly be seen in.

"Matthew," Montagu muttered, covering his face with his hand.

"What? Am I supposed to ignore the obvious?" St. Albans grinned widely, suddenly, and he was even more handsome smiling than when he was serious.

Johanna had not truly noticed at the house party. She had not wanted to notice. She would have married any of the men who offered to help her and her family. Now was no different, was it?

"You need money for your family, yes? I have plenty, and I am happy to help them."

"We are... my mother is starving." Tears flooded her eyes as she said the words aloud, choking her. "We barely made it through the winter. The house needs repairs. Everything needs repairs. The children do not have enough food or clothes—"

"Marry me, and none of you will ever want again." St. Albans' grin had faded at her words, and he lifted her hand to his lips to kiss her knuckles.

Johanna felt a flutter go through her belly, one that was different from those that came when she had gone without any food for too long.

"This is the most unusual proposal, but it does suit you somehow," Montagu said, shaking his head.

She turned to look at him because she needed someone else to tell her this was really happening. Someone who was not the man proposing to marry her for no good reason.

"He is serious, then?" She could hear the desperation, the hope in her voice.

"Utterly." Montagu answered immediately, and he seemed entirely sincere. "He would not propose without meaning it. I suppose you flipped for it?" The question was directed at St. Albans. Johanna did not understand what he meant, but the duke nodded his head.

At the house party, Johanna would have cried with joy at the prospect of marrying a rich duke. That he was young and handsome did not make a difference, though it was a relief. He did not seem cruel. She hoped he was as kind as his smile suggested. She had to believe that Lady Astrid would not have introduced him to marriage-minded debutantes otherwise.

Not that it mattered.

In order to save her family, she had been prepared to do far worse than marry a duke.

"Yes," she told him. "I will marry you."

The smile he flashed was blinding.

"Good. Now, tell me about your family."

Matthew

Lady Johanna's family was even worse off than they'd supposed. Matthew and Christian exchanged a glance when she told them about meeting Mr. Blash. The idea that he was providing for her family off his own income... Matthew thought it far more likely that he was supplementing his income with funds that should have gone to her family.

Clearly, she had not suspected anything, and he was loath to part her from that particularly charming naïveté before he had to. There was something very sweet and soft about her, despite the hard hand she'd been dealt. He would rather preserve that aspect of her, not crush it.

But he would certainly have someone look into Mr. Blash.

Matthew would get Lady Johanna settled in his home and introduce her to his grandmother and staff. Christian would head to her family's home and pack them up to bring them to Matthew's. He was more than happy to pay for whatever repairs were needed to their home while they were with him, so they could eventually return. He could sponsor her brother, and his grandmother would likely enjoy having young ladies to bring up.

In the meantime, having a happy, grateful bride—very much unlike his friend Nathanial, who had recently married and begun his married life rather coldly—sounded very nice to Matthew. He should have thought of this before. He had no need of a wife with a dowry of any kind, and this way her entire family would be grateful to him rather than considering it a social triumph to marry a duke.

Besides, he'd never saved anyone before.

It felt rather nice to be a hero.

And he got a wife out of it, to boot.

His friends would call it the devil's own luck, but the luck was all Matthew's.

Using the hand not holding Lady Johanna's, he quickly took his coin out and flipped it. The flip confirmed his thought, and he tucked the coin back into its pocket.

"I think a quick wedding would be best," he said, looking at Lady Johanna and giving her hand a squeeze. He liked holding her hand. Very husbandly. She was a beautiful woman, if a trifle delicate in her appearance. Surely regular meals would help with that. Likely some kind of fashion makeover. Matthew was certain he could leave that in the hands of his grandmother or perhaps Lady Astrid and the other duchesses. "Quick and quiet. Once you're my duchess, you'll have the protection of my name, so even if anyone recognizes you from this evening, they'll hold their tongue. If they have a chance to do so before the wedding, they may not. I would marry you anyway, but it will make things easier."

"Yes, that sounds best." Lady Johanna nodded her understanding. She seemed very serious-minded, which was not surprising after the tale she had told.

He wondered what it would take to make her smile. Likely, seeing her mother and siblings safe and well would be a good start.

"I would not want any rumors or scandal to touch your family name nor burden my brother and sisters. Though it will be several years before my sisters' come-outs."

The *ton* could have a long memory, but he did not point it out. He did not particularly care why she agreed, so long as she did.

"Good then. I'll acquire a special license as quickly as possible so we can be married without the banns being read. Once I have that, we can have the wedding as soon as your family arrives in London. My grandmother will be pleased to play hostess to them."

"Your grandmother is going to murder you," Christian commented, sounding more amused than anything else. Now that things were in motion, he was falling in line with Matthew's plans. Matthew was rather relieved it was Christian with him instead of one of their other friends. Christian was always good for a lark.

Gregory, the Duke of Clarence, might have gone along with things without protest, but he'd become much more serious since marrying. His duchess, Tiffany, was likely to influence his thoughts on the matter, and Matthew could not guess what she might think of his unusual method for procuring a bride. Her presence at Gregory's side was why it was just Matthew and Christian who had been following Drake instead of the three of them.

Matthew was uncertain what Drake would think. He'd been happy to see that Matthew had saved Lady Johanna, but proposing to her? Lady Astrid would likely approve, at least. Matthew knew she'd invited Lady Johanna to her house party with an eye to matchmaking. Unfortunately, Lady Johanna had had to leave rather precipitously, and now Matthew knew why. At least her mother was still alive. No woman should have to starve herself for her children's sake.

His mother had died in childbirth, and his father's second wife had not produced a child before she died of consumption a few years before his father's death. By which time his father had been searching for a third bride but had not found one to live up to his exacting standards.

Knowing his son was marrying the sister of an impoverished earl, who Matthew would be taking under his wing, would have had his father rolling in his grave. Another good reason for his choice.

"Will… will your grandmother not approve?" Lady Johanna asked in a soft whisper, sounding very worried. He had not realized she might think Christian was speaking of approval of her.

Neither had Christian.

"No, no, she'll approve of you, certainly," both of them rushed to reassure her.

"She will be very happy I am getting married, and she will have no qualms over your lineage nor your family's current situation," Matthew said quickly.

"You are not the reason she'll disapprove," Christian piled on. "She's going to be very annoyed with Matthew for rushing things, even if she understands the reasoning. She'll want the big church wedding and all the pomp and circumstance."

"I am hoping that having your sisters to take under her wing will improve her mood." Matthew grinned, giving her hand another squeeze. He glanced out of the carriage. They had finally reached Mayfair and were nearing his London home. "And the satisfaction of having me married off before this Season is over. Besides, we can call it an *exclusive* wedding. I'll tell her that Nathanial and Kalina set the precedent, so she cannot even blame me."

Christian rolled his eyes but did not disagree as the carriage came to a stop.

"I will make straight for Falmouth Heath in the morning," Christian reassured Lady Johanna. "With plenty of footmen and stableboys. I'll have your family to you as quickly as possible."

"Thank you, Your Grace," she said with heartfelt fervor, causing Matthew to frown.

He was the one making it possible. Stepping out of the carriage, he wondered at the small twinge in his chest that her gratitude toward Christian had caused. He'd never felt anything like it before. Turning back to the carriage, he held out his hand to help his new fiancée down the stairs.

She smiled at him, the light of the streetlamps making her violet eyes glow.

"Thank you, Your Grace." It was a shyer expression of gratitude than Christian had received, yet it felt deeper. That little twinge in Matthew's chest settled immediately.

"It is my pleasure," he said with satisfaction before giving Christian a nod. As they stepped away, the coachman closed the door and got back into position to take Christian to his own home. Matthew had no doubt he would be up early tomorrow to ride to the rescue of Lady Johanna's family.

The house was not as dark as he'd expected, but that was a good thing. Sometimes his grandmother had difficulty sleeping. Perhaps she was still up. Then he could get the introductions out of the way immediately.

His luck held, as it often did.

Holt, his butler, opened the door to admit them and did not blink twice at the fact that Matthew had a rather disheveled young lady on his arm. The man was rather used to Matthew arriving home in all sorts of situations. Grandmama was just coming down the stairs, and she came to a halt, her mouth dropping open at the sight of him. She was *not* as used to dealing with Matthew's more unusual appearances, as they had not occupied the same household until this Season.

"Hello, Grandmama," he said cheerfully. "You wanted me to tell you the moment I found my bride. Lady Johanna has done me the honor of agreeing to marry me."

CHAPTER THREE

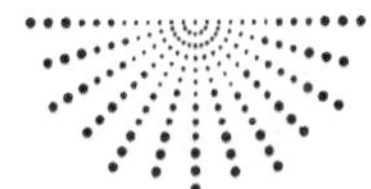

This was not how she would have chosen to meet the Duke of St. Albans' grandmother. She wanted to sink into the floor as the elegant older woman stared at them in pure shock. Johanna was beginning to realize the duke enjoyed shocking people. He was certainly very good at it.

"Lady Johanna, this is my grandmother, Lady Moira Stark."

Not a duchess, then; she must be his grandmother on his mother's side. Still, nobility. Despite the fact she'd never had an official come-out, Johanna *was* trained, to the best of her mother's ability. She sank into a curtsy she hoped was the proper degree and did her best not to wobble.

Thankfully, she had been practicing before the house party, and she managed to keep her balance.

"Matthew Ferdinand Cassius St. Albans!" Lady Stark might be in a dressing gown with a bonnet over her hair, but she did not need proper clothing to be intimidating. Johanna bounced up from her curtsy, quivering in place, and wondered if she should run—but she had nowhere to run to. "This is not how you introduce your fiancée to your grandmother!"

Relief bubbled up inside Johanna so fast and so strong, she nearly collapsed in a heap before locking her knees into place. His grandmother was upset about the introduction, not about Johanna or her appearance. She could have cried, she was so relieved.

St. Albans had quit her side, leaving Johanna in the middle of the foyer, bounding up the stairs to drop a kiss on his grandmother's cheek. She did not know if she felt abandoned or relieved that he had taken his grandmother's focus so completely.

"You did say immediately," he said cheerfully.

The older woman swatted him on the shoulder with her hand.

"You know this is not what I meant, you rapscallion!" Pursing her lips, Lady Stark glared at him.

He just chuckled, clearly unintimidated by his grandmother's ire.

Turning back to look down the stairs at Johanna, he held out his hand.

"Come, my lady, I'll show you to your room."

"You will not!" Lady Stark swatted him again and caused Johanna to stay in her place, swaying slightly since she had almost stepped forward. "Affianced or no, there will be no pre-wedding dallying under my roof."

"Technically, it is my roof."

"Get yourself to your own bed, and I will see to Lady Johanna," she concluded, ignoring his statement about the ownership of the house as thoroughly as he'd ignored the proprieties. Turning to look down the stairs, she smiled encouragingly at Johanna. "Come, my dear. There's a room just down the hall from me that you can use this evening, and tomorrow we'll have one prepared for you to use until your wedding."

"We'll be getting married by special license as soon as her family arrives," St. Albans said, striding away at a fast clip, though he somehow managed to look as though he was not running away from his grandmother.

Her eyes, which were bright blue, widened with fury as her nostrils flared. Johanna had been on her way up the stairs, following the lady's directions, but now she hung back.

Lady Stark closed her eyes, and her chest heaved beneath her dressing gown as she took a deep breath.

"I cannot murder the boy; his heir is a complete addlepate," she muttered to herself before opening her eyes again.

Johanna watched her mutely, still perched halfway up the stairs, still wondering if she should flee while she had the chance. But where would she flee to? St. Albans had promised to take care of her family. By the looks of the house and his grandmother's attire, he could well afford it.

And his grandmother seemed more outraged about the lack of a proper wedding than she was about Johanna's unexpected and disheveled appearance. Things could be far worse, even if her soon-to-be husband had just left her alone with his rather formidable grandmother.

Lady Stark turned her gaze to Johanna, and it swept over her with a calculating eye.

"*Lady* Johanna?" she asked, as if to be sure. Johanna could not blame her, considering her current attire, her lack of chaperone, and the late hour at which St. Albans had brought her to the house.

She steeled herself and nodded. "My brother is the Earl of Falmouth."

Swift calculations ran through the woman's eyes. She might be older, but she was sharp, and she recognized the name. Johanna could only imagine what other information she might remember about the family, but she was far too exhausted to care at this point.

If the woman kicked her out of the house, she would stay on the stoop until her family arrived, then she would figure out what to do. Though St. Albans had seemed very intent on marrying her.

"Come on then," Lady Stark said, turning. "Let's get you settled. Tomorrow, I want the full story."

Johanna was not sure she could give it. Hopefully, St. Albans would be awake tomorrow to make whatever explanation he desired, and Johanna could follow his lead.

That or she would wake up in the boarding house Mr. Blash had put her in and discover this had all been a very vivid dream. At this point, she was not sure which would be odder.

MATTHEW

The sharp rapping on Matthew's bedroom door just as he finished readying himself for bed made him sigh. He'd hoped that leaving Lady Johanna to his grandmama's auspices would distract her, but apparently not. His grandmama wanted an explanation.

"That will be all, Reedy, thank you," he said to his valet. "Let my grandmother in on your way out."

"Yes, Your Grace," Reedy said with a bow. Reed-thin, with light-brown hair, he lived up to his name. He was a very good valet for Matthew, adaptable and able to keep up with whatever wild starts Matthew had. They'd been together ever since Matthew had fired his previous valet, who had been his father's spy. Reedy was loyal to Matthew and no one else.

Grandmama swept into Matthew's bedroom like a gale wind and came to a halt in the middle, hands on her hips. Her glare could have wilted an entire field of crop.

"What did you do?" she demanded to know. "Where did you find that poor girl?"

"I saved her from a fate worse than death," Matthew replied, grinning, pleased to be able to defend himself so nimbly. Grandmama's eyes narrowed, and he quickly gave her an accounting of what had happened. He did leave out that he'd been following Drake, saying only that he'd been tailing a friend.

"She had better say the same thing tomorrow," Grandmama said, though much of her displeasure had dropped away. Something was still bothering her, though, he could tell. At least she no longer looked as though she wanted to whack him. It also did not seem as though she had definitively decided against it either.

While she didn't have nearly the strength of his father, her stinging slaps against his arm had always bothered him far more than his father's harsh punishments. Grandmama was rarely displeased with him, while his father always was.

"She will," Matthew reassured her. "I think she must have been quite desperate. We'll see the state of her family when they arrive, but I cannot imagine anything but pure desperation driving her to such acts. She was very quiet and very proper at Blackstone Manor."

"Hmm. Well. I suppose we will see." His grandmother sighed, her shoulders sagging. "I do want to see you married, you know."

"I know."

"An impoverished earl's sister… she may have some difficulty adjusting to running a ducal household."

"I am sure I can count on you to assist her." After all, his grandmother had been the lady of the house since his father died. She was speaking from experience, too—she had been thrown into the fire when he'd inherited, just as he had. Matthew had not expected to become the duke so soon, and his grandmother had never expected to have to run a ducal household. She'd been perfectly happy as the wife of an earl.

If anyone knew how difficult it was to adjust, it was her.

"Of course, I will render her all due assistance." Grandmama was still frowning.

"What?"

"You know that you cannot flip a coin for love, correct?"

"I didn't. I flipped my coin to choose my bride." Matthew laughed, patting his pocket where the coin in question lay. His grandparents had been a love match. His parents' marriage had not—it had been the one time his grandmother and his grandfather had fought, according to her. She'd wanted their daughter, his mother, to have a love match… but his mother had sided with his grandfather. She'd wanted to be a duchess.

She'd gotten her wish.

Matthew always wondered if she'd regretted it, or if perhaps his father had been different when she was alive.

His grandmother had said his mother had been content with her title, but she would have been happier with a love match. She'd tried to push the idea of a love match onto Matthew, too.

Personally, he did not see what difference it made, but he knew she was likely disappointed he was not interested in trying things her way.

"You cannot go through life making all your choices by coin!"

"I do not see why not." He shrugged. This was a constant argument between them. He could have written out their lines for them at this point. "It has not led me astray thus far."

"And what if it has this time?"

"Then I will deal with it. But I do not believe it has."

"Did you flip it for her at Blackstone Manor?"

Matthew hesitated. He had wondered at this as well.

"I did, but not to see if she should be my bride. I was choosing dance partners at that point." He shrugged. "Obviously, something changed. Maybe I was meant to wait 'til now."

"Does it not bother you to give up so much control of your life?" she asked, aghast. That was a new tack.

He paused to think about it for a moment before shaking his head.

"Since when have I truly had control, Grandmama? I was born to be a duke, and here I am." He spread his arms wide. "I did not choose any of this. Why should the rest of my life be any different?"

Grandmama snorted.

"Being born a duke only narrows your choices; it does not eradicate them. You are born into such a position and privilege that you have more choices than most. If you want to have a dearth of choices, you should try being a woman." With that, she turned on her heel and stalked out of his room.

The conversation left him slightly unsettled, which was a new sensation for him. Normally, he felt perfectly content with how he lived his life, even after arguments with his grandmother. He knew she did not approve of his coin-flipping, but it seemed to him it was no worse than the ways most people made their decisions.

Perhaps he had become overly reliant on it… but half of his punishments from his father had been for making the wrong decision.

Choices that he'd made on his own. When he'd started relying on luck, he'd been beaten less than when he'd been trying to do the right thing. The coin made better choices than he made when left to his own devices, so he relied on luck.

And that luck had gotten him out of many a belting.

While his father wasn't around to impose his ideas of what the right choice was anymore, Matthew still preferred to let his luck decide his path.

It had not let him down so far.

He'd saved his bride from a terrible fate and now would save her family as well. She would work hard to become a good duchess in gratitude. Considering how beautiful she was, conceiving an heir would be a pleasure, not a chore. Now that he had a bride—and presumably that would lead to an heir—taken care of, he could focus on helping his friends uncover who murdered their fathers.

And solve the mystery of what Drake was up to.

Feeling rather pleased with himself for a good day's work, Matthew took himself to bed. Tomorrow, he'd ensure Lady Johanna was well taken care of with his grandmother, then he would pay Drake a visit.

CHAPTER FOUR

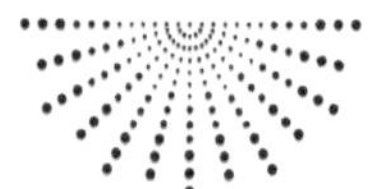

A knock on her door made Johanna jerk awake, and disorientation swirled around her. She had been sleeping so soundly, far more soundly than she could remember sleeping. For a moment, she thought she was still in the boarding house, but the bed was too big and comfortable, and the room far too large and well furnished.

Last night, she had not truly looked at it.

The door opened, and a maid poked her head in, smiling and bobbing a curtsy as she came through the door once she saw that Johanna was sitting up in bed. Dark hair and dark-eyed, she was slightly plump with apple-blossom cheeks and a wide smile that Johanna immediately envied. Draped over her arm was a length of lavender fabric.

"Good morning, my lady. My name is Nettie. Lady Stark sent me to take care of you." She bustled over to the drapes as she spoke, opening them and letting in the sunlight. It poured over the room, bathing it in soft light, revealing a feminine oasis of delicately carved furniture, an ornate carpet in lilac, cream, and grey lying across the floor. The bed she was in boasted a periwinkle coverlet and canopy, though the curtains were open as it was too warm to need them closed overnight.

Johanna did not know what to say as Nettie turned and looked at her expectantly. She'd never had her own maid, as she had not been old enough for one before they'd had to start letting the staff go.

"Good morning," she echoed after a moment since it was polite to do so. But she did not know what she could ask Nettie to take care of for her. She cast her gaze about. "Um, do you know where my dress is?"

The night rail she was wearing was one that Lady Stark had produced last night. Johanna had reassured the lady that she had no need of a dresser, and the lady had nodded her head and allowed Johanna to ready herself for bed. But at some point, her dress had disappeared, as it was no longer lying at the foot of the bed where she'd left it.

"Oh, yes, Mrs. Syme, the housekeeper, sent someone in this morning to get it." Nettie smiled sympathetically. "Rosa said you did not stir. You must have been exhausted."

"Yes." Exhausted and slightly disturbed now that she knew someone had been in the room with her, and she'd slept through it. That was certainly a measure of how tired she'd been, though. Normally, she awoke at any small sound in the middle of the night, always alert for bad news or for Charlotte crawling into bed with her.

She must have been more wrung out than she'd realized.

"Well, you're up now, and Lady Stark sent this day gown for you to wear today. She says that once you have broken your fast, you'll be going out to Bruton Street to visit her modiste." Nettie smiled through this whole recitation.

"Oh… I do not…" Johanna's voice trailed off. She did not have any money, but the Duke of St. Albans certainly did, and he would have a certain standard of dress for his wife, she was sure.

What was he getting out of this arrangement?

A wife, but he could have any woman of the *ton*, surely. Why her? Rather than bringing him a dowry, he had to spend money outfitting her. And he'd sent for her family.

What was he going to expect in return?

Last night, the choice had seemed simple. Now, she could not help but wonder if she was out of the pan and into the fire.

Lady Astrid had him as a guest. And the Duke of Montagu.

His grandmother had also seemed no-nonsense and entirely aware of the proprieties. She had not even let him escort Johanna to this room. Johanna blew out a long breath.

Whatever it was he wanted from her, if it saved her family, she would do it.

Nettie was still standing there, smiling and waiting patiently, holding up the lavender gown. Giving herself a small shake, Johanna got up and allowed Nettie to dress her, which was an entirely odd experience.

The maid not only had the gown, she also had undergarments for Johanna. Everything was too big for her, but it was better than nothing, and it was all far cleaner and newer than what she had been wearing. The lavender color made her eyes seem a bit paler than usual, as though they were shifting shades to match, but her skin and hair looked a bit brighter.

Nettie frowned over the lack of curls—it had taken Rose hours to craft an acceptable coiffure at Blackstone Manor—but skillfully braided the long, silky strands into an acceptable style. Johanna stared at herself in the mirror. She was as thin as ever, gaunt even, but somehow, she looked different.

"There we go," Nettie said triumphantly. "Would you like a touch of color for your cheeks, my lady? Nothing gaudy, of course, but I think it might brighten you a bit."

Because she had trusted Nettie thus far, she allowed the maid to put a bit of rouge on her cheeks, and she had to admit, she rather liked the effect. She looked healthier with a bit of color, more like she had as a child, though she'd never felt farther away from her childhood than she did at this moment.

"Let me show you to the dining room, my lady."

Seeming eager to show off her work, Nettie escorted Johanna through the halls. She chattered the whole time about the various portraits and artwork they passed, pointing in different directions to where Johanna would find rooms that might interest her. The house was massive, and Johanna just hoped she would be able to find her way to and from the dining room on her own, much less seeking out the study, the solarium, or the music room.

Though her own home was huge, so many of the rooms had been closed off over the years that she did not remember where most of them were. Some of them, her younger siblings had never seen before. Navigating through a large house was not something she had much experience with anymore. Blackstone Manor had been larger, but she'd had Rose with her, and it had made everything far less intimidating.

Now she was alone.

Thankfully, it did seem as though the way to the dining room was fairly straightforward. She thought she would be able to find her way back on her own.

As she came through the door with Nettie, the Duke of St. Albans and his grandmother abruptly cut off their conversation. He jumped to his feet when Johanna entered the room, staring at her. He was just as handsome in the daylight as he had been the night before, though he looked more at home in this elegant dining room than the shabby backstage of Mr. O'Connell's.

"Lady Johanna, Your Grace, my lady." Nettie sounded triumphant, very pleased with herself. Johanna was amused that she had not been far off the mark in thinking Nettie wanted to show off her work. She had to admit she would not look nearly so nice if Nettie had not been there to help her. Especially her hair.

"Your Grace, my lady," Johanna echoed, and curtsied, ducking her head to avoid the duke's intense scrutiny.

Was he regretting his decision? Was he pleased? She could not tell.

"Very nice, Nettie, thank you." Lady Stark smiled, and Nettie exited the room, appearing pleased. "Come, Johanna, sit and have something to eat. What would you like? Eggs? Sausage? Kippers?"

A sudden lump found its way into Johanna's throat as she sank down into her chair. Her mouth watered at the smells, but her stomach tightened at the thought of eating a single bite.

The same guilt had battered her at Blackstone Manor, but that had been before she knew her mother was starving herself. Now... she'd struggled to eat the food the boarding house had provided. The duke's food was too much. The quality so much higher. The options so much larger.

How was she supposed to eat eggs, sausage, and kippers when she knew her family had no such sustenance?

A tear rolled down her face, no matter that she tried to swallow back her sob, then another and another. Head bowed and hands clasped tight in her lap, she did her best to hide her reaction, but she could not look at either the duke or his grandmother because she could not control herself at all.

MATTHEW

What was she doing? Why was she crying?

Panic gripped Matthew as he stared at his bride. She looked lovely in her gown, though it did not fit her very well, and she had seemed happy enough until she'd been offered food. Shouldn't she want to eat? She'd said her family was starving. And she'd looked very thin herself, even before putting on a gown that was too big for her, which made her appear even less well fed.

He looked to his grandmother, who was sitting stiffly upright with an expression on her face that he'd never seen before. On someone else, he might have called it sympathy.

Then his grandmother looked back at him, and her expression changed, shooting him a look.

Help her, she mouthed.

Right.

How?

What did people do to help a crying woman? He'd never been in this situation before.

Matthew quickly took out his coin, but he did not know what to ask it.

His grandmother's face was slowly getting redder, and she looked like her head was about to explode.

Hug her.

Oh. That made sense. But he did flip the coin just in case, then hurried to get up and put his arm around Lady Johanna when it confirmed that was the right thing to do. The maneuver had the added benefit of putting the table between him and his grandmother. Just in case she decided to do something with her hands other than gripping the arms of her chair.

It was awkward crouching down to get in the right position, and Johanna felt incredibly frail under his arm. Even more so than she had last night. The sensation stirring in his breast felt... protective.

"Is there something else you would like?" he asked softly. "We can get you whatever you want."

Lady Johanna turned her head into his shoulder, which was nice, but she also started crying even harder, which was not. His grandmother dropped her head into her hands and took a deep breath. Matthew knew from experience that meant she thought he was mucking things up.

But it was not as though he had any experience in this sort of thing. He was doing his best.

Unfortunately, no further questions for his coin presented themselves to him.

"I am sorry," Lady Johanna said, straightening again, groping for the napkin. That was something he could do—Matthew handed the napkin to her. "Thank you. I am so sorry."

"Not to worry," Matthew said, getting back to his feet from the awkward crouch he'd been in, patting her shoulder. "I ah... is there anything I can do?" He would much rather she not start crying again. Maybe he should send for one of his friends, one with a wife. A woman other than his grandmother, since she expected Matthew to take care of this, and he was clearly not very good at it.

"You have already done everything... I just... there is so much food, and I started thinking about my family." She was turning weepy again.

How to stop it?

"Christian will see to it that they are fed," he quickly reassured her. "I promise."

That was an easy promise to make because he knew his friend. Christian would provide for their travel and their food the whole way to London, and Matthew would happily pay him back if Christian allowed. Which he might not. He would consider it part of his duty.

It should have made her happy, but she started crying again, this time holding the napkin to her face as her shoulders shook. He looked at his grandmother with a helpless plea in his eyes, and she sighed, shaking her head. Finally, she got to her feet and came around. Matthew quickly stepped back to allow her to take his place at Lady Johanna's side.

"Do not fret, my dear," his grandmother said soothingly, rubbing Lady Johanna's back. Oh. Maybe that was what she'd wanted him to do. He could have rubbed her back if he'd realized. "The boys will take care of everything. Your family is going to have plenty to eat from now on, and you need to eat to keep up your strength until they join us here."

Apparently, that was the right thing to say. Lady Johanna nodded, hiccupping, before getting herself under control again. His grandmother patted her back before returning to her place on the other side of the table, and Matthew sidled back to his seat.

Lady Johanna had more color to her face now—pink cheeks and eyes, the tip of her nose a delicate red—but she was as beautiful as ever. Matthew smiled at her, trying to appear reassuring, but she had ducked her head and was not paying attention to him.

Ah, well. They'd have the opportunity to get to know each other better once they were married.

Hopefully, there would be no more crying at breakfast once her family arrived, and she had no reason to be sad anymore.

"Once you are done breaking your fast, we shall go shopping," his grandmother announced.

Matthew understood he was not included in that 'we,' thankfully. He had his own plans for the day, such as procuring a special license and tracking down Drake to pepper him with questions.

"You shall need to be properly outfitted as befits a duchess. Matthew tells me that you are to marry as soon as your family arrives."

Lady Johanna glanced at him, and he nodded.

"First thing on my agenda is the special license." He smiled reassuringly at her. "Feel free to get whatever you need. Grandmama knows there is no budget for this."

Violet eyes widened, and she appeared at a loss for words. It was very generous of him, but he could afford it, and there was no reason his duchess should appear anything but top of the nines. Besides, he wanted to ensure no one would mistake her for the young woman in the brothel last night.

"Thank you, Your Grace," she whispered after a moment.

He smiled encouragingly at her.

"Now, let us talk about the wedding," Grandmama said.

Matthew nodded and pulled out his coin, much to his grandmama's obvious displeasure.

CHAPTER FIVE

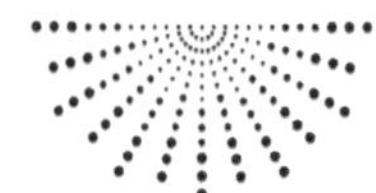

MATTHEW

Directly after breakfast, Matthew went to the mews to get his horse. Casper was a pure white stallion with strong lines and a good horse for London with his even temper, which was quite unusual for a stallion. Some gentlemen would have considered it a defect, regardless of whether they were in the city or the country, but Matthew liked Casper's steadiness, especially when in London. Plus, the coin had chosen him when Matthew had been picking out a horse.

He'd been brought to London from the Netherlands by a gentleman who had subsequently lost a horse in a game of cards to Matthew. He'd gone through the man's stables, one by one until the coin had picked Casper.

Casper whickered as he was brought out, his head bobbing up and down. Grinning, Matthew held out his hand to feed the horse a sugar cube before taking the reins from the stableboy.

First stop was the Archbishop of Canterbury for the special license. Thankfully, Charles had always had a soft spot for Matthew and was happy to issue one without any convincing needed beyond a donation to the church.

With that done, he headed for Drake's home. He could have

stopped on his way to the archbishop's office, but he'd felt it was too early to call. Securing the special license had not taken much time, but at least it was a little later.

And he had questions.

Dewbury, Drake's butler, let him in and went to get his master. Drake came down the stairs with a grumpy expression, wearing a dressing gown of burnt umber with copper embroidery and a black-fur ruff. Clearly, he'd just woken up and was not particularly happy about it. Maybe Matthew should have waited until later. This was what he got for not checking with his coin before arriving.

"What do you want?" Drake asked irritably, stalking into the drawing room and flopping inelegantly on the couch. A maid rushed in with a coffee cart before rushing away again. Dewbury came in and got a cup of coffee in Drake's hands before pouring one for Matthew.

He waited until the door was closed and Drake had taken at least two sips of coffee before answering.

"Good morning to you, too," Matthew said, leaning back in his chair. "I want to know what you were doing at that brothel last night."

"The same thing as you."

Matthew raised an eyebrow.

"You were buying a bride?"

Watching Drake choke on his coffee was strangely satisfying.

He stared at Matthew for a long moment, ignoring the droplets of coffee that now spattered the front of his robe.

"Lady Johanna?"

"We'll be married as soon as Christian brings her family to my London house." He smiled serenely as Drake scowled at him.

"You did not take advantage of her." It sounded more like an order than a request for information.

"Of course not. I'm going to marry her. My grandmother took Lady Johanna under her wing the moment we arrived home." Matthew tilted his head, studying Drake. "Besides, what do you care if I took advantage of a young lady? You were there, too, and you're engaged. So. What were you doing?"

"Seeing to some business."

It was not a real answer, but no matter how Matthew wheedled, Drake was not giving up any information.

Sighing, he finished his coffee.

"I should go. Do you know of any good private investigators?"

"Why?"

Matthew explained about Mr. Jamieson Blash, his disappearing act after Matthew had purchased her, and Matthew's suspicions based on what Lady Johanna had told him. Drake's countenance darkened with every word, turning into a real thundercloud. Which was another reason Matthew did not believe that Drake had been at the bawdy house for nefarious activities.

He might be a rake, but he had a keen sense for justice and defending those who could not defend themselves. In an earlier time, he would have made a wonderful knight.

Matthew would not have been a knight, of that he was sure. Though it had felt nice to rescue Lady Johanna.

Maybe he could have been a knight. If the coin said it was the right decision.

"I will take care of it," Drake said after a long moment.

"Take care of…"

"All of it. As soon as I have some information on Mr. Blash, I'll get it to you." Drake got to his feet, brushing the front of his robe even though the coffee had already soaked in. "You're going to have enough to do, what with planning a wedding."

"We've already started. It's going to be very quick, not much planning needed." Matthew shrugged, getting to his feet as well. "You'll be invited, of course."

"I expect nothing less." Drake cleared his throat. "Congratulations. She seemed rather nice at the house party, though I did not get much of a chance to speak with her. Astrid likes her."

"She is nice." Matthew smiled. He was getting more and more used to the idea of having a wife. Specifically, of having Lady Johanna as his wife. She was nice. Drake's fiancée liked her. The other ladies liked her.

Everything would be nice and comfortable and easy. Just the way he liked it.

Leaving Drake's, he decided to go for a ride in Hyde Park since he now had the time. First, he checked with the coin, and it landed heads up, confirming his choice. He absolutely trusted Drake would put an investigator on Mr. Blash, which meant that was handled. Perhaps he should have waited until later in the day to beard the dragon in his den, but it had worked out well enough. Next time, he'd check with the coin to make sure of it, though.

Feeling rather cheerful, he turned Casper toward Hyde Park. It was too late in the day to run. The park was already filling up with carriages and barouches as the lords and ladies of the *ton* came out to see and be seen. Matthew always enjoyed watching them, the carriages laid out in rows and filled with nobility, like colorful birds on display. Some of the ladies even had feathers in their caps.

He wondered if Lady Johanna could ride.

If her family was poor enough to be starving, they likely did not have horses, but they might have in the past. A question for another time. At some point, they would need to come through Hyde Park, either riding or in a carriage. It would cause comment if they did not.

Across the wide expanse of green, Matthew spotted another rider, instantly recognizable even from a distance by the tiny figure clinging to his shoulder. Matthew grinned and tugged on Casper's reins to send him in the direction of Zachary, the Duke of Grafton, and Monkey Sinclair.

The tiny monkey had been rescued by Zachary earlier this Season in a rather dramatic confrontation with his former owner. Upon acquiring his new pet, Zachary named him after their deceased friend, the former Duke of Northumberland. Sinclair would have hated it, which was why Zachary had done it. The two of them had been as close as brothers before Sinclair's death.

Matthew raised his hand to catch Zachary's attention, grinning when his friend saw him and nodded, turning his mount's head to intercept him.

"Good morning," Matthew said as he came alongside Zachary.

The other duke looked tired, as he often did these days. He was heartsick over the loss of Sinclair still, as they had been very close. It did not help that Zachary had also recently given his mistress her *conge.* Delilah Voight, Baroness Ashfield, was a widow he'd been involved with for years now, but when it came to marriage, Zachary was determined to do things properly. That meant the petticoat line and finding a young virgin to wed.

"Is it?" Zachary asked, not even pretending to be anything but melancholic. His dark hair and eyes already made him look broody, but now he appeared to be positively gothic. The only bit of brightness about him was the mustard pocket square tucked into the black jacket he wore—as, indeed, all of his clothing was currently an unrelenting black.

"Not for you, I take it?"

For a long moment, Zachary was silent as they rode beside each other. Then he stirred slightly.

"It was a long night."

"Oh?"

"Lady Annabelle and her parents came over for dinner," he said woodenly. Lady Annabelle was the woman Zachary's mother wanted him to marry, the daughter of her best friend and a sweet young thing.

If Zachary was not in love with another woman, she would probably be a perfectly acceptable choice.

"Anyone else?"

"My mother and uncle."

A family dinner. Delightful. Matthew sent his friend a look of sympathy. They might as well go ahead and formally announce the engagement once word of the dinner got out.

"The engagement announcement will run in the Gazette tomorrow." Zachary's wooden tone remained completely flat.

"Congratulations." Matthew thought about it for a moment. "Or condolences. Congratudolences?"

One corner of Zachary's mouth tipped up for just a moment before his expression fell again, which Matthew considered a monumental victory, given the circumstances.

"My mother is very happy." Zachary sounded exhausted rather than pleased. "The dinner went well, although afterward all I wanted was a stiff drink, and for some reason, Monkey Sinclair went berserk. He somehow managed to pick up the decanter, which was practically the same size as him, and throw it at the wall. The damn thing shattered, and that was that. It was good brandy, too."

No wonder the poor man looked peaked. Matthew took out his coin and deftly flipped it, not at all discomposed by being on the back of a horse. He'd had plenty of practice.

"Would you like to come for a visit?" he asked, after seeing the result. "You can meet my bride."

That raised Zachary out of his stupor, his head swinging so fast that he nearly knocked Monkey Sinclair off his shoulder. The tiny menace chittered, scolding him, and climbed up onto the top of his hat. Zachary did not seem to notice—or if he did, he did not mind the relocation.

"Your what?"

Matthew's coin had led him correctly. The news had knocked Zachary out of his melancholy; he had a real expression on his face— he was completely flummoxed.

"My bride. Lady Johanna Ashmore."

Zachary blinked rapidly, catching up.

"Lady Johanna from the Blackstone house party?" Though Zachary had not attended the actual party, he'd come out for Nathanial and Kalina's impromptu wedding and heard all about it. That he recognized Lady Johanna's name, though he had not met her, was a testament to his good memory.

"Yes." Matthew grinned. He did enjoy flummoxing his friends. "I picked up the special license this morning."

He patted the pocket it was in, hearing the faint crinkle of paper. The sound made him smile. Everything had fallen into place rather nicely, and now he could use his news to distract Zachary from his self-imposed misery. It was a good day.

Well, other than the crying at breakfast, but they'd made it through that well enough, and hopefully, once his bride's family joined them, there would not be a repeat.

"How did this happen?" Zachary was practically sputtering. "When? Why so quickly?"

Matthew did not need to flip his coin to know that discussing the manner in which he'd acquired his bride was not something he should brute about in public. But should he tell Zachary at all?

He flipped the coin.

Used to his ways, Zachary waited, albeit impatiently. He looked much more alert now.

Lifting his head, Matthew grinned.

"Come over, and I will tell you all about it." He was relieved the coin had gone that way. Keeping such a secret from his friends did not feel right, and Drake and Christian already knew.

"This, I cannot wait to hear," Zachary muttered as they angled their horses to the path out of the park.

Chances were, it was far too early for Grandmama and Lady Johanna to be back from shopping, but this way he could catch Zachary up... and question him to see if he knew anything about Drake's secretive activities.

CHAPTER SIX

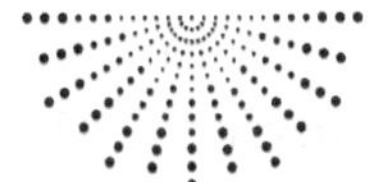

The carriage taking her and Lady Stark to Bruton Street was spacious and well sprung. The seats were soft, well-cushioned, and felt like luxury. It was a duke's carriage after all, which was why she felt so out of place in it.

I will have to get used to it if I am to be a duchess.

A prospect that sounded quite daunting now that she was actually betrothed. Though she'd attended the Blackstone house party, she had not realized until this moment that she had not had any real hope of a gentleman offering for her. She had never pictured herself as an actual bride to a duke. She'd been desperate and willing, but there had been a part of her that was sure it would be for naught.

Otherwise, she would have been as panicked then as she was now.

Somehow, selling her body for one night seemed an easier act than being a duchess for the rest of her life. Obviously, the latter was better than the former, but... she had no idea how to be a duchess. What if she did something horribly wrong? What if she shamed her new husband after all he had done for her?

Lady Stark did not seem concerned, and that was the only reason Johanna was not in a complete panic.

"I think violet," Lady Stark said suddenly, as if they had been having a conversation rather than sitting in complete silence.

"Violet?"

"Yes. To match your eyes." Lady Stark nodded, as if that explained everything.

Johanna could only blink said eyes in response, still uncertain what Lady Stark was speaking of.

Should she ask what would match her eyes?

Or would asking make her appear a ninny?

Was she supposed to understand what Lady Stark was speaking of?

Yet how could she do the right thing when she had no idea what her ladyship meant?

She had to ask. Even if it did make her look like a pinhead.

"What will match my eyes?" She kept her voice soft, low. After all, she did not want to anger her ladyship, who had already been far kinder than many women in her position might have been. Johanna did not want to take such kindness and generosity for granted.

"Your wardrobe." Leaning back against the seat, Lady Stark's gaze swept Johanna up and down. It did not feel judgmental in a lowering manner, but more as though Lady Stark was assessing Johanna's physical qualities rather than critiquing them. If she found them lacking, it did not show in her expression. "Yes. Violet as the base, certainly. No one is going to question your antecedents if they're focused on your eyes. They really are marvelous. Men will write poems."

"Poems?" Johanna echoed.

"About your eyes." Lady Stark flapped her hand. "Keep up, girl."

The idea of men writing her—*her*—poems was absurd, but she was not going to argue with Lady Stark. Not that she had much of a chance to, as the carriage lurched to a halt and one of the two footmen who had accompanied them appeared to open their door and help them down. Johanna held her breath as she did so but managed to reach the cobblestone street without any mishap.

Was it her imagination, or were passersby shooting her and Lady Stark glances?

It felt as though everyone was looking at her. Judging her. Waiting for her to fail. Johanna glanced around, and several hastily averted gazes did nothing to convince her otherwise.

"Come along, Johanna." Lady Stark's stern command had her hopping.

Perhaps she was to be a duchess, but she doubted that she would ever feel confident enough to take on Lady Stark.

Her feeling of confidence lessened even further when they walked into the modiste's. There were several ladies already inside, perusing the fabrics, while a smiling woman stood toward the back, watching them with an air of waiting to be needed. She brightened even further when she saw Lady Stark, her keen gaze taking in Johanna at the older lady's side. She hurried forward and curtsied deeply.

"Lady Stark."

"Madame Allard." Lady Stark looked around the room. "We need purples. Everything but the royal shade."

Johanna was beginning to realize this was Lady Stark's way of speaking. Madame Allard did not seem surprised, and she must have understood immediately what Lady Stark meant because she nodded.

"*Oui*, my lady." Madame Allard gestured at Johanna's face. "Those eyes! *Magnifique!*"

Feeling like everyone was looking at her, Johanna did her best not to shrink into herself. One of the other ladies, a beautiful blonde, was frowning at her with narrowed eyes and pursed lips. Her gaze was critical as it traveled over Johanna's current attire. Johanna knew the dress she was currently wearing was not particularly well-fitted.

Madame Allard noticed that, too. She frowned at Johanna.

"You must come to the back," she said, stepping aside and waving her hand at a curtain. "I will have my assistant work on the gown she is wearing now, and it will be ready by the time you leave."

"Perfect."

Lady Stark moved ahead, and Johanna followed in her wake, bemused and uncertain of what to do.

The assistant was going to fix her gown before they needed to leave? How long would this take?

Hours, it turned out.

Johanna had never had the benefit of a full fitting, and Lady Stark was determined to ensure she had everything she needed, from small clothes to ballgowns to pelisses that would not suit the weather for months. All in varying shades of purple or with purple patterning or purple trim.

"A riding habit, too," Lady Stark ordered, through the flurry of fabric and pins.

"I do not know how to ride," Johanna told her, because Lady Stark —or, really, the Duke of St. Albans—would already have been spending a fortune on the clothes they were ordering. Trying to guess at the cost made Johanna feel dizzy, so she had given up ages ago.

"You will learn."

The pronouncement was made with such confidence that Johanna did not dare argue.

She would learn.

Lady Stark had spoken.

Johanna was not against learning, but she was starting to feel over-whelmed by the number of things she needed to learn. Even ordering clothing like this was an experience in how little she knew about being a lady.

What looked best on her, what the current fashions were, what a lady should absolutely not wear… Lady Stark seemed to know it all, assisted deftly by Madame Allard, but it was definitely the lady leading the way in suggestions. She knew what she wanted Johanna to wear, and Johanna was grateful someone did.

By the time they were done, hours had passed, and Johanna was not at all surprised to be presented with her previous dress, which now fitted her perfectly. After listening to Lady Stark and Madame Allard's back and forth, she would not have expected anything less.

Although Lady Stark did not say that Johanna was to marry her grandson, Madame Allard seemed to understand that instinctively and did not even blink when Lady Stark ordered a wedding dress to be prepared immediately. A bonus was offered to have it done in two days, and all Madame Allard did was nod.

The modiste also provided Johanna with several more day dresses that had been altered to fit her perfectly and a promise that the wedding dress would be delivered in two days.

As they walked out into the main shop area again, Johanna felt as though she might list to the side and faint. It was sheer grit keeping her upright—that and her determination not to disappoint Lady Stark. Which was why she did not immediately notice Lady Astrid and her companions until the lady called out to her.

"Johanna! What are you doing here?" Lady Astrid's tone of shock cut through Johanna's exhaustion, jerking her back to attention.

"Shopping?" The answer came out as a question because Lady Astrid's query echoed so many of the thoughts tumbling through Johanna's mind.

What was she doing here? What was she thinking? How did she think she could ever be a duchess?

It is not as though I had another choice.

"Lady Astrid," Lady Stark greeted the startled redhead. They exchanged cheek kisses, then Lady Astrid came to do the same with Johanna.

"I apologize for my outburst," Lady Astrid said ruefully, stepping back from greeting Johanna. As always, the lady was impeccably attired, currently in a dark orange-and-black jacquard, with black gloves and a necklace of carved amber. The effect with her red hair was quite striking. "I did not expect to see you in London. How is your mother?"

Tears sprang into Johanna's eyes—another measure of her exhaustion—and she felt her throat clog.

Lady Stark patted her on the shoulder, bolstering her.

"She is better," Johanna managed to answer, feeling as though she was trying to speak through a foghorn. "No longer ill." Only starving. Which would soon be remedied. Surely, if Lady Stark was willing to spend so much on clothing, she and the duke would see to it that Johanna's family was well fed, too. They'd certainly reassured her as such during breakfast this morning.

"I am so glad to hear that." Lady Astrid clasped Johanna's hands, utterly sincere in her relief, which made Johanna want to cry again.

She did not know what she had done to attract Lady Astrid's friendship, but she was so grateful for it. Lady Stark cleared her throat, gave Lady Astrid a pointed look, and glanced at the women beside her. Lady Astrid started as she realized she had forgotten to make introductions.

"Oh, please excuse my poor manners, Lady Stark. I was so startled to see Lady Johanna here and concerned about her mother, I forgot myself."

"Of course, Astrid." Lady Stark smiled reassuringly.

"Allow me to introduce my companions," Lady Astrid said, stepping back from Johanna to give her a better view of the other two ladies. "This is Hu Jiumei, who prefers to be called Mei, and Miss Jeanne Yates. And this is Lady Stark, the Dowager Countess of Pike, and Lady Johanna Ashmore, sister of the Earl of Falmouth."

"Best wishes on your engagement, Miss Yates," Lady Stark said, smiling at the starry-eyed young brunette. "I saw the announcement in the Gazette this morning."

"Thank you! It is all thanks to Mei and her grandmother. They are wonderful matchmakers," Miss Yates gushed, looking adoringly at the young Chinese woman who was quietly standing beside her and Lady Astrid. Dressed in English fashion, her forest-green gown hugged her body, emphasizing the slight tan of her skin and the depth of her dark eyes. A long sheet of black hair hung straight down her back, exactly as Johanna's would without the expertise of a maid to curl it.

"Lady Stark." Mei dipped a curtsy. "Lady Johanna. It is truly my grandmother who is the matchmaker. I but assist."

Something about the look that Lady Astrid shot Mei made Johanna question that assertion, but the lady did not speak up to argue.

"We are here to choose a wedding gown." Miss Yates beamed, practically bouncing on her toes.

She was clearly very excited about her upcoming nuptials. Far more than Johanna was about her own. But she'd also obviously had a say in her match, even if she had chosen to use a matchmaker. At least she had not been purchased off a stage by her groom-to-be.

"Best wishes to you." Johanna echoed Lady Stark's words.

"Thank you!"

They did not get to speak further with Miss Yates as one of Madame Allard's assistants came over to draw the young lady away. Lady Astrid lingered, though Mei accompanied her client to go examine some bolts of fabric.

"Now that I know you are in London, you must come to call. I gather we have a *lot* to catch up on," Lady Astrid said, sliding a glance at Lady Stark. She was quick to put two and two together, although Johanna knew that she could not possibly guess how it had come about. The curiosity in her eyes was hard to miss. "Tea. Tomorrow at two."

It was a command, not a question.

Johanna looked to Lady Stark. She had no idea what the duke's grandmother had planned for tomorrow, or if there were other things she should be doing.

"She will be there," Lady Stark said.

"My mother is having some friends over, if you would like to join them as well, Lady Stark." Lady Astrid smiled widely at her.

"No, no. I have my own plans for tomorrow afternoon, but it will be good for Johanna to be with her friends."

"Very well." Lady Astrid focused on Johanna again. "I will see you tomorrow." Nodding her head firmly, Lady Astrid swanned off after Miss Yates and Mei.

Seemingly pleased, Lady Stark led Johanna out of the shop. The footmen who had come in to fetch their boxes followed them and loaded up the carriage while the coachman helped Lady Stark and Johanna inside it.

"How close are you with Lady Astrid?" Lady Stark asked as soon as they were both seated. She had a gaze like a hawk, and Johanna felt very much like a mouse.

"She is a neighbor, of a sort." Johanna had not seen much of the other lady while they were growing up, though she knew where Blackstone Manor was.

"But you attended her house party." Lady Stark tapped her lower lip with her fan, obviously thinking.

Johanna was not certain if she was supposed to reply, so she just nodded. She assumed the duke had told his grandmother about how they'd met before… well, before. "It is a good connection. She seemed pleased to see you with me. She'll know what that means. But you should not tell her the full story. Tell her Matthew sought you out."

Johanna nodded again. She understood why Lady Stark wanted her to lie. It was the story they would tell the *ton* as a whole. Although she felt bad about lying to Lady Astrid when the lady had been so kind to her. She'd run into Johanna on a visit home during the Season and had been quite pleasant in conversation. The invitation to her house party had arrived several days later, an unexpected boon.

It did not mean that she could trust Lady Astrid with the scandalous truth of how the duke had found Johanna again.

"Good. That's settled." The older woman nodded decisively, and the carriage lurched into motion. "On to Bond Street."

"Bond Street?"

"Yes, you need hats. And gloves. Reticules."

More shopping. Johanna wanted to sag in her seat, but she doubted that was how a duchess would behave. Besides, she should be grateful to Lady Stark for taking the time to ensure that Johanna was properly outfitted. Straightening her spine, she rolled her shoulders back, trying to summon some energy.

Watching her, Lady Stark frowned.

"Perhaps something to eat on the way—and you will eat, girl." She stabbed the end of her fan toward Johanna. "Your family will not be saved by you starving yourself while you are here."

The guilt that thinking of eating had stirred was not assuaged, but she understood Lady Stark's point. Johanna nodded meekly.

She would eat. And try not to think *too* hard about her family.

They would be here soon enough, and eating soon enough, and it would not do anyone any good if she did not eat until then.

"Good." Lady Stark nodded again, resting her fan down in her lap, clearly pleased that the world was being sorted to her order.

Johanna could only hope to have that kind of confidence one day. And her energy. She did not look nearly half as tired as Johanna felt, despite her age. If she could keep onward, Johanna could do no less.

CHAPTER SEVEN

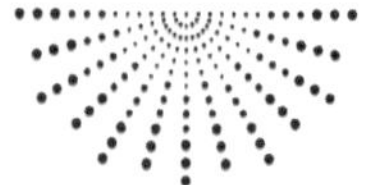

MATTHEW

It was several hours into Zachary's visit when Matthew's grandmama and bride-to-be finally returned home. He and Zachary had moved from the billiards room, where they'd done the harder conversations about their brides—and, in Zachary's case, about his former mistress Delilah—to the library for more comforting surrounds and lighter conversation.

Though Matthew supposed most people would not consider Drake's activities and the mystery of their father's murders to be lighter conversation. It was more that they were not so emotionally engaged. Truthfully, Matthew was not particularly emotionally engaged in any of the topics, but Zachary certainly was, especially when it came to Delilah.

Not that they got anywhere on any of the topics.

Zachary had no more idea what Drake was up to than Christian and Matthew did. He'd been shocked to hear about the state of the bawdy house they'd followed Drake to, and completely unsurprised that Drake had refused to speak about it when Matthew approached him earlier.

Neither were there any new clues as to the murder of their fathers.

They knew the Duke of Clarence's steward had something to do with it—in revenge for the rape of his niece, a maid in the Clarence household, that left her with child. But the man had fled. Drake had sent investigators after him, but so far, they had not returned with any more information.

The next clue they'd found was in the debts of the Duke of Hereford's father, a profligate gambler who left his family nearly as poorly off as Johanna's with his reckless spending. He'd died in massive debt to multiple establishments and noblemen. One of them had invited him to the hunting lodge where he'd died.

Why a man, who was owed such a massive sum of money, would issue such an invitation…

Well, the Earl of Cornwall had lived to tell the tale, but the Duke of Hereford had not. It could have been coincidence, but it needed looking into.

Which was why Christian, Drake, and Matthew had been in the Warrens the night Matthew rescued Johanna. They'd all said they were headed home after not finding Cornwall, but Drake had not gone in the correct direction, and Christian and Matthew had followed him. Which meant that they still needed to track down the earl, but without further information from him, they had very little to go on.

So, by the time Grandmama and Lady Johanna arrived, they were a welcome respite from talking in circles about the mystery.

"Well, now," Zachary murmured, reaching up to pet Monkey Sinclair as he and Matthew strolled into the foyer. "They have been busy."

Very.

Lady Johanna looked even paler than she had this morning and like she was holding herself up through pure willpower, but she was also smiling at his grandmama, so he took that as a good sign. She looked… better. Even though she appeared exhausted. There was something about her that was different, although he could not quite place his finger on it.

Perhaps just that she'd had the benefit of a shopping excursion.

Women did like shopping, so he understood. Which he appreciated; without his mother's and then his grandmother's prodding, he would likely have ended up naked with an empty house and no idea why. Matthew was good at making impulse purchases, not so good at ensuring the things he needed on a day-to-day basis were at hand. That was left up to the ladies of the household, and men were not allowed to stick their noses into the ladies' arena. He shuddered to imagine how his grandmother would react if he even made the attempt.

It looked as though his grandmother was jumping right into teaching Lady Johanna everything she needed to know.

"Did you get everything you needed?" he asked, approaching his grandmother and dropping a kiss on her cheek.

"For now." She beamed up at him. "It was a lovely day. Johanna did very well."

"I am glad to hear that." He turned to where Zachary was making his bow to Lady Johanna, which she returned with a very deep curtsy. Once she was married to him, she would not need to curtsy so deeply, and he was rather looking forward to that. There was something very pleasurable about sharing his power and position with a woman who had been through so much.

"Lady Johanna, a pleasure to meet you," Zachary said, bowing over her hand. "And might I add, you look positively stunning. That shade of purple ribbon is inspired next to your eyes, like a field of violets on a warm summer afternoon."

"You see?" Grandmama said, giving Lady Johanna a significant nod. "Poetry."

"I... ah... thank you." Lady Johanna's violet eyes were very wide. They really were unusual. The way she smiled at Zachary made something twinge in Matthew's chest. "That is very kind of you to say, Your Grace."

"It is very easy to speak the truth, my lady. And please, call me Zachary as you are to be Matthew's wife, and we will be friends."

"Then you must call me Johanna. I must admit, I am not used to such formalities."

Her guileless response made Zachary laugh.

"The formalities are something you will certainly have to get used to once you are a duchess," he told her. "Everyone will insist on it. Though we can be less formal among close friends, of course."

Some of the rakishness Zachary was known for—well, had been known for before Delilah—seemed to be coming through in his smile, and Matthew scowled. His chest did that same clenching thing it had when she'd smiled at Christian. Zachary was already engaged to one woman and in love with another, so he did not need to make up to Lady Johanna.

No, not lady, just *Johanna*.

Because if Zachary could call her Johanna, then Matthew certainly could. He was the one who was going to marry her after all.

Which was why he quickly claimed her hand from Zachary and put it on his arm. Zachary smirked at him for some reason.

"The ribbon does bring out your eyes very nicely," Matthew said. If there was one thing he was good at, it was colors. He might not like to shop, but he did enjoy quality clothing and fashion, even if he found the process of purchasing it to be tedious. "I'm sure it is not just the ribbon that you got."

"I think we got everything," she replied with a quiet smile that did something quite odd to Matthew's chest when she directed it at him. "In every shade of violet, except the royal purple."

"No one will complain when they see her eyes," Grandmama said, sounding almost maliciously triumphant. "Not many ladies could do so, but she will be a duchess and her sons in line for the crown, even if they are very far down the line."

Because he was standing right beside her, looking into said eyes as his grandmother spoke, Matthew saw the startled shock that filled them at her words. He was so used to knowing his place in line to the throne that he did not think of it, but obviously, Johanna had not considered that her sons would be as well.

Which made him feel even better about his coin choosing her for his bride. Though she'd been at Blackstone Manor for the house party, to which Lady Astrid had exclusively invited dukes of the unwed variety, Johanna had not been duke hunting for dynasty reasons. He fully believed it was the financial straits that had her searching for a husband, and the rank of a duke had not been a necessity.

That part he put up to Lady Astrid's machinations. Because if she could enhance a friend's future, she would. So, why not a duke?

It had not worked out precisely the way Lady Astrid had intended, but he was sure that she would be pleased with the end result.

"If anyone complains, send them to me," he said gallantly. After all, it was his duty to protect his wife. And the idea of someone being anything but kind to Johanna, after all she'd been through… well. He would take much pleasure in playing the knight errant for her again.

"Thank you…" Her voice trailed off as if she was uncertain what to call him now. Especially after Zachary told her to call him by his given name, but Matthew was the one she was engaged to.

He leaned in, lowering his voice so that only she could hear him.

"You should call me Matthew." He whispered his name like it was a secret, just for them, and for just a moment, it felt like his grandmama and Zachary faded away from the room, and it really was him and Johanna alone.

Matthew. She mouthed his name, rather than saying it aloud, her perfect pink lips forming the syllables in a manner that made his heart beat faster. He might have completely lost his head and done something shocking like kiss her right in front of the others, if not for the supper gong. It jolted him out of his reverie, and both of them pulled back.

Grandmama looked eminently pleased, though she quickly turned to Zachary.

"You'll join us for supper, of course," she said. "Unless you have another engagement."

"Of course," Zachary replied, smiling. "Nothing that I must rush to, though I am expected at Lady Chesterham's ball later this evening."

Which gave Zachary the opportunity to get to know Johanna better, which benefited Matthew as well. Both of them were able to speak with her and Zachary; including Grandmama in the conversation as well meant there were as many stories about Matthew being told as Johanna told of her own childhood. Matthew noted that his fiancée was more than happy to talk of the past during the time her father had been alive and much more loath to speak of anything in more recent times.

Which allowed him to deduce that things had only gone downhill once her brother's guardian took over managing the estate and the estate's funds. Tomorrow, he would check to ensure that Drake had sent someone to dig into Mr. Blash. Well, he would flip his coin to see if it was the right day to check in with Drake, in case giving him more time would be more appropriate.

Supper ended, and Zachary excused himself to get ready for his evening. Grandmama had announced over the meal that she'd cried off events for the next few days while they got Johanna sorted. After all, she could not attend a ball without the proper attire.

"The ballgowns will not be ready for several more days," Grandmama said with obvious regret.

"That is fine with me," Matthew said jovially. He did not need to go to any more balls anyway, now that he had his bride. Unless he was likely to find Cornwall there, although any of his friends who were still on the hunt could take on that duty. It was unlikely Cornwall would be found in a ballroom, though, and far more likely he'd turn up at a gambling hall. Which was where Matthew excelled, as long as he had not been banned for his uncommonly good luck.

His grandmother cast a gimlet eye at him but did not remark on his response.

"Hyde Park tomorrow," she announced. "The ladies will want to meet Johanna before your wedding."

Matthew winced but saw his grandmother's point. Johanna should be introduced to the other *grande dames,* the terrifying array of the older ladies of the *ton.* Socially savvy and occasionally savage, they would be far less harsh if Johanna had been introduced to them before Matthew married her. An elopement out of nowhere would have them out for blood.

The *ton* ran on talk, and the *grande dames* ran the gossip.

"Sounds as though your day will be busy—"

"You are coming too, Matthew."

"Ah. Right. Of course."

Damn.

So close.

But Grandmama had spoken, and there was nothing to do but grin and bear it.

At least with Johanna at his side, he would not be mobbed by young ladies, the way it often happened when he or one of the other eligible dukes stepped foot in a ballroom. Matthew was very much looking forward to no longer being surrounded by debutantes eager to make his acquaintance. Being crowded in made it very difficult to flip his coin when he wanted to decide which to talk to.

CHAPTER EIGHT

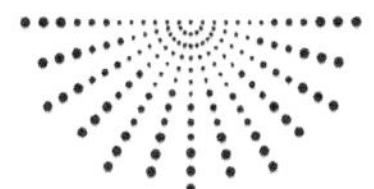

Hyde Park was beautiful and incredibly intimidating despite that beauty.

As so many things had been since coming to London. The engagement announcement had run in the Gazette that morning, and the number of carriages—and passersby on foot—that crowded around the St. Albans landau was massive. Johanna sat poker-straight beside the duke, a smile on her lips, all while wishing she could hide... but every eye was on her, watching her every move, and some of them were clearly finding her wanting.

She did not blame them. Especially the young ladies who appeared very disappointed that the duke had been poached from their pool, and by someone they'd never met before. Johanna felt very much like an animal in the zoo, on display, although the animals could at least do what they wished, and no one would think twice about it.

Johanna knew that one wrong move on her part in front of such an audience and the gossip would be horrendous. Not at all how she wanted to repay the duke and his grandmother for rescuing her.

"Yes, Lady Astrid's house party," Lady Stark said, nodding knowingly at another grey-haired woman, who lowered her lorgnette to study Johanna intently over the wire frame. "They're neighbors of Falmouth's, you know. Matthew came back to London without her, but he could not stop thinking of her, and…" Lady Stark shrugged as if to say *here we are.*

"And why did you not properly debut, young lady?" the woman asked. Johanna had already forgotten her name, among the many that had been given to her during introductions, and she hoped she would not be required to use it.

"My mother has been ill," she said quietly, as Lady Stark had instructed her to.

"Which is why I am currently her chaperone," Lady Stark said, smoothly sliding back into the conversation. "The rest of the family will be arriving shortly for the wedding, of course."

And because they could not keep living where they had been. But Johanna could not say that, of course.

According to Lady Stark, she and the Duke of St. Albans had a highly romantic story—love nearly at first sight, the duke languishing without her once he'd returned from the house party, then running off to fetch her when he could not bear to be apart.

"I bet his blasted coin told him to," one of the young ladies muttered, just loud enough for Johanna to hear, though it was likely out of Lady Stark's earshot. Especially since she was still talking to the lady with the lorgnette.

Since Johanna was fairly certain the debutante was not wrong, she just pretended not to have heard the remark. Already she'd noted the duke's predilection for letting his lucky coin lead his way, and there had been enough *sotto voce* jests from those around the carriage about whether or not he'd consulted the coin for his bride that she'd realized his habit was mostly common knowledge.

"Your eyes are like pools of violet," one of the young men said, stepping up to the side of the landau. He was younger than the duke and very handsome, with floppy blond hair and kind hazel eyes. Unlike the duke, who wore a jacket of plum with a light-plum waistcoat, the young man was clothed in nearly all black, except the crisp white of his shirt. "Your hair like spun cornsilk."

"That does not even make sense," the duke said, suddenly leaning forward and glaring at the young man from across Johanna. "You cannot have pools of violet; flowers are not a liquid."

The young man frowned back at him, his feathers ruffled from being interrupted.

"It's poetry, Your Grace, it does not have to be exact," he said haughtily.

"It should also not be poppycock." St. Albans made a waving motion at him, dismissing the young man entirely. "Go work on your verse and stop bothering my fiancée."

Johanna was not particularly bothered, more bemused that Lady Stark had been correct about the poetry, but she did not want her soon-to-be husband to be upset with her, either. Something about the poet was upsetting him because he was not the genial, smiling figure that she had come to know him for.

"Thank you for the poetry," she said to the young man, whose face fell as he recognized the dismissal in her voice as well. "But we must be getting on soon, I think. I have an invitation to tea that I should not miss."

Lady Stark—despite being deep in conversation with one of her friends—had sharp ears. She heard Johanna's remark and immediately took out her pocket watch to consult.

"Oh, yes, tea. We must be going."

Despite Lady Stark's announcement, it took another half hour to untangle themselves from the crowd, and Johanna was very relieved she'd said something. She had only been trying to rescue the young man from the duke's displeasure and spare his feelings, but it turned out she had spoken true about needing to leave to make it to Lady Astrid's in time for tea.

Even with that, she was a few minutes late.

The duke escorted her up to the house, with an explanation that he would take his grandmother home. His hand held on to hers for a moment longer than was quite polite, and she stared up at him as the oddest expression crossed his face.

He really was very handsome. Much more so than the poet in

Hyde Park. Even now, when he was being more serious rather than smiling. His dark eyes studied hers, his eyelids drooping for just a moment...

Johanna's breath caught in her throat. Surely, he was not going to kiss her, standing here on the Blackstones' stoop, his grandmother watching them from the landau.

The door opened, and the butler was standing there.

"Your Grace," he said immediately, bowing deeply and breaking the moment. Johanna's breath left her in a rush of air as the duke nodded, then released her hand.

"I'll return in a few hours for you," he said sharply, turning on his heel and hurrying back to the carriage.

The behavior seemed quite unlike him... but then, she did not know him all that well, did she?

"Lady Johanna. Welcome to the London house," the butler said, leading her in. "The young ladies are having their tea in the conservatory."

Something about the way he said it as she followed him down the hall made her think that there was probably a group of older ladies with Lady Astrid's mother, also having tea, elsewhere in the house.

The conservatory was lush with greenery and bright with flowers, the subtle scents wreathing through the air. The path through the potted plants and beds of flowers was a pretty mix of stones that was aesthetically pleasing despite the mix of shapes, sizes, and colors.

Laughter reached Johanna's ears before she saw the other ladies, and she steeled herself... before being suffused with relief when they passed by a large fronded plant to find a clearing among the greenery where a table had been set, and she saw the women gathered. The cream tablecloth had a copper silk runner on it, a large orange and dark-yellow flower arrangement in the center, and piles of small sandwiches, scones, and biscuits on serving platters spread about its surface. There were six chairs around the table, five of which had an occupant already in them.

Lady Astrid sat directly across from the path's entrance, so she saw Johanna the moment she appeared.

"Ah, you made it!" she said, getting to her feet and coming around the table with her hands spread out in front of her.

"I am so sorry I am late," Johanna said, exchanging cheek kisses. The butler had already melted away among the greenery. "I was in Hyde Park with Lady Stark and the duke…"

"Enough said." Lady Astrid laughed, pulling Johanna's arm through hers to escort her to the table. Her red hair was piled loosely on top of her head, several strands having worked their way loose and brushing against the amber and cream stripes of her gown. The necklace around her throat was a simple amber drop, which matched her earbobs. "It must have been a Herculean task to escape that in time."

"It was," Johanna said fervently, making everyone laugh. Some of the tension that had wound its way around her chest loosened. She recognized all the ladies there, though Lady Astrid made introductions anyway, which helped dispel the initial awkwardness.

Mei, whom she'd met the day before, sat serenely sipping her tea, not at all perturbed to be surrounded by nobility. The matchmaker was the only one who was not of the *ton*, but she seemed perfectly comfortable sitting there, clothed in an emerald outfit much like the one she'd been wearing yesterday, but more brightly colored. Her hair was pulled back into a bun today, held in place with carved wooden sticks that were both simple and lovely.

Baroness Ashfield, who immediately requested that Johanna call her Delilah, was the eldest of the group, though only by a few years. She was a widow, the younger daughter of an earl, and a stunning beauty. Her hair was as dark as Johanna's was light, her eyes a bright amber that became almost golden when the light hit them, and she had a sultry, throaty voice that made Johanna feel positively squeaky in comparison. The canary-yellow day dress she was wearing made her eyes appear even brighter and lighter and gave her dusky complexion a soft glow.

"I must be Tiffany to you," the Duchess of Clarence said, right after Delilah made her request for given names. Another stunning beauty, she was a true English rose, with her hair caught somewhere between blonde and brown, hazel eyes, and a pink-and-cream complexion. She was garbed in cornflower blue and was even more sumptuously curved than Delilah.

The Duchess of Hereford, who had been introduced as Miss Little at the house party, was still wearing her signature pink with pink diamond jewelry to set off her darker coloring. Mahogany skin, raven-wing-black hair, and midnight eyes were stunning against the lighter shade of dusky rose.

"And I am Kalina," she said, smiling brightly with welcome. Miss Little, who had been bolder than Johanna but far shyer than Delilah at the house party, seemed to have come into her own with newfound confidence.

Johanna only hoped she could do as well. Perhaps there was something about actually becoming a duchess that automatically made one more confident. At the moment, she did not particularly feel like she belonged with this group of elegant ladies. Even Mei seemed more comfortable than Johanna felt, despite not being a noble, much less a duchess or soon-to-be duchess.

But she smiled and greeted them and hoped they did not see how her stomach was churning or her hands were shaking. If they did, they were kind enough not to look at her askance. She put a finger sandwich and a scone on her plate and hoped no one noticed she was crumbling the scone between her fingers rather than eating it.

Not from guilt, this time, but from sheer nerves.

"Gregory and I saw the announcement in the Gazette this morning," Tiffany said, smiling in the same friendly way that she had at the house party. "We are so happy for you, but we are dying to know how it came about."

"Especially since you had to leave the house party early," Kalina said sympathetically. "We were all hoping to spend more time with you there."

Tiffany laughed. "Yes, you missed all the excitement."

"Excitement?" Johanna echoed curiously. She had not realized something had happened after she left, other than Kalina's engagement to the Duke of Hereford.

"Oh yes, Kalina's scandalous manner of snagging a duke," Delilah teased, making Kalina roll her eyes.

"My father's, you mean." She looked at Johanna. "Most of the *ton* does not know and think that Nathanial and I were a love match from the beginning, but everyone else who was at the house party knows the truth. My father noticed the growing feelings between myself and Hereford but knew that Hereford was not considering me for his wife because of the scandal around my grandfather disowning my father. As well as my newness to the *ton* since he has three younger sisters who all need to debut and be guided through their Seasons."

"Which all of us are more than capable of helping with, if you even require it. Nathanial was being foolish," Lady Astrid said with a tone that made Johanna glad she was not the Duke of Hereford. Lady Astrid had little patience for 'nonsense,' which is what she clearly considered Hereford's reticence over Kalina.

"Yes, well. My father decided the best way to handle the situation was to get Nathanial drunk and leave him in my bed," Kalina said in exasperation while Johanna's mouth dropped open in shock.

She'd heard of mothers attempting such tactics, though usually it was to leave the young lady in the gentleman's bed, and it was an extremely risky maneuver relying on the gentleman's honor to offer for her after being so heinously tricked. This was the first she'd heard of a father attempting such a thing.

"I am a *very* deep sleeper. I did not even wake the night that you left, and apparently, everyone else did."

"It was rather noisy, I'm so sorry," Johanna said, glancing at Lady Astrid, who waved her hand as if to wave Johanna's guilt away.

"You needed to attend your mother. Think nothing of it. No one else did, especially after Kalina woke us all screaming when she found Nathanial in bed with her." Lady Astrid smirked while the others laughed. Kalina included.

"You try waking with an unexpected naked man in your bed," Kalina retorted.

"He was naked?" Johanna's hands flew to her mouth in shock.

"Well, not entirely," Kalina admitted. "But I did not know that. And he was not wearing very much."

"The best ones never do," Lady Delilah quipped, causing another round of laughter. Once again, Johanna was uncertain whether she belonged among these ladies. Not because of their stations, but because of their experience in marital matters.

Hopefully, she would feel more like she belonged once she had the experience as well.

"So," Lady Astrid said, putting down her teacup and leaning eagerly toward Johanna. "You must tell us exactly what happened with Matthew. Did the two of you have a *tête-à-tête* at the house party?"

"Oh... ah no." Johanna shrugged and relayed the story that Lady Stark had given the rest of the ton. Which had them all sitting back and frowning at each other.

"That does not sound like Matthew," Delilah said skeptically.

"Well... I believe he used his coin to make the actual decisions," Johanna tempered. These ladies clearly knew the duke better than the crowd at Hyde Park, and even they had guessed about the coin.

"That does sound more like Matthew." Tiffany giggled. "I cannot believe it finally said yes. Every time he asks it questions about a lady —should he be introduced, should he ask her to dance, should he court her—it inevitably comes back with an eventual denial."

"That would make sense with the odds," Mei said, finally speaking up.

Johanna got the feeling she was very happy sitting, listening, and observing, but not because she was intimidated by the august company. She was just content that way.

"Yes, but Matthew always defies the odds," Lady Astrid explained. "That's why the *ton* calls him the Lord of Luck."

"Should it not be 'Duke of Luck'?" Mei asked, frowning.

"Yes, but the alliteration is too appealing to adhere to his actual title. And Matthew is very easygoing, so he does not object."

"I wonder what made him think of you again," Kalina said, tilting her head as she looked at Johanna. "I will admit, I am somewhat disappointed. I was hoping to have another secret scandal on our hands."

"Another secret scandal?"

They told her about Tiffany's marriage, too. Not quite as scandalous as Kalina's, though a kiss in the library during a ball from a stranger who turned out to be her brother's closest friend, which led to immediate fisticuffs in the library, did sound very exciting.

That was also when Johanna learned that both situations had been covered up, so the *ton* at large had no idea the reasons behind the hasty marriage. In Tiffany's case, it was put about that she and Gregory had been secretly engaged because she was supposed to be enjoying her first Season and confirming he was who she wanted before the announcement was made. The public scandal of the kiss dimmed very quickly in light of the more romantic explanation, especially as they truly had fallen in love.

Kalina's story was somewhat similar in that the *ton* was under the impression that she and Hereford had fallen in love during the house party and married in haste due to desire rather than necessity. The other guests of the house party had been completely discreet, and nary a rumor had arisen about their marriage since their return to London.

"Though we did not actually fall in love until we were back in London," Kalina confided. "But we were acting the part beforehand."

Their honesty with her made Johanna's guilt stir.

"It is possible Lady Stark had a similar idea to cover the real story of how the duke and I became engaged..." Johanna admitted. They had been truthful with her, giving her their trust, and she could do no less when faced with their vulnerability.

She did exactly what Lady Stark would have advised against and told them the truth.

CHAPTER NINE

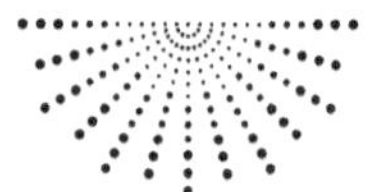

Telling the truth ended up having unintended consequences, and Johanna felt awful.

"I am certain Drake had other reasons for being there," Delilah reassured Lady Astrid, who was gripping her teacup's delicate handle so tightly, it was a wonder the china did not shatter.

"It is no matter to me how *Lucifer* conducts himself," Lady Astrid said haughtily, even though, by the way her face had paled and her entire demeanor changed, it was clear she was very much affected by hearing that her betrothed had been in the same bawdy house as Matthew and the Duke of Montagu. Even more so that Johanna could not give her an explanation of what he was doing there, exactly, or why he disappeared back into the house while the other two dukes escorted her out. "We are not married yet, after all. What he does with his time is no concern of mine."

All the other ladies cast worried glances at her, but it was clear she did not want to talk about it.

"I am so sorry to hear about your family," Kalina said, taking some of the attention off Lady Astrid. Out of the corner of Johanna's eye, she saw Lady Astrid relax when everyone was no longer staring at her, trying to gauge her reaction. The lady's shoulders slumped. "Hereford's estate was in similar straits when he married me. There is a lot of work to reinvigorate everything, but I am sure Matthew will be able to help."

"He certainly has the money to invest," Delilah said with a snort of amusement. "And if he needs more, he'll just visit the tables. The man has the devil's own luck, I swear."

"Do not ever bet against him," Tiffany chimed in, looking at Johanna.

As if she would ever think to do such a thing. She would not even know what to bet. Or what to bet on.

Mei, who had been silent again up to this point, reached out to put a gentle hand on Johanna's arm.

"Thank you for sharing with us. I am sure that could not have been easy," she said softly.

The tension that had been stirring in Johanna's stomach as her desire to be as honest with them as they had been with her versus knowing that Lady Stark would be displeased—and likely the duke as well—settled under that one sentence. She was not sure what the right thing to do had been, but Mei's quiet acknowledgment that sharing the truth had been a difficult decision somehow helped.

"Yes." Lady Astrid nodded. "The truth. It is very important that we are able to share things with each other. Finding true friends can be very difficult, especially in the viper's nest that is the *ton*. But we are going to be married to the tragic dukes—and Mei is possibly going to help with matching them, and Delilah... well, Zachary is a wooden spoon, but I still have hope he'll come around."

"You may hope all you want, but it does not mean I would take him," Delilah said with an indelicate snort. "Did you not see the announcement in the Gazette this morning? His engagement is official. There's no way out of that short of death or dishonor. And that's if I would even accept him after all of this, which I would not. I am *done* with that man."

"He certainly does not deserve you, but the heart wants what the heart wants," Lady Astrid sighed, a very resigned sound. "But my point is—"

Whatever her point was, she never got to say it because they were interrupted by the sudden arrival of her butler and Johanna's fiancé.

"The Duke of St. Albans," the butler announced, with Matthew looming beside him. His normal grin was absent from his face, and his gaze immediately sought her out.

Johanna's stomach flipped over as their eyes met, her heart beating a little faster as her chest tightened. When he looked at her like that, it felt strangely difficult to breathe.

When she blinked, the spell was broken.

"My apologies for interrupting, ladies," he said with a rakish grin that managed to be charming, self-deprecating, yet not at all apologetic. "But I must collect Lady Johanna from you earlier than expected." He looked directly at her again, but this time without the sizzle in the air between them. "Your family has arrived in London."

Johanna was on her feet before she even realized what she was doing.

"Oh, dear..." she said, hesitating, looking down at the teacup she was still holding. Thankfully, most of the tea was already gone, and not a drop was spilled.

"Go! No need to stand on ceremony," Lady Astrid said. "We can speak more later. You need to see to your family."

Yes, of course, that was the right thing to do. Johanna was relieved to hear it, even though leaving so abruptly felt very rude. At least the others were all encouraging and completely sincere about it. She felt as though she must be mucking things up left and right, but thankfully, everyone was very forgiving of any missteps she was making.

At least, among this crowd. She had the feeling it would have been very different at Hyde Park.

"Thank you so much for... well, for everything," she said, setting her cup and saucer down on the table. They clattered a little as she set them down, her fingers feeling nerveless. Her family was here!

Far sooner than she'd thought they would be, to be honest, even with Rose's efficiency. The need to see them, to hold them, to hug them, and see for herself that everyone was hale and hearty made her want to run. But duchesses did not flee tea parties just because their family was nearby. Even if she had not seen them in days and had no idea how everyone was doing.

"We will see you again, soon," Lady Astrid promised sweetly, getting to her feet to embrace Johanna and give her a kiss on the cheek. "Go, tend to your family. There is time enough for our discussion later."

Breathlessly, Johanna walked as quickly as she could over to the duke, who held out his arm for her to take. Although she was looking forward to spending more time with the other ladies, right now, all she wanted to do was go to his home and see her people.

MATTHEW

Being sent to fetch his fiancée was a responsibility Matthew had been happy to handle, especially when compared with the hustle and bustle of getting the Falmouth household settled into *his* household. They did not have much in the way of possessions—which was why Christian said it had been rather easy to get it all packed up—but Matthew was not used to being around children.

They were loud.

And full of questions.

Letting Grandmama take charge of assigning rooms and sorting out who needed what, while Matthew fetched Johanna, was a relief in comparison. Christian had also fled the scene almost moments after arriving, although that might have had something to do with the glares Miss Belle kept sending him.

The two had not gotten on at the house party, either. Unlike the vast majority of ladies, young and old, Miss Belle had proven to be ruthlessly immune to the *ton's* acknowledged Adonis. Neither his looks nor his charm had affected her, much to the rest of the dukes' amusement.

"How was everyone? How did they look?" Johanna asked anxiously once they were in the carriage.

Fortunately, those were questions Matthew knew how to answer.

"They looked well," he reassured her. "Grandmama was sending for a doctor to see to your mother when I left. She appeared weak, but not ill, but Grandmama is thorough."

"As long as he does not want to bleed her." Johanna shook her head. "My mother acted as a kind of medicine woman for our local community, and Rose studied with her, and she is adamant that Mother not be bled."

Something that cost Johanna to ensure, Matthew thought, from the tension in her voice and the way she held herself as she said the words. Someone had certainly wanted to use leeches, but Johanna had held the line, probably wondering all the while if she was making the right decision or dooming her mother. And she did not even have a coin to help her make the choice.

"Dr. Syme is considered rather... eccentric by some of his peers," Matthew reassured her. "He does not use leeches or purges of any kind. But Grandmama has found him to be extremely knowledgeable, and whatever diagnosis and recommendation he makes, you and Miss Belle will be consulted before anything is enacted."

"Thank you." The tremulous smile on her lips was more than worth such an easy promise. Matthew decided against telling her that he would also consult his coin. Not everyone understood his faith in his luck to steer his course.

But he also knew that it was her decision. He would consult the coin to see if he needed to try to convince her to another one.

Hopefully, there would be no need.

The house was still bustling when they returned, though the noise had moved from the foyer to farther into the house. Not just the children, but also the sound of the staff, who had come together to set things up. There were going to be a lot more people for supper than anticipated.

"Johanna!" The young man who appeared at the top of the stairs looked as though he wanted to pelt down them to his sister, but he held himself together and kept to a slightly more staid pace. She, however, rushed to meet him at the bottom of the stairs, throwing her arms around him.

"Micah!"

Matthew hung back as they hugged, curious about and slightly envious of the interaction. He'd always wanted a sibling. Someone to share the burden of his father's focus, though perhaps that had not been very gracious to wish upon someone else. But it would have been nice not to be so alone.

"How is everyone?"

"Good. We're good. Mother is fine." The young man's bright gaze moved to Matthew. "I hear we have you to thank for our relocation, Your Grace."

Although he was young, Micah Ashmore, Earl of Falmouth, obviously had his pride. Like his sister, he had the pale white-blond hair and stunning violet eyes, but his skin was not quite as translucent, and his jaw was more square. The threadbare clothing he wore did nothing to detract from his quiet dignity.

He sounded torn between gratitude at being saved and a kind of resigned embarrassment that it had been necessary.

"We're happy to host you for our wedding," Matthew said, coming forward to shake the young man's hand. "Also, I was hoping I could speak to you beforehand. As the man of the house."

Falmouth blinked in surprise, then nodded, squaring his shoulders. Because he was the man of the house, even if he had not been able to act as such. Behind him, Johanna smiled at Matthew in a manner that had him wishing they were alone…

But it was not to be.

Turning slightly, Falmouth looked at his sister again.

"Mother is asking for you." The words were barely out of his mouth before another of the siblings appeared at the top of the stairs. The middle sister, Bridget, Matthew thought her name was. She had the eyes as well, but her hair was a darker blonde, more wheat and honey than cornsilk.

"Johanna! Mother is asking for you."

"Micah just told me," Johanna responded, with only a touch of exasperation in her voice. "I am coming."

She glanced at Matthew, who nodded. He certainly was not going to keep her from her mother or from checking on the rest of her family.

"Your brother and I will be in the library," he told her.

Falmouth puffed up his chest a little, and Matthew hid a smile.

The young man had inherited his title even earlier and more unexpectedly than Matthew had, and although his title was a much lower one than a duke's, that only made Matthew's acknowledgment of him as a man count even more.

Johanna nodded, appearing relieved, and hurried up the stairs to her sister, who greeted her with another fierce hug before pulling her down the hall.

Matthew was not certain which rooms his grandmama had put everyone in, but he knew he would find out later.

"This way," he said to Falmouth, pulling his attention back to the matter at hand. "How was the journey to London?"

"Rather trying, though I have very little to compare it to," Falmouth replied seriously. Now that his sisters had disappeared from sight, the smile had fallen away from his lips. Matthew felt for him. "This is my first time in London."

Through some gentle probing, Matthew found out that the prior earl had meant to take his heir to London for the first time the year he'd died. An unfortunate circumstance, as the young man's new guardian decided that Falmouth had no need to visit London after his mourning was over. He should stay on the estate and learn about it.

Except that Mr. Blash was rarely there to teach him anything, and all Falmouth learned was how everything was falling into disrepair.

Sitting on one of the chairs in Matthew's library, head hanging, shoulder slumped, it was easy to see how defeated the young man already was. Matthew could not imagine being in such circumstances, and he was grateful his own road had been far different. Even though his father had been a righteous old bastard, and often cruel to boot, he'd ensured that Matthew never wanted for anything physically or materially.

"Falmouth, I need to speak to you man to man," Matthew said, bracing his elbows on his knees and leaning forward. "I did not have the chance to ask for your blessing before proposing to your sister."

"You have it," Falmouth said immediately. He gave Matthew a look. "Though I am not entirely sure you need it. Your Grace."

The side of Matthew's lip twitched, despite his desire to remain serious.

"Thank you. I would prefer to have the blessings of your family."

"As if we should be so foolish as to turn down a duke." Falmouth snorted, then colored as he realized what he was saying, what he was implying.

Matthew just chortled.

There really was something to be said about the impulsiveness of youth. Although Falmouth would need to learn to hold his tongue amongst the rest of the *ton*, right now, he reminded Matthew of himself at that age. However, he was not going to punish Falmouth for his blunt honesty the way that Matthew's father had him.

"Well, I am still happy to have your blessing." He cleared his throat. "As we are soon-to-be family, I wanted to speak frankly to you about Mr. Blash."

An expression flashed across Falmouth's face, too quickly for Matthew to tell what it was, but he got the distinct impression that there was not much love lost between Falmouth and his guardian.

"What about him?" The young man's tone was carefully neutral, guarded, in a completely different manner than his open bluntness from a moment ago.

"I believe he's stealing from you."

CHAPTER TEN

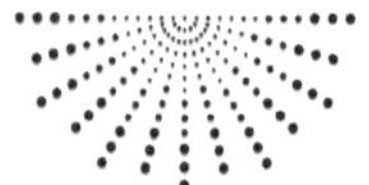

"This house is amazing!" Bridget whispered, pulling Johanna down the hall by her hand. "You're going to marry a duke? Did you meet him at that house party? Is that why you came to London, to beg him to marry you? How did you convince him to say yes? Did you know that Charlotte and I get our own maid? And mama gets one! And Rose gets one! And Micah has a footman now! His own footman! What are we supposed to do with them? Do you have your own maid? Do you have more than one since you're going to be a duchess? Will I have to call you 'Your Grace' or can I still call you Johanna?"

The rapid pace of questions was normal for Bridget, and Johanna did not even attempt to answer them. There was no point; Bridget would just keep talking over her even if she did. Besides which, most of it was Bridget working through her nerves.

Her grip on Johanna's hand was very tight. She was nervous, and it was coming out in the barrage of questions, which she was using to distract herself.

Johanna got quieter as she became unsettled, while Bridget got louder.

Her questions came to an abrupt halt when they turned the corner and saw Lady Stark and Rose in the corridor, speaking with their heads together. Johanna's heart stuttered for a moment. Not everyone was accepting of Rose as part of their family, given that she was illegitimate, even though she was obviously acknowledged. Someone as high on the instep as Lady Stark... She had been kind to Johanna, but would that extend to her cousin when she'd been born on the wrong side of the sheets?

To her relief, when Rose looked up, there was a slight smile on her face. Rose did not smile unless she meant it. She must like Lady Stark, and she would not like Lady Stark unless the lady was treating her well.

"There you are," Rose said, brightening even more when she saw Johanna. She hurried forward with her arms outstretched in front of her.

The hug Johanna gave her was even tighter than those she'd exchanged with her siblings. Though Micah was her brother and Bridget her sister by blood, Rose was her sister of the heart. The two of them had leaned on each other over the past few years, and Johanna did not know how she would have gotten through them without Rose.

"Everything is well?" she whispered in Rose's ear.

"Everything is well."

The sigh of relief Johanna exhaled left her feeling like a stiff wind could knock her over. Rose would not say that unless it was the truth. She always spoke the truth, no matter how unpleasant.

Mother was in no worse condition than Johanna had left her in; otherwise, Rose would have said something.

Hopefully, that meant it was not too late.

Bridget pulled on Johanna's arm.

"Johanna! Mama!"

"Ladies do not pull on people," Lady Stark announced, giving Bridget a gimlet eye, though there was no malice in her gaze. "They might gently touch someone on the shoulder or hand to give a wordless reminder. Come along, dear. Your sister will see your mama, and I will see to you and your sister. We have work to do."

Looking somewhat bewildered, Bridget immediately followed in Lady Stark's wake, much to Johanna's astonishment. There was just something about the duke's grandmother that made it impossible to say no to her, even for a normally rebellious and rambunctious thirteen-year-old girl.

"I never thought I would see the day," Rose whispered, clearly thinking along the same lines, as Lady Stark and Bridget went around the corner.

"Neither did I." Johanna gave herself a little shake. "Has mama eaten... anything?"

"She has." Rose's gaze shifted slightly. "Montagu brought us food for supper when he arrived, after he realized what we had to offer."

Even though what they had to offer would have been extremely sparse and not up to snuff for a duke, Rose obviously took exception to the duke's rejection of it. Or maybe it was just because it was that particular duke who had shown up on the Falmouth doorstep. Montagu *had* rubbed her the wrong way from the first.

"She is eating, but..." Rose's voice trailed off, and she frowned before shaking her head. "Something is upsetting her since we arrived. I do not know what. But she was also, well... she was not able to speak much before we arrived. Regular meals have helped bring her back to herself, so it's possible she was unsettled before as well, and I did not realize."

"She will not tell you why?" Johanna asked with a frown. In some ways, her mother and Rose were closer than she was with her mother. It was unheard of for Johanna's mother to insist on only speaking of something with Johanna, especially because she knew that Johanna would tell Rose.

Rose shook her head, and a little thread of tension wound its way through Johanna's stomach. An extremely unwelcome one.

Something very dire must be afoot.

"Very well. I should go see what she wants from me then," Johanna said, mostly because she could not imagine what her mother would wish to tell her but not Rose. Not knowing was going to drive both of them batty.

"Do. I will find Lady Stark and the girls." A ghost of a smile lit Rose's face again. "I am most curious to hear what she thinks they'll need to learn to become ladies."

Quite a bit, Johanna would imagine. Their mother had been too ill to give them lessons, and Rose and Johanna too busy to have time to spare for such things. Rose strode off down the hall as Johanna squared her shoulders and went into her mother's room.

The room itself was beautiful, very much like Johanna's, but decorated with soothing blues and creams. Just stepping inside helped to calm some of her nerves. Her mother lay in the huge four-poster bed, looking impossibly small on such a large piece of furniture. Pillows were piled up behind her, helping to prop her up in a sitting position.

"I told you, I want— Oh, Johanna," her mother said, her tone going from peevish to relieved. Her eyes widened. "I almost did not recognize you."

Johanna glided forward.

"Lady Stark, the duke's grandmother, took me shopping," she told her mother, settling down on the bed beside her and taking her mother's slim hand into her own. The fragile bones felt sharp against her palm. "I believe she plans to outfit me as a duchess by the end of this week."

Rather than smiling back, her mother looked more agitated at this pronouncement.

"It is the Duke of St. Albans whose house we're in, yes?" she asked. Johanna nodded, and fear lit up her mother's eyes. "You cannot marry him."

Johanna just stared at her mother for a moment, aghast. This was literally the answer to all of their prayers, and her mother was telling her not to marry him? Her mother stared back at her, her grip tightening on Johanna's hand, as though willing Johanna to say that she would not.

"What? Why not?" Her mother could not just make such pronouncements, given the circumstances, and expect Johanna to fall in line. She'd always done her best to be a good and dutiful daughter, but her mother had literally been starving herself to death. What else was Johanna supposed to do?

Exactly what I had been about to do, and if mother knew that...

"You cannot marry him." Her mother's voice dropped to a whisper, eyes darting this way and that, as if seeking to see whether they were alone... but there was no one in the room but the two of them. The fear and worry in her mother's expression was the only thing that kept Johanna from growing angry with her.

"But why not?"

Her mother's gaze met hers again, terrified, quelling Johanna's impatience.

"Because I killed his father," she whispered.

<u>*Matthew*</u>

Watching the young earl pacing back and forth, muttering under his breath, Matthew wondered if he should interrupt. Surreptitiously, he pulled his coin from his pocket and gave it a quick flip.

No. This was something the young man needed to work through on his own.

Matthew did not envy him the task.

Hard enough to feel as though he was too young to be much use at his own position, and that he was ill-trained for it, hard enough to see his elder sister shouldering more than her fair share of the burden, but to discover that it might not have been necessary? While Matthew did not have proof—yet—he had a gut feeling about Mr. Blash, and he would be shocked to discover he was wrong.

"That bastard." Falmouth punched his fist into his palm, likely in lieu of being able to plow it into his guardian's face. "I asked him—I *asked* him—to show me the accounts. Even if they were failing, I thought that I could learn from them. He kept putting me off or forgetting them, and the last time I insisted..."

His voice trailed off.

"What happened then?" Matthew asked, spurred on by pure curiosity.

Falmouth's shoulders slumped.

"He has not returned since." He raked his hand through his hair. "I am so stupid. I should have realized he was doing it on purpose."

"You are not stupid at all; you trusted him. He turned out to be unworthy of your trust, but you could not know that at the time." Matthew gave his coin another flip. Ah, yes, good. He got up from his seat, sliding the coin back into his pocket, and went over to clap the young man on the shoulder. He was not even a young man, truly, still more a boy on the cusp of manhood. He had his title and the responsibility that came with it but without the control he would one day have once he reached his majority. "It was not your fault that your father left your guardianship to the wrong man. Nor was it his, if he had no reason to think that this man was anything other than honorable."

"I suppose that's true. But what do I do now?" The young earl turned to look at Matthew, pleading for guidance in his eyes.

Which was the first time in Matthew's life that he'd ever found himself in such a position. Would it disturb Falmouth if he pulled out his coin and flipped it? Then again, Matthew had no proof that his coin worked for anyone else's life. Though it had predicted Nathanial and Kalina's happy marriage.

But that was just one instance. While Matthew was happy to rely on his for himself, he did not want to reassure anyone else that they could live their life by *his* luck.

Especially someone who was so down on their luck as the Earl of Falmouth already was.

"I ah... well. I have someone investigating Mr. Blash. Well, I have a friend who has sent an investigator after him. Drake. The Duke of Ormonde. He's got the right sort of contacts. And, well... give me a moment." Matthew turned around so he could flip his coin in front of him, with his back to Falmouth, so he could not see exactly what Matthew was doing. He would learn soon enough, Matthew was certain, but right now did not seem like the time to try to explain, especially when no one was there to vouch for the explanation. He turned back around. "Yes, we'll search for Mr. Blash and look into his activities, and in the meantime, you can stay here and learn from me."

"You'll be my tutor?"

"Well, in certain things. We should hire a real tutor for you, though, as well." Matthew eyed him. "And you'll need to attend university. Grandmama will know what to do."

If she did not already have a tutor in mind, she would ask one of her myriad contacts to suggest someone, he was sure.

"Grandmama will know what?" As if mentioning her had summoned her, his grandmother swept into the room with the younger two girls trailing after her. Matthew was not certain of their ages, but the one with honey-wheat hair was a little older and a little bigger. That would be Bridget. The youngest, Charlotte, was like a wraith. She was dressed in all white, which nearly matched her white-blonde hair, and her eyes were a lighter violet than either of her siblings, making her appear even more washed out, almost ghostly. The somber expression on her face did nothing to dispel the impression.

"Where to get a tutor for the earl." Matthew gestured at his soon-to-be brother-in-law, who appeared both eager and hopeful.

"Ah, yes. A tutor for Micah and a governess for Bridget and Charlotte." Grandmama tapped her lower lip as she went to sit on one of the chairs.

"We do not need a governess," Bridget protested immediately, crossing her arms over her chest. Beside her, her younger sister shifted silently back and forth on the balls of her feet, swaying slightly in a wind that no one else felt. It was more than a little eerie, and Matthew felt keenly uncomfortable looking at her.

"You need what I say you need, and you certainly need a governess. And a dancing instructor. We should discuss what instrument you'll learn as well." Grandmama pointed at the chair next to Micah. "Sit."

Unsurprisingly, despite the mutinous expression on her face, Bridget went and sat. Charlotte trailed after her like a silent specter.

Matthew hoped his bride was having a less fraught discussion with her mother than he was with the rest of her family.

CHAPTER ELEVEN

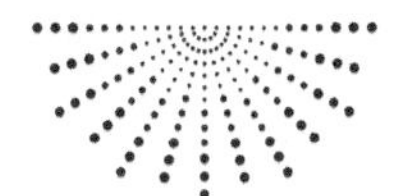

JOHANNA

Staring at her mother, Johanna shook her head. She could not have just heard what she thought she heard, but just in case her mother said it again… She got to her feet, snatching up one of the blankets on the foot of the bed and hurrying over to the door to press the material against the crack along the bottom. The last thing she needed was for someone to overhear her mother confessing to murdering a duke.

That was a hanging offense.

Turning around, she stared at her mother, who was still looking back at her with fear in her eyes.

"We have to escape here, Johanna," her mother whispered. "You have to gather your brother and sisters, and we have to escape."

"And go where, mother?" Johanna wrung her hands in front of her and shook her head, swiftly returning to her mother's bedside so they could speak quietly. The fear that was in her mother's eyes shook her, yet she worried about far more than what her mother had just said.

There would be consequences if she was overheard, but she also now worried that the lack of food and the condition of the family had driven her mother to madness. Johanna was not sure which would be worse—if her mother was overheard and believed, in which case she would be hanged or if her mother was overheard and declared mad. She would be sent away to somewhere Johanna could not help her, if that was the case.

Either way, there would be a stain on the family.

"Anywhere but here." Her mother reached for Johanna's hand and closed her claw-like fingers around it, her grip surprisingly strong in her desperation. "You cannot marry a man whose father I killed. He'll find out."

Johanna reached up with her other hand and pressed it to her mother's forehead. She was warm to the touch, but not feverish. Still. Whatever her mother was thinking, she was not in her right mind at the moment.

"You are imagining things, mother. The former Duke of St. Albans died in a fire," she said gently. "Did you ever even meet him?"

She knew her mother had not. How and where would she have met a duke?

"No, it was the Duke of Clarence's steward," her mother said, her voice going higher with stress and fear as she spoke. "Remember that winter when I suddenly had money? It was because I sold my sleeping potions to the Duke of Clarence's steward. He sought me out, and I did not care why. I did not ask. We needed the money. But a few weeks later, the dukes were dead. They were all dead."

"In a fire," Johanna said soothingly, repressing a little shudder. It did seem a terrible way to die, but that had nothing to do with her mother or sleeping potions. "It was a horrible, tragic accident, not murder."

"I thought the potions must be for the duchess or perhaps for the steward himself, as he looked unwell, but he never came back for more." Mother gripped Johanna's hand tighter, pulling her forward. "He must have given the dukes the sleeping potions to ensure they slept through the fire. To ensure they died."

First, she claimed she'd killed the dukes, now a murderous steward?

"It was an accident," Johanna said firmly. She'd heard enough comments today about the former dukes to know that not one soul suspected any kind of foul play. The loss of so many dukes at once had been a shocking accident. If there was more to it and no culprit caught, the gossip would have been rampant. "You are imagining guilt where there is none, mother. Perhaps the potions did not work, and that is why he did not return for more."

Of course her mother immediately looked affronted.

"My potions always work."

They did, as far as Johanna knew, when her mother had been able to make them. That did not change the facts, though. And the fact was that her mother was making up an utterly fantastical story in her head and feeling guilt for no reason. Though the emotion behind it was real, it was also misplaced.

"I will let you rest," she said gently. There was no point in arguing with her mother when she was like this. "We will speak more tomorrow."

"You cannot marry him, Johanna."

Holding back her arguments—because she *had* to marry the Duke of St. Albans, no matter what her mother said—Johanna got to her feet and pressed a kiss to her mother's forehead. Thankfully, it seemed as though her mother was running out of energy now that she had spoken to Johanna. Her eyelids drooped, even though she frowned.

"We will talk more tomorrow," Johanna said.

Hopefully, a good night's rest and a full belly would help her mother's mental state. Otherwise, Johanna was going to have to find some way to hide that her mother was losing her mind from the duke and his grandmother, and neither of them seemed feeble-minded.

At least her mother had had the sense not to blurt out such things in front of the others. She'd waited for Johanna.

Going to the door, Johanna picked up the blanket and draped it over the arm of a chair that was nearby. She glanced at her mother, who was watching her through half-lidded eyes. The expression on her face said she was unsatisfied, but she did not speak up to stop Johanna from leaving. Her slumped shoulders spoke of her exhaustion.

Opening the door, Johanna jolted when she realized there were people on the other side of it. Rose and a young man with brown hair and brown eyes that were framed by spectacles. He was neatly dressed, obviously not aristocracy by the quality, but well-to-do. There was a large black bag in his hand.

As his gaze met Johanna's, he smiled.

"My lady," he said, with a short bow. "I am Dr. Syme."

Johanna tried not to let her conflicting feelings show on her face—her worry that he and Rose had overheard some of her conversation with her mother, her dubiousness over the doctor's youth, or her surprise that someone was in the hall at all.

"Lady Johanna," she said faintly. "Um…"

"The others went to the library," Rose told her. "I wanted to accompany Dr. Syme." The warmth in her voice with which she said his name was all Johanna needed to know about how Rose felt toward the doctor. She approved of him, which assuaged most of Johanna's worries.

Rose clearly intended to supervise Dr. Syme's visit, but if she was already so warm toward him, Johanna could rest easily that it would not be a fight about how her mother was to be treated.

"Yes, and when we are done, I would like to keep speaking to you about the poultice." Dr. Syme beamed at Rose with interest in his gaze —not the kind of interest a man might have for a beautiful woman, but the interest of knowledge. He might be young, but he was clearly energetic and excited about his craft.

The fact he was willing to speak to Rose about such things, and learn from her, spoke well of him. That Rose seemed pleased with him meant he was competent and clever.

"I am happy to." Rose smiled back at him. "Come, I will introduce you to the countess."

She gave Johanna a nod as they walked past. Rose would take care of Johanna's mother, leaving her free to go find her siblings. Johanna let out a long breath as she held still for a moment in the hallway, trying to soothe her fraught emotions.

It did not sound like her mother was immediately blurting out a confession to murdering a duke to the doctor and Rose, so there was that at least.

The library.

Johanna strode down the hall, stopping a maid to point her in the right direction. Instead, the maid immediately abandoned her duties and showed Johanna herself, which she had not meant to have happen but was grateful for. She made a mental note to remember that maid for the future.

Johanna was not certain what she could do for her, but once she was the duchess, surely there would be something. Lady Stark had made it sound as though she would have dominion over the household. A daunting thought, but one which was made more appealing by knowing she could reward the staff when it was deserved.

"No." Bridget's voice drifted out of the open door, stubborn as always.

"Yes." Lady Stark's response was unbothered but firm.

Oh, dear. Bridget was arguing with Lady Stark? Johanna rushed into the room, pushing a smile that she did not feel onto her lips.

Lady Stark and Bridget appeared to be in a staring contest, while the duke and Micah watched with fascination but also appeared to be sitting as still as they could so as not to draw attention. Charlotte, as usual, was staring off into space, in her own little world. She was perfectly still on the large chair she and Bridget were sharing, her legs hanging down, feet hovering several inches above the floor.

"Hello," Johanna said brightly. "What are we talking about?"

"French," Bridget and Lady Stark said at the same time without breaking their eye contact, as if that explained everything.

Johanna looked at Micah.

"Lady Stark says we'll need to learn some French," he said tentatively, with a wary look at Bridget, whose scowl deepened.

"I am already going to have to learn dancing, embroidery, an instrument, math, reading, and geography; the line must be drawn somewhere," she said dramatically, breaking her gaze away from Lady Stark so that she could look at Johanna. "You are going to be the duchess. Tell her I do not have to learn French."

"That… is not… I am not…" Johanna fumbled over her words.

It was a good thing Bridget was not old enough to marry; she was already in the works to be a tiny despot. The last thing she needed was a duke as a husband to give her a taste of real power.

"Every young lady needs French, unless they wish for others to be able to speak about them without knowing what they are saying." Lady Stark arched her eyebrow.

Bridget's mouth opened. Closed. She frowned even more fiercely. Then her chin tipped up.

"I will learn French," she declared. "But that is it. No more lessons."

"No more lessons for now," Lady Stark agreed.

Bridget did not seem to pick up on the significance of the last two words, thankfully. She relaxed, pleased.

"I am going to learn the flute," she told Johanna. "What instrument do you play?"

"Ah… well." Johanna cast her mind back to her childhood. "I believe I mostly sang. Mother would play the piano, and I would sing." That was before their father had died.

"Oh." Bridget tilted her head. "I think I remember that. You do have a nice singing voice."

"Thankfully, you do not have to take singing lessons," Micah teased her. "You will sound much better with a flute instead. She has the singing voice of a donkey."

"Micah," Johanna said reprovingly as Bridget's face flushed hot. "That was ungentlemanly." It was true, but it was not gentlemanly to say so.

Micah looked at the duke, who raised his eyebrows at him.

"Sorry, Bridget," Micah said immediately, rather than arguing. As annoying as it was to have Micah listening to the duke rather than to Johanna, at least the duke had agreed with her.

Bridget sniffed and turned up her nose. Charlotte hummed under her breath, still staring into space, hands folded neatly in her lap.

"What instrument is Charlotte going to learn?" Johanna asked, hoping to turn the subject.

Everyone looked at Charlotte.

She blinked. Focused. Smiled at Johanna.

"Violin," she said, then her eyes unfocused again, and she went right back to humming. Which was very Charlotte.

Both Lady Stark and the duke appeared mildly concerned, but they would become accustomed to her ways. Or not. Charlotte had a tendency to fade into the background, something Johanna suspected she did deliberately. It allowed her to do as she pleased without being bothered most of the time. Bridget drew focus; Charlotte avoided it. Except for when she was trying to deliberately unsettle someone, which she was very good at and which also assured they would leave her alone.

"Well, then, that's settled." Johanna smiled again, trying to hide her worry that the duke might change his mind now that he'd met her family and realized everything he was taking on. Lady Stark seemed up to the challenge, but it was… a lot.

Her, her siblings' educations, her mother's health…

What was he getting out of this that he could not get from another young lady? One with fewer burdens accompanying her?

"Tomorrow we will go shopping. You all need to be properly outfitted," Lady Stark said. "Then, the day after that—"

"The wedding," the duke said.

Johanna could have melted into a puddle with relief. Whatever his reasons, he was not changing his mind. Could he really be that determined to follow a course set forth for him by a coin? Perhaps it was truly *her* lucky coin and not his because she could not see how any of this was lucky for *him.*

His grandmother glared at him.

"That is too soon."

"Her family is here, are they not? We do not need to waste time. The dress should be ready by then." He shrugged. "Besides, the faster we move, the more the gossip will be about the wedding and not about why the entire Falmouth household is living in *this* house. Or why Lady Johanna arrived before them. Or—"

"Enough." Lady Stark cut him off with a wave of her hand. She scowled at him. "I imagine you have a reason for that day?"

The duke's hand brushed over the pocket where Johanna had realized he kept his coin. He touched that pocket a lot, even when he was not using the coin.

"Yes."

"Very well." Her clipped tone said she was displeased, yet she did not argue with him, which Johanna found fascinating. Lady Stark did not seem the type to indulge fancies, but she indulged the duke and his coin. "The wedding will be the day after tomorrow."

"Will we have our new dresses by then?" Bridget asked, making Johanna groan softly.

Her mercenary little sister. Though she supposed she could not blame her for asking. They truly did not have anything appropriate to wear to a duke's wedding.

"Yes, you certainly will." Lady Stark and Bridget somehow looked very alike in that moment, despite their features being entirely different, and Johanna had a flash of what Bridget might be like in the future.

God help them all.

CHAPTER TWELVE

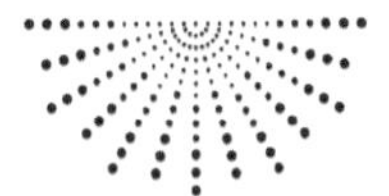

Supper with the Ashmores was a lively affair. Bridget and his grandmother were constantly butting heads, yet there was a certain amount of respect there. Having her at the table meant that his grandmother's focus was less on him, which he appreciated.

Micah had about a thousand questions, but thankfully, they were the kind of questions Matthew did feel comfortable answering. What would he be learning, what was university like, what did he need to know to run an estate, that sort of thing. The kinds of things a young man might be interested in.

To Matthew's surprise, he rather enjoyed playing mentor.

On his left, Johanna and her cousin Rose had their heads bent together. From the snippets he overheard, they appeared to mostly be speaking of Dr. Syme—who they seemed to approve of—and Johanna's mother's condition. Dr. Syme was worried that there was more to it than mere lack of food, which had Johanna worried.

Matthew hoped her mother would be well enough to attend the wedding, at least. He would like to meet her, but invading a woman's bedroom when it was a sickroom as well was hardly polite. Especially as they had *not* already been introduced.

He quickly flipped his coin.

No, he should not try to introduce himself while she was abed. Very well, then.

He lifted his head to pay attention to the conversation happening between his grandmother and Johanna's sisters, which was beginning to become rather heated.

"What about Rose?" Bridget asked, gesturing to her cousin, who was still talking quietly with Johanna.

"Of course Rose will come with us," Grandmama told Bridget. "She will need dresses too."

"See?" Bridget said, directing her comment across the table and snagging both Johanna and Rose's attention. "Rose, you have to come with us."

"I have what I need," Rose said, frowning. "It is not as though I will be appearing in public."

"Why not?"

"Because Johanna does not need a companion anymore now that she has Lady Stark to chaperone her."

"But how else are you going to find a husband?" Bridget asked exasperatedly.

"Who says I want one?" Rose snorted. "I certainly am not going to find one among the *ton*."

"Why not?"

A sudden silence fell over the group at Bridget's question. Not that many people had been talking before; they'd all become too distracted by Bridget and Rose's back and forth, but the quiet was somehow more fraught than normal. Matthew glanced at Micah, who was suddenly very interested in his dinner plate. Grandmama had averted her gaze, studying one of the paintings on the wall.

Rose glanced at him, then at his grandmother. Though her dusky skin did not show it, he got the feeling she was blushing. Beside her, Johanna put her fingers on the back of Rose's hand and leaned forward.

"Bridget, if Rose does not want to marry, then she does not have to."

"I just do not understand why she would not want to." Bridget pouted, slumping in her seat.

Matthew could explain it to her, but how illegitimate children came to be was not really proper mealtime discussion. His grandmother would likely have a conniption. Though with her connection to him, Rose might very well be able to attract a gentleman if she so wished. A younger son, perhaps. Maybe even a baron or viscount looking for a connection to a duke. She seemed a perfectly lovely young woman, so as far as he was concerned, she should have what she wanted.

The way she cared for her cousins and her aunt was especially admirable.

"Not everyone wants to be married," Johanna said firmly. "However, regardless of Rose's marital ambitions, I do agree that some new dresses for Rose are in order."

With that, the subject was changed, and Bridget, Johanna, and Grandmama set about leaning on Rose to update her wardrobe. Their combined efforts had her agreeing, with exasperation, not long after.

Supper concluded, followed by a few quiet moments where he and Micah were able to sit in blessed silence before joining the ladies in the drawing room. Matthew took the opportunity to offer to walk Johanna to her room—after a quick coin flip to reassure himself it was the correct decision. While her room was not that far from her family's, they were in a separate hallway, as her room had been placed closest to his grandmother's, while her family was too large to be all hosted in the same hall.

It was not a trip taken entirely alone, since they were still nearby, and Matthew was relieved to leave the younger siblings and Rose to their rooms while he escorted Johanna further on.

"How is your mother?" he asked, feeling rather awkward. He'd wanted a few moments alone with his bride, yet now that he had them, he was not certain how to progress. His hand brushed over his pocket.

"Ah... well, I think." Johanna's face turned away so he could not see her expression for a moment, before she faced forward again. "Rose seems pleased with Dr. Syme. Rest and a slow reintroduction to normal food was his recommendation."

"I am very glad to hear that. I am sorry she could not join us for dinner tonight."

"Yes, well." Johanna's face tilted away from him again. "Hopefully one day soon."

There was something in her voice, but he was not certain what it meant.

They came to a halt in front of her door. She was still looking away from him. Matthew quietly slid his coin from his pocket and gave it a quick flip, happily getting the answer he wanted.

"Johanna."

Her head jerked up, and her wide violet eyes looked up at him, meeting his gaze. There was... fear? Anxiousness? Worry?

Matthew did his best to smile reassuringly, even as his heart was beating a little faster in his chest. While he'd enjoyed playing the part of a charming rake, a cheerful lover who never overstayed his welcome, he'd never had to seduce a virgin before. Kissing debutantes had never been his speed.

But his bride-to-be was both.

"I would like to kiss you."

Her pink tongue flicked out across her lower lip as her eyes widened even more, which he had not realized was possible.

"You would?" she whispered.

"I would." He stepped to the side, turning toward her, and her head tilted back to hold his gaze.

The difference in their heights gave him a delightful view of her bosom as she sucked in a breath. He carefully slid one arm around her back, his other hand coming up to cup her chin and hold her in place. Had she ever been kissed before? Was he the first?

Not exactly questions he could ask a lady.

Matthew lowered his lips to hers. They were warm and soft beneath his, slightly parted, and he felt his desire stir at the tentative touch. In his arms, she felt even more fragile than before, so much smaller than him, yet when her hands came to rest on his arms, it felt as though her palms seared him through the fabric of his coat.

Her lips pressed more firmly against his.

She was kissing him back.

When his grip on her tightened, she gasped, and he slid his tongue between her lips, claiming her mouth with his own as a pulsing need for her awoke in him. He wanted her—badly. More than he thought he would, considering this was a marriage of convenience on both their parts.

But she was a beautiful woman. Thin, but soft against his body as they were pressed together. Her tongue was hesitant but willing. She tasted like sugar. And Matthew had not been with a woman in far too long, ever since he realized any woman in his bed might start getting ideas about staying there now that he'd inherited his title.

Johanna was going to be his duchess, though.

He was going to marry her the day after tomorrow.

Would it really be that bad to anticipate their vows…

The feeling of being watched crept along Matthew's skin, raising the little hairs on the back of his neck and dashing cold water over his growing desire.

Lifting his head, he held Johanna upright as she gasped, shivering against him, and looked over her shoulder at the ghost-like waif standing at the end of the hallway staring at them.

JOHANNA

Reeling from the duke's kiss, her body on fire with a thousand new sensations, it took Johanna a moment to realize he was no longer focused on her. His body stiffened, his arm still holding her up but no longer with the same kind of grip. She turned and saw Charlotte at the end of the hall, standing silent witness to Johanna's first kiss, and heat bloomed in her cheeks.

"Charlotte!" Her voice sounded strange to her ears. Shriller than normal, certainly. But different in an ineffable way. The difference between a woman who had never been kissed and a woman who had just experienced a first kiss that had sent her senses flying.

Without saying a word, her youngest sister glided away, back out of sight.

Johanna groaned, turning back to the duke but unable to look him in the eye. She rested her forehead against his shoulder, closing her eyes. She'd dreamed of her first kiss—what young woman had not?—but she'd never expected it to be like that. With his body so hard and strong against hers, his lips demanding but gentle—and his tongue in her mouth! She also had not imagined what might come after, nor had she anticipated having it witnessed by her youngest sister.

"Is she always like that?" the duke asked hesitantly. He still had not stepped away, his arms were still around her, and Johanna had to admit she rather liked it. Especially as her body throbbed pleasantly, feeling as though her senses had awakened from slumber.

The sensations coursing through her made it difficult to focus on what he was saying.

"Like what?" she asked.

"Ah… she is a bit…"

"Creepy?"

"Well…"

The answer was yes, she could tell, but he was too much of a gentleman to say so. Johanna let out a long breath, straightening up. To her surprise and delight, he did not let go of her when she did but continued to hold her close against him. She could not escape his arms, and she did not want to. With her own hands still on his biceps, she could feel the strength of them beneath her fingers. Her breasts felt as though they were swelling against him, aching and needy, and there was a pulsing in her core that went along with the throbbing between her legs.

Johanna shivered as their gazes met. There was something hot and needy in his dark eyes, the same thing she'd seen right before he kissed her.

"Yes, she has always been that way," she murmured.

"Ah. Well." Rather than answering, his gazed dropped to her lips.

Johanna leaned in. She desperately wanted him to kiss her again, but she did not know if she should say so. If she could say so.

Thankfully, that was all it took.

His lips claimed hers again, and the resurgence of sensations made her legs tremble, her knees nearly giving out from under her. Her hands slid up over the supple fabric of his coat so she could wrap her arms around his neck. The kiss deepened, his tongue thrusting into her mouth, dancing with hers, and Johanna found herself backing up step by step until she was crushed between him and the wall.

She rather liked being crushed.

If this was what being with a man was like, it was not so bad...

Though she knew her reaction was because it was *this* man. Her savior. Her knight in shining armor. He'd saved not only her, but her entire family.

It would not have been like this with any other man.

But with Matthew...

She wanted him. And she wanted to give him everything.

He was hard, all over, as he pressed against her, rocking his hips into her body and making her gasp as his lips moved from hers to leave a fiery trail of kisses along her jaw before he reached her sensitive throat. Johanna closed her eyes, tilting her head back to give him better access as one of his hands slid down to cup her bottom, while the other moved up to stroke the side of her breast.

Every part of her was on fire. Throbbing. Aching. *Needing.*

"Charlotte!" Rose's scolding tone had Johanna jerking back to her senses and the realization that she and the duke were *still* in the hallway. Both their heads whipped around, his hands frozen in place on her body, but thankfully, the end of the hall was empty.

"Not here," the duke muttered. And groaned. Closing his eyes, he lowered his forehead to hers.

"Your Grace?" she whispered back.

His eyes flew open.

"Matthew," he told her, softly but firmly. "You call me Matthew."

The sudden fluttering inside her chest had nothing to do with her physical reactions to him.

"Matthew."

"Matthew. Unhand that girl, immediately." Lady Stark's appalled tones made both of them jerk upright, and the duke practically flew back, several steps away from Johanna. The world felt cold without him pressed up against her, though the throbbing did not immediately go away. "You are not ravishing her before your ring is properly on her finger, young man. Now scat."

The imperious older woman waved her hand. Despite her obvious displeasure, the duke managed a bow as he sighed with resignation.

"It is not ravishing her if she agrees to it, Grandmama," he said cheekily, striding forward to give Lady Stark a kiss on the cheek. "And I *am* marrying her, as quickly as possible."

She made a hmphing noise as he passed by her. Turning, the duke —Matthew—looked at Johanna over his grandmother's shoulder and seared her with that single glance. What he had been going to do, Johanna was not entirely certain, but she wished he'd been able to do it. She would certainly have agreed to it.

"To bed with you," Lady Stark said, waving her hand at Johanna. "You two will behave under my roof."

"My roof, technically." Matthew's voice drifted back down the hall, even though he'd turned the corner.

"Do not worry, I do not blame you," Lady Stark told Johanna, continuing on as if she had not heard the duke, even though her hearing seemed to be perfectly fine. "That grandson of mine is a charmer through and through, and it is not as if you would know how to repel such advances. If you even wanted to."

Johanna's cheeks felt as though they were on fire and not in the way the duke had made her feel on fire. She had not wanted to repel his advances, and she was very much afraid Lady Stark knew that Johanna would have let him do whatever he wanted, right there in the hallway. That's how out of control she'd been.

"You will learn," Lady Stark said, nodding firmly. "There is a proper way for a duke and duchess to behave, and making love in the hallway is certainly not it."

"Yes, my lady," Johanna finally managed to respond, faintly.

"Now, go to bed. Tomorrow will be busy."

The only problem with Lady Stark's command was that once Johanna was in bed, her body still itched and yearned, and she had no idea what to do about it. It took much tossing and turning before she finally managed to fall asleep… and once she did, she dreamed of the duke and his kiss.

CHAPTER THIRTEEN

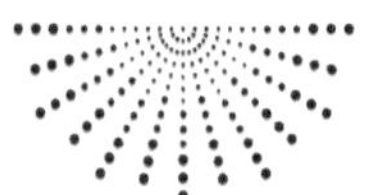

"What was it like?" Rose asked in a low whisper, glancing at Lady Stark, where she was speaking with the shopkeeper about bonnets for Bridget and Charlotte. They'd barely been able to speak privately during the day, so they took every opportunity for Johanna to catch Rose up on what had transpired between her and the duke.

It was all Johanna had to offer to get Rose to speak to her, once she'd admitted to Rose the real manner in which the duke had found her. Her cousin and best friend had been furious to know that Johanna was going to offer herself up in such a manner, and that she had not even tried consulting with Rose on other options. Despite the fact that Rose had not been there to consult with.

If Mr. Blash was smart, he would stay well away from the Falmouth household from now on. The duke seemed very displeased with him, but it was Rose's retribution he would really need to fear.

Telling Rose about the duke kissing her last night was the first thing that had broken through her cousin's icy façade. Neither of them had been kissed before yesterday.

"It was..." Johanna groped for the right description. 'Wet' did not nearly do it justice despite its accuracy, because it did not encompass any of the emotions or the reaction she'd had. 'Hot' had the same problem. "Magical."

Both of them giggled, and Johanna flushed from head to toe with the remembered sensations. Her body still felt as though it was buzzing. Especially after seeing him at breakfast this morning. She'd barely been able to look at him. When she had, he'd winked, and she'd felt like hiding under the table.

"Then there should be no problem on the wedding night," Rose said, sounding relieved.

Though neither she nor Johanna had been kissed, they knew a bit about what to expect between a man and a woman. Women had come seeking Johanna's mother for certain herbs and potions to help keep them from getting with child, as well as for assistance with births. Not the normal occupation for a countess, but Johanna's mother had been happy to assist. As such, Johanna knew the basics of what went on between a man and a woman.

But she had not known that it would feel so... so...

Good.

Especially because there had been instances for the young women visiting her mother where it had certainly not been good for them. A sobering thought, but also a relief that she would not experience such a thing. Because of her knight. Her duke.

"Rose. Come here. Gloves." Lady Stark beckoned.

Rose obeyed with a sigh and a sardonic look at Johanna.

She shrugged.

She was certainly not going to apologize for sharing her good fortune with her cousin and sisters. If Lady Stark wanted to outfit them all, then Lady Stark would outfit them all.

A tug on her sleeve made her look down.

Charlotte. Clad in all light grey. With her light coloring, the effect was very... creepy. As Johanna had told Matthew. Though she had not admitted that she'd always rather liked that about Charlotte. Her youngest sister walked to the beat of her own drum, and Johanna admired that about her.

"Yes, darling?" she asked gently, leaning down so Charlotte would not have to raise her voice to be heard. She liked to speak softly, when she spoke at all, perhaps because Micah and Bridget tended to make enough noise for all of them.

"Mama's wrong," Charlotte told her quite seriously. "You need to marry the duke."

Turning in place, though she did not seem to actually move her feet when she did so, Charlotte glided away. A shiver went down Johanna's spine. Yes, her youngest sister was a touch eerie at times. As if those violet eyes knew things other people did not. Even though Johanna knew the same was occasionally said about her, with Charlotte... she was not certain they were incorrect.

"What was that about?" Bridget asked from behind Johanna. Straightening, Johanna turned and cast a gimlet eye at her middle sister.

Charlotte could be unsettling just by being herself, but Bridget would deliberately work to discombobulate a person.

"She's glad I'm marrying the duke," Johanna said simply, rather than getting further into what Charlotte might have meant and what she might have overheard.

"So am I." Bridget preened, holding out her hands, which were covered with a fetching pair of kid gloves, a fawn color that nearly matched her hair. "Look at these gloves! We have whole new wardrobes, Johanna!" She spun in place, too delighted to remember to be ladylike.

Johanna could not help but laugh. It had been so long since her sisters had anything to be happy over, especially when it came to their clothing or fripperies. And Bridget did love her clothing and fripperies.

"Do not be gauche, Bridget," Lady Stark said. "It is not done to rub others' noses in your good fortune."

"I am sorry, Lady Stark." Bridget beamed at her, not appearing sorry at all. "I am just so happy. Thank you so much for your generosity. Today is the best day of my life."

Happy and winsome enough that the shopkeeper and other ladies in the shop were all smiling at her, some with sympathy after the set-down Lady Stark had given her. Even Lady Stark was not immune to Bridget's charm, though she did her best to hide her smile. Johanna could have told her it was not worth the attempt—even the hint of a smile and Bridget became incorrigible.

If she was not also sweet, generous, and genuinely appreciative, she would have been insufferable.

"Gunter's," Lady Stark declared. "For ice cream."

Bridget cheered, and Johanna could not stop herself from making a very small cheering sound of her own. It truly was a wonderful day.

And tomorrow she would marry a duke. Bridget might be excited, but Johanna was still terrified.

Still, if last night was anything to go by, there were some parts of being a duchess that she thought she might enjoy.

MATTHEW

Spending time with Micah Ashfield was rather enjoyable, Matthew found. While part of him felt as though he should be looking for the Earl of Cornwall and finding out why he'd invited the Duke of Hereford to the hunting lodge where he'd died, it was nice to help someone with their problems for a bit instead.

First, he took Micah to the tailor, which thankfully did not require much input from him since they were well equipped to outfit the earl without Matthew's opinion. After that, it was several stops at shops for other necessities, by which time Micah was beginning to look a bit apprehensive.

"Is something amiss?" Matthew asked him. "Was there something else you needed?" He did not like seeing the young man's exuberance dimmed.

Micah shook his head.

"You have already done too much," he said quietly, ducking his head down and glancing at Matthew as they walked along the street. The passersby were paying very little attention to them, other than those who recognized Matthew and made their acknowledgments.

Several glanced at Micah's startlingly light hair with interest, but no more than that. "I am not sure I can ever repay you."

"You do not need to," Matthew reassured him, feeling utterly generous. He'd already flipped his coin and knew that he was paying for everything, as a gift. "I am marrying your sister. It is only expected from the *ton* that I would take you under my wing and ensure you and your family are provided for."

For a long moment, Micah was silent, processing that thought as they ambled down the road.

"I feel as though I should not lean on you, though," he replied quietly. "I am going to be an earl."

"When you reach your majority, that might be true," Matthew agreed cheerfully. "But you will always be able to come to me with any questions you have. We are going to be family."

Though he would not have gone to his own father with questions, Matthew had good friends who he could approach with any of his issues. He had seen some of their relationships with their fathers and knew what was possible. Not that Micah was his son, but he could fill the role in some manner, especially as Micah's guardian had proven to be deficient.

Even if the man was not stealing from the estate, suggesting that Johanna sell herself at such an auction as they'd attempted…

The man was a scoundrel and a reprobate from that alone.

"You should also cultivate a group of friends. You'll find them at university, most likely, or among your peers," Matthew explained as a man who fit such a description appeared at the corner. The Duke of Ormonde was also out for a walk today… or perhaps, going by his disheveled appearance and unshaven jawline, on his way home from the night before. "Come along."

Matthew picked up the pace, and Micah followed him with alacrity.

"Ormonde!" Matthew called out before Drake could cross the street, not caring that it was gauche. Perhaps he should have checked with his coin, but there was not enough time, and he did not want Drake to disappear into the crowd.

The other man paused and turned, his expression clearing when he saw that it was Matthew hailing him. His eyes flicked to Matthew's side, where Micah was coming along.

"St. Albans," he said with a formal nod. "And Falmouth, I presume."

"The Duke of Ormonde," Matthew told Micah, who breathlessly made his bow.

Despite his rumpled clothing and hairy face, Drake made a rather imposing figure in his black attire, relieved only by the starchy white of his shirt and the copper pocket square tucked over his breast. There was always something about him that exuded high amounts of confidence, even for a duke.

"I was hoping to catch you," Matthew said. "I was wondering if you'd sent out the investigators yet."

"Sent, and they have returned." Drake's dark gaze flicked over Matthew and Micah. "I was going to visit you this afternoon. You might as well come with me. This is not a discussion for the street."

Which was how Micah ended up visiting the Duke of Ormonde's household with Matthew and learned that not only had his former guardian been stealing from them, but he'd fled to the Americas already. He'd boarded the ship yesterday and was currently far out of their reach.

Micah knew a startling number of curses for a youth in a household full of women, and he fair blistered the air with them as he paced around in a rage afterward.

Neither of the dukes stopped him. They both understood that kind of anger. If anything, Drake looked upon him more companionably once he'd settled back down.

"There is nothing to be done for now," Drake told Micah once he'd sat, slumping in his seat with a weariness in his expression that went far beyond his years. He really was far too thin. Living in Matthew's household, under his grandmother's wing, should help rectify that. "I will send men after him, and we will have him returned to England to pay for his crimes when we can. In the meantime, we will have Matthew appointed as your new guardian and recover what funds we can."

"But why would you do all this for me?" Micah asked, looking at Drake with utter bewilderment. "I know Matthew is to be my brother-in-law and feels responsible… but why are you doing this?"

"Because sometimes everyone needs some help, and when we receive it, it is our responsibility to either repay it or to pay it forward," Drake explained calmly, handing the young man a glass of water to sip from.

Micah pondered this when there was a knock at the door, and Drake's butler came in with a silver tray balanced on one hand.

"The mail, Your Grace," he intoned somberly, holding the tray out in front of him with a small bow so that Drake could pick up the stack of letters and cards. Having performed his service, he immediately exited back out of the room.

The duke shuffled through them quickly and raised his eyebrows before lifting a single invitation from the pile.

"Your wedding is tomorrow?" he asked Matthew. "And a dinner tonight, in lieu of an engagement ball."

"Really?" Matthew asked, trying to lean forward and see what was written there. "That must be my grandmother's doing. I did not realize we were to host anything tonight. What time?"

Drake snorted his amusement, shaking his head as he handed the invitation over for Micah to see.

"I will be there," he said. "I am looking forward to being properly introduced to your bride."

Since the last time he'd seen her had been immediately following Matthew's purchase of her at the auction. If Micah caught the reference, it did not show on his face.

"If Grandmama is inviting you, she is probably inviting the others," Matthew said, scanning over the invitation.

"The others?" Micah asked.

"The tragic dukes," Drake explained. He grimaced when Micah shook his head in confusion, and Matthew shrugged. He had not told the story to his bride's family, because it did not seem of any importance. "Those of us who inherited our titles early when our fathers were killed in a fire at the hunting lodge they were visiting."

"That's terrible, I'm so sorry," Micah replied, with all the sad fervor of someone who understood completely—because of course he did. "What a terrible accident."

Drake and Matthew exchanged glances.

"Actually," Drake said, leaning forward to brace his elbows against his knees, before Matthew could flip his coin to decide whether to tell Micah. "There is something you should know, as your sister is marrying Matthew and you are the man of the house…"

Because it had been no accident, though that was the official verdict of the investigation. So far, it did not seem as though there was any further danger, but there was always the chance of something they'd missed. Or of stirring things up now that they were investigating their fathers' deaths, if the culprit got wind of what they were doing.

It was unlikely Johanna would be put in any danger by marrying Matthew, but there was always the chance. Her brother, even if he had not reached his majority, should know the truth.

Matthew supposed that eventually he would need to tell Johanna as well.

Pulling out his coin, he gave it a quick flip as Drake filled Micah in.

Apparently, it would have to wait for another day.

CHAPTER FOURTEEN

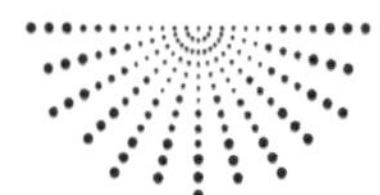

JOHANNA

Wearing one of her new gowns, a beautiful eggplant color trimmed with silver, Johanna turned back and forth to look at herself in the mirror, her eyes wide at the vision before her.

"You look perfect," Nettie said proudly, as she should since Johanna's current appearance was mostly due to Nettie's skills.

"Thank you, Nettie."

There was a knock on the door, and Nettie immediately jumped.

"I'll get that!"

Johanna was grateful because she could not stop staring at herself. She looked like a lady. A real lady. The way she had been trying to look when she'd gone to the Blackstone house party. Then, she'd been a tawdry, cheap imitation of what a lady of the *ton* looked like. An out-of-date one, at that.

Now...

She truly did look like an earl's sister. A duke's soon-to-be duchess.

If only she felt as different on the inside as she looked on the outside.

"Ah, perfect," Lady Stark said as soon as she came through the door, Rose following in her wake. She was also wearing a new gown. It had been made for another lady who decided that the dark maroon silk did not flatter her, fortunately for Rose. Though Johanna could tell her cousin was uncomfortable with the low-cut neckline and the richness of the dress, she looked stunning in it. "Just as you should look, but with one small touch missing."

Lady Stark gestured at Rose, who handed over a box she was carrying. Johanna had been so distracted by their combined finery that she had not even noticed Rose was holding anything.

Now Lady Stark came forward, a gleam in her eye that was almost predatory.

"Sit."

Future duchess or not, Johanna sat. Immediately.

Lady Stark moved behind Johanna, so they could both see her in the vanity looking glass, which framed Johanna's upper body perfectly. The light grey of Lady Stark's dress behind her made for a perfect foil of colors.

Opening the box, Lady Stark took something out of it before setting it on the vanity in front of Johanna. She did not get more than a glimpse of purple and sparkles before something was draped around her neck.

"Oh," she said softly, her fingers reaching up to the cool stones as they settled on her collarbone. The array of sparkling purple stones was lighter than her dress, but complemented it well and enhanced the effect the dark purple hue had on her eyes.

"Amethysts," Lady Stark said smugly. "Just the trick for you. Rubies for Rose eventually, but not tonight."

"Not ever," Rose muttered, but Lady Stark did not even twitch, ignoring Rose's rejection of her suggestion.

"They're beautiful… but… I cannot…"

"You can and you will. These are from the family's set, which will be yours after tomorrow. They might as well have been made for you," Lady Stark said matter-of-factly. "Now, the earrings and brooch. We will save the tiara for tomorrow."

Johanna took a deep breath, but she could tell Lady Stark was not going to be denied. Arguing would be a waste of breath.

Besides, Lady Stark was correct. Adding the earrings and brooch completed the look.

Now she really did appear to be a duchess.

But she felt like a child wearing her mother's clothing for play.

"You look beautiful," Rose said, coming to Johanna's side and putting her hand on Johanna's shoulder as if sensing her need for reassurance. Rose often seemed to know exactly what Johanna needed even before Johanna did. Not the words, but the comforting hand, the touch of someone who knew her and believed in her and would be there for her no matter what happened. That was what Johanna needed right now, and somehow, Rose had known it.

The touch settled her, and she took a deep breath. She was still her, no matter what she wore or what title she had, and she would do her best. As she always had. That was all she could do.

"Thank you," she murmured, reaching up to put her hand over Rose's. They gave each other a quick squeeze.

"Guests should be arriving shortly," Lady Stark said, sweeping out of the room as quickly as she'd come in.

Johanna looked up at Rose, bemused.

"Do you think we are meant to follow her?"

"I assume so," Rose said, sounding both exasperated and entertained.

"Most certainly," Nettie chimed in, nodding her head.

Johanna got to her feet and strode out, arm in arm with Rose. She was so grateful for her cousin's presence. She did not know how she would be able to do this without her.

"Your mother began running a fever this afternoon," Rose said in a low voice. "Dr. Syme has already attended her and did not seem worried. Did you know he is the housekeeper's nephew?"

"I did not." How interesting. She wondered if the family connection was why the duke had a young, different kind of doctor in attendance. "I should go see her."

"Not before supper." Rose squeezed her arm. "She was sleeping when I peeked in on her, and you do not want to disturb her rest. There has been a great deal of upheaval around her the past few days."

Upheaval and delusions. Worry that her mother might say something in front of someone else trickled through Johanna, but she did not know what she could do about it. Her mother had already been gripped with nerves before she'd been feverish… perhaps that was what had precipitated her belief that she'd caused a duke's death?

In any case, her mother's absence from this dinner might not be the worst thing, even though Johanna did not wish her ill health.

"Do you think she will be able to attend the wedding tomorrow?" Johanna whispered as they neared the staircase. She could already hear her brother's and sisters' voices echoing in the foyer.

"I do not know. We will have to see how she is doing tomorrow. I will ensure she has some willow bark tea tonight."

"Thank you." Johanna could almost taste the flavor of the tea herself the moment Rose mentioned it—it was what her mother always gave them for a fever, and Johanna had never liked it.

They reached the top of the stairs, and she looked down at her family and could not help her smile. Micah was so handsome, standing stiffly beside the duke, in a coat that was actually fitted to him. When had he grown into a young man? Bridget and Charlotte were still in short skirts, of course, but they both somehow looked older than they had before, now that they were properly clothed.

Johanna's heart ached inside her chest, and she reached up to touch her fingertips to her breast to try to relieve the pressure.

Her siblings were growing up and leaving childhood behind, and she was so relieved to have them here in the duke's London home rather than at their crumbling estate. Which was an awful feeling to have because that had been their home for their whole lives, but for the first time in a long time, she was truly able to feel real hope for the future.

That things would be different.

That they would have enough to eat. That Micah could get the education he deserved. That Bridget and Charlotte would get the lessons they needed and the futures they were born for. The weight, which had felt so heavy on her shoulders for so many years, had lessened overnight when the duke had purchased her.

He was an honorable man. A good man.

Johanna finally let her gaze rest on him and felt her breath catch in her throat, her heart no longer tight in her chest but racing within it. The dark grey of his jacket was set off by a plum-and-silver waistcoat and a matching plum cravat tied around his neck, only a couple shades off from the color of her own gown. They were not matching, but they would appear coordinated beside each other—and she knew exactly who had done the coordinating. Lady Stark appeared particularly smug in her place beside the duke.

The stiff points of his starched white collar framed his jawline. A silver cravat pin with an amethyst topper was just beneath his chin, holding the complicated knot in place. His dark hair waved back from his face, so that his burning gaze was completely unobscured as he drank in the sight of her coming down the stairs.

"He is looking at you as though you are a pudding and he wants to devour you," Rose murmured beneath her breath.

Yes, he was.

And Johanna realized she was all too happy to be devoured.

The two men moved to the bottom of the stairs as she and Rose descended, the duke's gaze never leaving Johanna's as he took his place. Micah moved into position on Rose's side, watching the duke for cues. He really had grown so much, but Johanna could not focus on him when the duke held all her attention at that moment.

Her skin tingled, her stomach swooping as she released her arm from Rose's and took his hand.

"My lady." He bowed over her hand, turning it so that when he pressed his lips against her skin, it was against the inside of her wrist.

Butterflies exploded in her stomach as her breathing stopped for a moment, her heart pounding so hard in her chest that it felt impossible that no one could hear it. No one else seemed to notice anything amiss, though.

"Johanna, look at me!" Bridget spun in place, arms out around her, skirt billowing. She was beaming as she came to a halt.

"You look beautiful," Johanna said honestly as the duke pulled her hand onto his arm, so they were standing side by side, her fingers now resting on his wrist with his hand over hers. His very nearness made her feel breathless, but she did her best to hide her reaction to him.

She doubted duchesses were overwhelmed by the mere presence of their husbands.

Perhaps she would be able to watch the others tonight to see how they behaved. When Lady Stark had suggested the dinner, Johanna had been anxious until she'd realized the guest list was all the duke's friends and their families, which meant Lady Astrid and her friends. Now, Johanna's friends or at least women she was hoping would be her friends.

They had seemed to accept her as one of their own, and she'd already told them her biggest secret.

As if her thoughts summoned them, there was a knock at the front door. Johanna squared her shoulders to meet their guests as the butler moved to answer it. Beside her, the duke smiled in anticipation, which helped her to relax. He did not seem nervous at all.

Matthew

Having a table full of dinner guests was more enjoyable than Matthew had anticipated. He was sorry his bride's mother could not join them, but he knew she had been doing poorly before she arrived in London. The travel must not have agreed with her.

Beside him, Johanna was resplendent in her new gown, with violet jewels at her throat and ears. When she'd first come down the stairs, Matthew had had a burning desire to see her in nothing but those jewels. It was all he could do not to stare at her throughout the meal, imagining peeling her clothing from her body one piece at a time to reveal what was underneath until she was completely bare before him, clad in nothing but the amethysts.

A fantasy he'd forced himself to abandon because it made for uncomfortable sitting when they were surrounded by company.

At one end of the table were the younger crew. Nathanial had brought his sisters, as promised, to meet Bridget and Charlotte. They seemed to be getting along splendidly. Beside them were Micah, Ashwin Little, and Rupert Blackstone. The latter two had formed a fast friendship already but were very welcoming to Micah.

Julianna, Nathanial's eldest sister, who should have debuted this year but was prevented from doing so by the dire straits of their finances, seemed thrilled to be included in such a supper. Since it was a family affair, she could attend without raising any eyebrows.

Seated next to Sebastian, the two of them looked to be in rather close conversation. Sebastian had proven to be rather picky about his prospective wife; perhaps he'd found a suitable match in Julianna? The rest of the dukes and their wives were spread about the table, with Matthew's grandmama between Sebastian and Nathanial.

"I am not cabbage-headed," Lady Astrid said from beside Matthew, cutting through his musings. She was gripping her fork like she wanted to stab Drake with it.

"I called you *mon petit chou*, I did not call you cabbage-*headed*. It is an endearment." Not that Drake sounded particularly fond of his betrothed as he spoke the words through gritted teeth. "Though if you do not want to be called cabbage-headed, then stop acting cabbage-headed."

"You do not need to call me anything."

"Like you do not need to call me Lucifer?" Drake's response was droll, while Lady Astrid was living up to the fiery nature of her hair.

Matthew could all but feel her simmering at his side.

"I call things as I see them," she responded tartly. "If you do not want to be called Lucifer, then stop acting as—"

"I am not the devil," Drake snapped back at her, apparently not enjoying having his own words tossed back at him. "I was trying out an endearment; you do not have to be such a shrew."

"I would rather be a shrew than a cabbage."

"Should we be worried about them?" Johanna asked, leaning into Matthew to murmur the question. She was not the only one now watching the back-and-forth between the squabbling two. Why his grandmama had insisted on putting them beside each other at the table, just because they were engaged, Matthew did not know.

Grandmama was now turning her head to stare reprovingly at them, not that either noticed. Matthew should likely intervene… probably. He quickly took out his coin and flipped it beneath the table, unsurprised by the answer he received.

Reaching over, he plucked the fork from Lady Astrid's hand, causing her head to whip around, fire in her eyes as she glared at him.

"Just in case you start to mistake Drake for the next course," he told her with a grin.

For a moment, he thought she was going to burn even hotter, but then she laughed, her shoulders relaxing. Beyond her, Drake looked torn between exasperation and relief at the interruption.

"He is far too sinewy to be pleasant to eat," Lady Astrid said, her lips curving into a smile, her voice no longer tight with tension.

"It's a well-known fact that dukes need tenderizing," he replied with a wink, making her laugh again.

Now Drake frowned, then sighed. Shaking his head, he turned to speak with Tiffany, the Duchess of Clarence, who was on his right. Matthew felt Johanna relax as well, and her focus was drawn away by a question from Christian, who was seated on her other side. His grandmama nodded approvingly at Matthew before returning to her discussion with Nathanial.

Leaning over, Lady Astrid's focus now on Matthew, her green eyes with their unusual gold flecks bore into his.

"Are you going to need tenderizing when it comes to Johanna?" she asked quietly but sternly. It was not exactly a threat, yet Matthew knew exactly who would do the tenderizing if she decided he did, and he had no desire to be stuck with her fork.

"She has nothing to fear from me," he reassured her.

"She told me how you rescued her."

That was a surprise and took Matthew aback for a moment. But he supposed ladies did talk, and if Johanna was going to reveal their secret to anyone, the other duchesses were a good choice. Not that Lady Astrid was a duchess yet, but that was how he thought of her.

The other dukes would know, so it only seemed right that their wives should as well.

"I was happy to." He glanced over his shoulder at where his soon-to-be wife was listening to something Christian was saying. "No young woman should have been left in those circumstances."

"I agree. Thank you for saving her."

"It was all my pleasure," Matthew said sincerely. And he felt like it was going to be even more his pleasure once he wedded her and was finally able to bed her, satiating the desire that had risen up so unexpectedly strong inside him.

Even though they were speaking with their dinner companions, rather than each other, he was acutely aware of her presence at his side. And when the evening ended, and they parted ways, all he could think about was the fact that tomorrow night, he would finally have her beside him all night, in his bed.

He could hardly wait.

CHAPTER FIFTEEN

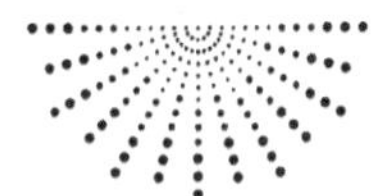

The morning of his wedding dawned bright, without a cloud in the sky. Matthew took that as a good sign. Rather than breaking his fast in the dining room, he ordered a tray in. The quiet was rather nice. Plus, it was bad luck to see his bride on their wedding day, so he flipped his coin to see if he should attend breakfast and discovered he should not.

So, a tray in his room it was.

He was not entirely surprised when his Grandmama stopped by to speak with him, not long after he finished eating. She did not even raise an eyebrow at finding him still in his dressing gown.

"Matthew." She sighed as she sat down on one of his chairs. "Are you sure you know what you are about?"

Blinking, he tilted his head at her.

"What do you mean, Grandmama? I thought you liked Johanna. You certainly are spending my money as if you do."

"I would spend the money regardless, as she and her family need to be brought up to snuff if she is going to be your bride," she said reprovingly. "But you are moving very quickly. The poor girl is over-whelmed. Her family is overwhelmed. You have moved them from their own home and are thrusting them into the heart of the *ton*, unprepared and untrained."

"They are overwhelmed?" He had seen no evidence of any such thing.

"Yes. Well, not Bridget." Grandmama waved her hand. "I do not think Napoleon's armies could have overwhelmed that girl. But the rest of them…"

"If they are overwhelmed, they are bearing up incredibly well."

"Perhaps." She pursed her lips, and he knew that she had not yet gotten around to what she really wanted to say. Which was unusual for her, as normally she went straight to the point. She only avoided it when she thought he might take it badly. "More to the point, are you sure you want to marry her?"

"Of course." He realized his hand was smoothing over the pocket where his coin rested, and he quickly dropped his hand into his lap. Grandmama, of course, saw everything anyway, and she raised her eyebrow at him. "I have already said I would, and I see no reason to change my mind. She is perfectly suitable."

Besides, his coin had told him to.

Which he knew was his grandmother's real objection.

"What I am saying is that you cannot flip a coin for love," she finally said, sounding exasperated.

Yes, he'd been correct, although he was surprised by her assumption.

"Oh, I know," he reassured her. "I flipped it for a bride."

The expression on her face was very odd. If she was not his grandmother, he would think she wanted to stick him with a fork, the way Lady Astrid would with Drake. She closed her eyes for a moment, and he knew that she was calling on her patience, though he did not entirely understand why.

Matthew waited. If she had a point to make, she would do so when she was ready.

Finally, she opened her eyes again.

"I want you to be happy, Matthew," she said firmly, and he nodded.

Happy was also what he wanted. "I would like you to have a love match. Like your friends."

"You know those were not truly love matches."

"They became such."

Had they? Matthew had not realized. Or perhaps it was just his grandmother being fanciful. Of course, Gregory and Nathanial liked their wives. Nathanial had forgiven Kalina for trapping him—or, rather, he now believed it was her father who had trapped him and he'd forgiven her father. Gregory was married to Sebastian's sister, so of course he was going to do everything he could to keep her happy.

But love?

That seemed unlikely.

He would have to ask them.

"Do you think you could one day love Johanna?" Grandmama asked wistfully.

"I do not know." It was the honest answer.

"Don't you dare take out that coin to flip it for this!" Her sharp order made him drop his hand.

Which was for the best, as he had not realized that he was reaching for the coin until she'd told him not to. Still, he did not see what was wrong with using his coin to ask if he would fall in love with his wife.

"I was not going to."

It was a lie, and they both knew it.

"Promise me, Matthew." Grandmama gave him that hard look that let him know she was not going to leave him alone until he did as she asked. "Promise me that you will not flip that coin for love. That is not how love works."

"I promise," he said. It did not matter anyway. They were getting married; that had nothing to do with love.

His grandmother looked at him as though she was uncertain he was telling her the truth, but after a moment, she sighed and nodded.

"Very well. I will see you at the chapel. Do not be late."

"Of course."

He was not going to miss out on his wedding because he was certainly not going to miss out on his wedding night.

<hr>

JOHANNA

Rather than going down to breakfast, Johanna took a tray in her room. She was far too nervous to face anyone over the breakfast table. The thought of dealing with her siblings and their questions was too much. Besides, she wanted some peace and quiet before her life changed even more than it already had.

Just being in this room made her feel anxious. Knowing that tonight she would be moving to the duchess' room... and knowing she was going to have to fulfill her marital duties...

That was both exciting and nerve-racking.

The knock on her door did not surprise her.

"Come in," she called.

The door opened a crack, and Rose slipped in, a frown on her face.

"You did not come down to breakfast," she said, coming into the room. She pulled one of the extra chairs over to where Johanna was sitting at the window seat, settling on the other side of Johanna's breakfast tray. She was dressed in a cream gown with a misty red overgown, the combination lightening the scarlet hue so it was not so bright.

"I wanted to eat here and gather my thoughts." Johanna gestured at the tray, which was admittedly still quite full. She had not managed to eat more than a few bites, even without the distractions of the rest of her family.

"Doing more of the latter than the former, I see." Rose pushed the plate toward Johanna.

With an internal sigh, Johanna leaned forward and picked up the piece of toast that she'd nibbled on. She could nibble a little more.

"Your mother's fever is holding steady. It has not gone down, but it has not gone up."

Nodding, Johanna sighed. She had looked in on her mother earlier, but her mother had been sleeping peacefully, and she had not wanted to disturb her rest. As much as she wanted her mother to be at her wedding, this might be for the best. This way, she would not have to worry about her mother saying something she should not in the middle of it. Some of the tension she was feeling receded.

Yes. Perhaps it was better that her mother not attend.

Once mother was feeling better, surely this delusion about being a part of the deaths of the dukes would go away.

"What of Bridget and Charlotte?"

"Bridget is *in alt* at the idea of being your flower girl. Charlotte is… Charlotte. I think they enjoyed meeting Emma and Fiona last night." Rose's lips quirked. "Did you know that Fiona had a squirrel in her pocket while she was here?"

Johanna's mouth dropped open in shock and slight horror at the realization of what could have gone wrong.

"I did not," she said faintly.

"Do not worry, I mentioned it to Kalina, and she promised to ensure Fiona would not sneak any animals into the wedding with her." Rose smiled. "Apparently, she is a great animal lover and spends a lot of time taking care of injured ones, which is how she got the squirrel."

"Do you think Lady Stark knew?" Johanna asked, her hand drifting up to her mouth. "She must not have. Can you imagine how she would have reacted? I hope Charlotte does not get any ideas…"

"I do not think Charlotte's interests include bringing home scores of animals," Rose reassured her with a smirk. She picked up a piece of fruit to eat from Johanna's tray. "Micah was worried you did not come down to breakfast, but I reassured him that you were probably resting before the hubbub."

Her poor brother. Too young to properly be the earl, yet feeling all the weight of it.

"Thank you. I probably should have thought about how they would react, but… I just needed some quiet."

"Understandably. And by this evening, you will be a married woman." Rose glanced around the room. "Have your things already been moved?"

"What things I had." Most of her wardrobe was still on its way from the modiste, although the wedding gown should be delivered at any moment. Once it was, she would get dressed. She smoothed her hands over the skirt of the day gown she'd put on to eat her breakfast and let out a long breath. "I cannot believe I am to be in the duchess' rooms tonight."

"Are you worried about tonight?" Rose's eyes glinted with curiosity.

"Of course," Johanna admitted. "I mean, theoretically, I know what to do. But I do not actually *know* what to do. If you know what I mean."

"Strangely, I think I do. Do you *want* to do it?"

"I… I think I do." She felt the blush rise in her cheeks, lowering her voice even though it was just the two of them in the room together. "Last night I had another dream about him. Kissing me. Touching me. It was… I woke up tingling."

"That is a good sign, then, I would think. Not that I know." Rose smiled impishly. "But it seems as though it should be."

"I think so."

The sharp rapping sound on her door made both of them jump, and Johanna's piece of toast went flying from her nerveless fingers. Thankfully, it landed on the tray in front of her. Unfortunately, it landed in her tea.

"Johanna, your gown is here." Lady Stark swept into the room, followed by Nettie and several maids, one of whom was holding a box. "Oh, good, Rose, you're here." Her gaze swept over Rose's attire as she got to her feet. "You look perfect. Well done, dear."

Johanna fished her toast out of her tea and set it back on the plate. Well, at least no one was going to expect her to eat it now. No one wanted to eat soggy toast.

"Now, girl, let's get you ready for your wedding day."

It was a flurry of activity around her, which became even more chaotic when Bridget and Charlotte came in. Not that Charlotte added to the chaos, but Bridget certainly did. She was right in the middle of things with her opinions as the maids worked on getting Johanna dressed and her hair properly coiffed.

Yesterday's jewels were brought out again. They sparkled against the ribbed silk of her lilac wedding gown, and her eyes appeared even lighter and brighter in reflection of both. With Johanna's hair curled and pinned, Nettie carefully lifted the amethyst tiara into place. It shimmered against her hair.

"You look like a fairy queen," Charlotte whispered, appearing at Johanna's side in the mirror, staring wide-eyed at her.

"I do?"

Charlotte nodded.

"You do," Bridget confirmed, pushing her way to stand on Johanna's other side. "And we are your fairy princesses."

Charlotte made a face at the description but did not protest.

Truthfully, Charlotte looked more like a fairy princess than Bridget, but Johanna was not going to burst her sister's joy. They'd had precious little of it over the years.

"You all look splendid," Lady Stark pronounced. "But we must move now, or we are going to be late."

Flutters zipped through Johanna's stomach. Late for her wedding. To a duke.

Her *wedding.* To a *duke.*

She took as deep a breath as her stays would allow, feeling her bosom expand upward as she did so. It did not help as much as she would have hoped. It rather felt as though her soul had left her body, though it continued to move and breathe, dragging her along with it.

In a few hours, she would be the Duchess of St. Albans.

Lifting her chin, she steeled herself. It was what she had to do to save her family, no matter how little she felt ready to take on the role of a duchess.

CHAPTER SIXTEEN

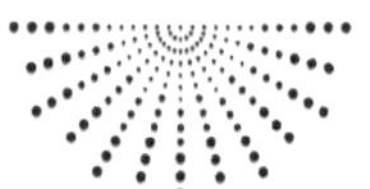

M̲A̲T̲T̲H̲E̲W̲

Waiting at the end of the aisle of the small chapel, Christian by his side, Matthew rolled his shoulders. His jacket felt uncommonly tight in a manner it had not before. The gathered guests filled the pews since the chapel was not all that large. Matthew was glad not to have the full might of the *ton* watching him from St. George's.

The *ton* would be disappointed, he was sure, since this made two ducal weddings in a row that they missed, but he was glad of their absence. Besides, they should have gotten their fill from the pomp and circumstances of Gregory and Tiffany's wedding; they did not need his as well. Matthew had no interest in feeding the voracious appetite of the *ton* more than necessary.

In fact, he was rather looking forward to being a boring married man of the *ton*, which would have much less expectation being pushed on him than a single duke in need of a wife. Granted, there would be interest in his heir, but as Matthew was also interested in the process of begetting one, he did not mind that as much.

He was very eager to start tonight.

The doors at the back of the chapel opened, and he straightened to attention. Out of the corner of his eye, he saw Christian doing the same thing.

Bridget and Charlotte came in, side by side, walking with stately elegance. Bridget was smiling widely, chin up, beaming as she glided down the aisle. Charlotte appeared fierce, her expression solemn, her wide, pale violet eyes staring at him intently as she walked beside her sister.

"Is it just me, or is the little one rather spooky?" Christian murmured in his ear.

It was not just him, but Matthew could not answer him without turning toward him, and he was a little afraid to take his eyes off Charlotte.

They got to the end of the aisle and took their seats next to his grandmama, which meant he could relax now that they were under her eye. She nodded approvingly at them, and Bridget preened while Charlotte remained serious and unaffected.

Miss Belle appeared at the back of the chapel, beautifully regal, gowned in a rosy hue that matched her given name. Matthew was aware of Christian stirring beside him. The two of them truly did seem to cause each other discomfort, but Christian was who he'd wanted standing beside him for his wedding, and he did not think Johanna would have chosen anyone other than Miss Belle to stand up with her.

If she was discomfited by the sight of Christian at the altar beside Matthew, it did not show in her demeanor as she came down the aisle and took her place. Her focus immediately went to the doors as the music changed and swelled.

Matthew felt his breath catch in his throat. He'd seen other men standing in this position, waiting, and he had never wondered how they felt. Never thought they might feel any differently than they normally did.

Maybe they did not.

But he suddenly felt a surge of anticipation, of momentous occasion, the way he sometimes felt when his coin was spinning in the air while he waited for the outcome of an important decision. As if the whole world had come to a brief halt, waiting with bated breath for the dice to fall.

She appeared at the back of the chapel on her brother's arm, but Matthew barely saw Micah. Johanna took all his attention.

The veil covering her face could not obscure her beauty. The pale netting nearly matched her hair beneath it, blending together, though the sparkle of the amethysts in her tiara shone through. The dress she was wearing was pale purple, though not quite lavender, and clung to her figure. Her amethyst necklace rested on the white lace that decorated the silk, adding a matching glitter to her tiara.

As she came closer, more of her features came into focus.

Her wide violet eyes.

Her pink bow of a mouth.

The slight blush in her cheeks.

After Micah completed the portion of the ceremony where he gave her away to Matthew, he stepped away, leaving Johanna's hand in Matthew's. She took her place across from him, her fingers still held in his.

The way she was looking at him reminded him of when he'd seen her a few days ago, on the stage about to be sold.

And he'd purchased her.

Not for a night, but for the rest of his life.

Which was only hitting him now at this moment.

Thankfully, he did not need to do much but say the appropriate answers at the appropriate times, prompted by Father Michael. He had not realized how very struck he would be by this moment, looking at the woman he was tying himself to.

His wife.

JOHANNA

The wedding went by in a blur. The vows, the brief press of the duke's lips against hers, then she was a duchess. But she did not feel any different. She still felt like herself.

Uncertain and as though she was playacting at being a duchess.

But she held her head high as they thanked their guests for coming and moved to the wedding brunch. At which, she found herself fascinated by their guests and not just because she was trying to distract herself, but because they were truly fascinating.

The Duke of Grafton had come with his fiancée, Lady Annabelle Walsh, and his mother. While no one was unkind to Lady Annabelle, it did not seem that the future duchess was part of the group of women who had pulled Johanna into their circle. Which made her feel bad for Lady Annabelle, but considering the way Grafton was staring at Delilah, and the way she was pointedly ignoring him, was enough to make it clear why Lady Annabelle was excluded.

It was not her fault, but the fault of the circumstances.

Then there was the Duke of Ormonde and his insistence on dogging *his* betrothed's footsteps, despite Lady Astrid's obvious annoyance with him. She was growing more and more peevish as he hung about her, while he became more and more stoic as she poked and prodded at his pride. Johanna was not sure what to do about that, but Lady Stark sailed in, claiming the duke's arm and pulling him away to speak to the Duke of Hereford.

"I swear, Lucifer is trying to drive me mad before the wedding," Lady Astrid muttered to Johanna, shaking her head. "He has gone from avoiding me to clinging to me like a limpet."

"Perhaps something has changed in his feelings for you?" Johanna suggested. She did not know the duke well enough to tell, but there must be some reason for it.

"More likely, he hopes to drive me to the madhouse rather than having to wed me. Perhaps all these weddings are getting under his skin as he realizes ours approaches." Lady Astrid tossed her head, a bit like a fractious horse.

They both quieted as the Duke of Bolton approached. Johanna felt her nerves rise. He was so very intimidating, so very serious, and there was an air about him that seemed even heavier with tragedy than the other dukes. His grey morning jacket hung on broad shoulders over a white shirt, with a forest-green waistcoat and matching cravat. The effect was effortlessly elegant.

"Lady Astrid," he said with a bow. "Duchess. Felicitations on this happy day."

"Thank you," Johanna replied, uncertain of what else to say to him. Fortunately—or perhaps unfortunately, given the topic she chose—Lady Astrid had no such qualms.

"Your Grace." Lady Astrid smirked at him. "How goes the search on the marriage mart? You realize you and Christian are the last dukes standing at this point. The debutantes and their mamas will be growing quite desperate once news of this morning reaches their ears."

Bolton shuddered.

"Thank you for the reminder," he said dryly.

"If you need assistance, you can always speak with Mei," Lady Astrid said, tilting her head in the direction of the matchmaker, who was standing off to the side speaking with Delilah and Kalina. According to Mei, her grandmother was the real matchmaker, and she provided assistance, but Johanna had noticed Lady Astrid always spoke as if it was truly Mei making the matches.

For a moment, Johanna thought the duke would roll his eyes, but instead, he shook his head and his shoulders at the same time, as though shaking off Lady Astrid's suggestion.

"I am a duke." He had straightened up, stretching his already impressive height higher and looking down his nose at Lady Astrid. "I do not require the assistance of a matchmaker to find a willing bride, just because it will give your friend the cachet of matching a duke."

"Then why are you not engaged yet?" Lady Astrid raised her eyebrow at him. "If it is so easy to find a willing bride?"

Johanna gulped, nervously peeking at the duke again to see his reaction. Should she try to intervene in this conversation and end it? What would a duchess do?

Perhaps Lady Astrid was not the duchess to try to emulate. Johanna was not sure she could stomach the confrontations the lady appeared to thrive on.

Thankfully, the duke was either used to Lady Astrid's blunt manner or unbothered by it. Johanna would bet on the former, as he seemed a very upright and proper kind of gentleman.

"Just because a lady is willing to become a duchess does not mean she would be a suitable one. I am trying to choose the right bride. One who will be a wife I can be… content with."

"Which is exactly what Mei can assist you with," Lady Astrid said triumphantly. "Helping narrow down your options, especially as she can become far more familiar with the contenders than you can. She will see sides of the debutantes that you do not."

Bolton opened his mouth, already starting to shake his head, then stopped. Frowned.

"Think about it," Lady Astrid said, reaching out to pat Bolton's arm. "Come, Johanna, we should go speak with Delilah."

Johanna allowed herself to be carted off, thankful not to be left alone with the duke.

As they approached, Delilah smiled. She exchanged air kisses with both of them before Johanna moved on to greet Mei and Kalina, who were standing beside the baroness.

"Thank you for being here," she said to them, feeling herself relax a bit more now that she was with the ladies instead of the dukes. Especially Mei and Delilah, who were not duchesses and had no expectations to be.

"I was honored to be included with such august company," Mei told her with a smile, brushing a lock of long black hair back from her face. The jade green and gold gown she was wearing matched the jade and gold sticks that held up half her hair in a bun, while the rest hung nearly to her waist. "I am sorry my grandmother could not make it; she has been unwell."

"Oh dear, I am so sorry to hear that," Johanna said sympathetically. "My mother as well. The doctor that ah, Matthew, uses has been very helpful, and Rose has quite a bit of knowledge of healing, if you would like to speak with her about your grandmother."

Mei brightened. "I might do that. My grandmother can be very stubborn about seeing a doctor, especially one we do not know, but a recommendation may help."

"Dr. Syme is very good," Lady Astrid assured her. "We use his services as well." She glanced around. "But that is not what we wanted to talk to Johanna about. We should move to the retiring room for some privacy."

If anyone thought it odd that the majority of women in the room left at the same time, no one said anything. Johanna did catch a glimpse of Lady Annabelle's wistful expression as they left before she turned to say something to the Duchess of Grafton. Her heart went out to the other woman... but she also knew she would consider Delilah's feelings first.

Tiffany came in only a moment after they'd arrived.

"I did not miss anything, did I?" she asked earnestly, patting her chestnut locks and smoothing back some of the flyaway hairs. The cornflower blue gown she was wearing looked particularly well on her, highlighting the very English rose type of beauty she possessed.

"You did not," Kalina reassured her. "We have barely stepped foot inside."

"What would she have missed?" Johanna asked, her nervousness starting to creep up again now that she was alone with the other women. None of them seemed unhappy with her, but she still did not know what to expect from them, either. She pressed her hands together in front of her.

The door opened again, and Rose came in, frowning. Her expression lightened when she saw Johanna, but while Johanna was anxious, Rose appeared ready to rush to Johanna's defense if necessary. She really would take on any members of the nobility if she needed to. Just seeing her helped Johanna feel better.

"We wanted to talk to you about tonight," Tiffany explained, after glancing at the others. Surprisingly, Lady Astrid seemed content to let the other woman take the lead, and when Johanna realized what Tiffany meant—the *wedding* night, which Lady Astrid had not yet experienced—she understood why.

"Oh." A hot blush flushed her cheeks, impossible to hide with her pale skin.

"We were uncertain if you knew what to expect," Delilah said, sitting down in one of the chairs. The elaborate black patterns on her watered silk dress of buttercup yellow were quite pretty against the green chair, as though she was a flower in the forest.

"My mother did a particularly poor job of preparing me." Tiffany made a face, taking a seat on the chaise beside Kalina.

Kalina smiled. "My mother did a better job, but I found it rather difficult to speak with *her* about it. I think sometimes it is easier with our peers than with our mothers."

"I... think I know what to expect," Johanna said, exchanging a glance with Rose. "My mother and Rose have helped many women when it comes to... ah..." She groped for the correct word.

"Bedroom matters?" Tiffany suggested.

"Lovemaking?" Kalina smiled.

"I believe men call it fucking," Lady Astrid said, making Delilah choke on a laugh.

"That is a very crude word, but yes," Tiffany agreed with a sigh. She shook her head, giving Lady Astrid a sidelong glance, but she did not ask how the unmarried woman knew the word.

"Yes," Johanna said, trying to ignore the heat that was still filling her cheeks. "That. I believe I have the basic idea."

"It can feel very good for many women, if the gentleman knows what he's about," Delilah told her in a reassuring manner, as though she wanted to be sure Johanna knew it was possible. "Matthew has a reputation as a charmer. You should have no problems with him."

"We did not want you to be afraid," Tiffany said. There was an expression on her face that made Johanna wonder... she had said her mother did not do a good job of preparing her. Had Tiffany been afraid?

"I am not afraid," she said quickly. Perhaps too quickly. The speculation in their gazes increased. "Matthew has kissed me, and it was... well..." Her face was getting hotter and hotter.

Kalina laughed.

"Well, if he is as good with his mouth as all that..." She left the words hanging, and Johanna did not quite understand, but she found herself giggling along with the others.

Beside her, Rose had relaxed completely, though she seemed fascinated by the discussion. She was likely soaking up what tidbits the other ladies were willing to drop, just as Johanna was.

"It was a very nice kiss." Her face was surely about to burst into flame, but she did not want the other ladies to worry about her and Matthew tonight. It was reassuring to know they were willing to talk about such things, in case she had any questions in the future.

"In that case, there's only one other thing we want to mention—" Before Tiffany could get any further, the door to the retiring room burst open, and Bridget barreled in before coming to an abrupt halt.

"What are you all doing in here?" she asked peevishly. "You have been gone for ages. Lady Stark is very displeased."

'Later,' Tiffany mouthed at Johanna as all the women made their excuses and started trickling out of the room.

As curious as she was, Johanna nodded. Curiosity could wait. Right now, she needed to return to her duties as the Duke of St. Alban's new duchess.

CHAPTER SEVENTEEN

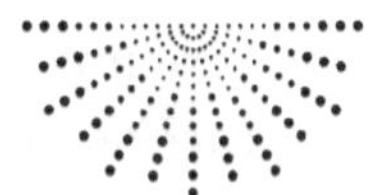

It seemed an egregious wrong to schedule weddings in the morning and force the groom to wait the entire afternoon for the wedding night, yet that was how things were done. Once they said goodbye to their guests, there was a flurry of activity as the maids finished setting up the duchess' rooms to Johanna and his grandmother's specifications. More dresses also arrived, which needed to be put away.

Matthew flipped his coin. To his relief, he no longer had to hang around waiting; instead, he flipped it a few more times until he got the direction to stay in, but to visit the billiards room. Micah and Bridget were there, finishing up a game, which Micah appeared to have let Bridget win.

Taking the next turn, Matthew was shocked to find that Micah had certainly *not* let Bridget win. Where a girl her age had found someone to teach her billiards, he did not know, but she had enough skill to give his luck a run for its money. He won by the skin of his teeth and made a mental note to bring some of his friends in to play her.

Watching them be humbled by a girl still in short skirts and braids would be extremely entertaining. Especially since no one but Micah and Charlotte had witnessed his own showing.

By supper, everyone was tired, making it rather quiet. Matthew could not help but steal glances at Johanna during the breaks in conversation. Or when there was conversation.

She had changed into a gown of white silk with a violet pattern repeated over and over across its surface, trimmed in an even darker purple. The effect with her white-blonde hair and purple eyes was quite fetching. The tiara had been removed, but the amethysts around her neck and dangling from her ears remained.

Watching her now, knowing that he was finally going to have her all to himself soon… it was very distracting.

He wanted her all to himself.

Which, he supposed, was a good thing to feel about his wife, if a trifle unexpected. When he'd thought about having a wife, he had not truly thought in terms of desire. Especially when faced with the debutantes of the *ton*, none of whom had stirred desire in him when he'd been trying to choose his bride. Some of them had been quite pretty, but they had not stirred him the way she did.

Though, to be fair, neither had Johanna when he'd met her at Blackstone Abbey. He'd thought she was beautiful, of course, because she was, but he had not felt the way he did now.

Maybe it was the difference of knowing that she was his wife.

Maybe it was because they'd already kissed.

Or maybe there was just a touch of excitement from the experience of simultaneously purchasing her and saving her.

He did enjoy knowing that he'd been her white knight, like something out of Arthurian legend. Perhaps a touch different in circumstances, but he thought the end result was much the same. She'd been saved from a dreadful fate, and he'd been the hero who saved her.

Now he would receive his just reward—her hand in marriage and her in his bed. Really, not a bad deal all around.

Though he could see she was nervous as dinner ended, and he escorted her back to their rooms. Her hand felt light as a feather on his arm, and she kept peeking up at him with consternation. Had she been able to talk to her mother about the wedding night?

Matthew was assailed with sudden worry. He might be her hero, but he'd never bedded a virgin. He knew, theoretically, that it should be about the same as bedding any other woman but that he should take extra care to be gentle. Was there anything else he should do?

Damnation, he should have asked Gregory and Nathanial some questions.

But they had kissed, and it had been exhilarating. He could start there. And his coin would not steer him wrong.

Feeling much assured, Matthew smiled as he halted at her door. Johanna took a deep breath before looking up at him.

"Go," he said softly, lifting his free hand to tuck his fingers under her chin and lift it so that her mouth was accessible. He brushed his lips over hers, softly. Gently. Barely a touch because he did not want to become overcome with desire in the hallway the way he had before. "I will join you shortly."

Her breath caught, but she nodded, violet eyes wide. Matthew could not help himself. He kissed her again, this time a touch more firmly, but pulled away before the kiss could become more heated.

Opening the door to her room for her, he caught a glimpse of her maid before he shut it behind her. His desire pushed against the strict control he'd held it under, but Matthew forced himself to close the door and walk away.

His valet was waiting for him, and Matthew quickly shucked off his clothing and got into his dressing gown, a splendid affair of plum and gold velvet trimmed with fur. Tucking his coin into one of the deep pockets as his valet exited, taking Matthew's laundry with him, he paused.

A virgin.

Perhaps it was best to flip for what he should do now before even entering her room. So he could go in with a plan.

Kissing?

Yes, apparently. That made sense.

Straight to bedding from there?

No.

Disappointing, but understandable.

Perhaps her breasts.

Yes.

Then to the bedding?

No.

Ah, his mouth.

Yes.

Matthew grinned at the head side of his coin. He did enjoy using his tongue. It seemed proper he should know how his wife's pussy tasted before he claimed it.

Very well. That was a good start. Kissing her lips, her breasts, and her pussy, then he would see where his coin wanted him to go from there. Already his blood was heating at the very thought of being able to touch her all over, however he wanted. His bride. His wife.

His cock was certainly ready for her.

Cinching the tie of his robe, he went over to the adjoining door between their rooms and knocked before opening it, to give warning he was coming in. Two steps in and he paused, arrested by the sight of her in her own dressing gown. Hers was made of long falls of lavender silk and silver lace that clung to her body. Her hair had been let out of its coiffure and fell around her in gentle waves. She stood in the middle of the room, near the bed, with her hands clasped together in front of her.

Nettie, the maid, was already letting herself out of the bedroom door, shutting it firmly behind her and leaving the two of them alone.

Glancing nervously at him, Johanna dropped her gaze almost immediately.

A virgin.

Start with kissing.

Right.

He wanted to kiss her all over.

JOHANNA

The duke entering her room while she was wearing practically nothing was utterly nerve -racking. Johanna felt like she could barely breathe as his dark gaze moved over her. The silky feel of her nightrail and robe against her skin was doing wicked things to her senses. Even as she shifted slightly in place, she could feel her nipples pebbling against the soft fabric, and she moved her arms to hide them.

"You look beautiful," the duke said, moving to her again. Despite the hunger in his eyes, there was also gentleness. The same kind of protectiveness she'd seen the night of the auction, which soothed some of her nerves.

As he approached, it felt like her entire body lit up, acutely attuned to his presence. She swayed forward a little, though she could not gather the courage to actually step toward him.

"Thank you," she whispered, and rallied. "You look very handsome."

He chuckled, and once again his fingers moved under her chin, tipping her head back in that manner that made her feel both breathless and wildly excited.

"I am glad you think so," he told her, right before he kissed her.

Johanna felt her whole body shiver as their lips met, her insides clenching in response. Lifting her hands to his chest, she could feel his heart beating beneath her palm, the soft velvet of his robe gentle against her hand. It was not just their lips, either; the hot, hard press of his body against the length of hers made her tremble. His other arm went around her, holding her in place. Holding her so she could not step away.

Not that she wanted to, but something about not being _able_ to made the whole thing more exciting.

His tongue slid into her mouth, dancing with hers, and she kissed him back as best she could. Heard him—felt him—groan, his hold tightening on her. The hardness of his body against hers, the feel of his muscles flexing, made her very aware of how vulnerable she was to him... and rather than feeling afraid, it stirred her excitement, the ache that was growing inside her even further.

It throbbed and pulsed within her, stealing away her breath as much as his kiss did. She leaned against him, as much because she wanted to feel him against her as because she was uncertain her legs would hold her up much longer.

With a groan that was muffled by the fusion of their mouths, he hauled her around, spinning her, and started moving her back.

Toward the bed.

Her heart started to pound in her chest even harder than it already was. It was a wonder it did not pound its way right out of her skin, it was beating so hard.

His hands moved on her, and silk slipped from her shoulders, leaving her in nothing but the silky nightrail. Johanna shuddered, arching with a gasp as his lips moved from her mouth to her throat. The thin silk between them meant her nipples rubbed against the velvet of his robe, the soft silk amplifying the sensation and hardening them even further. They tingled, throbbing, and she pressed her thighs together as her knees went weak.

The grip on her shifted as he moved her back, and she fell slightly, ending up sitting on the bed before him, her thighs spread wide rather than primly together because he was standing between them. He dropped to his knees in front of her, slipping the nightrail from her shoulders.

Johanna whimpered as her breasts were bared to him, even before he kissed the top slope of one. No man had ever seen her like this, and now he was not only seeing her, but touching her, kissing her...

One hand closed around one breast as the other reached behind her, pulling her forward. Gasping as his teeth scraped over her soft flesh, she buried her hands in his dark hair as she held onto his head for dear life. The sensations coursing through her threatened to drown her.

How could one person possibly hold so much sensation and not go mad?

"Oh!" she cried out as his mouth closed around her nipple and sucked, his hand squeezing her other breast, pinching that nipple between his fingers. It was too much and not enough, all at once. Her nipples throbbed, her core pulsing in time with them, yet it felt as though there was something more that she needed, that her body craved. The demand, without knowing what the desire was for, was wildly frustrating.

Her breath caught in her throat as his teeth nibbled on her taut bud, testing her, teasing her. Then his mouth moved to the other breast, his hands switching places so he could continue to caress the breast his mouth was not attending.

It was pure pleasure, yet utter torment as her insides writhed with unfulfilled need. The ache between her legs kept growing, even though he had not touched her there yet.

She was dizzy, coming apart at the seams, yet he kept going. His mouth kept going. Down her quivering stomach, over her skin.

Johanna gasped as he lifted her legs, making her fall back against the bed, staring up at the canopy above her as he lifted the skirt of her nightrail. The fabric made a silky river across her stomach, and she closed her eyes, covering them with her hands, her face burning hot as she realized he could see *everything*.

Intimately.

The silky blonde fur over her mound. The soft folds between her legs. The place where she throbbed and ached the most. Could he tell? Did he know?

"Beautiful," he murmured, pressing a kiss to her inner thigh, which elicited a sound she'd never made before.

Everywhere he touched her felt seared to the bone. She tried to close her legs, but he was between them, and his arms moved to curve around them, holding her spread open for him.

"Just relax," he murmured. "I'm going to make you feel so good, my duchess."

There was something about the way he called her his duchess that made it feel like so much more than a title.

Not that she had time to ponder what he did mean by it; almost as soon as he said the words, his mouth lowered between her legs. He was kissing her *there*. Johanna had not known such a thing was even possible, and she shrieked in combined shock and pleasure as his tongue slid up her center. Her thighs immediately tried to close, but he was still holding them open, his fingers digging into her soft flesh, forcing her to allow him to taste her. He began to lick and suckle, making her gasp and writhe for him. It was utterly wicked. Sinful even.

And it felt so very good.

The ache that had been so confusingly insistent now had a focal point. The itch she hadn't known how to scratch was now being licked, sucked, and satisfied. Johanna's head whipped back and forth as she moaned, her hands pressing down tightly on her eyes as if to hide her shameful response to what he was doing to her. Although licking her down there had to be shameful as well, yet he apparently had no qualms about it.

The pleasure spiraled higher and higher, his tongue driving her wild, then he sucked on a spot that made her nearly levitate off the bed. She gasped, her hands flying to hold on to the bedsheet beneath her as she writhed for him, rubbing herself shamelessly against his mouth and tongue as wave after wave of inexpressible ecstasy rolled over her until she was utterly limp.

All that, yet there was still more.

Her mind reeled. He had not even taken her virginity yet.

CHAPTER EIGHTEEN

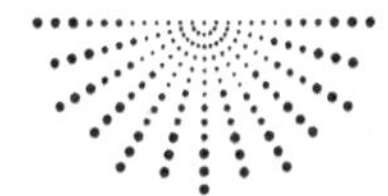

MATTHEW

The sweet taste of his wife's pussy could easily become addictive. As could the sound of her gasps. Her moans. Her little noises of surprise. The way she tried to hide when he first lowered his mouth between her thighs.

His cock was throbbing, eager to be inside of her, to hear those noises when wrapped in the slick heat of her body, to feel her coming apart while impaled on his shaft.

Lifting his head from her sweetness, he grinned as he looked up the length of her body. The fall of silk over her stomach did little to hide her breasts, tipped with the pink nubbins of her nipples, and the way her lips were parted as she panted for breath.

Reaching into his pocket, her legs still draped over his shoulders, he gave his coin a quick, small flip.

Not time to bed her yet.

Which was disappointing.

His mouth again?

Apparently yes.

Matthew tucked his coin back into his pocket.

Once more unto the breach.

J̲O̲H̲A̲N̲N̲A̲

She did not know what she'd expected after the tumultuous pleasure. Her body was still buzzing, but her muscles were completely limp. Closing her eyes, she tried to slow her breathing.

That had been...

There were not words.

Then she felt his hands sliding up her body, her legs still spread wide with his head between them, and she gasped as he gave her another soft lick. His hands closed over her breasts, squeezing, kneading, and her back arched involuntarily, pushing her breasts against his touch.

His tongue parted her center once again, finding that sensitive spot that had sent her reeling. It throbbed, her toes curling at the sensation, and she cried out as her hands gripped the bedsheet again. She was so much more sensitive than she had been before; she could not possibly take any more stimulation, yet there was nothing she could do to stop him.

All she could do was cry out and writhe as he used his tongue to drive her to new heights of rapture.

M̲A̲T̲T̲H̲E̲W̲

The insistent ache in his cock as his wife erupted in passion again was almost painful. Reaching down with one hand, he gave himself a hard squeeze to ease some of the need, moving his hand up and down, though he was not going to let himself come yet.

Not until he was inside her.

He gave the coin another flip.

Bloody hell, really?

He must be missing something.

Ah, yes, *fingers*.

Very well then.

He still had one hand on her breast, and he gave the soft mound a gentle caress, rolling her nipple between his fingers while she shuddered and moaned.

"Oh, please…" Her voice was soft as a sigh, catching in her throat.

Tucking his coin back into his pocket, Matthew shifted his position, going up higher on his knees so he could get a better view of her as he pressed his fingers to her sweet pussy.

Watching her mouth fall open as he began to slide two of them into her slick softness.

JOHANNA

Oh, this was…

She mewled, her insides clenching as his fingers pushed inside her.

Inside her.

She could feel him within her, and it was horrifically intimate. Excitingly invasive.

And all the while, she was so sensitive, she could feel tears beginning to slide down her temples into her hair; she could barely stand any more pleasure.

"Please," she begged again, breathlessly, uselessly.

His fingers did not stop. They stroked. Pushed in deeper. And his other hand squeezed her breast, caressing, kneading. His fingers toyed with her nipple. Pinching. Pulling. Tugging. There was a direct line of sensation straight down to her core where he was now moving his hand back and forth, thrusting his fingers into her while she shuddered around him.

The heel of his hand rubbed against her, his fingers pressing on a spot deep within her.

The sensations roiling through her somehow felt deeper. More encompassing. And Johanna was quite sure she was losing her mind.

MATTHEW

Surely now…

He slid his fingers from his wife's virgin pussy, bringing them up to clean them off with his tongue. The sweet flavor of her already coated the inside of his mouth, but he was correct in thinking he was addicted. He could not get enough of it; he was enjoying tasting her on his fingers nearly as much as he had at the source.

That was not what he really wanted, though. His cock felt as though it was about to explode if he did not sink inside her immediately.

Digging into his pocket, he gripped his coin tightly.

Surely now…

He flipped it.

Finally.

JOHANNA

Every ounce of strength had been drained from her body.

She did not have any voice left.

She barely had breath left.

If her husband wished her to move, he would have to lift her limbs for her because she could not possibly. In fact, she was not certain she would ever be able to get out of this bed again. Perhaps this was where she would spend her life as his duchess. Limp and useless from his ministrations on their wedding night.

Had the other duchesses experienced this?

How did they manage to function properly afterward?

A shadow fell across her as her legs shifted, and Johanna's eyes focused on the man looming over her. One leg was still on his shoulder, the other sliding down to drape over the edge of the bed. His dark eyes blazed, hot with passion as he looked down at her. Johanna whimpered as his hand slid from her thigh up to her ankle.

Turning his head, he kissed the side of her leg, just above her ankle, and she felt it in the marrow of her bones. She was so sensitive, it did not matter where he touched her; her body pulsed in response.

Which was when she realized his dressing gown was gone and he was naked. When had that happened? She had not even noticed it slipping off.

Now she could see his full upper body. His muscular shoulders. The dark hair sprinkled over his chest and down his stomach... though she could not see any lower than that due to her current position. Rubbing her leg, he leaned forward, bending it back toward her.

Something thick and hard nudged at the entrance he'd just been exploring with his fingers.

"Look at me, sweetness," he ordered in a soft murmur. "Do not close your eyes. Just look at me."

Johanna felt caught in his gaze as the part of him at her entrance began to push, making her gasp as she opened for him, stretching far wider than she had for his fingers. He leaned forward over her, his demanding gaze boring into her helpless one as he began to slide into her.

He was too big, but she did not have the strength to stop him.

Did not have the breath to tell him.

And she did not want to.

Whatever air she'd managed to breathe in was being pushed out of her by the sensation of him filling her.

Because of their intimately connected gazes, she could see the pleasure that filled his eyes just before he closed them and groaned. His hips moved, thrusting forward, his hands holding her in place so she could not do more than clench around him and gasp as he went deeper inside her.

It hurt, it ached, yet it felt good, too.

She could feel him within her.

And she was so, so, so very glad he was the one who'd purchased her from the auction block.

The idea of another man, a stranger, being inside her like this... She did not know how she would have been able to bear it. He'd saved her in more ways than one.

"Bloody hell." He groaned, shuddering, his eyes flicking close for just a moment before meeting her gaze again. The need in them seared her to the bone, and she whimpered as her limbs twitched. Leaning forward, he pressed the leg on his chest toward her body, the other hanging down beside him, able to feel his hairy thigh against her silky skin. "Your pussy is perfect, sweetness."

He rocked again, as if to emphasize where he was speaking of, not that Johanna needed much explanation. There did not seem to be a response expected, which was good because she had no idea how to reply to such a brazen statement. How was one supposed to talk to a man who was currently filling her?

All she could do was whimper, which seemed to satisfy him as he thrust forward, deep into her, his body finally coming to rest against hers. She could feel the coarse hairs surrounding his manhood now rubbing against the sensitive folds of her pussy. Could feel his shaft so deep inside her, while her muscles clenched and shuddered around him, touching parts of her she did not know could be touched.

When his hands slid up to cover her breasts, she gasped, closing her eyes involuntarily as the sensations pulsed through her. His thumbs rubbed over her nipples as he kneaded her breasts, holding himself in place, as though allowing her to adjust to her new proportions.

Then, finally, he began to move.

It was… indescribable.

The pull of him retreating, the shocking sensations as he thrust back in, his guttural groan vibrating through her. He moved with slow, sure strokes, making her gasp and shudder every time he buried himself inside her. His body rubbed against all her sensitive bits, which were almost too raw to bear… yet she must bear it.

She wanted to give him the same pleasure he'd given her.

Wanted him to have whatever he desired from her. From her body. Not just because she was his wife, but because he'd saved her. Because he made her feel… like this.

As he began to move harder, faster, she cried out. Her fingers curled in the bedsheet, her arms too tired to lift up to reach for him the way she wanted to. All she could do was lie beneath him, taking his hard thrusts, fighting off the impending rise of sensation. She could not possibly live through another little explosion... yet she could feel one coming.

"That's it, sweetness," he said, encouraging her as his hand moved to cover her hip, his thumb pressing against the terrible, wonderful spot just above where he had impaled her. "Come for me, little violet. Come all over your husband's cock."

The rubbing press of his thumb had as much to do with the shocking swell of her pleasure as his words did. She cried out, unable to stop herself, as he masterfully brought her to the peak and pushed her over it yet again. The spasms of her body around his... cock made him feel even bigger inside her, and she would be willing to swear he hardened even further as he pumped himself back and forth within her several more times.

His groan, his shudders, as he buried himself inside her and let her muscles work over his length, were as heated as her own. Johanna lay limp, breathless beneath him, watching his jaw clench, then his expression go slack with relief and erotic rapture.

Letting out a shuddering groan, he lowered his head to hers, allowing the leg that had been propped up on his shoulder to slip down. Even that movement made her shudder and gasp as his body shifted against hers. Their foreheads pressed together, breath mingling, the feel of his hard body covering hers strangely comforting.

Lips brushed over hers, and Johanna closed her eyes, letting out a sigh into his gentle kiss. His hands stroked her sides, sending more little tremors through her body, though he was not trying to arouse her again. She could feel him inside her, shrinking, softening. Even that sensation made her whimper.

By the time he withdrew completely and returned to run a warm, damp cloth between her legs, she was almost asleep. Dimly, she was aware of him cleaning her. Stroking her. Crawling into bed with her and wrapping his body around hers, like she was snuggled into a warm cave.

Perfectly happy, still in awe that her terrible fate had been so perfectly reversed to good fortune, Johanna breathed out a sigh of relief.

The only cloud on the horizon was her mother's health… especially if she continued to hold on to the delusions she'd confessed to Johanna. But she could not think about that now. Somehow, they would make it through. They always had, and now she was a duchess married to the luckiest man in the *ton*.

This was going to be the start of a wonderful new life.

CHAPTER NINETEEN

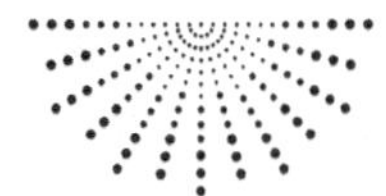

Matthew

Next to his wife was a very nice way to wake up, Matthew decided the moment he stirred. She was warm and soft against him, her silky hair tickling his nose, his hand over her breast, and his cock very nicely wedged between her buttocks. If he'd known that waking up next to a woman was this enjoyable, he might have done it sooner.

Though likely not.

He had not wanted to give any of the women he'd seduced ideas if they were widows. And the other ladies... well, they discouraged gentlemen from staying overnight, anyway. Their husbands tended to object. Not because they were jealous, but the lack of discretion was very impolite.

Now, Matthew could not help but wonder what those husbands were doing, choosing not to warm their wives' beds themselves. He could not imagine letting _his_ wife's bed go empty. Not after tonight.

Keeping her satisfied was going to be very enjoyable. He was quite happy to ensure she did not find any rakes or _roues_ of the _ton_ tempting.

Pressing a kiss to the back of her neck, he rocked the hard ridge of his cock between her buttocks, enjoying her soft moan. She was not quite awake yet, he could tell. Shifting the angle of his hips, he slid himself between her silky thighs, felt the hint of moisture rub along the top of his shaft.

Desire swelled as he pressed another kiss to the back of her neck, fondling her breast… then he froze.

He had not flipped his coin.

The ache in his balls protested the sudden interruption to fulfilling his desires, but…

How could he have forgotten to flip his coin?

It was very early. And his wife's body tucked up next to his was very tempting. Obviously, the combination of just waking up and distraction had been detrimental to his usual processes.

Which meant he needed to stop what he was doing right now and flip his coin before proceeding further. Just to make sure.

Surely, I can decide to fuck my wife without flipping for it.

But could he?

Should he?

What if it somehow went horribly wrong?

Gritting his teeth, Matthew forced his hand to release its hold on the soft swell of Johanna's breast. He turned over toward her nightstand, where his coin rested, glinting silver against the dark wood. He had laid it down there last night, within easy reach, easy for him to find in the morning, so at least he did not have to leave the bed to hunt for it.

"What are you doing?"

Matthew froze at the sound of his wife's sleepy voice, his hand closing around the coin, hiding it within his fist.

"Ah…" He truly was not entirely awake yet. No wonder he had almost forgotten his coin. He turned back to her, feeling entirely sheepish, unsure of how she would react to what he was doing.

Looking delightfully rumpled, a slight pink mark across her cheek where it had been pressed against the pillow, Johanna blinked at him in confusion.

"Were you…" Her voice trailed off, and she blushed, tugging the bedsheets up, even though she was currently decently covered.

"I was planning on continuing our explorations of each other this morning, yes," he confessed. Well, he was planning on doing it as long as the coin confirmed it was the correct choice.

"Our…" Her blush deepened, going from light pink to a very dark rose, and she blinked rather rapidly. "I, um… I am not sure I can… I am rather sore." The blurted words were full of apology, but it was Matthew who realized he should be apologetic. Granted, he was not used to bedding virgins, but he had seen the smears of blood on his cock last night and when he'd cleaned her afterward.

Of course she was sore.

What an arse he was.

"I am sorry," he said, shaking his head. "I did not think." Internally sighing, because his cock was still hard, Matthew tried to decide what to ask his coin next. Return to his room, perhaps? "I will take my leave of you."

"You do not have to go. Is there… is there something else we could do that would um, help your condition?" If her face had been pink before, it was bright red now. "You used your mouth on me last night. Could I not, um, do the same? In some manner?"

The contrast between her embarrassment and her brazen offer was even more titillating than if she'd thrown herself at him. Matthew could not help but be fascinated by the generous offer. Not at all what he would have expected from a debutante. Then again, she was not like any other debutante.

Leaning forward, he tilted his head back so he could press a kiss to her lips.

"There is indeed," he murmured, pulling away a bit. "Ah…"

But he wanted to use his coin. His hand moved involuntarily, though he did not actually lift it up, and his fingers remained tightly closed around it. The urge was nearly impossible to resist. Mostly, he did not care what others thought of his proclivities, but for some reason, right now, in this moment, he cared about what she thought.

"Do you need to flip for it?" she asked, cocking her head to the side, but it was not the way people normally asked him. There was no mockery in her voice, no judgment. She was completely matter-of-fact and perhaps a little curious, but in a manner that put him at ease rather than raising his hackles in defensiveness.

"You do not mind?" His grip on the coin tightened and relaxed. "I would feel better."

"You flipped to save me."

"I flipped to marry you," he corrected her. It seemed important for her to know that he would have saved her, regardless. Even if the coin had said not to, he would have found a way. Have Christian do it. Or Drake.

But he was glad it had been him.

A slow smile curved the edges of her lips, and she drew her knees up under the covers, wrapping her arms around them. She was completely covered this way, and he had the strongest urge to tug those sheets down and reveal her body to him all over again. But it depended on what his coin said. For the first time, he was starting to see his friends' point about using it for *everything*. It might be nice to just do what he wanted.

"Then I have no objections. I am very happy with its outcomes so far. And I am curious what will happen if you flip it and it says that I should not um... do anything for you." The lingering blush in her cheeks as she tried to speak around her offer, rather than repeating it outright, was utterly delightful.

Matthew was very much looking forward to teaching her to say utterly filthy things to him in the future, but for the moment, he was content to flip his coin and have her *do* something utterly filthy.

Hopefully.

"Then I will ask it if I should use my mouth on your pussy," he replied, deliberately being blunt, just so he could watch her cheeks flush hot again. He was not disappointed. Shaking her head, her arms tightened around her knees in front of her.

"I do not think I can take any more of that either. Wait..." She blinked. "Is that why... last night..."

"Yes." He flipped the coin into the air. "Heads, I get your mouth on my cock. Tails, you get mine on your cunt. And I promise, you will be able to take it."

Matthew lifted his hand from where it was covering the coin on the back of his arm and grinned. Sliding the coin off his hand, he reached over to put it down on the nightstand as he spoke.

"Your mouth."

"My mouth." She whispered the words.

"Not to worry, little violet," he said, shifting his position on the bed so that he was sitting beside her, his back against the headboard, his legs stretched out on the bed, feet shoulder-width apart. The sheets were pressed to her front, so her back was bare, covered only with the silky fall of her long, white-blonde hair. He ran his fingers through the silky strands, then up her side to curl around her neck and draw her to him, finishing his sentence just before he kissed her. "I will direct you."

<hr>

JOHANNA

The brush of her husband's lips over hers sent a thrill through Johanna. Though she was very sore between her legs when she pressed them together, she could not deny the flutter in her core as he touched her. His strong fingers around the back of her neck, the way he guided her with his grip, made her body come alive in response.

She recognized the sensations—the tingling, the way her skin prickled—from the night before. More pleasure seemed impossible to endure, yet there was some part of her body that absolutely alighted at the possibility.

The pressure on her neck increased, and Johanna's head drifted away from her husband's lips and down toward his chest. The bedsheet was still clutched to her own chest as she was moved, though it hardly mattered as her breasts were now hanging beneath her, the long length of her hair brushing over his thighs.

The curtain of hair helped give her some confidence as she got her first truly good look at his cock, hiding her while she looked her fill. He was so very different from her. The dark thatch of hair around the stalk of his manhood was coarser than the rest of his body, even more so than that of his legs, and from it grew a hard bloom with a reddish-purplish knob at the top.

He had paused in his pressure on her neck, as if realizing she wanted to look at him and giving her the time to do so.

Taking one of her hands in his free one, he moved it to his cock, wrapping her fingers around the stalk and groaning with pleasure as her cheeks heated in another fiery blush. He felt hot and hard in her hand, almost as though he was pulsing against her palm.

"This is the shaft," he said, before moving her hand up to the top. "This is the crown, or the head. Bloody hell, that feels good." He groaned again, and a rush of pleasure went through Johanna.

Was this how he felt when he made her moan and whimper? Did her pleasure bring him a rush of his own?

Tentatively, she flicked out her tongue along the crown, right where the small slit was, and was rewarded when her husband hissed between his teeth and his grip on the back of her neck tightened. Johanna felt very much like a naughty little kitten while he was holding her like this… and to her surprise, even though she'd always been one to follow the rules, right now she was enjoying feeling very naughty indeed. Perhaps because it was obvious, the duke was receiving pleasure from her wickedness.

"Yes, lick my cock, sweetness." He tightened his hand around hers on his shaft, guiding her fingers up and down as he pumped his cock with her palm. Emboldened, Johanna flicked her tongue out to lick him again, swiping the flat of her tongue over his crown. He groaned, squeezing her hand even harder around him. "All around the head. Good girl."

Oh my.

The heat that flushed through Johanna at his praise had nothing to do with a blush. It was like her whole body turned red, but she could see from her hand and arm that was not true… it just felt that way. Her insides were suddenly throbbing, the way they had last night when he'd been touching her. Licking her.

All from a couple of words.

From being told she was a good girl.

Which was something she had always strived to be, but it was far more wicked, far more perverse to be told she was a good girl for doing… this. Which just made her want to do it more. She licked all around the crown, exploring him with her tongue, before brazenly closing her mouth around it.

Groaning, his hand pushed on the back of her neck, forcing her mouth further down on his shaft until her lips met their hands. He tasted salty and sweet at the same time, the sensations of him being in her mouth both shocking and exciting.

"Bloody hell. That's it, sweetness." His fingers massaged her neck as he guided her back up, then pushed her mouth back down, so he was thrusting between her lips the same way he'd thrust inside her last night.

Johanna licked and sucked as best she could, squeezing the base of his cock, moving her hand the way his hand was directing her.

"Ah, fuck… love… I'm going to come. Swallow me…"

Swallow what?

She had her answer almost as soon as the question flitted through her head. Salty fluid spurted onto her tongue, and she would have jerked back in surprise had he not been holding her in place. It did not taste *bad* exactly, but it did not taste very good either, and the texture was very strange… yet the way he was groaning, the way he shuddered as she did indeed swallow him, made it more than worth it.

The grip on her neck lessened, and she lifted her head. Her lips felt swollen, her mouth felt… used, but in a manner she rather liked. When he guided her back toward him and pressed his lips to her forehead in a gentle kiss, she closed her eyes and sighed happily. This was so nice. So unexpectedly nice.

Then he pulled her against him, nestling her head on his shoulder, cuddling her on his lap, and Johanna could have cried at how utterly wonderful it felt to rest all her burdens on his broad shoulders and strong chest. Her family was taken care of. Her siblings would be fed. Her mother would not starve.

And somehow, she had ended up with the most wonderful husband in the world.

It felt like all her dreams were coming true.

Whatever he needed of her to be his duchess, whatever he wanted from her as his wife, she would happily do. All she wanted was to stay in this blissful little bubble forever.

Unfortunately, reality was suddenly knocking at her door.

Both of them jumped, and Matthew's arms tightened protectively around her, which made her heart feel like it did a little swoony loop in her chest. There was a muffled voice, which she could not make out the words, but she could easily hear Bridget's response.

"She's my sister. Why can I not go into her room?" The indignity in her sister's voice would have been enough to make Johanna laugh under other circumstances. She could feel a chuckle rumbling through Matthew's chest.

"I shall go, but we should make sure to keep your door locked from now on," he murmured, caressing her back in a manner that made her want to ask him to stay… but she really did not think she could handle another bout of pleasure. Nor did she think her impatient sister would wait very long.

The duke pressed another kiss to Johanna's forehead as he shifted her off his lap. His cock was no longer hard and long, but had softened, now smaller and less fearsome, resting on the sack beneath it like a cat upon a cushion. Johanna very much wanted to explore the difference and touch him while he was like this… but that would have to wait as well.

She waited until he had exited through the door to his room before scrambling up to grab her robe and cover herself. Bridget was still arguing with someone outside the door—she thought it might be Nettie and was even more grateful for the maid—and Johanna rushed to open it. The soreness between her legs was even more amplified now that she was moving, but it made her smile, too.

It was like feeling her husband's touch on her when he was not even in the room.

Right now, at this moment, it felt like nothing could ever go wrong again. Her fortune had finally turned by marrying the Lord of Luck.

CHAPTER TWENTY

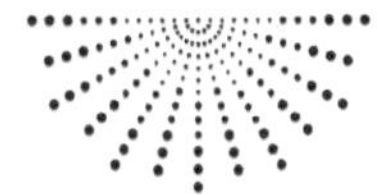

MATTHEW

Married life was definitely for him, Matthew decided, humming under his breath as Reedy helped him dress for the day. He would very much like to go on a honeymoon, he decided. Somewhere he and Johanna could be together without her family. Though he did not think that she would be ready to leave them quite yet, now that they'd just been reunited.

While Reedy brushed off his jacket, Matthew quickly flipped his coin.

No, not yet.

But something to do in the future. Something they could look forward to. Would she like Paris? Maybe Greece to see some of the ruins. Or Italy. He'd always wanted to go to Venice. Or they could stay closer to home and visit Scotland or Ireland. Whatever she wanted.

He doubted she'd had the opportunity to travel before. Oh, the things he could teach her... both in and out of the bedroom. It was going to be very enjoyable spoiling her, then reaping his rewards in pleasure. While he'd never really thought about bedding a virgin before, there truly was something rather titillating about being able to teach her what he liked. Especially because she was so enthusiastic, something that had undone him when she'd put her mouth on him this morning.

Her enthusiasm was his favorite part. Matthew had known she would do her duty—she seemed a very dutiful sort—but he'd always understood that wives and mistresses or lovers were very different creatures. While it had been clear she did not have any experience in what she was doing, she had not appeared to consider it a duty, either.

"All done, Your Grace," Reedy said, nodding as he gave Matthew a quick, final look over. "You are looking very fine for your first day as a married man."

"I am feeling very fine," Matthew replied, grinning. "I ah, expect that I will be a bit late returning to my room tomorrow morning as well. Or perhaps the door might be locked when you arrive."

"Thank you for informing me, Your Grace. Your schedule is my schedule."

Matthew knew Reedy did have his own schedule, no matter what he said. It might shift now that there was a duchess in residence, though. And if he and Johanna were in his room tonight rather than hers, they would likely not have to worry about her sister knocking on his door. Not even Bridget was that brazen. Probably. Hopefully.

Tugging on the cuff of his jacket, Matthew headed to the door. He was very hungry and eager to break his fast. Last night and this morning had helped him work up a mighty appetite.

Stepping into the hall, he almost screamed like one of the maids seeing a mouse when he was confronted with a tiny, pale, wraithlike figure. She was holding some kind of doll that was as pale as she was. She stared at him, watching as he jumped back, her light violet eyes as eerie as the rest of her. Matthew managed to straighten and square his shoulders, despite the way his heart was pounding in his chest.

"Good morning, Charlotte," he said seriously, speaking around the lump in his throat.

Giving him a long, long look as if she could see all the filthy things he'd done to her sister—and did not approve—she turned and glided away. Even though he could see her feet because she was in short skirts, she looked like she was gliding. It was entirely unnerving.

"That child is unnerving," Reedy muttered, echoing Matthew's thought.

At least he knew it was not just him. He supposed he was going to have to get used to having her acting like a ghost in his house, for now. Maybe if he expected it, it would be less startling in the moment.

Or she could stop being so bloody creepy, but he was not sure how to make that happen. And a little afraid of what she might do if he tried. The other siblings seemed to accept her as a matter of course. They were likely just used to her. He would have to get used to her, too.

Taking a deep breath, he gave himself a little shake, then smiled as his wife's door opened, and she came out with her other sister. No one could accuse Bridget of being ghostly. Johanna's head lifted, and their gazes met, and Matthew found himself unable to stop the grin that spread across his face. Not that he particularly wanted to. Unlike several of his friends, he did not have an aversion to smiling.

"Good morning," he said formally to both ladies, though his focus was wholly on his wife. She was quite fetching in a violet and lavender sprigged muslin gown that made the most of her ivory skin and pale hair. Bridget's brighter coloring made Johanna appear even more ethereal beside her. Like a fairy queen... one he was allowed to touch in any way he wanted.

One day, he truly was going to have to take her to bed while she was wearing nothing but jewels and a tiara. Last night, her dressing gown had been very nice, but he had a specific image in his head he would like to indulge in.

"Good morning," his wife said, in a slightly lower voice than her sister, her cheeks turning that lovely shade of pink he so enjoyed.

"May I escort you ladies to the dining room?" He grinned as he held out his arms, one for each of them to take. Johanna was more sedate, more demure, while Bridget was bouncing exuberance on his arm.

"Thank you, Your Grace," Bridget said cheekily, as they began to move down the hallway. "It is very kind of you to escort us." The manner in which she said it was more teasing than sincere, and Matthew answered her in kind.

"I know."

Her peal of laughter rang down the hallway, though it did not delight him quite as much as the softer laugh it elicited from his wife.

JOHANNA

Breakfast as a married lady, officially a duchess, did not feel all that different from breakfasts before. The largest difference was the parts of her body that were more tender than she was used to and how much more aware of them she was. Rose kept shooting her curious glances, and she knew her cousin was dying to ask about the wedding night.

Johanna did not know how she was going to bring herself to talk about it to Rose. Not just because it was so very unladylike, but also because some of the intimacies just did not seem right to share. Which was unlike her because she and Rose shared almost everything. Their burdens, their dreams, their worries… but Johanna found herself wanting to keep last night for just herself. Well, for herself and Matthew. It felt wrong to include someone else in it.

Though she knew she was going to need to speak with Rose about at least some of it to quell her cousin's curiosity.

As they were finishing breakfast, a footman came in with a tray for Matthew, who glanced at the cards and coughed.

"Excuse me, ladies," he said, wiping his mouth with his napkin and getting to his feet. His demeanor was suddenly quite a bit more serious than it had been, the smile gone from his lips. "And Micah. Some of my friends have come to call on urgent business. I will leave you to it."

With a half-bow, he departed before any of them could truly respond, and Johanna blinked in surprise.

"What serious business could he have the day after his wedding?" Bridget asked, looking around the table as if one of them might have an explanation. Johanna only shook her head because she had no idea. She looked curiously at Lady Stark, wondering if his grandmother might have an inkling.

"Men always think all of their business is serious," Lady Stark said, but she was frowning. She shook her head. "We have our own business to be about today. Bridget and Charlotte, your dance instructor will be here in an hour, so make yourselves ready for him."

"How do we do that?" Bridget asked.

Lady Stark opened her mouth, then closed it. "I will accompany you to your rooms. Johanna, you and Rose are welcome to join us if you wish."

"I will as soon as I check on Mother," Johanna said. She was woefully aware of how long it had been since she'd danced.

"I appreciate the offer, but I do not think such lessons are necessary for someone like me," Rose said, although she did not sound very sorry about it.

"What's wrong with you?" Bridget asked, narrowing her eyes at Rose. "Why would I need to learn to dance, and you do not?" Charlotte was frowning too, and she'd sat up straight, her pale eyes focused on Rose, waiting to hear her answer. Although she had not protested taking the lessons, it was very possible that both girls would stage a rebellion if they thought they were unnecessary.

They did not truly understand how much they owed Lady Stark and the duke—and Johanna hoped they never really did. A little inkling might have been helpful right now, though.

Both Johanna and Rose glanced at each other. They'd all been apart from Society, unable to accept any invitations until now. Neither Bridget nor Charlotte truly understood how Rose would be viewed by Society; in their household, she had *always* been treated as their family because she was. They did not understand that, because she was illegitimate, not everyone would view her that way.

Lady Stark had gone rigid, looking as though she was biting her tongue, but she gave them a sharp look as if to say *explain this, or I will.*

"I… you are going to be a young lady of the *ton*," Rose said after a moment. "Young ladies of the *ton* dance."

"Are you not a young lady of the *ton?*" Bridget was like a dog with a bone. "I know Johanna did not have a debut, but that was because we were poor. Now we are not."

"Bridget, you cannot just say things like that!" Johanna was aghast, and she shot an apologetic look at Lady Stark.

"At least not in public," Lady Stark agreed. "Young ladies are not so blunt with their words, and it is not polite to talk about finances in mixed company."

"Well, we are not in public, we are at the breakfast table," Bridget replied ruthlessly. "And the duke has left, so Micah is the only man left, and he knows we were poor."

"Still are," Micah added cheerfully. Johanna sent him a dire look he completely ignored. "I do not know if the duke will be able to get the money Blash stole from us back. We are reliant on his generosity for now."

"Johanna is his wife, so is it not her generosity?"

As usual, Bridget was asking questions Johanna did not know how to answer. She looked at Rose, then at Lady Stark.

"Not exactly," Johanna said at the same time Rose spoke.

"I will take the dance lessons," her cousin announced, obviously exasperated. "Even though I will never need them."

"I still want to know why you will never need them."

"Because I am illegitimate, Bridget," Rose huffed, tilting her chin up as she sat back in her seat, crossing her arms over her chest.

Johanna's heart ached, and she wished she was beside her cousin so she could hold Rose's hand. It did not matter to her that Rose's parents had not been married; it never had.

"My parents were not married, so even though I am your cousin, none of the noblemen will marry me because I am a bastard, and my grandparents were from Africa, not England. No nobleman will want to tie themselves to someone with my lineage. They want a young English woman who is part of the nobility and without any scandal to their heritage."

For a long moment, silence reigned over the table, and it seemed that Bridget had been quelled by Rose's blunt honestly. Then she frowned fiercely, shaking her head and slumping back with her arms crossed over her chest, looking remarkably like Rose despite the difference in their coloring.

"Well, then, they are all pinheads, and I do not want to marry any of them either." She sniffed, tilting her nose up into the air. "Therefore, I do not need to learn to dance."

"Oh yes, you do," Rose replied grimly, in the tone of voice that let Bridget know she was serious. When she sounded like that, Johanna already knew that she was going to get her way, and so did Bridget. She scowled, but before she could start trying to argue with Rose, Charlotte put her hand atop Rose's arm.

"I will marry you, Rose," she said earnestly, if quietly.

Immediately, Rose melted. They all did. Charlotte's moments of unexpected sweetness usually had that effect. Even Lady Stark's expression softened as she looked at Charlotte with a kind of amazement—as this was likely her first time seeing this side of Charlotte.

"Thank you, darling," Rose said, patting Charlotte's hand. "That will not be necessary. I do plan to find a husband, just not among the nobility."

"All right." Charlotte smiled, then pulled her hand away, returning to her picking at her breakfast. Even with the abundance of food set before them, she barely ate. Johanna did not know if it was because she truly was not hungry or perhaps just not used to eating or if there was some other kind of odd thought process happening inside her head. She made a mental note to speak with Charlotte about it later. There was no need to eat sparingly anymore.

"I think you should marry a duke," Bridget said. "That way, we do not have to rely on Matthew alone to support us."

"A duke would not want to marry me, were you not listening?" Rose shook her head in exasperation. "Perhaps *you* should marry a duke."

"Are there any dukes who are not married that we did not meet at Johanna's wedding?" Bridget asked, looking at Lady Stark, who shook her head in amusement. She did not seem scandalized by Bridget's outrageousness, thankfully. "Then they are all likely to be married by the time I am ready to wed one of them."

"They are going to marry proper young ladies who befit their stations," Rose told her firmly.

"Johanna is not a proper young lady who befits a duke's station," Bridget replied, undeterred. "We are too poor, and she never had a debut. The Duchess of Hereford is *also* not a proper young lady who befitted a duke's station. I heard yesterday that the duke did not want to marry her because of a scandal around her family, but then he had to marry her because of a scandal with her. Which makes no sense to me, but that is what her brother said."

There was another long silence. Johanna knew what Kalina's brother meant, and now that she knew intimately something of the kind of scandal Hereford had with her before their marriage, she knew she was absolutely not going to explain it to Bridget. Certainly not with Charlotte in the room, even if she wanted to make the attempt.

"It is time to get ready," Lady Stark announced, cutting off the conversation with brisk efficiency, rather than letting Bridget continue to lead them where she wanted to go. She got to her feet, putting Johanna in mind of a battleship, moving with determination and no intention of stopping. "Johanna, come join us after you have seen to your mother. Come along, Rose."

"I... yes, of course." Rose shot Johanna a look, but she merely shrugged.

It was not the worst thing to put off talking to Rose about her wedding night since she still did not know exactly what she would say. And she did not need Rose in order to check on her mother. Besides, if her mother reacted badly to the fact that Johanna had married the duke yesterday, despite what she'd said, it was better if Rose was not there.

CHAPTER TWENTY-ONE

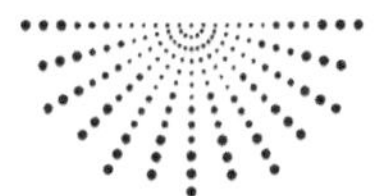

MATTHEW

Drake and Zachary were waiting for him in the foyer, both of them dressed and ready for the day. Monkey Sinclair sat on Zachary's shoulder, as usual, his yellow ribbon dangling from his collar.

"Apologies for interrupting the day after your wedding," Zachary said regretfully. "Last night, my uncle mentioned seeing Cornwall back in town. We want to do the rounds of the clubs today and possibly the hells tonight to try to track him down, but…"

"But my presence there is less likely to cause comment than yours. Especially as you are newly engaged."

Zachary flinched at the reminder, raking his hand through his long dark hair. The dark yellow waistcoat under his grey jacket was fitted perfectly to him, shifting as he moved.

"And even though you are newly married," Drake said. "Christian and Sebastian are going around to some of the more vaunted haunts for gentlemen of the _ton_. White's, Hyde Park, and the like. Nathanial is not at-home to visitors at the moment, so we left him a note. Gregory and Zachary will be attending events with their ladies, in case Cornwall acts completely out of character. Which leaves you and me…"

"We will not cause comment at the gaming hells and the like."

Matthew sighed. Even the day after his wedding, no one would question the Lord of Luck trying his hand at the tables.

Perhaps they would think he was testing his luck now that his life had changed so drastically. Or trying to win a big pot to gift his new wife with something outrageous. The important thing was that the theories would have nothing to do with their fathers' deaths, and no one would think twice about Matthew approaching Cornwall at a gaming table.

It was important to all of them that no one know they were investigating.

Firstly, because an investigation had already been completed, and the *ton* was convinced the tragic deaths of such a large group of dukes was an accident. Gossip had died down rather quickly. Learning that it had been a conspiracy to murder would do more than set a fox among hens; it would cast a shadow on all the heirs.

Perhaps Matthew was naïve, but he fully trusted his friends, and he did not think any of them had anything to do with the explosion and subsequent fire that had killed all their fathers. Some of them did not have the best relationships with their fathers—Nathanial, for one— and if it was just *his* father who had died... well, truth be told, most of the *ton* would likely have shrugged their shoulders and privately said it was for the best, even if Nathanial was guilty.

But Nathanial would not have done that to the other dukes. And he was the one who had come up with the clue about Cornwall, who had invited the former Duke of Hereford to the party at the hunting lodge, despite being owed a very large debt from Nathanial's father.

It was suspicious, and until Drake's men managed to track down Gregory's old steward—who they *knew* had something to do with it— Cornwall was their only clue. That also meant they had to tread delicately because it was not as though the earl would be eager to implicate himself in the death of so many dukes.

Secondly, several of them now had wives and heirs. Not to mention mothers or grandmothers. If they were known to be investigating, all of them could be in danger. Nathanial and Gregory's wives knew the truth, of course. Matthew would need to tell his wife eventually, too.

"Flip your coin to see if you're coming with me," Drake ordered impatiently.

Matthew pulled it out of his pocket and did as Drake asked. He was unsurprised by the answer.

"I am." It only made sense after all.

He gave the coin another flip. He would not be telling his wife the truth about his father and the other duke's fathers today. Which also made sense. It was her first day as his duchess. Better to let her get used to the household first, then ease her into things.

"What was that for?" Zachary asked, frowning at him.

"Nothing to do with this. Just a private matter." Matthew tucked his coin back into his pocket. "Well, gentlemen, shall we?" He gestured to the door.

He glanced around for Holt, who was coming back from the hallway.

"Holt, let my grandmother and wife know that I have gone out with the Dukes of Grafton and Ormonde, and I expect I'll return rather late this evening."

Though Holt's expression did not change one iota, Matthew got the distinct impression that the butler was displeased with his announcement. It was likely not well done of him to leave his new wife on her first day as his duchess, but his grandmama would have things well in hand. Matthew was not sure what he would be able to add to it.

The ladies ran the household; he would likely be rather useless hanging about.

"Yes, Your Grace," he said, nonetheless, because he was a butler, and that's what butlers did.

Matthew nodded at him and followed Drake and Zachary out the door. Drake was waiting for him on the other side, though Zachary was already making his way down the street.

"How is married life?" Drake asked, falling into step beside him.

"Much nicer than I anticipated," Matthew replied, eyeing his friend. Drake was the contemporary who intimidated him the most, if he was being honest. While all of them had been bonded together by the tragedy that had befallen them, sometimes, he felt like that was all he had in common with Drake. "You should try it soon."

"I will. Soon enough." Drake scowled, but not at Matthew. At a point in the street in front of him. Likely, he was also being hounded by his mother as well. One of the dangers of being betrothed to the daughter of her closest friend. Lady Astrid was no wilting flower either.

Personally, Matthew did not blame Drake for putting it off, now that he thought about it. He could not imagine Lady Astrid being nearly as nice or obliging as Johanna was. Lady Astrid was known to the *ton* as an Original; friendship with her was highly desired, but she was rather choosy with her friends, and no one knew exactly what her criteria was. After all, she'd invited Lady Johanna to her house party, and before that, Matthew had never even heard of the Ashmores. Trying to memorize Debrett's book of Peerage had never been one of his aspirations. His grandmama handled the connections for him.

"Right, well. I suppose I would not be rushing toward it, either."

Now Drake did frown at him, turning his head with a quizzical expression on his face and pinning Matthew with his dark eyes.

"Your marriage was the definition of rushed."

"Ah… well." He had meant that he would not rush to marry Lady Astrid, but despite the way he dragged his feet, Drake could become rather prickly over his betrothed. Matthew would prefer not to draw his ire if they were going to spend the day together. "That was really the coin, though. Not me."

Drake's expression softened, and he shook his head.

"You know, you do not have to do what the coin tells you to. You have a choice."

"Of course I do. But why would I choose to do the opposite when it has never steered me wrong?" Matthew shrugged. "I am not one to fight the whims of fate."

Which made Drake frown again, and Matthew realized that could apply to his situation, seeing as he was certainly fighting marrying the woman his parents had fated him for. So, Matthew had stuck his foot in it after all. Ah, well. It was not as though Drake was the most humorous fellow; it was hard to tell the difference between Drake in a good mood and Drake in a bad mood, anyway.

"Speaking of, where should we go first?" Matthew dug into his pocket for his coin. Beside him, Drake sighed, but obligingly slowed to wait and see what direction the coin would point them in.

Matthew appreciated that about him.

JOHANNA

Walking down the hallway alone, Johanna steeled herself. Hopefully, her mother was better this morning. Both in body and in mind. As much as part of her wanted Rose by her side, she was also relieved she would not have to explain anything to Rose if her mother said something shocking again.

When she reached the door, Johanna took a deep breath and squared her shoulders, lifting her chin. She was a grown woman, and she did not need her mother's permission or blessing to marry. Especially when doing so had saved her mother's life.

Opening the door, Johanna stepped inside. Her heart softened as soon as she saw her mother lying there in bed, pale as ever, head nestled against the pillow. Her mother's eyes opened as Johanna approached.

"Good morning, Mother, how are you feeling today?" Johanna asked gently, stepping to the bedside and reaching out a hand to feel her mother's forehead.

Damp, but cool. Johanna breathed a sigh of relief. The fever must have broken in the night, helped by the tea.

Her mother grabbed her by the wrist in a faster movement than Johanna would have thought she could manage, and it was all she could do not to jump back and pull away as her mother stared up at her with wide, violet eyes.

"Did you do it?" she asked, her voice a low hiss.

"Do what?" Johanna's heart sank. Whatever madness had gripped her mother, she worried it had nothing to do with the fever.

"Did you marry him? The duke? I heard the maids talking. They said you married him yesterday."

"I did." Johanna said it as gently as she could. "But—"

Before she could say anything else, her mother had released her wrist and was turning over.

"Then we are all doomed."

Taking a deep breath, Johanna tried to gather her thoughts. She had no idea how to handle her mother when she was like this. The threat of doom was gone. Johanna had saved them from doom with her marriage to Matthew. She closed her eyes and felt her nails biting into the palms of her hands.

While it did feel as though the lovely dream of being safe under Matthew's care could disappear at any moment, the truth was that there was no reason to think it would. She was so tired of being afraid. So tired of scrambling for a few more days of sustenance and hope.

Why could her mother not see those days were over?

Perhaps it was fear of having to return to them that had prompted her to make up wild stories in her mind. Perhaps she was too frightened to trust that all of this would not be taken away again.

Johanna could understand that. The very thought of losing everything she'd just gained by her marriage made her feel sick to her stomach.

She did not know how to reassure her mother. Only time would be able to ease the fear entirely. Johanna unclenched her hands and let out a long, slow breath.

"Everything will be well, Mother," she said softly, putting her hand on her mother's shoulder. There was no response, verbally or physically. "You will see. Just do not speak of this to anyone else."

Her mother sniffed but did not argue, which Johanna presumed was the best she could hope for at the moment. There was a small throbbing in her head, not quite an ache but like the beginning of one.

Everything else in her life was so wonderful, she felt like she'd been swept into a fairy tale. She'd been rescued from a terrible fate, married to a handsome duke, and would have no worries for the rest of her life... Her mother's fears and the terrible fantasy she'd conjured up because of it were the only fly in the ointment.

Perhaps she could find a way to bring the conversation around to the old duke with Lady Stark in the room. Surely, hearing from Lady Stark that the entire *ton* knew the dukes' deaths had been accidents would help convince her mother to be reasonable. Why this thing had stuck so in her mind, Johanna could not countenance.

It was sheer madness to think that her sleeping potions had anything to do with their deaths, even if they had been purchased by one of their stewards. Of course Johanna did not wish to expose her mother's madness. Lack of food must have done something to her. Hopefully, having it in plentiful amounts now would be healing.

At the very least, Johanna could be grateful that her mother did not seem eager to speak of it to anyone but Johanna herself. Hopefully, it would stay that way, especially as Johanna and the duke were already married, and the marriage had been thoroughly consummated. There was nothing to be done about that.

Tucking the covers in around her mother, Johanna sighed and left the room. As much as she wanted to convince her mother, it was obviously useless to make the attempt today when she was so upset. Maybe tomorrow she would be able to be more reasonable.

In the meantime, Johanna wanted to be the best duchess possible, and right now, that meant joining her sisters in learning how to dance.

CHAPTER TWENTY-TWO

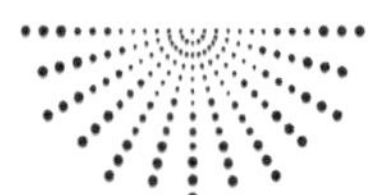

When her husband did not appear by suppertime, Johanna was becoming worried, but his grandmother waved her hand.

"He's newly married, dear. When he gets home, you will tell him that the expectations of a married gentleman and an unwed gentleman are very different and that he will need to start returning home at a reasonable time." Lady Stark was very confident in how the duke should be managed.

Johanna was not feeling so confident in her ability to manage him, but she supposed she would have to at least try.

Whatever his business was, it must have been important. She should not take it as a slight against herself.

Her sister, on the other hand, had no such reasonable compunction.

"What do you mean he is not joining us for supper?" Bridget appeared even more put out at the revelation than Johanna had been. Seated at the table, she leaned back against her chair, crossing her arms over her chest. Beside her, Micah appeared disappointed as well, though he was far more quiet about it. "He is your husband, and he is supposed to be here."

"He was called away for something important this morning, remember?" Johanna reminded her gently, though part of her felt very much the same. "I am sure he would be here if he could."

"Well, I think it is very ill done of him."

"It depends on how important his business is," Rose muttered, but the look of disapproval on her face said she agreed more with Bridget than Johanna.

"He will learn," Lady Stark said, though she looked as though she wanted to smile. At least she did not seem put out at Bridget's criticism of her grandson. "It is his first time being a husband, after all."

Bridget thought about that for a moment, tilting her head to the side.

"That is true. Should he not have learned from his father, though?"

Lady Stark sniffed.

"Unfortunately, his father was not the paragon he thought he was, at least not when it came to family. I would be surprised if he showed up for a meal with Matthew and my daughter more than once a fortnight." There was a dark look in her eyes. "Though I doubt either of them missed him and would have been happy to have his presence afflict their suppers even more sparsely."

Frowning, Bridget looked to Johanna, who shook her head, mystified. Obviously, Lady Stark had not cared very much for her son-in-law, duke or not. It did explain why Matthew might not have thought that attending supper this evening was very important. If his father had rarely been around for meals… while Matthew had already taken quite a few with her and her family.

But unlike Matthew and his mother, she truly enjoyed his presence. Apparently, her siblings did, too. Even Charlotte was hanging on to every word being spoken, absorbing all of it without commentary.

"Our father attended every supper with us, even if he was not there for the other meals," Bridget announced. "That's the kind of husband I want."

Johanna started at Bridget's pronouncement because she had not thought Bridget would remember that. Although their father was not a forbidden topic in their household, they did not often speak of him.

Perhaps Johanna or Micah had said something about it once, and Bridget remembered *that*.

"The desire for your husband's company will very likely depend on whether you enjoy his company," Lady Stark said.

"Why would I marry a man whose company I do not enjoy?" Bridget appeared taken aback at the very notion.

"Many reasons." Lady Stark waved her hand. "While some couples at our rank marry for affection, there are all sorts of other reasons, too. Connections, money, alliances… and a man during courtship is often quite different from a man during marriage, unfortunately."

"You mean they are dishonest?"

"Yes," Lady Stark stated bluntly. "Which is something to keep in mind after you debut and men begin to court you."

Johanna found the back-and-forth between Bridget and Lady Stark fascinating. Her mother had not spoken so baldly about marriage with Johanna. Their parents had been a love match, and that was what she and her siblings had grown up hearing about.

Stymied by Lady Stark's truthfulness, Bridget subsided, appearing to be deep in thought. Johanna smiled inwardly and turned to Micah.

"How was your reading today?" she asked him. Though he did not have a tutor—yet—she knew that he'd set himself the task of reading the entirety of *The Iliad*, which had been their father's favorite book. He'd found a copy of it in Matthew's library yesterday and asked to borrow it.

That neatly turned the conversation away from Matthew's absence and the topic of marriages for the rest of the meal, to Johanna's relief. Even though they had only come together a few days ago, she was already used to his presence, and it made her sad to look at his empty seat. Despite the fact she had not married for love—she had married for a multitude of the reasons Lady Stark had listed—the truth was that she did rather like her husband.

She liked being around him. She liked speaking with him. She liked touching him.

And after last night and this morning, she would have very much liked to have his company.

Perhaps he did not feel the same way, though. Or perhaps the business he was attending to was very important. She was curious what he might have to do with the other dukes, but she was uncertain if it was her place to ask.

Once supper finished, they retired to the drawing room. Lady Stark allowed herself to be drawn into a game of spilikins with Bridget and Charlotte, much to Rose and Johanna's amusement. Micah tucked himself into an armchair with his book.

She and Rose sat by the window seat—not because she was watching for Matthew's return, it was just the most convenient spot—to work on their needlework by lamplight.

Matthew

The usual luck Matthew lived by was not aiding their search. Cornwall was in neither of the two establishments they visited. Matthew mentally shrugged and flipped his coin again. Perhaps they should be looking elsewhere, but he and Drake were the only ones among their coterie who could search at this level. Any of the others walking into these rooms would cause comment and curiosity.

Even now, they were getting occasional sidelong looks, although perhaps that was because it was so early in the day.

"Perhaps he is not awake yet," Matthew murmured to Drake as they left The Fiddling Magpie, the second location they'd tried. "Has anyone checked his house?"

Drake shot him a sharp look.

"Of course I did. And his mistress' house. And his mother's."

Well, trust Drake to be thorough. Matthew shrugged and sighed, pulling out his coin to see what direction they should head in next.

"Maybe we should try using something other than your luck for the moment," Drake said dryly. "Let's go to the Pearl and Buck next since it is on the next street over."

Nodding, Matthew flipped his coin anyway, then grinned at Drake.

"I agree."

Pressing his lips together, Drake looked like he was trying not to smile. Truth be told, Matthew was enjoying this excursion with him more than he'd thought he would. As serious as he was, Drake also seemed unbothered and amused by Matthew's coin.

He also did not do some of the things that Matthew would have expected. Though the doxies had recognized him at the Magpie, he had not leered at them or made any coarse remarks, though Matthew was fairly certain he'd seen Drake slipping one of them a pouch. He would be willing to bet his lucky coin that the pouch had been full of money.

What Drake was up to with the seedy venues he frequented, Matthew was not sure, but he was becoming more and more certain that it had nothing to do with bedding as many ladybirds as he could before his wedding night. No matter what Drake said. He was up to something.

But Matthew had bigger mysteries to attend to at the moment than why Drake was so determined to present himself as the worst of dissolute rakes before he finally wedded Lady Astrid.

"Tomorrow, I am going to start sorting through Falmouth's finances," he told Drake. "To see what I can recover for him. Would you like to help?"

For a moment, he thought Drake was going to say yes, then the other man shook his head regretfully.

"Unfortunately, I have other matters I must attend to. Let me know if you need some extra weight to lean on the bankers."

"I will." One did not look a gift duke in the mouth, after all, even if one was already a duke. Two dukes were better than one and all that.

They walked into the Pearl and Buck, and it took a moment for Matthew's eyes to adjust. Despite the brightness of the day, the interior of the bar was dark, even in the front room where patrons were doing no more than eating and drinking. The windows were shuttered, only bits of light seeping in from the outside.

It was not very crowded, and they quickly made their way past the suspicious bartender to the much larger backroom. Here, the windows had heavy, dark curtains drawn over them, and the only light came from flickering flames in the lamps. There were more men back here, possibly having stayed overnight, some of them not even realizing it was midmorning already.

Matthew elbowed Drake in the side and nodded to a table in the corner where a group of four gentlemen were playing hazard. Cornwall sat with them, looking fresher than his companions, and Matthew would be willing to bet that he had recently arrived.

They did not make straight for him, so as not to cause alarm, but separated and sat down at two of the other tables instead. The crowd was a mix between noblemen and wealthy merchants or their sons. Names were not needed, though one of the men immediately got up after he sat down, obviously recognizing the Lord of Luck.

Matthew grinned, unbothered.

He did not stay at any one table for too long—doing so had a tendency to enrage the other players. Just long enough to win a handy sum at each before moving on. Anyone who did not recognize him would assume he was leaving before his lucky streak could end—not knowing that it would not. Anyone who did recognize him was grateful he only lightened their purses a little before leaving.

Eventually, he managed to end up at the same table as Cornwall, with Drake at the table beside them. The earl looked up as Matthew came to the seat beside him, a fleeting expression crossing his face that made Matthew think the earl meant to flee.

"Cornwall," he said, clapping his hand on the man's shoulder and grinning widely, keeping the earl in his seat as Matthew sat beside him. Seeing Matthew's friendly demeanor, the earl seemed to relax. "How goes it? You missed the tournament at the Tramp's Den."

"I did. Business to attend at home. You know how it goes." Cornwall seemed resigned to losing some of his money to Matthew.

The other two players seemed vaguely familiar, though he could not place either of them. They clearly knew each other, and they seemed to recognize him and, like Cornwall, were resigned to losing a few hands. They had likely noted that he did not stay in any one place for too long, so they might as well play, then they could continue on at this table once he left. Matthew could practically read their thoughts as he'd watched so many others make the same calculation.

"I do indeed," Matthew replied jovially. "It's been a busy Season. I just got married yesterday, you know."

Cornwall jerked in surprise as he picked up his cards. "I did not. Congratulations."

"Thank you." Matthew looked at his own hand and smiled. He always smiled, so it did not really matter what the others thought. "This Season is full of ducal weddings. First Clarence, then Hereford, and now myself. I cannot help but wonder who will be next."

"Care to make a wager on it?" one of the other men, a swarthy fellow with dark hair, asked and his companion nudged him in the side with his elbow. "What? He cannot be lucky at everything. There's no way to know which of the tragic dukes will fall to the altar next."

Cornwall winced at the mention of the tragic dukes, his head dropping to look at his cards, but it also hid his expression. Matthew pretended not to notice. He could tell Drake was listening closely at the next table, even if his attention appeared to be fully on the game in front of him.

"You might be surprised." Matthew grinned, pulling out his coin and rubbing its surface. "Would you care to make the wager?"

The other man eyed him. His companion shook his head ruefully at the folly.

"Let's focus on the game at hand," the other man said after a moment. "No need to make wagers right now, I s'pose."

Matthew shrugged, because it made no difference to him. He was curious which of his friends would be next, but without the wager, he was not certain his luck would work on informing him.

"Condolences for your father," the swarthy fellow said. "I did not mean to be callous."

"That is alright," Matthew replied cheerfully. He was feeling *quite* cheerful and very much in debt to the swarthy fellow. How lucky that the man was bringing up the exact right things Matthew wanted to speak with Cornwall about. "It was a tragic accident, but I believe we've all since recovered. And it could have been worse. You were there, weren't you, Cornwall?" Matthew already knew he had not been, but he wanted to see how Cornwall reacted.

The earl jerked, his face paling as his head snapped up so he could look at Matthew.

"I... What?"

Now the other two were looking at him with interest, too.

"You were there when the elder dukes died?" the swarthy fellow asked. Despite his apology to Matthew, he was obviously rabidly curious about the whole thing. Matthew could not blame him. He could not think of a single time in history when so many British dukes had been lost at the same time.

"I, ah, no." Cornwall shook his head vehemently. "I was invited, but I did not attend. I fell sick at the last moment. I... sometimes wonder if being there, if I might have been able to... help." There was heavy guilt in his voice and his face as he swallowed hard, and Matthew got the impression he truly felt as though he should have been there.

Which was interesting.

"I apologize for bringing it up," he said. "Hereford said that you'd invited his father, and I assumed."

"I *should* have been there." Cornwall looked down at his cards, but it did not seem as though he was truly seeing them. The guilt was still writ large over his expression.

Across the table, Drake looked over at them with a frown, his gaze connecting with Matthew.

Whatever was going on with Cornwall, it was not what they'd expected.

CHAPTER TWENTY-THREE

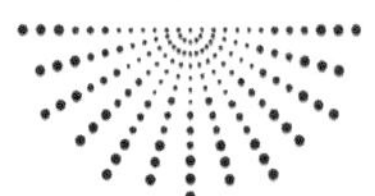

MATTHEW

Seeing Cornwall's maudlin reaction, Matthew worried about pushing too hard, especially in front of witnesses, and when he gave his coin a surreptitious flip, it agreed. So, he let the topic of the hunting lodge, his father, and the other dukes drop. As they played, Cornwall rallied, but it was clear his focus was not entirely on the game. He was not playing at his usual level.

After taking some of their money, Matthew moved on, but kept an eye on Cornwall. As did Drake.

When the earl got to his feet, Matthew quickly flipped his coin again, then got to his feet to follow the earl. He sauntered from the room as if he'd just had enough of playing, and grinned when he heard the sigh of relief behind him. No one was going to question his departure.

"Cornwall," he called out, catching the man halfway through the room. The earl stopped and turned, and his face fell when he saw who was speaking. "A moment of your time, if you will?"

Obviously bracing himself, Cornwall nodded. Perhaps he thought Matthew would want to harangue him for his father's death, but hopefully, Matthew would be able to put the other man's mind at ease quickly enough.

"Let me buy you a drink," Matthew said, signaling to the barkeep before gesturing at an empty table nearby. The pub side was still fairly empty, giving them a nice selection of seating and plenty of tables between them and the other patrons.

Cornwall looked at Matthew, confusion clear in his expression, but he slowly sat down. "You want to buy me a drink?"

"You seem upset." Matthew shrugged. Besides, a drink would likely loosen Cornwall's tongue more than anything else.

The barkeep brought two mugs over and slid them in front of Matthew and Cornwall. Cornwall immediately took his in both hands, his fingers curling around the handle and the mug, pulling it in front of him as his head dropped down to stare into its depths. Bringing his own to his lips, Matthew took a sip and was pleasantly surprised at the taste.

"You know my father's death was not your fault," he said conversationally, to open the topic.

If Cornwall knew anything useful when he had not been there was questionable, but now that they'd tracked him down, Matthew felt as though he should at least attempt to find out if Cornwall knew anything. They did not have any other clues at the moment, unless Drake's men finally tracked down Gregory's former steward, Arthur Montblanc.

At the very least, he could discover why Cornwall had invited the former Duke of Hereford, who had already owed him a great sum of money, to the trip. Perhaps Cornwall's guilt was because he had not known the other dukes would die as well. The note Montblanc had left Gregory certainly indicated he had not fully understood what he had become involved in. He'd wanted justice for his niece, who had been raped by Gregory's father, but there was no reason for him to have a grudge against any of the other dukes.

Perhaps Cornwall had wanted to punish Nathanial's father for lack of payment and had realized he would never get his money anyway, but he had not meant for the others to perish as well.

"I know." Cornwall finally lifted the mug and took a large swig. "I do know that." He sounded grim but firm, as though he was repeating words to himself he'd said before but did not quite believe yet.

"If you were there, you might have died alongside him and the other dukes," Matthew pointed out.

"I know. I do keep thinking, though…" Cornwall's voice trailed off, and he stared down into the mug again.

Drake stepped into the pub as Cornwall fell silent again and nodded to Matthew.

"Ah, here is Ormonde," Matthew said cheerfully, as if he had just noticed Drake and not as if they'd come here together for a purpose. Lifting his hand, he gave Drake a wave. "He will tell you. Ormonde, Cornwall here is feeling a surfeit of guilt because he was invited to the trip with our fathers but was too ill to attend."

Moving to the empty chair beside Cornwall, Drake tilted his head. He looked slightly exasperated—likely wondering what Matthew had been saying when he was not there to listen—but he did not remonstrate him.

"No reason for that," Drake said, keeping his voice amiable and matching Matthew's tone. "It would have done the country no good to have you dead, too."

"Yes, but not everyone died." Cornwall shook his head. "Your fathers. Some of the servants. None of the other noblemen. The dukes were all in the same section of the cabin. I asked Martingale."

Martingale, being the marquess who had hosted the event. He'd survived, as had the other two marquesses and the other earl who had attended, just as Cornwall said. They'd been on the other side of the lodging when the explosion happened.

"I did as well," Drake said with a nod. "My understanding is he felt they should all be grouped together by rank." And if Drake accepted that understanding, Matthew knew it had been thoroughly investigated. It was also hardly an unusual state of affairs. "It was poor luck they were on the side where the explosion and fire hit hardest."

Although his tone was neutral, it was also tight, and Matthew shot him a sympathetic look. Drake, along with Zachary and Sebastian, truly grieved his father as they had been rather close. Whereas Matthew's feelings were much more complicated. It was true he'd respected his father, but in many ways, the death of his pater had given him more relief than anything else. He was somewhere between them and Nathanial—who likely would have done a jig on his father's grave if not for the deaths of the other dukes—in his feelings.

"Poor luck and an extremely unhappy accident." Cornwall took another large swig of his drink and shook his head. "I cannot help but think... if I had not invited Hereford... his is the death that can be attributed to me."

"Nathanial did say his father owed you a great deal of money," Drake said delicately, leaning forward onto his elbows as he folded his arms on the table in front of him.

"He did." Cornwall shook his head. "But no sum is worth a man's life."

"Were you hoping he might bring the funds with him when you invited him?" Matthew asked.

Cornwall nodded.

"Though I did not have much hope of it. Either way, I would not be gambling with him, but I thought perhaps I could collect... and if anyone chose to include him in a game after that, well, that was at their own peril." He looked away, pensive. "It seemed like a good idea at the time, though I had been drinking when it was suggested to me."

"It was suggested to you?" Drake asked, drolly casual, as if he had not a care in the world.

If Cornwall realized he was being interrogated, he did not show it. If anything, he seemed almost relieved to talk, as though he'd been carrying around a great weight inside him that he could finally put down.

Drake asked most of the questions, getting Cornwall to tell them everything, though there was not much to tell. He'd been out with friends, playing and drinking, and at some point during the evening, the discussion had gone round to the hunting lodge. One of them told him that Hereford had recently come into some winnings and suggested that Cornwall invite him to the lodge, so as to have a place to collect the debt.

"I played with him—Hereford—the very next night, and he confirmed that he was recently flush, but he did not have the money on him at the moment. So, I invited him to join us at the hunting lodge and pay me back then." Cornwall snorted. "I doubt he did, though."

By the time they finished, Cornwall was completely foxed, yet seemed happier than he had been earlier. His load was lightened after telling them everything, at least some of his guilt absolved. Perhaps because they had not condemned him. Drake was more frustrated than anything because he did not have the knowledge they sought.

He could not even remember who had suggested that he invite Hereford to the lodge. Possibly Carmathan. Possibly the Earl of Hatchett. Possibly the Earl of Conyngham. Possibly the former Duke of Grafton or his brother, the Marquess of Selter. Or possibly someone else whom he could not remember being present that night.

It did at least give them a list to start with, though Matthew was not certain that suggesting Hereford be invited to a gathering was an indication of anything nefarious. On the other hand, it was not as if they had anything else to investigate. At the very least, if they fully investigated, they could mark off the possibility.

Helping Cornwall stumble back to his carriage, practically carrying him between them, they got him tucked away and watched it roll down the street before looking at each other. Drake took a deep breath, then tilted his head back to look up at the sky. The sun was much lower now.

"We should gather the others to discuss," he said, his head dropping back down. "Let's go to my house. I will send them notes to come and meet us."

"My home is closer," Matthew pointed out. "So is Hereford House."

"But full of people, including your new wife." Drake glanced at him. "And after Kalina was eavesdropping on Nathanial, I do not believe conversations there will be very secure either. The ladies are getting far too involved in the investigations. Only Hatchett is married among the men Cornwall spoke of, and he and his wife are hardly close; therefore, we do not need the ladies to question *their* wives. I would rather keep them out of it."

"Fair enough," Matthew agreed, seeing his point. "I do not think we need to be concerned Johanna will try to listen to us, as I have not told her about our investigation, but there are others in the house." Including Charlotte, who seemed to appear wherever she willed, even if she was not supposed to be there, or Bridget, who he could absolutely imagine listening at keyholes.

So, Drake made a good point.

"She might know anyway," Drake said dryly. "The ladies have already befriended her. As she is your wife, they may feel it is their duty to inform her, in case you do not."

Matthew shrugged.

"The coin said not to tell her today. Not that I particularly want to, anyway. It is not exactly a cheerful subject, especially so soon after our wedding. We should be joyful this week, should we not?" He thought about it for a moment, then shrugged again. "Yes, I think it is better that I wait to tell her. That is probably why my coin keeps putting it off."

Especially because Drake was correct; there was no need to involve the ladies in this part of their investigation. If Nathanial and Gregory chose to inform their wives of the discussion later, that would be up to them. Matthew certainly did not feel the need to tell his wife at the moment; his coin would let him know when the right time was.

They returned to Drake's house and quickly sent out the notes, discussing their impressions between the two of them. They both agreed Cornwall was telling the truth and that he'd not been part of the plot to kill Nathanial's father—he'd still been trying to get the money owed him. His guilt was all to do with feeling as though he might have been able to do something if he'd been there, but none of that had basis in reality.

None of the men who had been on the other side of the Lodge had been able to reach any of the dukes—the fire had been too fierce.

Neither Matthew nor Drake blamed any of them, as long as they had not been involved in the actual setting of the fire. Which, at the moment, there was no proof of.

To their surprise, Nathanial arrived rather quickly and joined them in Drake's library, though they decided not to update him till the rest of their group came. Better to do it all at once. Instead, Matthew teased his friend about being unavailable that morning for the investigation, and Nathanial teased him back about *being* available now that he had a wife.

Thankfully, the other dukes trickled in not long after, and Drake quickly gave them a rundown of the little information Cornwall had divulged.

"I think Conyngham could very well be involved," Zachary said immediately, frowning and reaching up to stroke Monkey Sinclair's back. The little monkey chittered at him and jumped up onto the back of the wingback armchair he was sitting in. "I've never trusted him."

"Just because he has taken your place in Delilah's bed does not mean he was involved in murdering your father," Drake said, sounding exasperated and shooting Zachary a look. "Your uncle was also among those Cornwall named."

"Yes, but what reason would he have for killing his own brother?" Zachary shook his head. "I have always felt Conyngham was a shady type of character."

"You have not," Gregory replied, obviously amused. He shook his head and took a sip of his brandy, crossing his arms over his chest as he leaned against the mantle beside Sebastian. "You do not even believe what you are saying. I agree, we should look into him, but what would his motive even be? It's not as though he knew you would give Delilah her congé so you could marry someone else, and he could become her new lover."

"And it is not as if he's in love with her," Christian added from his place beside Zachary in another wingback chair. "Conyngham is a rake through and through. I think he's bedded more ladies of the *ton* than I have. Not that I've been keeping score."

"Of course not." Sebastian shot him a bemused look. "I agree we should try to speak with all of them, if only because they might remember who encouraged Cornwall to issue the invitation."

"Which may or may not mean anything, but at least it's something we can *do* right now," Christian said, echoing Matthew's earlier thoughts. He shot Zachary a look as the other man began to open his mouth. "*I* will take Conyngham. Certainly, *you* should not."

"Very well," Zachary said irritably, appearing very put out that no one was willing to jump on board his theory. Monkey Sinclair climbed from the back of the chair on top of his head and patted his forehead with a tiny paw. Sighing, Zachary reached up to encourage the monkey onto his hand instead. "Tiny menace. At least he's not throwing food or my drinks now. He ran off with the scone from my breakfast this morning. I am starving."

Drake glanced at the clock.

"You should all stay for supper, and we can discuss who will speak with whom."

The others quickly agreed, so Matthew did as well, after a quick flip of his coin. He would have liked to have gone home to see his wife... but this was important. Besides, she had plenty of other company for dinner between his grandmother, her siblings, and her cousin. He would join her in bed later this evening.

CHAPTER TWENTY-FOUR

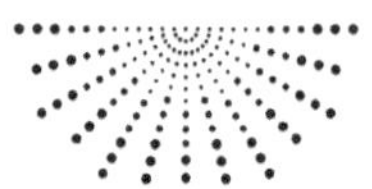

Getting ready for bed, Johanna tried not to feel put out that she had not seen her husband since this morning. After all, he was a duke. He was a busy and important man. The fact that he was also a very affectionate, amiable, cheerful sort of man did not change the fact that he had a multitude of responsibilities, and her presence in his life was both entirely new and in some ways unexpected. He'd been around the house the past several days already.

Yet she also could not deny that her heart jumped and her pulse raced with happiness when there was a knock on the adjoining door between their rooms before it quickly opened as Nettie was finishing up with her hair. Seated in front of the vanity, Johanna looked into the mirror and saw her husband appear over Nettie's shoulder.

He was not wearing a dressing gown. Instead, he was in nothing but his linen shirt, which gaped open at the neck with the top button undone. Seeing him only partly dressed made the heat in her cheeks rise, and Nettie blushed as well, quickly averting her gaze as she dropped into a curtsy.

"Your Grace."

"That will be all, Nettie," he said, coming up behind them and holding his hand out for the hairbrush Nettie was holding. She dropped it immediately into his hand and scampered for the door before Johanna could say a word.

"Was she finished?" Johanna asked him, amused as the door closed behind the retreating maid.

"It does not matter; I am happy to do it for you," he said, stepping into the place where Nettie had been before. "I am sorry I missed supper. There was some rather important business my friends and I needed to attend to today."

"That is alright." Though she wondered what the business was, she was not sure it was her place to ask him if he was not offering the information. Especially right now, as he was so intently focused on her hair. She did not want to trouble him as he tilted his head this way and that, before finally laying the brush against her silky strands. The sensation of the brush moving over her hair had abruptly changed in a manner she could not quite define.

When Nettie had been brushing her hair, it had been easy for Johanna's mind to wander. Now that it was her husband doing so, she found herself acutely focused on the feel of the bristles moving through her hair, the long strokes tugging gently on the strands. She could feel them all the way down her neck and through the rest of her body.

Meeting his gaze in the mirror, she felt her blush creeping up her entire body and into her cheeks. As intimate as the many things they'd already done had been, there was something even more so about having him perform such a mundane, daily task—yet again, a task which no man had ever done for her. Not even her father.

"I hope everything is well," she said finally, giving him the opening to talk about his business if he so desired.

"Well enough. Did you miss me today?" he asked in a low voice, his gaze steady on hers even as he continued to pull the brush through the long, pale wealth of her hair, the edges of his lips curved up in a smile. The change of subject did not bother her, though she remained curious.

Still, she could not help but take a jab at him since he had disappeared for the entire day after their wedding.

Johanna widened her eyes at him with an acutely innocent expression on her face.

"Oh, were you not about?" She kept her tone light and teasing, as if she had not noticed.

There was a long pause. She worried she'd overstepped and was about to apologize when the smile on his face broadened into a wide grin. His chuckle started low and turned into laughter after a few seconds, allowing Johanna the freedom to giggle as well.

"I did not realize you were so cheeky," he said, wagging the brush he was holding at her in the mirror. "You'd best be careful, or I will use this on more than your hair."

"What do you mean?" Her giggles stopped with her confusion. "Where?" What else could he use a hairbrush on other than hair?

The brush, which he'd been about to use on her hair again, hovered just above it as his head jerked up to look at her in the mirror.

"I ah, meant on your bottom."

"My bottom?" Now she was even more confused. There was no hair on her bottom. It would have made more sense if he had said 'on her womanhood', though the hair there did not need brushing.

"To spank you," he clarified.

"I do not know what that means," she confessed. She'd never heard the word before.

"Ah, well, it means I would smack the hairbrush against your bottom."

"And that is enjoyable?"

"Well, no, it would be meant to be punishment for being cheeky." He lifted the brush and inspected it while Johanna turned the notion over in her mind, uncertain how she felt about it. "Probably not with the brush, to be fair, that would be rather harsh for just being cheeky. But I was not intending to, anyway. I was just teasing."

"So, it would hurt."

"Yes. And no. Some women rather enjoy it." He shrugged and

started brushing her hair again, leaving her feeling aroused and confused at the same time. "I know Gregory and Nathanial have both spanked their wives, and they seem to have no complaints."

"Tiffany and Kalina?" Johanna was rather aghast; she could not imagine either Gregory or Nathanial hurting either of them. Perhaps it did not hurt very much. Though she was uncertain how it could hurt, yet a woman could still enjoy it. "Have you ever been spanked?"

"No. My father used to belt me," he said matter-of-factly. "But he did not think spankings were harsh enough discipline for a boy. It hurt like the dickens. When I was very young, I would scream the house down, but eventually, I learned to be quiet. Do not worry, I would never use a belt on you."

Johanna's stomach had flipped over for another reason entirely now as her heart went out to the young boy that he'd been, and anger roused in her breast at his father.

"You mean your father used to hit you with a belt until you screamed when you were naughty?" The very idea made her clench her fingers in her lap. How dare a man do that to a young boy? She could not imagine allowing anyone to do such a thing to Micah.

"Naughty, did not complete my lessons, did something wrong..." The way Matthew said it sent chills up her spine, as if he had accepted that it was his due that his father hurt him. "Eventually, I found my coin when I was in secondary school, and that helped a lot. That or he'd given up on me, by then; I could never decide which."

"Is that... do you plan to do that to our children?"

"Oh, no." Matthew shook his head. "It was not effective at all, I don't think. And I rather hated my father, and I do not want our children to hate me. I do not think my father liked me very much; he just needed an heir, and I had a lot to learn to be the heir he wanted. I do not have those same expectations of my heir. I do things very differently from my father, and so far, all has gone well." Now he sounded positively cheerful, and it was all Johanna could do not to shake her head in wonder.

Her parents had never used any kind of punishment that had hurt her, Rose, or any of her younger siblings. Johanna had never even heard of such a thing. Some of the women who visited her mother for potions talked of terrible things, but nothing like hitting a child for being naughty. Nor had they spoken of being spanked as punishment. Or because they enjoyed it.

It was all very confusing.

The one thing she did feel very sure of was that her husband would not hurt her. And that it was a miracle he was as warm and cheerful as he was.

"Do you want to spank me?" she asked.

The brush stroke paused, and he looked up at her in the mirror again.

"Do you want me to?" He sounded more curious than eager, but to be fair, that was how Johanna was feeling as well.

"I do not know. I want to know how it feels. How you felt."

"I never want you to know how I felt." He shook his head. "It is very different, what my father did to me and what Gregory does with Tiffany or Nathanial with Kalina. It would be very different with you and me."

"Do all husbands spank their wives?"

"I do not know. It's hardly proper to go round asking them." Matthew chuckled at the thought, which made Johanna smile, too. There was nothing she could do about how his father had treated him as a child, but at least she could make him smile now.

Staring at him in the mirror as he refocused his attention on her hair, she considered his words. She wanted to know something of what he'd been through. She was also curious as to his very confident statement about Tiffany and Kalina, though, apparently, the topic was not a common one among gentlemen. The dukes were very close, though, in their friendships. They must be comfortable talking about subjects that were not for lesser acquaintances.

"There," he said with some satisfaction. "That is done."

Grinning widely, he moved around the side of her chair to place the hairbrush on her vanity and held out his hand to help her to her feet.

Putting her hand in his, she let him pull her to standing, their bodies now nearly flush against each other with just their hands between them. She tilted her head back to look up at him.

"Matthew," she said, only a little breathless. "I would like you to spank me."

MATTHEW

Of all the things he thought his wife might request on the second night of their marriage, a spanking was not one of them.

"I… are you sure?"

She tilted her head, looking up at him with a serious expression, though he would swear mischief was dancing in her violet eyes. The filmy nightrail she was wearing beneath the thin silk of her _peignoir_ did little to hide her body from him, and his cock was already as hard as a rock. He very much wanted to strip her down… and now he very much wanted to give her a spanking. But he could not quite believe _she_ wanted him to give her one.

"Well," she said, wrinkling her nose. "I _was_ very cheeky. I am not normally cheeky."

"That is true." But he rather liked that she was cheeky with him. It made him feel like she was comfortable with him in a manner she was not with others. "I would prefer to give you a nice spanking, though."

"What is a nice spanking?"

The earnestness with which she asked was adorable. He found her naïve curiosity to be utterly entrancing. Most young ladies her age had been trained on what was and was not socially acceptable, what they could and could not say. Johanna's family must have been very on the outside of social events, even at home, for some time because she was far too inquisitive for Society.

"One that is for fun, not for punishment. It… hurts less." Matthew had been rather appalled when he'd first realized that he was aroused by spanking a woman, though he'd also quickly learned that there were varying degrees to which a woman liked being spanked. He was not a very good disciplinarian, but he enjoyed a nice pink bottom as much as the next man. Though he did not think he could ever use a belt on a woman, he had no objections to a flogger, a good, sturdy hairbrush, or a paddle, though one lover had told him he wielded such things far too lightly.

"Then that is what I want," Johanna said, nodding her head firmly. The mischief was still dancing in her eyes, though she seemed nervy as well. Matthew grinned and slid one arm around her waist to pull her more firmly against him, their hands trapped between them, so he could lower his lips to hers with a kiss.

"As you wish," he replied softly, just before their lips met.

It only took a moment of kissing her before he slid his hand out from between them, so he could hold her in both arms. One hand splayed out across her back, while the other skimmed over the back of her silken robe to curve over her buttocks. She shuddered against him, sliding her hands up to wind them about his neck as she pressed closer to him, the hard ridge of his cock digging into her soft belly.

With a groan, Matthew hoisted her up against him, making her squeak in surprise as she wrapped her legs around him. Holding her buttocks with both hands, he held her in front of him as he pivoted and began carrying her to the adjoining door between their rooms.

"Where are we going?" she asked, even though the answer was somewhat obvious.

"My room. If I am going to spank you, I certainly do not want one of your sisters coming in during the middle of it. Or interrupting our morning tomorrow." He grinned, pressing a kiss to her throat as he moved them through the doors and into his space.

Besides, if he was honest, he wanted her in *his* bed. Though hers was very nice, there was something nicely proprietary about having her in his space rather than hers. Very primeval and whatnot.

She shuddered against him, and he gave her buttocks a good squeeze as he kicked the door shut behind him.

CHAPTER TWENTY-FIVE

Heart pounding in her chest, Johanna clung to her husband's neck, her thighs tight around his body, with her ankles locked together behind his back as he carried her toward his bed. This was her first time in his room, and it was difficult to do more than catch a glimpse of it, she was so focused on him.

The brief impression she got was a great deal of heavy, dark wood, dark plum curtains and bedspread, and a thick Persian rug was large enough to cover the majority of the open floor space. A masculine space that seemed almost too somber for her husband's open charm and warmth.

There was not much time for her to really look around, though, before they reached the bed, and he was spinning around to sit on it with her legs still wrapped around him. Despite the fact she could have sat on his lap at this point, his hands still cupped her buttocks.

What would it feel like when he spanked them?

Dark eyes bore into hers.

"Are you sure you want this?"

"Yes." She sounded much surer than she felt, but she was too curious to back out now. Besides… "I was very cheeky."

Matthew chuckled and squeezed her bottom.

"I like you cheeky with me. You're still my good girl."

The heat that flushed through her had nothing to do with the way he was touching her. Just being called his good girl made her want to melt as much as his hands on her did—if not more. Johanna leaned toward him, daring to press her lips to his, and he groaned as he pulled her closer to him, kissing her back.

Running her fingers through his hair, Johanna enjoyed the thrilling sensation of being atop him, of feeling his cock pressing into her stomach while his hands kneaded her buttocks. The silky material of her peignoir and nightrail amplified the sensations as it slid over her skin every time she moved. She shifted atop him so her legs were no longer wrapped around his torso but rather bent at the knee, so she was kneeling over his thighs, her lower legs completely uncovered by fabric.

Matthew groaned and pulled away from the kiss.

"If I am going to spank you, it needs to be now," he said gruffly, pulling her up from his lap, then back down. Johanna found herself across his lap rather than straddling it, her stomach over his thighs, his cock pressing into her side. The bed supported her upper body and her legs, and she shivered as she felt silk slide over her skin, baring her bottom to him.

She did not understand why it had to be now, but she was hardly going to protest.

Especially as his hand glided over her bare skin, cupping her bottom… then lifting and coming down with a sharp smack.

Johanna gasped, more at the surprise than the sting. It did hurt, a bit, but it was not the same as any pain she'd ever felt before. Perhaps because she had asked for it. Knew it was coming.

His hand came down on her other cheek, and she dropped her head against the bedcover, trying to understand why something that hurt also felt so good. Felt so exciting.

Then his hand came down again. And again. Johanna moaned as he began to pepper her backside with sharp, crisp swats that both stung and aroused. She was beginning to understand what he meant by an enjoyable spanking. It felt as though she was being warmed all over.

Every time his hand came down, it stung, but it almost immediately receded into a steady, throbbing warmth that went straight through her core, making her pussy clench. She could feel it when she moved her legs, rubbing the slippery lips of her womanhood together, her insides quivering with arousal. Little whimpers began to escape her lips as she lifted her hips, begging for more with her body.

Then the swats shifted, from her buttocks to the very sensitive spot just beneath them. Johanna gasped as she lurched forward, trying to get away. Matthew's arm braced across her back, pinning her in place on his lap. The sting was far sharper, yet her body still had the same reaction of aroused excitement.

"Ow!" She squirmed against his hold as he began to spread the swats down the backs of her thighs.

"You are my good girl, are you not, kitten?"

Johanna felt very much like the naughty kitten he'd just called her. Just as she had when he'd been holding the back of her neck. And she liked it just as much as she liked being called his good girl.

"Yes, Matthew."

"Say it." His hand snapped against her thighs again. "I want to hear you say you're my good girl."

"I'm your good girl." She moaned as he returned to her bottom, giving the hot skin there two sharp swats—one on each heated cheek.

"Tell me you're my kitten."

"I'm your kitten."

Another two swats of reward, making her moan and lift her hips again. She much preferred being spanked on her bottom than her thighs. Her thighs made it very easy for her to imagine how it could become a punishment.

Thankfully, she did not need a punishment.

Because she was her husband's good, cheeky girl. His kitten.

She liked that.

Kittens could be quite cheeky, but they were still good kittens.

Matthew's hand came down on her bottom again, but instead of lifting immediately, he rubbed the swat into her sore skin. Johanna moaned and pushed her buttocks back against his touch, her insides throbbing. It felt like she was so empty, and she needed to be filled.

"What does my wife want tonight?" he asked, continuing to rub his hand over the hot skin of her bottom, as if he wanted to feel how well he had done. "Would you like to lick my cock and drink my cream and be my kitten like this morning? Or would you like to be properly fucked like only a good girl can be?"

Johanna hesitated. She was rather sore still, she suspected. But she also felt empty, like she wanted to be filled. Yet at the same time, she'd enjoyed having him in her mouth this morning, and surely that would not make her sorer...

How to decide?

Peeking shyly over her shoulder at him, through her curtain of hair, she smiled hopefully.

"Can we use your coin to decide?"

The hand that had been rubbing her buttocks paused.

He stared at her.

For a moment, she thought he was going to be upset that she was asking to use his coin, but then he cleared his throat.

"We can, indeed."

He kept one arm across her back as he leaned over to snag his coin from the nightstand. Johanna was still spread across his lap, waiting for him to flip it... which he did, then rather than using the back of his hand to see the final outcome of the coin, he slapped it against her bottom. She giggled, even as she squirmed at the sting.

Turning his head to look at her again, he grinned.

"The coin says you shall be fucked like my good girl tonight."

MATTHEW

The fact that his wife wanted to use his coin to decide on her continuing erotic education this evening made Matthew far happier than he could say. Others had asked about using his coin before, but always for things for their own benefit, and he was loath to allow them. After all, he did not want to be blamed if the coin only worked for him and the outcome was not what they desired.

Besides, many of those who had privately asked him had also sniggered at him for using it before that.

However, this was a decision for both him and Johanna, and she had never once mocked him for using the coin. She'd never indicated that she thought poorly of him for it.

And there was something very satisfying about smacking the coin down onto her bottom to decide on how they would be ending their night. Heads—her mouth, Tails… well. Self-explanatory, really.

"I should see if I should start with *my* mouth," he said, picking the coin up and flipping it again, enjoying the sound of her giggling as she wiggled her bottom at him. It did not feel as though she was laughing at him, just that she was enjoying herself so much that she was giggling.

Matthew got the feeling she had not had much cause for her joy in recent years, and he liked that she was certainly doing so now.

Smacking the coin down on her opposite cheek, he grinned at the answer.

"What does it say?" Johanna asked, trying to push herself up and twist to see, though the position would be impossible. The coin was already starting to slide off the curve of her buttock when Matthew caught it.

Rather than answering her verbally, Matthew quickly changed his hold on her and toppled her back onto the bed, so she was on her back, with her upper body resting against the pile of pillows and cushions at the head of his bed. The lavender silk of her nightrail and peignoir slithered over her skin, sliding between her thighs to cover her pussy from his gaze.

Setting the coin back on the nightstand, Matthew leaned over to give her a kiss, brushing his lips over hers, before he began moving his mouth down her body. As he did so, he pushed the peignoir off her shoulders, so only the thin fabric of the nightrail was between her skin and his mouth.

The creamy lace over her breasts was quite fetching, allowing a hint of pink nipple to peek through, and rather than pulling the top of her nightrail down, Matthew closed his mouth over her nipple through the lace. She gasped, her hands sliding through his hair as he sucked on the hard bud, running his tongue over the lace, teasing the nubbin with both his mouth and the fabric. He could feel her squirming delightfully beneath him, her thighs tightening around him as her body arched in reaction.

Switching breasts, Matthew let his hands move down to her bottom, which was still hot against his palms, and gave her cheeks a rough squeeze. Whimpering, she shuddered in reaction as he kneaded the hot flesh, rocking his groin against hers. His cock ached in response, but it would have to wait.

Lifting his head from her breast, he stripped off his shirt before moving lower, draping her legs over his shoulders as he tugged the silk of her nightrail away from her glistening pink pussy. The hair on her mound was a bit darker than that of her head, but still brightly blonde, providing a sweet frame for her pink, pouting lips, slick with her arousal.

Matthew lowered his head between her thighs as his hands moved up her sides to close over her breasts. She moaned again, her hips lifting to meet his tongue, fingers tugging on his hair as he began to feast.

JOHANNA

Hot need coursed through Johanna as her husband began to lick and suckle on her, making her cry out and thrust her breasts up into his hands. He squeezed the soft mounds, the lacy wet fabric moving over her nipples, stimulating them, followed almost immediately by the silk as she shifted and writhed. The contrast was wildly stimulating, adding to the pleasure of his mouth working over her flesh.

"Oh, please..." she moaned, shuddering as he sucked on a particularly sensitive spot, making her toes curl and her knees flex, digging her heels into his muscled back.

Her bottom was exquisitely sensitive, throbbing in a manner she was not used to, adding to the assault of sensations on her senses. No wonder some women enjoyed being spanked. At least, the way her husband had done it to her. She was hot and sensitive and drowning in pleasure from every side.

Every part of her tingled.

Every part of her throbbed.

And every part of her burst into pure ecstasy as his hands tightened on her breasts, his mouth closing around the part of her that was most sensitive and sucking *hard.* Johanna cried out, shuddering, squirming in place against his hold, her grip on his hair so tight, it was a wonder she did not pull any out in her throes of passion.

Wave after wave washed over her, stealing her breath and senses, until she was limp and panting.

Only then did her husband lift his mouth from her, looming over her. One hand grabbed hold of her ankle, kissing her leg just above where his fingers gripped her, as she stared up at him. Her bosom heaved as she caught her breath, already replete and satiated.

"My turn," he said with a wicked grin that made her insides clench.

CHAPTER TWENTY-SIX

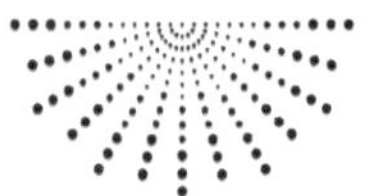

MATTHEW

Freeing his cock from his breeches, Matthew shucked them off completely before pulling Johanna's nightrail and peignoir from her as well, leaving them both entirely naked. Placing himself over her, between her thighs, he felt the head of his cock rub along the wet seam of her pussy as he pressed his lips to hers, claiming her mouth with a deep kiss. Letting her taste her own pleasure on his tongue.

She kissed him back, a little more hesitantly than before, more curious as she tasted herself. Her hands moved over his chest, feeling him. Exploring him. Matthew groaned, rocking forward and pressing the tip of his cock to her heat. Pushing in slowly.

He did not want to hurt her, after all.

Johanna moaned, her fingers curling, nails scratching over his skin as he began to slide inside her. Matthew deepened the kiss, his tongue dancing with hers, as the wet heat of her pussy enveloped him. She was so slick, so smooth, her muscles clenching around him as he entered her.

With a groan, he pulled back slightly, then thrust in again, going deeper this time. She moaned, shuddering in his arms, her hips coming up to meet his thrust, allowing him to slide even more easily inside her.

"That's my good girl," he murmured, moving his lips away from hers and leaving a trail of kisses along her jaw. Her head tilted back, opening the long line of her throat to him, and she whimpered. He could feel the way her pussy spasmed around him when he called her his good girl, and his cock throbbed in response.

Braced on one forearm, his other hand slid over her body, up to cup her breast and give the mound a gentle caress as he nipped at her neck, his cock sliding all the way home inside her. Fully buried in the slick grasp of her pussy, Matthew rocked, pressing himself against her pleasure nub as he toyed with her nipple and kissed her throat.

"Oh…" She let out a little cry of passion as he fondled her, her muscles rippling around the length of his shaft.

"Tell me you're my good girl, kitten."

"I'm your good girl, Matthew." She whispered the words, almost shyly, which, for some reason, was even more alluring than if she'd been brazen and confident.

Knowing she was saying it just for him, that she was doing it because it pleased him, made him feel excessively powerful. Groaning, he pulled his hips back and thrust back in, making her cry out again.

"Good girls get their husband's cock." He nuzzled his nose along the length of her throat as he shifted his position, bracing himself on both arms, so he could begin slowly fucking her. Pulling halfway out, then thrusting back in, slowly but firmly, until he could rock his body against hers, trapping the pearl of her clit between their bodies and rubbing against it. He could feel the way her pussy clenched every time he did. "Say it, kitten. Tell me that you're a good girl who wants your husband's cock."

"Oh…" She sucked in a breath and let go of him, covering her face with her hands even as he thrust into her.

Chuckling, Matthew reached up to pull her hands away from her face, wrapping his fingers around her wrists to reveal her flaming blush as he pinned her hands on either side of her head. No longer able to hide herself behind them, she closed her eyes, biting her lip as she arched beneath him. She was so bright pink, the color had traveled down her throat and was creating splotchy areas across her chest.

"Look at me, kitten," he ordered.

Wide, violet eyes opened and stared up at him, filled with arousal and a kind of panic.

"Be a good girl. Tell me that you're a good girl who wants your husband's cock." He thrust into her again, a little harder, a little faster this time to emphasize what she was asking for.

Another whimper came from her throat.

"I…" she whispered. Matthew thrust again and then ground himself against her, stimulating her folds and nubbin, but slowly so she could not find her peak. The next words came out much louder, clearer, almost like a sob. "I'm a good girl!"

"And what does my good girl want?"

"Your cock!"

Her eyelashes fluttered shut, but Matthew did not scold her. He was far too aroused. Pinning her hands down, threading his fingers through hers, he pressed his lips to her open mouth as he began to ride her, hard and fast. She was so slick, so soft around his cock.

Matthew felt the base of his spine begin to tingle, his balls tightening, and he groaned against her kiss before pulling away; it was too difficult to both kiss her and fuck her at the pace he wanted. His wife arched beneath him, her soft cries urging him onward.

"Oh… oh… Matthew!"

His name on her lips, said in passion, was his undoing. Letting loose the reins on control, Matthew wallowed in the splendor of her clenching heat, giving himself over entirely to the desires riding him.

She was perfect.

JOHANNA

The words her husband wanted from her, the way he began to move atop her, within her when she said his name… Johanna could feel her ecstasy rising yet again. She was now sore, inside and out, between her bottom and her pussy, and somehow, all of that contributed to increasing her rapture. As if the scrape of pain somehow sharpened the edge of her pleasure.

"Come for me," he ordered as that pleasure threatened to swamp her senses. "Be my good girl and come all over my cock."

It felt like the coming that he called it—like something great and terrible and uncontrollable brought forth from the depths within her.

Every part of her body tensed, bowing, aching, then shattered as that tension released in a tumult of exquisite agony. It went on and on and on, waves of it cresting and crashing over her, tumbling her senses about as her husband thrust deep inside her again and again.

Finally, he buried himself within her with a cry, head bowing over hers, her body throbbing around him as he began to pulse. Pinned beneath him, unable to hold him, Johanna could do naught but shudder and squirm under his hard body, feeling the thick shaft inside her throbbing as he emptied himself into her channel. It was hedonistic glory as they shattered apart together and almost more than she could stand.

Feeling him go lax atop her, the sound of his heavy breathing mingling with her own, Johanna shuddered as she opened, then closed, her eyes again. There was not much to see other than the canopy of his bed above them, anyway. His heavy weight atop her was cozy. Reassuring almost. Rather than pinned to the bed, she felt protected, as though his body was a safe haven around hers.

"Mmm." He turned his head, nuzzling the side of her neck, his fingers relaxing their grip on her wrists. "You *are* my very good girl."

Johanna turned her head to meet his lips with her own. The warm flush of happiness that went through her had nothing to do with arousal and everything to do with pleasure at his words. At being his very good girl.

The kiss they shared was sweet. Tender.

When he broke away, he rested his forehead against hers for a long moment.

"Stay right here," he whispered as he pushed himself up.

She shuddered as she felt him slide out from within her, the sensation sending a frisson of pleasure through her. Drawing her legs together, she turned on her side to drowsily watch him as he went to the wash basin and got a cloth to clean himself. He returned a moment later with one for her, and she blushed bright pink all over again as she had to spread her legs for him to tend to her.

Then he came back to the bed and curled up around her, drawing the covers over both of them. His front was pressed against her back, one arm tucked around her to hold her close.

A soft kiss pressed against the back of her neck, and she smiled, squirming to snuggle back against him. Her sore bottom tingled, but it did not hurt.

"Did you enjoy your day?" he asked softly in the darkness.

"Oh, yes." She found it easy to relax in the dark and speak fairly frankly with him. It was hard not to relax with a man who had seen her at her worst and married her, anyway. "Your grandmother and Mrs. Syme were very helpful in walking me through arranging the menu for this week. Bridget and Charlotte's dance lessons went as well as could be hoped for."

Matthew chuckled at the way she said it, and Johanna could not help but smile as well. Thankfully, Bridget was very good at picking up movements easily. The largest problem with her had been convincing her that she needed to wait for everyone else to do so as well. Charlotte was very graceful but not very good at paying attention to when the music was starting, which had caused several small collisions before the dance instructor decided she was too young and had her sit and observe for now.

Since Charlotte was very happy sitting and staring off into space—Johanna did not for one second believe she was observing—the dance lessons went a good bit more easily after that. Rose and Johanna joined in, and Rose enjoyed herself more than she likely wanted to admit. It was more difficult for Johanna to enjoy herself because she very much wanted to be perfect, and of course, such perfection could not be immediately achieved.

"Once they're ready, I can have some of my friends come over to give them partners to practice with."

"Charlotte will not need one; she has been relegated to observer until she's older, but that will likely be very helpful for Bridget, Rose, and me," Johanna replied. "Thank you."

"Of course." He sighed happily into her hair, tightening his arm around her and taking a deep breath. "Happy to help. You and Rose will likely need us sooner rather than later if you are to attend balls beginning next week. I believe Grandmama will insist on it."

He was not wrong. She'd already made noises about attending and showing off Johanna as the new duchess. The very idea made Johanna's stomach cramp, but she knew it was part of her new duties. At least she would have Matthew and Lady Stark by her side, and she would hopefully have some friends in the crowd.

"And… how did your day go?" she asked tentatively, unsure if she should be prodding into his business, but he had asked first. It would be rude not to respond in kind. "Were you able to conclude your business?"

"No, unfortunately." He hummed under his breath, and she felt the vibrations against her back. "We made some progress on it, though. I ah, had to go into some unsavory places. If you hear about me visiting anywhere untoward, be assured I was only there to help my friends. Not for any other purposes."

"Very well." She was not certain what he meant by that, but obviously, he worried about what she would think if she found out.

Perhaps he meant more places like Mr. O'Connell's. Certainly, Johanna would not expect him to come home with any more *brides*, but she would have no objection to him rescuing other young ladies in desperate circumstances. If that was what he'd been doing. It was a noble reason to visit unsavory establishments.

She yawned, and he hugged her tightly.

"Hush," he ordered. "Get some sleep."

Although she wanted to ask more questions, she closed her eyes, truly exhausted. More questions could wait until tomorrow.

Right now, she wanted to enjoy being in her husband's arms. It was the perfect moment. Her very own happy ending to what had been a number of terrible years.

Even now, she could scarcely believe it was happening. It seemed hardly possible that everything would be so simple, yet here she was, happily resting in the arms of her duke, who was everything she could have wished for in a husband. The only fly in the ointment were her mother's absurd claims, but at this moment, she found it impossible to think that would not resolve itself at some point… her mother would come round to sense, eventually.

Johanna yawned again as she drifted off to sleep, safe and soundly protected in her husband's embrace.

CHAPTER TWENTY-SEVEN

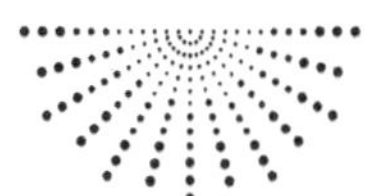

Once again, Matthew awoke randy and ready. Once again, his wife was too sore to accommodate him with her pussy but happily used her mouth for his pleasure. Why were so many men against married life? Why had *he* been so against rushing to marry? This was wonderful.

In the future, Matthew would not allow himself to be so influenced by the attitudes of others.

Though he supposed his wife could just be different from other wives. After all, most wives were not rescued in the manner she had been. Perhaps this was her showing her gratitude.

Which... Matthew did not enjoy that idea as much as he had when he'd first rescued her. Gratitude was all well and good, but truth be told, he did not just like marriage more than he'd expected. He liked his wife. She was loving. Kind. Warm. Willing to do anything for her family. Open-minded. She did not judge the use of his coin; in fact, she'd joined him in it.

If he was the type to write out a list of attributes for a wife, she would have checked every single box and some he would not have thought of.

Sighing, he leaned his head back against the headboard, stroking her hair as she fell to her side, resting her head against his stomach as his cock slowly deflated. She really did remind him of a kitten... and he very much enjoyed making her purr.

Matthew realized, at that moment, that he very much wanted his wife to like him as much as he liked her.

But how could he tell?

"We should probably get dressed and go to breakfast," she murmured, though she did not actually move. "My sisters will come looking for us if we take too long."

"Mmm." Matthew ran his fingers through the silky strands of her hair, looking down at where she rested on her stomach, facing away from him. She did enjoy what they did. He felt sure of that much. He could ensure she received as much pleasure as he did. And she had been very enthusiastic yesterday and this morning about taking him in her mouth.

After all, she had been the one to suggest it yesterday.

But...

Did she like him?

How did one ask such a question?

He'd never been in this position before, and he did not like it.

Would his coin work for this? He eyed where it rested on the nightstand.

It was not a decision. And it had to do with her, not him. Therefore, he could not be certain he could rely on the coin's answer.

Blast.

Matthew pushed the thoughts away for now. That was something he could ponder another time. At the moment, she seemed to like him. Not just out of gratitude. Perhaps there were things he could do to make sure she liked him. The normal things gentlemen did during courtship, since they had skipped over that.

Not poetry.

But flowers. Jewelry.

"Do you have dancing lessons again today?" he asked hopefully. She had seemed enthusiastic about him and his friends joining the lessons. If she had them today, he could join them today. If the coin confirmed that decision. Dancing with ladies was part of courting them.

"Not today. I am learning more about the household with your grandmother and Mrs. Syme. I believe we are going in to have our ballgowns fitted as well. And I should check on my mother at some point." She sighed.

"Should I stop in to see your mother as well?" he asked, hoping she did not think him a neglectful husband for not having done so yet.

"Oh, no." Johanna sat up, shaking her head. Which had the delightful side effect of jiggling her breasts in a very distracting manner.

Matthew was distracted enough that he almost forgot the question he'd just asked that she was saying no to.

"I do not think she would be comfortable meeting you when she is… indisposed."

"I feel the same," he replied agreeably, somewhat relieved, still focused on his wife's beautiful breasts. This was the first time she'd been so exposed to him without trying to cover herself, and he was quite enjoying it. "But I also feel as though I have been a bad son-in-law when she is in the house, and I still have not met her."

"I am hopeful she will be able to meet you soon." Something in Johanna's voice had Matthew lifting his gaze to meet hers, but she was already looking away and moving to the edge of the bed. "But we should ready for the day now. I will certainly look in on her today and see how she is doing."

Picking up her nightrail and peignoir from the floor, Johanna clutched them to her chest as she hurried to the adjoining door and disappeared through it. While Matthew enjoyed the sight of her delectable backside, he did not get to watch it nearly long enough. She was in too much of a hurry.

He wondered if she would always be so modest or if the need for it in front of him would eventually wear off.

Sighing, he rang for Reedy to come and help him get ready to meet the day. While he was waiting for his manservant, he flipped his coin several times to see what he might do with his time today.

Spend some time with Micah—the boy could assist Matthew on estate business and learn from him at the same time.

Matthew was not one of the dukes who would be completing the next part of their investigation. Zachary would be speaking with his uncle, of course, and Christian would be tracking down Conyngham. Drake had said he would approach Hatchett, who was belligerent at the best of times, and all of them were happy to leave the earl to him. Sebastian had volunteered to take on Carmathan.

Which rather left Matthew, Gregory, and Nathanial at loose ends. Because, as married men, they ostensibly had responsibilities toward their wives. But Matthew's wife did not need him today.

Perhaps he could visit his friends later and see what they had found out.

The coin flipped through the air and landed four separate times.

No to Drake. No to Zachary. No to Christian. Yes to Sebastian. How very interesting. Well, so be it. At least he had a plan for the day now. Micah in the morning, he could seek out Sebastian in the after-noon, and then hopefully be home in time for supper this evening.

Matthew smiled as Reedy knocked, then entered the room. It was good to have a plan.

***

JOHANNA

Scurrying into her bedroom, Johanna pressed her hands against her chest, feeling strangely winded even though she had not moved very far. The panic that had sparked when Matthew had asked about meeting her mother…

Hopefully, her mother was in her right mind today.

It felt like there was a huge lump in Johanna's throat as she closed her eyes, leaning against the wardrobe. The hard wood helped her remain upright. Somehow she'd brazen through. She must.

Everything was going so well; surely, Mother must have recovered by now. Physically *and* mentally. Johanna knew that was not how life worked, yet everything was finally falling into place. Her mother was the last missing piece; then everything would be wonderful. Far better than she'd ever dreamed it could be.

Giving herself a shake, Johanna froze as she realized she'd just run naked from her husband's room. Of course, it was not as though he had not seen her naked by now. But she had not even given it a thought because she'd been so quick to flee once he'd started asking about her mother.

Leaning against her bedpost, she caught her breath.

She had not been lying when she told Matthew that they needed to get dressed; otherwise, her siblings were likely to come looking for her. So, that was what she did. She rang for Nettie and gathered herself, shaking off the worry that had crept up on her when she'd realized Matthew wanted to meet her mother.

Because of course he did.

Thankfully, her mother being confined to her bedroom was a good reason not to allow it yet.

A knock at the door distracted Johanna from her worries. Nettie came bustling in to get her ready for the day. It seemed to go in a whirlwind, from getting dressed to eating breakfast with the family, exchanging small, secret glances with her husband as they did so. Afterward, Matthew asked Micah if he would like to join him in his study, to which Micah very quickly expressed his interest.

Seeing the two of them together, Matthew smiling at Micah, who beamed up at him in pure hero worship, made Johanna's heart melt.

Both her husband and his grandmother seemed to relish having her family in the house, which did much to ease any guilt that might have reared its head over the duke being forced to support them. As soon as they were done eating, Bridget and Charlotte were rounded up by Lady Stark, who said they could come and see what she was teaching Johanna and Rose until their new governess arrived.

Unsurprisingly, Bridget was not particularly interested in the kinds and colors of linens that were available to the household, no matter how Lady Stark tried to explain their importance. Especially if

Johanna were to ever throw a ball. Thankfully, the girls' governess, a Miss Marjorie Swift, arrived midmorning, and they went to meet her. Lady Stark's explanations sped up considerably after Bridget was no longer there with a thousand questions irrelevant to the topic at hand.

They were interrupted by the butler, Holt, as they were going through the different sets of tableware that were available.

"Excuse me, ladies, Your Grace." He bowed. "Are you at-home this afternoon? Lady Astrid Blackstone and their Graces the Duchesses of Clarence and Hereford have come calling."

"Goodness," Lady Stark said, blinking in surprise and exchanging a glance with Mrs. Syme. "Is it that time already? I should very much like to retire to my chamber for a bit of a rest. Johanna, you may hostess them if you wish."

"I do. Rose and I are at-home," Johanna said, nodding immediately. Although she was rather tired, she did not want to turn away Lady Astrid or the other two duchesses who had befriended her on their first visit with her as the lady of the house. "Put them in the drawing room, please, Holt. Mrs. Syme, could you ready some tea and a tray for us?"

She glanced at Lady Stark, who nodded approvingly. Holt and Mrs. Syme both quickly left to follow her requests.

"You have this all in hand, I am certain." Lady Stark smiled and lifted her hand to pat Johanna's cheek. "You are doing very well, my dear. Enjoy some time with your friends, and we can get back to this tomorrow. Without Bridget and Charlotte. I do enjoy Bridget's energy, but she must learn where to best apply it."

"Thank you, Lady Stark. And I fully agree about Bridget." Her sister was a handful. Johanna could not help but wonder how training her up to be a debutante at this point would go. She hoped Miss Swift had a strong backbone. On the other hand, she could not imagine Lady Stark choosing a governess who did not.

Smiling, Lady Stark swept from the room and turned down the hall in the opposite direction of the drawing room, so Johanna and Rose were able to walk arm in arm toward the front of the house.

"Running this large a household is… daunting," Rose said, shaking her head. "Yet I do greatly prefer deciding which foods and which linens over trying to scrape up *any* food at all."

"As do I." Johanna blew out a breath. "It feels like a dream, coming from wondering how we were going to get Mama through the summer… how any of us were going to make it through the winter, and being here, now."

"A wonderful dream, I hope?" Rose asked, eyeing her. She did seem to like Matthew quite a bit more than she liked some of the other dukes they'd met, but her protectiveness over Johanna had not ceased simply because she was now a married duchess.

"Very much so," Johanna assured her. "Like stepping from a nightmare into the most wonderful dream in the world."

"Good." Rose nodded her head firmly. "I was a bit worried; he is very cavalier for a duke, but he seems quite caring, and that is a point in his favor. He's good with Micah and the girls."

The sound of light laughter came from the drawing room as they approached, effectively ending their conversation. Johanna felt her heart lighten even more as they reached the doorway and saw their friends waiting inside.

All three ladies smiled happily when they saw Johanna and Rose, getting to their feet to greet them.

As always, Lady Astrid looked impeccable in a deep-orange shade that put Johanna in mind of a sunset, especially when set against her red hair. The Cairngorm crystal jewelry around her throat added a bit of shimmer to her appearance.

Beside her, Tiffany, Duchess of Clarence, was stunning in a bright sapphire-blue that matched the single sapphire on a silver chain and the drop earbobs hanging from her ears. Her cheeks were pink with happiness as she embraced Johanna and exchanged air kisses.

The Kalina, the Duchess of Hereford, was next to exchange kisses of greetings with Johanna and Rose. Herdark-pink rose dress trimmed with cream was the height of fashion, setting off her mahogany skin and dark hair and eyes. Kalina's father had fallen in love with her mother after moving to India, and she took after her mother in looks.

The effortlessness with which they wielded their beauty and confidence made Johanna feel even more intimidated, despite their warm welcome. It was easier to forget that she was now a duchess when she was not surrounded by fellow duchesses.

"How is married life suiting you?" Tiffany asked as they sat down again, just as a maid came in with the tea cart.

"Very well, I believe," Johanna replied, smiling and thanking the maid as she set down the tray. "Tea, anyone?"

Once they were all served some tea, and Lady Astrid had picked up a biscuit, a silence fell over them. The other three women looked at each other, as if they had something to say but were not certain how to begin.

Johanna glanced at Rose, who raised her eyebrow back at Johanna. Obviously, she sensed something was amiss, too.

"Well." Lady Astrid cleared her throat, setting down her teacup, the biscuit precariously perched on the edge of the saucer. "We did come here to speak to you about something particular."

She paused, as if searching for the right words.

Tiffany jumped in. "Actually, we were hoping to speak to you before you and Matthew were married, although once we heard your story of how he rescued you, it was not as though you could do otherwise." Tiffany shook her head. "So, it did not matter that it ended up having to wait."

"What had to wait?" Johanna asked, feeling her nerves rising.

"Nothing terrible, well, not terrible for us," Kalina reassured her, glancing at the other two. "But it is possible that marrying Matthew may have put you in danger, though so far there has been nothing... but you know how his father and the other dukes all died in a tragic accident?"

"Yes." The kernel of anxiety that had sunk into the pit of her stomach began to rise, and she clutched onto the teacup in front of her as though the tighter she held it, the safer she would be.

A feeling of utter foreboding filled her, growing wider and darker with every passing moment. Something terrible loomed over her future. She wanted to stop them from speaking, yet she knew she could not.

"It was no accident," Tiffany said, glancing away, her voice full of grief and anger. "My father and the other dukes were murdered."

"Murdered?" Rose asked, alarmed, while Johanna mouthed the word, unable to draw the breath she needed to actually speak it aloud. The bands of fate, the terrible luck that had befallen her family, were tightening around her chest all over again.

She knew.

She knew what they were going to say before they could say it. Johanna could feel the awful certainty closing around her, and she could not speak. She felt too overwhelmed… too acutely aware of her mother resting in the house, only one floor and two hallways away.

"Murdered," Lady Astrid confirmed grimly. "The dukes know. We know. Delilah and Mei know. And now you two."

"So far, nothing has happened that indicates any of us is in any danger of the same fate," Kalina rushed to reassure them. "There have been no threats and no indication that whatever motivated the death of those dukes has anything to do with their heirs."

"But there has been a threat, of sorts," Tiffany said, heaving a sigh. "If we investigate. Which, of course, our husbands are. Though they are keeping it as secretive as possible."

"They even tried keeping it a secret from us." Lady Astrid snorted and shook her head. She eyed Johanna and Rose. "From your expressions, I assume Matthew has not said anything to you."

Johanna shook her head, and so did Rose, although she shot Johanna another glance, pressing her lips together. She was clearly displeased with Matthew keeping Johanna in the dark. Johanna just felt sick to her stomach.

"How do you know what happened?" Rose asked.

"Well, we did not know until fairly recently. Tiffany overheard Sebastian and Gregory speaking of it, and things went on from there." Lady Astrid huffed. "She told me. We told Kalina and Delilah— although it looks as though Delilah did not strictly need to know, since Zachary is a dunce. And I told Mei because I felt that if she was going to matchmake any of them, she should know what the young lady she matched them with might be getting into."

"But Johanna had to marry Matthew after... well, after he purchased her at that awful auction." Rose shook her head. "I know he saved her from a terrible fate, and I am grateful for that, but how can we be sure she has not jumped from the frying pan into the fire now?"

"We cannot," Tiffany said grimly. "All we can tell you is what we know so far, so that you can be on your guard in case there is any danger."

Rose nodded, leaning forward, obviously intent on defending Johanna by whatever means necessary. Johanna wished she could be so fierce, but right now, all she felt was faint. And it was about to get so much worse.

"A lot of what we know begins with the note my husband's steward left him, the night he fled."

I sold my sleeping potions to the Duke of Clarence's steward. Johanna's mother's voice echoed in her head. *I killed his father.*

Oh God. She was going to be sick.

CHAPTER TWENTY-EIGHT

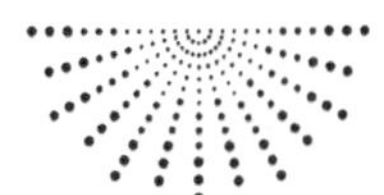

It felt like Johanna's entire world was crashing down around her while she sat in a drawing room, sipping tea and pretending she was not dying inside. Her heart was not pounding, it felt very much like it had stopped as her skin had gone clammy and her mind utterly blank with panic. Yet somehow, her arm moved to lift the tea cup to her lips, as though she were some kind of puppet.

Rose had no hesitation in asking questions because she did not know that Johanna's mother was involved.

Rose had not heard the confession.

Johanna had not told Rose because it was so ludicrous... but now, it was sounding as though her mother's wild theories might hold the truth.

"Initially, Gregory was actually under suspicion of having murdered his father," Tiffany explained. "His father was... well, he was not a very kind husband or father, and he was..." She trailed off, groping for words.

"He was altogether awful," Lady Astrid said bluntly. "Do not look at me like that, Tiffany. Gregory would say the same thing."

"Yes, though it seems wrong to speak ill of the dead, especially when I never met the man to form an opinion myself."

"I met him once, and trust me, that was enough." Lady Astrid made a face. "To make a long story short, he fathered several children on various maids, whom he ravished, then did nothing to care for them or their mothers after they were born."

Glancing at Rose, Johanna reached out to take her cousin's hand. Her uncle might not have been the best father, but her mother had been willing, and he had wanted to provide his daughter with her family, illegitimate or not. While he was absent from her life even after her mother passed, he had ensured she was taken care of. Rose's chin tipped up. If she was bothered by being reminded of her own circumstances, it did not show in her expression.

"One of them was the steward's niece." Tiffany's face became quite drawn. "She was… is very traumatized by what he put her through. According to Montblanc—that's the steward—he wanted justice and knew he would not get it from the courts, so he took matters into his own hands. But in that same letter, he also claimed he did not understand what he was getting into."

"We think there must be a conspiracy," Kalina said softly, glancing at the others. "A group working together. Gregory swears up and down that Montblanc would never have had any part of murdering men he had no quarrel with. He believes if Montblanc had known the full extent of the damage that would be done, he would have turned himself in beforehand."

"But we cannot know for certain because he has fled." Lady Astrid flexed her fingers, looking peeved at the man for fleeing the hangman's noose.

Johanna felt her stomach turn over again. It was a wonder she had not lost her breakfast already as the revelations came, one after another. Perhaps it was not just for Rose's sake that she had reached for her cousin's hand because now she was squeezing it tightly on her own.

"There are certainly reasons for some of the dukes to have been targeted."

"Nathanial's father was a reprobate in an entirely different way from Gregory's," Kalina offered up. "The amount of money he owed to various men *and* gambling establishments. And after a certain point, they must have known they were not going to get it back, no matter how long he lived."

"Then why would they keep allowing him to gamble with them?" asked Rose.

Tiffany shot her an amused look. "It is no easy thing to say no to a duke."

The expression on Rose's face turned mulish. If anyone could say no to a duke, Johanna would wager it was Rose. For herself, on the other hand, she was not certain she would be able to.

Already, she had proven to be very poor at saying anything but yes to her husband. Not that she had *wanted* to say no. But she pitied the mere mortals who felt as though they had no choice but to acquiesce to a duke's desire to join their game, even if he already owed them a princely sum of money.

"What about Matthew's father?" Rose asked, glancing at Johanna and giving her hand a squeeze back. Clearly, she was concerned about what must be going through Johanna's head right now, and she was not even privy to all the possibilities.

Tiffany and Kalina both looked at Lady Astrid, who shrugged.

"He was the kind of gentleman who very few people had anything to say about. From what I know, he was very strict with Matthew. Old fashioned. Believed in leading with a firm hand."

It was all Johanna could do to bite her tongue against telling them what kind of father the old duke had been to Matthew, but she did not think it was her place to say. He had spoken to her in confidence, and she was not willing to break it.

Although... did that not give her husband good reason to have murdered his father as well?

She could not imagine...

But what if his coin had told him to?

Dizziness assailed her. Good lord, was it possible that both her mother *and* her husband had something to do with the dead dukes?

"Drake's father was a good man. A very good man," Lady Astrid said sadly. "I have trouble imagining why someone would have wanted him dead, unless they had nefarious designs on something they thought he would notice. Drake is much the same. At least, I thought he was." She rolled her eyes. "Clearly, grief and the knowledge that he is about to be married has broiled what there was of his brain."

"What about Chris… I mean, what about Montagu's father?" Rose asked. Johanna was grateful her cousin was able to take the lead on the questions. She could barely think, but she did want to know more.

"His reputation was that of an upstanding man and duke," Lady Astrid said with a shrug. "But so was Gregory's father. I only met him a few times, and I did not find him out of the ordinary in any way. I do know he was very disappointed in Christian's levity about life. He was a very serious sort himself."

"That leaves, who?" Rose looked around at them. "Grafton?"

"Grafton, Northumberland, and my father." Tiffany smiled wanly. "What reason for any of them, we do not know. Like the Duke of Montagu, they were just ordinary sorts. If Sebastian has suspicions or has come across anyone who hated our father enough to want to kill him, he has not shared that with me."

"Unsurprising," Lady Astrid said, rolling her eyes. "The men are telling us as little as possible."

"They were up to something yesterday," Kalina said. "Nathanial received a message from Drake and ended up joining them for dinner, but all he would tell me is that he does not think their investigation is going anywhere."

Johanna did not know whether to feel relieved.

She did not want to worry that her mother might hang for her part in whatever had happened. Like the steward, she had not known what she was getting into. She had also told Johanna that she had not asked.

Would ignorance be enough to save her? Or would the dukes be looking for a scapegoat?

While Johanna did not believe Matthew would *want* her mother to be blamed or to hang, he was also one of only seven dukes who would have a say. Possibly eight, if Northumberland's heir weighed in on the death of his uncle in the fire. Matthew might not be able to control what happened.

And would he look at Johanna the same if he knew that her mother had a hand in his father's death?

There did not seem to be much love between Matthew and his father, but that did not mean that he would have no feeling about his murder.

Worse—would her mother's fate hang on the flip of Matthew's coin? Pure luck and chance. Considering how Matthew made so many of his decisions, how much of her life had already been twisted up by the mere flip of his coin, Johanna could not reject that possibility. It was all too likely.

She had not saved her mother from starvation only to see her die on the noose.

But at the same time, she could not help but look at Tiffany and see the real grief at the loss of her father. Justice demanded they solve the mystery and find the culprits. The *true* culprits.

Could they do that without Johanna risking her mother?

She did not know.

"Well." Lady Astrid gave herself a shake. "We will discover what they are up to soon enough, I am sure. They are never as discreet as they think they are. We've all decided to tell each other everything we discover from our husbands—or soon-to-be husband in my case. Can we count on you for the same?"

"Yes," Johanna said immediately, relieved that she could make such a promise. "Of course."

If Matthew told her anything, or if she overheard anything that he was saying, she could happily tell her friends. The promise was not about things she might discover from *other* sources. Because, of course, none of them suspected anyone in her family might have anything to do with the demise of the previous dukes.

"In the meantime, are you coming out of seclusion soon?" Kalina asked. "I would love for you and Matthew to attend my upcoming ball. It is my first one as Nathanial's hostess."

That she was nervous about it was obvious, even to Johanna.

Which made her feel a little less nervous, at least about social matters. Ruthlessly, she boxed up the fear and anxiousness that their revelations had sparked, the way she had back when she'd been dealing with her siblings and keeping how badly off they were from them.

Right now, she needed to get through this visit. She could fall apart later.

The way she always did.

"Yes," she said immediately, pushing a smile onto her lips. "Lady Stark says we must leave the house soon or we will be overrun *here* by curious visitors."

"She is not wrong. The suddenness of your marriage is the talk of the *ton*," Lady Astrid confirmed with a glance at the others. "We have managed to keep them at bay with some talk of my house party and your meeting there, but since there is not much to tell, that will not satisfy them for long. They will want to see you for themselves."

"Another duke off the marriage mart is a big deal," Tiffany agreed, a small smile alighting on her lips. "My brother is finding himself in more pursuit than ever, yet no closer to finding a wife. He is growing desperate enough, I think he may soon hire Lady Hu and Mei to help him."

"Oh, I hope so," Lady Astrid said immediately, a wicked grin on her face as she literally rubbed her hands together. "I would love to rub his nose in it that he did need a matchmaker's help after all."

"Well, that will not help if he thinks you might do so," Tiffany told her, exasperated.

"I will wait until the actual wedding to enjoy my glory," Lady Astrid assured her.

Johanna laughed with the others, a smile upon her face, even as her heart wailed within her.

MATTHEW

Laughter from the drawing room assured Matthew that his wife was well taken care of for company when the note from Drake arrived, summoning him to the club. His lessons with Micah done for the morning, Matthew did not hesitate to take his hat and cane and quit the house for a bit—well, after confirming his plan of action with his coin. Hopefully, he could be home in time for supper this evening.

He was very hopeful someone might have come up with something. Being left out of questioning the gentlemen Cornwall had named had seemed the best course of action at the time, but being out of the informational loop was rather bothersome. Matthew wanted to know what was going on.

Drake had commandeered one of the private rooms at White's, and Matthew was surprised to find that he was not the first to arrive. Sebastian, Gregory, and Drake were all already there, glasses in hand, ensconced in large wingback chairs that had been set up in a circle.

"Matthew." Drake nodded a greeting and handed Matthew a glass of brandy from where he was seated beside the drink tray. "How goes it?"

"I need to be home by supper," he replied, taking both the drink and a seat. "Grandmama and Johanna were put out by my absence last night."

"Tiffany was not best pleased, either," Gregory agreed. "And we are not even as newly wed as Matthew and Johanna."

"Yes, but you and Tiffany are a love match," Sebastian said, swirling his drink in his snifter. "Matthew and Johanna are not."

"Neither were Tiffany and I at the beginning. That was the falsehood we put about to save her reputation, remember?"

"I am trying to forget all about your scandalous behavior with my sister, actually, thank you," Sebastian replied dryly. He turned to Matthew, cocking his head. "It has only been two days of marriage. Less than a week since you rescued her. Surely, you are not in love already."

"I do not think there needs to be love for a new wife to desire her husband to be around for suppertime the day after their wedding," Drake interjected, which Matthew was grateful for because he did not exactly know how to answer Sebastian.

He had not married Johanna for love. But he did like her. Quite a bit. He was not particularly interested in pursuing or bedding any other woman. In fact, he rather wanted to be around for suppertime this evening. He did not want to miss another meal with her if he did not have to.

He wanted her to be happy.

From what he'd seen of Gregory and Nathanial, that was how they conducted themselves, and they were both now love matches, though neither had started as one. Was it possible he was falling in love with his wife?

The desire to pull out his coin and flip it made his fingers twitch, but he managed to resist.

"I pity the woman who takes a chance on you if you do not think you need to be there for supper so soon after your wedding," Gregory told Sebastian. He was grinning, but there was some sincerity to his words.

"Any woman would be lucky to marry a duke."

"Then why have you not chosen one yet?"

"I am trying to do things *properly*, unlike some of us." Sebastian glared at his closest friend. Since Gregory had been caught in a compromising position with Sebastian's sister at the very first ball of the Season, he had a point. Not that it bothered Gregory, who just grinned at him.

"Who has done things properly at this point, other than Drake? And look how miserable he is. Do you want to be miserable like Drake?" Gregory gestured at the man in question, who glowered at him.

Thankfully, Gregory was saved from whatever retribution Drake and Sebastian may have come up with by the arrival of more of their friends. Christian and Zachary came in, interrupting whatever might have followed, and they had not even gotten settled when Nathanial arrived and completed their coterie.

They sat in their chairs with their brandy, and Matthew wondered if the Knights of the Round Table had ever felt like this. And if this group were the knights, who was their King Arthur?

"Right then," Drake said, drawing everyone's attention to him. "Who has managed to track down their quarry?"

CHAPTER TWENTY-NINE

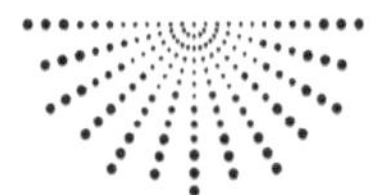

"I do not believe Conyngham suggested Cornwall invite Nathanial's father to the hunting lodge—no matter what some people might think," Christian said, sending an amused look at Zachary, who made a face but did not protest. He did reach up to stroke Monkey Sinclair, who petted his head in return, as though the little creature thought Zachary could use some comforting.

He probably could, considering that anytime Conyngham came up, Zachary would likely only be able to think about how he was Delilah's new lover.

Zachary was another of their group who was doing things 'properly', now that Matthew thought about it. And, as Gregory pointed out about Drake, he seemed quite miserable. Gregory seemed to have come to the same conclusion. He leaned over to elbow Sebastian, nodding at Zachary to point him out to the other man, and mouthing the word 'miserable.' Sebastian glowered at him and took another sip of his brandy.

Perhaps there really was something to marrying to cover up a scandal. It had worked out well enough for Gregory and Nathanial, and so far, Matthew was quite happy with his marriage. All of them had been able to skip over the tediousness of actual courtship as well.

Though Matthew did want to do some of that for Johanna, he thought it would be much more enjoyable with the pressure off. He did not need to worry about whether she would want to marry him at the end of it—she already had.

"Carmathan does not believe he was there for the discussion," Sebastian said quickly, turning away from Gregory. "He would have remembered and told Nathanial if he'd known who had pushed Cornwall to make the invitation."

"I believe that; he was very open with me about everything," Nathanial said. "But it is good to have confirmation."

"It is," Drake agreed. "Hatchett was belligerent, as usual, and asked why he would have paid attention to what the former Hereford was doing with his time."

All of them snorted. That sounded like Hatchett. Zachary was still stroking Monkey Sinclair, who made a similar snorting sound to the rest of them. Considering the little monkey had been rescued from Hatchett—after Lady Hatchett brought him to a ball to show him off, only to have him bite her husband and flee—perhaps it was possible he recognized the man's name.

"Conyngham was not sure, but he actually thought it might have been your uncle who suggested it, or your father," Christian said, almost apologetically as he turned to Zachary. "But it was a while ago, and he would not be willing to swear to either statement."

"Of course he did," Zachary grumbled. Closing his eyes, he took a deep breath. The little monkey on his shoulder lay its tiny head against his, like the tiniest hug in the world. Matthew thought it rather adorable. "I know, I know. I should not hold it against him that he replaced me in Delilah's bed after I gave her her congé."

"You should not," Christian agreed cheerfully. "If you wanted her, you should have kept her."

"I could not do that without marrying her, and mother would have thrown a fit." Zachary shook his head. "Not just a fit. I do not know what she would have done. She was so sunk in melancholy, and now she is happy again…" His voice trailed off.

Drake leaned over to clap him on the shoulder; thankfully, the one opposite where the monkey was sitting was the one beside him.

"You did what you felt must be done," he said, almost gently. "Now, all you can do is keep moving forward on the path you've chosen." Although he was speaking to Zachary, it felt almost as though his words were more profound, more meaningful than that. Like maybe he was speaking to himself as well.

Which, of course, made Matthew wonder even more just *what* Drake was up to visiting all these brothels and such.

"My uncle had to go back to his estate for a visit, but he should return the day after tomorrow, and I will ask him then," Zachary said with a sigh, leaning back in his chair. "Thankfully, it is a quick visit. I swear, he is the only one with any sense when it comes to this wedding. Thankfully, he backed me on waiting 'til next Season."

"Next Season? That seems uncommonly long." Nathanial frowned at him.

"Says the man who married by special license," Zachary replied dryly. "Compared to you and Matthew, any amount of waiting is long."

"Tiffany and I had the banns properly read, and we still managed the big hullabaloo." Gregory smiled widely. His gaze unfocused for a moment, like he was remembering, and was quite happy about it.

"To an extent," Zachary agreed with a nod. "But you were also marrying quickly due to scandal, even if you waited for the banns. If I am going to do this properly, then I am going to do this *properly*, and I will not be rushed into it."

"Are you sure you are not just trying to delay the inevitable?" Matthew asked curiously. It seemed to him that Zachary might as well get it over with, especially if his mother and Lady Annabelle and her mother were pushing him. Which it seemed they must be if his uncle was the only one backing his desire to take a longer planning period.

Zachary shot him a dark look, and Matthew shrugged.

"We were all thinking it," Christian admitted, coming to Matthew's defense. "Matthew was just the only one to say it."

He did seem to struggle the most with not saying aloud the things he should not.

"I am trying to do this *properly*," Zachary said with gritted stubbornness. "And I am not taking nearly as long about it as Drake is."

Everyone turned to look at Drake. That was true enough. He glowered back at them.

"Why are we talking about Zachary's wedding plans?" Drake asked. "That is not what I gathered us here for."

"Well, what else are we to talk about?" Gregory responded with a shrug. "There is not much we can do until we know if Zachary's uncle is the one who suggested Cornwall invite Hereford. And then what? We still have nothing other than that information. But what reason would the Marquess of Selter have to do away with the former Hereford? And if it was Zachary's father who suggested the invitation, the same question remains."

"We have no further clues," Sebastian agreed, though he was clearly more unhappy about the situation than Gregory was. Then again, Sebastian had been close with his father. Gregory had hated his. "Not unless your men have finally caught up with Montblanc."

"Not yet." Drake was grim. "He is uncommonly good at hiding himself." He looked over at Matthew. "I did receive a message that several of them have picked up on Mr. Blash's trail and expect to apprehend him shortly. They may even have him by now."

Matthew immediately perked up. That was good news indeed. At least he would be able to tell Micah and Johanna that things were happening in justice for them.

"That is all well and good," Sebastian said irritably. "But where does that leave us? We have nothing more to go on. It seems we have hit a dead end."

"We keep going with what we must do and look for more threads to pull," Drake told him, as grim-faced as Sebastian was. "My men will keep looking for Montblanc. I am not giving up on finding who murdered my father. Not ever."

All of them nodded their agreement. Matthew would be there right alongside his friends, even if he was more invested for their sakes than his own.

As Drake and Zachary began comparing notes on long engagements, and Sebastian and Christian bent their heads together to discuss something quietly, Matthew flipped his coin, then sidled over to where Nathanial and Gregory were. Perhaps it was not unexpected that they were separating by marital status, and it did make things easier on him.

"Ah... I have a rather indelicate question," he said, drawing both of their interest.

"This should be good," Gregory murmured, making Nathanial chuckle. "Welcome to the club of married men."

"Thank you. Ah, that is what my question is about."

"Oh, dear, did the wedding night go that poorly?" Gregory jested.

Matthew rolled his eyes.

"The wedding night was wonderful, thank you," he said dryly, while Nathanial covered his smile with a quick sip of his drink. "I was wondering... I was wondering about love."

His two fellow married dukes both paused.

"What about it?" Nathanial asked after a moment.

"Well, neither of you was in love with your wife when you married her, even though we all said it was a love match. But you both seem very happy now. I know you like your wives, but... do you love them? And how do you know?"

Nathanial and Gregory looked at each other.

"I do love Tiffany," Gregory said after a long moment. "I do not know that I did not love her when I married her, I just did not recognize the feeling as such. It's about... wanting her happiness as much as my own. More even. And being willing to do whatever is needed to bring that about."

"I was furious with Kalina when I married her, but there was something between us even before that," Nathanial admitted. "You knew. That's why you flipped your coin for us."

"I did." Matthew frowned. He was not certain whether any of this applied to him and Johanna. There had not been a connection before they married. Not truly. Maybe the day before. But he did want her to be happy.

Did he want her happiness more than he wanted his own?

Why could they both not just be happy?

Before he could ask more questions, Drake announced that he had to take his leave. As Matthew was determined to be home by supper-time this evening, and the others all seemed ready to depart as well, that ended the conversation. He was not certain he had learned anything.

But he did think about it all the way home, ready to examine his feelings once he saw his wife again.

Which led to a bit of disappointment when he was informed that the duchess had requested a tray in her room rather than coming to join the family for supper. He did not find out until he had already joined the others in the dining room, which meant that he could not politely do the same.

"Johanna gets terrible megrims sometimes," Bridget told him seriously. "Even Rose's tonics do not work."

"They help, but…" Rose sighed, looking a bit guilty, as though she thought she should be able to cure whatever ailed Johanna. "No, they cannot always work the way they should. I am uncertain what brought it on today. We were having such a good day."

Matthew frowned. He'd thought they were having a good day as well. Perhaps Rose was wrong about the cause.

"Well, I was not." Bridget scowled and poked at her meal. "If anyone should be having a megrim, it should be me."

"You are perfectly well; you are just stubborn," Grandmama told her. "Which is not a bad quality, but it needs to be properly applied. Balking at learning necessary lessons from your governess is not properly applying it."

"But it's boring!"

"So is much of life, which means the lesson to be learned there is patience. Something you are in great need of if you want to succeed in life."

Micah snickered, which made Bridget scowl at him. She lifted her chin, sitting up straighter, obviously trying to mimic what she thought a proper lady should look like. Beside her, Charlotte cocked her head at her sister, giving her a little glare.

"I like the lessons," Charlotte said. "I want to be able to read more."

Bridget made a face.

"It is very good to be able to read. If you cannot read, then you cannot know what others write about," Grandmama said. "Many secrets are written in notes to people."

The face Bridget was making immediately changed from annoyed disgust to something much more contemplative. Matthew shook his head. His grandmother had certainly figured out how to motivate Bridget, but he was no longer sure that was a good thing.

At least he could leave Johanna's siblings in his grandmother's capable hands while he tended to his wife.

JOHANNA

Curled up on her bed, hugging her pillow to her chest, Johanna felt utterly exhausted. Containing her emotions all afternoon in front of the other ladies had taken every bit of energy she possessed. Trying to have a meal with her family, Lady Stark, and her husband… out of the question.

Rose would know something was wrong because she knew Johanna's 'headaches' formerly came from the stress of trying to handle the family's finances and food. Now, Rose would surely suspect it was some kind of stress again, but she could not possibly guess at the reason behind it. And Johanna could not confide in her. That was not fair to Rose.

Would it be conspiracy to cover up a murder if she did?

Johanna did not know, but she would not risk it. Bad enough she and her mother were already involved, both unwittingly. She would not do the same thing to someone else, especially not Rose.

If the worst happened, and Johanna and her mother were… not

around... Rose would take care of the others. But for that to happen, she could not be a part of this. Not even tangentially.

Her head really did hurt, but it was as much from worry and crying as any physical pain. Johanna did not know what to do, and there was no one she could ask. No one she was sure she could trust. Other than Rose, but she had good reasons for keeping quiet there.

As much as she'd wanted to tell the other ladies today, how could she? They were keeping one secret for her already but one that impacted no one but her. Tiffany's father was among those dead. Had Johanna's mother supplied the sleeping potion that caused his death?

Moaning, Johanna rolled her face into her pillow, feeling her shoulders heave even as no more tears were able to come. Her well had run dry. She should drink something, eat something, but she was too nauseous, and the tray sat untouched by her bedside, the food growing colder, her drink growing warmer with every passing minute.

At some point, she would have to gather herself. Face everyone again. She knew it. She'd done it hundreds of times before.

Though she had not had a husband. Or his sharp-eyed grandmother. And she'd been able to confide in Rose.

What am I going to do?

There was a knock on her door, and it opened immediately following, making Johanna stiffen.

"Johanna? Kitten?"

Oh no.

It was her husband.

Johanna held perfectly still and closed her eyes, not responding because she did not know what to say. She wanted so badly to be his kitten, his good girl, but how could she be when she was withholding information from him? Incredibly important information?

But how was she supposed to choose between her mother and her husband?

She could hear him coming closer to the bed. Felt his hand on her arm. Could not help the sniffle that came up, which ruined the illusion of sleep. Still, she kept her face averted.

"Poor kitten, does your head hurt so badly then?" He rubbed his hand over her arm, then up to the back of her neck. His touch was gentle, soothing, and even though she did not deserve it, she could not help but sink into it.

Closing her eyes, she let her mind empty as his hand moved up her neck to the base of her skull, pressing his fingers into the space between them. It felt better than it should, which made her feel all the more guilty.

"You have not eaten." There was a hint of scolding in his voice. "You will feel better if you eat something. Roll over."

The order was clear, and Johanna found herself rolling over. The sympathy on her husband's face was nearly enough to make her start crying again. He looked so serious, so concerned.

Lifting his hand to her cheek, he swiped away at the tiny bit of moisture beneath her eyes. Johanna knew she must look terrible, yet if he thought so, it did not show in his expression.

"Something to drink first," he said.

She found herself being propped up on several pillows behind her back, then Matthew held her glass to her lips. When she lifted her hands to take it, he frowned and shook his head. Somewhat exasperated, but also not wanting to antagonize him, she let her hands drop into her lap while she drank.

Then he took the plate from her tray and fed her supper, one bite at a time.

She did feel better, even though she did not want to. Did not deserve to. Johanna frowned at him.

"I can hold my own fork," she mumbled between bites.

"But you do not have to because I am here to do it for you." He raised his eyebrow at her. "Now, be my good girl and take another bite."

Johanna did as he said, though her chest felt like it was breaking apart at the idea that, once he knew the truth, he would never call her his good girl again.

CHAPTER THIRTY

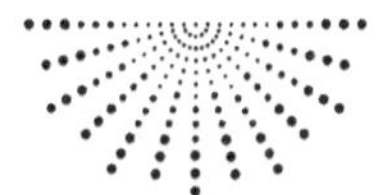

MATTHEW

Curled up around his wife, in her bed, listening to her breathe, Matthew wondered if this was what love felt like.

He pondered what Gregory and Nathanial had said.

Last night, he had enjoyed taking care of Johanna. He had wanted her happiness and to take away all her pain and discomfort.

Going by their actions, he could see some similarities. They doted on their wives, the same way Matthew did on Johanna. They wanted to take care of them, to make them smile, to ease their burdens. That was how Matthew felt about his wife as well. But he'd felt that from the moment he saw her on stage at the auction. He certainly could not have been in love with her then; he'd had no thought but to rescue her.

That had been the right thing to do, though. Not an indicator of love. He would have rescued any young woman he'd seen in such dire straits.

On the other hand, would he have thought to _marry_ any young woman?

He ran his fingers through his wife's silken hair, gently stroking the strands as he pondered the situation.

Then, he'd flipped his coin, deciding whether to bid on her or not; he had not asked the coin whether or not to bid on her but whether or not he should marry her. Granted, he had been searching for a wife at the time. But had such a thought come into his mind because he already loved her?

Unlikely.

He did not think he felt the same way about her that day as he did right now, for instance. There had been pity and a desire to protect a young lady in terrible circumstances, but he'd had no urge to cuddle her at that moment. Not the way he was cuddling her now. If she'd had a megrim, he would have felt badly for her, but he did not think he would have been overwhelmed by the desire to try to make it better for her.

So, no. He did not think it had been love at first sight, nor second sight, since technically, he'd met her at the house party originally. He had not paid her much attention while they were there. His coin had not even indicated he should dance with her at the time.

He wondered what would have happened if he'd asked it about marrying her then.

Perhaps the timing had not been right.

Matthew did not often question how his coin worked, but right now, he could not help but wonder why she could not have been spared the night of the auction. Was wanting her to have been spared that also love?

How did one know for certain?

He glanced over at his coin on the side table, but Johanna's head was pillowed on his arm. He would not be able to reach for it without disturbing her. The itch to do so remained, but he forced himself to stay still. Letting her sleep was more important than his coin.

Last night had been difficult for her. Rose had mentioned she occasionally had megrims. Hopefully, they did not happen too often. Matthew did not like to see her laid so low.

Leaning forward, he pressed a kiss to the back of her shoulder. He was not trying to wake her; he just... wanted to kiss her. And that was where he could reach. His cock was hard, as it always was in the morning, but he was not going to touch her like that unless he was completely assured that she was well.

With a soft sigh in her sleep, Johanna snuggled back against him. She felt so small, so frail in his arms. Perhaps Dr. Syme would have a suggestion for her head, something that Rose had not yet thought of.

"Matthew?" Her voice was soft, sleepy.

Blast. He hoped he had not woken her with the kiss.

"Shh. You do not need to be up yet." He kissed her shoulder again, in the same spot as before. An apology for waking her.

Yawning, she shifted so she could turn onto her back, one hand coming up to find his. The arm that was under her head shifted so he could curl his fingers around hers. Half-lidded violet eyes met his, and she smiled at him. The smile gave him a wave of relief. Surely, if she was smiling, that meant she was feeling better.

"Good morning," he said in a low voice, just in case her head still hurt, leaning forward to kiss the tip of her nose.

"Good morning." She tilted her head back, and he obligingly gave her a kiss on the lips, a very brief one.

"Are you feeling much improved?" he asked.

Her eyes widened, some emotion twisting her expression, then disappearing almost as quickly as it had come on. There was something different about the way she looked at him, though he could not quite put his finger on it. A kind of wariness?

Perhaps she thought he meant to push her for marital relations, and her head was still not fully recovered.

"I am," she said after a moment. "I am sorry about last night."

"Do not be," he reassured her. "You could not help it. Rose said you sometimes get megrims."

"I... yes." She gave herself a little shake, turning into him and pulling his hand with her so that it was wrapped around her shoulders. Matthew's cock stirred as she pressed herself against him. "I *am* much improved this morning, though."

Breathlessly, she pressed her body and her lips against his, and Matthew groaned.

His wife's head was so much improved that they spent the

morning with her learning how to ride *him*. Which meant Matthew got to enjoy seeing her bounce up and down on his cock, her pale hair falling around her body, breasts jiggling, as she moaned and worked herself to frenzied pleasure. With his hands gripping her hips, he thrust up into her as she ground down atop him, crying out with pleasure together.

Married life certainly was most enjoyable.

JOHANNA

Guilt surged inside Johanna after her husband returned to his own bedroom. She was still throbbing from the pleasure he'd brought her to—the pleasure she did not deserve. She was not lying to him exactly, but it was a lie of omission at the very least.

Thankfully, being married meant Rose would not come barging into her room this morning, demanding explanations. Johanna needed to think of something to tell her. She wondered if her cousin would believe that she'd truly had a *megrim*. One could always hope.

Perhaps she could convince Rose that she was afraid of facing the *ton*, and that's what had caused her absence from supper. There was some truth to that, although it was not nearly as stressful as trying to figure out how to feed the family had been.

Staring up at the ceiling, Johanna took a deep breath, acutely aware of her breasts and the sweet ache between her thighs. First things first. She needed to speak with her mother today. Alone.

She had not bothered to question her mother before. There had been no point since she had not believed for a moment that her mother was in her right mind when speaking of such a wild notion as being involved in the murder of eight dukes. Now, she needed to know everything her mother knew.

Perhaps there would be something there to absolve her mother of all blame. She could only hope.

She wished she had questioned her mother before... but it was no use. She'd made what seemed like the practical decision of not indulging her mother's absurdity, and now she was paying the piper. At the very least, she could be there to support her mother and hopefully guide her husband into acknowledging that there was no way her mother could have known what her potions would be used for.

Giving herself a shake, Johanna forced herself to get up and ring for Nettie. Forcing herself out of bed was nothing new. She was used to that feeling. It was very odd to ring for her maid afterward to help ready herself for the day. That was new.

If only she could return to that blissful moment this morning when she'd awoken in Matthew's arms, having forgotten about the events of the prior day for a few glorious seconds... but reality must be faced. That was a lesson she'd learned years ago.

She'd done what she could to please her husband this morning, which had assuaged very little of her guilt, and now she had to take the next step.

"Good morning, Your Grace," Nettie said cheerfully as she entered the room. It was soothing to have her bustling around, getting Johanna ready for the day, the patter of her conversation distracting Johanna from her own troubles. Bridget and Charlotte had both gotten up early this morning, and Charlotte had startled a footman in the library, causing him to run through the house, crying out about a ghost in the library.

According to Nettie, Bridget had found the entire incident hilarious, while Charlotte had done nothing but smile serenely and continue to glide about. Lady Stark had given the staff a rather stern talking-to about putting too much belief in the supernatural.

It was an eventful morning already, and it had barely started.

"It would help if she wore some colors, but..." Nettie shrugged, her fingers flying as she worked her magic on Johanna's hair.

Rose had missed the whole thing because she'd been in Johanna's mother's room, visiting her before breaking her fast. Thus, Nettie had not seen her reaction to the morning's excitement, if she even knew yet.

Micah was still abed.

Nettie had seen Matthew's valet going into his room just ahead of

Johanna ringing for her. She reported that with a wink to Johanna in the mirror, causing Johanna to blush furiously.

Once Nettie was done with her, Johanna dismissed the maid with her thanks and headed to her mother's room. She did not know whether or not to hope Rose was still there visiting. If Rose was, obviously, Johanna would not be able to question her mother, and a large part of her did not want to… but at the same time, another part of her wanted to get it over with as quickly as possible.

Pressing her lips together outside her mother's room, Johanna took a deep breath through her nose before opening her mouth to exhale. It did help some.

Easing the door open, she peeked inside.

No Rose.

Again, she did not know if she was relieved or disappointed.

Slipping into the room, she closed the door behind her and quickly took the chair beside the door, propping it against the frame. If someone attempted to enter the room, the chair would not stop them but *would* slow them, and the noise would alert Johanna to their presence.

Her mother was still in bed, on her side, facing away from the door.

"Mother," Johanna said softly, approaching quietly in case her mother had fallen back asleep.

But her mother rolled over. Her mouth tightened when she saw who it was.

"Mother, I am sorry I did not believe you," Johanna said, her stomach turning over. She sat down on the edge of the bed and reached for her mother's hand. "You were correct. The dukes were murdered."

Tears filled her mother's eyes.

"I knew it." There was a hint of a wail in her voice, but she kept it quiet. Her fingers closed around Johanna's, squeezing them tight. "I knew it."

"You did not mean to, though. You did not know." Johanna could hear her own desperation in her words. Knew that her mother could as well.

"That may not be enough to save me."

"I know. But I do not believe my husband would…" Johanna's voice trailed off. She did not believe Matthew would wish harm upon her mother. And she would do what she could to ensure he came to the conclusion she wanted him to. But there were no guarantees in life, and she knew that more than anyone.

"But he might. Even if he does not, there are seven other dukes with a say in the matter." Her mother closed her eyes and swallowed.

"Perhaps only six," Johanna said quietly. She had not met the new Duke of Northumberland, unlike the others. But the son of the duke who died at the hunting lodge had been lost at sea. Whether or not his heir might be as invested as he would have been… "But that is enough." She was grasping at faint hope, and she knew it.

"One will be enough to send me to the hangman's noose." Her mother shook her head. A tear slid from beneath her lashes. "Though I worry more about how it would affect you and the others. You should have let me die, Johanna. I was ready."

"No." Johanna squeezed her mother's hand. "Not when there was another way. And there may be another way now, too. Tell me everything you know."

"I already have."

"Then tell me again." Johanna took a deep breath. "I am listening now. I promise."

CHAPTER THIRTY-ONE

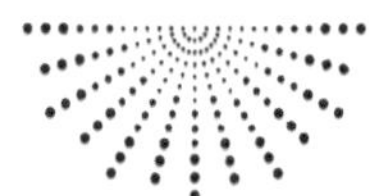

Matthew

There was something amiss with his wife. Ever since her megrim, she'd been... well, she'd been herself, but there was something amiss.

Matthew was not certain anyone else knew it, either. He did not think he would be able to describe the difference if asked. There was just something off about her. The only other person who seemed suspicious was Rose, but he could not even be sure of that. Rose always watched Johanna closely.

Perhaps it was the upcoming ball.

Which his wife *did* seem nervous about. Though so did Rose. They were both attending quite a few of Bridget's dance lessons, which Charlotte was now joining in on because she thought they looked fun. Her joining had spurred Bridget to take them more seriously, as she did not want to be outdone by her younger sister. As promised, Matthew brought in several of his friends to assist the day before the ball. Christian, Sebastian, and Zachary all answered his call. Not only that, but Nathanial brought his sisters, Fiona and Emma, and Kalina's brother, Ashwin, as well. Which meant Micah came to join them to practice.

It was a very full dance lesson.

"You cannot just dance with me," Johanna protested as Matthew took her hand for the third song in a row. "You need to dance with the others as well."

"At the actual ball, yes, but not during the lessons." Matthew glanced around. "Besides, everyone has their partners already."

Micah was with Emma, Ashwin with Bridget—and looking appropriately terrified of her—Sebastian had claimed Fiona, and Zachary was bowing over Charlotte's hand, which left Rose glaring at Christian as if daring him to ask her to dance. She'd already partnered with Micah and Ashwin for the first two dances.

"Go dance with Rose," Johanna commanded. "She'll dance with you."

Sighing and trying not to feel as though his wife was avoiding his company—a feeling he'd had the past few days, ever since her megrim, despite her company in his bed every night—Matthew obliged. He stepped beside Christian, who appeared increasingly frustrated at Rose's disinterest in his company, which was not something he was used to. As the acknowledged Adonis of the *ton*... ladies chased him, not the other way round.

"Would you just dance with me?" Christian asked in a low voice, his brow furrowed, not seeming to register Matthew's presence at his side. To be fair, Rose was glaring so hard at Christian, her arms crossed over the deep red fabric of her dress, she did not seem to notice Matthew either.

"No."

"Why not?"

"Because."

"That is not a reason!"

Matthew cleared his throat. Both of them whipped their heads in his direction, clearly startled he was now beside them. He smiled disarmingly.

"Johanna says we cannot dance three songs in a row. Christian, would you oblige my wife in partnering her for this one?"

"Of course," Christian said, straightening up and squaring his shoulders. "It will be a pleasure to dance with a lady who is *not* a termagant."

Rose audibly gasped, though she did not have time to respond before Christian had swiftly moved out of earshot. Instead, she ended up muttering something under her breath that Matthew was certain was horribly unflattering. He smiled at her genially. Rose was as prickly as the stems of the flower from which she got her name, but he did like her quite a bit.

Whether or not she liked him was up for debate, but she seemed to tolerate him for Johanna's sake, and she had expressed her gratitude for the attention he paid Micah.

"My lady," he said, holding out his hand as Christian took his place with Johanna, and the music began to start.

"I am not a lady." Exasperated, Rose did not uncross her arms. "I was helping Micah and Ashwin learn how to dance. You do not need my assistance."

"But Johanna will be put out with me if I do not dance with you," he pointed out, still holding out his hand, smiling widely. "Besides, I wish to speak with you privately. About her. This is as good an opportunity as ever."

Curiosity piqued, Rose's mouth set in a mulish line before she sighed and let her guard drop, placing her hand in his with clear reluctance. Matthew could not help but be amused. He put his hand on her waist, and they moved into the steps of the country dance, joining the others. It was the perfect opportunity to speak with her as this particular dance did not require them to switch partners.

"What about Johanna?" Rose asked in a low voice, glancing over at where Christian and Johanna were now dancing. He said something to make Johanna laugh. Matthew felt his chest constrict, though not as much as it had when he and Johanna had first married.

Now he recognized the emotion for what it was—jealousy. He no longer worried that his wife would like one of his friends better than him, though. He just wanted to be the one making her laugh. But he liked hearing her laugh regardless of whether he was the instigator or not.

"Does she seem… different to you?"

Rose glanced over at Johanna again, her feet stepping perfectly into place, despite her distraction. She really was a very good dancer. Perfect for Micah and Ashwin, who may have overestimated their abilities after dancing with her; both of them were now floundering with Emma and Bridget. Matthew winced as Ashwin and Bridget crashed into each other rather than stepping away from each other, and the dance instructor immediately went to untangle them and walk them through the correct steps.

"Different how?" Rose's tone was guarded, but since she did not immediately deny it, Matthew felt more certain that Rose had noticed it too.

"I cannot put my finger on it, but she has been different ever since the evening of her megrim. It is not in how she behaves. She is doing everything the same as she was before. But she is… different." He could feel his mounting frustration in his words. "I do not know how to explain it."

Rose let out a long breath of air as they circled around each other, looking up at him. For the first time, Matthew thought he might actually see approval in her expression when she looked at him, which was a rather lofty feeling. Rose's approval was not easily won.

"Yes," she said, nodding her head. She glanced over at Johanna, who was smiling widely at Christian as they danced together, looking for all the world as if everything was just fine. But Matthew knew better. So did Rose. "Yes, she is different. Something is wrong. But she will not tell me what."

JOHANNA

"Why is your cousin so…" The Duke of Montagu's voice trailed off, and he snapped his mouth shut, clenching his jaw so tightly she could practically hear his teeth grinding together. His blond hair waved back from his handsome face, a face that likely caused many a female heart to flutter but had had very little effect on Rose.

Even Johanna thought him one of the most handsome men she'd ever seen, but if Rose had noticed it, she'd never indicated so. Perhaps Rose preferred darker features, rather than Montagu's blond Adonis. Johanna might recognize him as a gorgeous creature, but she preferred her husband's dark locks and wide smile to Montagu's more calculated charm.

"Delightful?" Johanna suggested with an impish smile.

Though her mother's secret was always hovering in the back of her mind now, it was easier to relax in front of someone who was not her husband or Rose. Though she liked the Duke of Montagu, he did not know her very well. It was unlikely he would realize something was amiss with her.

She thought—hoped—she was fooling Matthew, but sometimes, he looked at her in such a way, she felt certain he suspected something. Rose definitely did. But Johanna was still keeping her mother's secret, and her mother was still not leaving her room. Not because she was too weak or sick, but because she was too afraid. Which left Dr. Syme and Rose at a loss. They could find nothing wrong with her, yet her mother insisted she remain abed.

Johanna wished she could do the same. It would be so much easier to just avoid everyone rather than having to pretend everything was fine. At least she had quite a bit of practice at it. Her siblings suspected nothing.

"Yes," Christian said dryly. "Delightful is exactly the word I was looking for."

She could not help but laugh at his aggrieved tone of voice.

"I think you are perhaps a little too used to ladies falling at your feet for your handsome looks," Johanna said, smiling up at him as they moved through the steps. Thankfully, this was a dance in which she was well versed, unlike some of the others. Her parents had taught them to her the year before her father passed. "It will take more than a pretty face to turn Rose's head."

"I am not trying to turn her head, I am just… trying to be polite." Christian frowned down at Johanna. "Does she think I am trying to turn her head?"

"I have no idea. But Rose is very guarded when it comes to gentlemen." Guarded and with very little personal experience. Not from lack of offers, but the majority of the offers were not honorable.

Being illegitimate but acknowledged, raised with her cousins, Rose knew what those offers meant. And from helping Johanna's mother with the women who visited, seeking potions and other assistance, she knew how hard life could be, especially for mothers of bastards who were unacknowledged. In many ways, Rose had been lucky.

She would not risk a child of hers being less lucky.

"I just wanted to dance with her, not court her," Christian huffed. "She's very prickly."

"With good reason, I assure you. Some gentlemen are not so gentlemanly," Johanna reminded him gently.

The sudden fire in his eyes and the way he puffed up were completely unexpected.

"Has someone been bothering her?" He growled the words, his head whipping around to look at Rose. Both she and Matthew were focused on their own conversation, thankfully, and did not notice. "Who? I'll—"

"No, no." Johanna patted his chest, just above his scarlet pocket square, to get his attention before Rose could see his reaction and think something terrible. He turned his burning blue gaze back to Johanna, where it smoldered with a kind of protective fire that took her aback in its intensity. "No one has been bothering her. Not here. There were a few men in the past, but not for months. Rose is not one to suffer fools."

The fire banked almost immediately, and he quite quickly turned back into the affable, charming Duke of Montagu. But Johanna did not think she would forget how quickly he'd turned knight-protector when he'd thought Rose's honor was being threatened. She should not have forgotten; he had also been there the night she was rescued from the brothel and had participated in guarding her along with Matthew.

Both of them could be quite fierce, despite their normally easygoing demeanors, when the situation called for it.

The dance came to a close, and Johanna curtsied as Christian bowed.

Thankfully, her husband was across the room, which meant it was easy enough for her to end up paired with the Duke of Bolton next, rather than Matthew. It was not that she did not want to dance with her husband, but she also wanted to dance with each of his friends to try to get a measure of who they were as men.

Sometimes, there were hidden depths, such as with Christian.

Would they be the kind of men to blame her mother for providing sleeping potions that were likely used on their fathers?

Johanna was not certain it was something she could deduce, but she had to try. Dancing with them at least gave her a few moments of private conversation with each of them, to get to know them a little better. It also gave her a reprieve from her husband's far too perceptive stare.

The Duke of Grafton was polite but distant. There was a sadness that clung to him even when he smiled. Whether it was the loss of his father or the ending of his relationship with Delilah—who displayed a similar air of heartbreak whenever *his* name came up—Johanna could not be sure. He was most open when speaking of his monkey, who he informed her he'd named after Sinclair, the previous Duke of Northumberland. Which made Johanna think that might be the cause of his melancholy. Or perhaps all of it.

How difficult it must have been, losing their fathers together, then losing Sinclair to the sea… and then to break things off with Delilah so he could court an appropriate debutante to please his mother. Of course, he did not say all of this to her, but she could read between the lines of his conversation, and all the gossip her friends had imparted about him supported her thoughts.

He was most comfortable speaking about his monkey, which he'd named after his friend.

"He'd have hated it, of course," Zachary said, smiling ruefully. "For a while, it was almost like a dare, to see if he'd show up to shout at me about it."

"I know the feeling," Johanna replied with fully sympathy. "When my father passed, sometimes I would do something naughty, thinking he might come in at any moment and catch me."

"Exactly." Zachary shrugged. "It is a harmless bit of fantasy, I suppose. It does help me keep the memory of him alive, although Monkey Sinclair is far more mischievous than he ever was."

The dance with him ended, and despite their conversation, Johanna was not certain she knew much more about him than she had before. He was a stalwart friend and a man trying to do the right thing, no matter how much misery it caused him. On the other hand, that could very well work against her and her mother if he thought the right thing was that her mother be punished.

And he truly missed his father, she could tell. Which might mean he would want punishment.

The Duke of Bolton was very much like both his sister and Zachary in missing his father. He did not have quite the same air of sadness about him as Zachary, though. Johanna felt a kind of anger emanating from him, rather than grief, though she could not think of why. It did make her rather wary, though.

A man holding back such anger... would it spill over onto targets other than where it belonged?

Was she willing to risk it?

Johanna could not help but be relieved when the gentlemen were called away by the Duke of Ormonde's arrival. He was not there to join the dance lesson but to speak with them, and the dukes all bowed very nicely before they quit the lesson.

She wished she felt more certain about how they would feel about her mother, but at least now that they'd left the room, she had a bit of space to breathe. Even so, she could feel Rose's eyes on her, watching her.

Eventually, she was going to have to figure out what to do... and who she could trust.

CHAPTER THIRTY-TWO

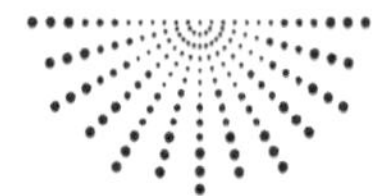

Should he ask his wife what was the matter? Matthew ran his fingers over his lucky coin as Reedy tied his cravat in place. It was very possible that after tonight's ball, she would be back to herself. Perhaps he should wait until tomorrow to decide if he should ask.

"Everything all right, Your Grace?" Reedy murmured, stepping back and eyeing Matthew curiously.

"Yes, yes, everything is fine." Matthew studied himself in the mirror. The dark plum and silver of his waistcoat was set off nicely by his black jacket and the crisp white of his shirt. The cravat was several shades lighter plum and pinned with an amethyst-and-diamond cravat pin set in silver.

He looked very fine indeed, with his dark hair swept back from his face and his jawline cleanly shaven and framed by the stiff points of his collar. As far as appearances went, Grandmama should have no complaints about how he looked for his return to the ballrooms, this time as a married man.

Reedy nodded his head, though he still appeared skeptical.

Very much like how Matthew felt about his wife at the moment.

"Is there anything else I can do for you, Your Grace?" Reedy asked.

"No, Reedy, thank you. That will be all." Matthew continued to look at himself in the mirror as Reedy left, turning back and forth and examining his reflection. He felt unaccountably anxious for this evening.

Which made no sense.

He had been far less nervous attending balls when he was looking for a wife, which was the whole point of going to these events. Why was he so nervy now that he had one?

Perhaps because it seemed to mean so much to Johanna. Was this another indication of love? That he cared because she did?

That seemed possible.

His hand drifted to the pocket of his waistcoat, fingers dipping in to rub over the familiar metal circle of his lucky coin.

Am I in love with my wife?

That was the question.

He did not even realize he'd pulled the coin out and flipped it until it was turning in the air. It was so habitual, he had not done it consciously. Startled, he jerked back, and for the first time in his life, he missed catching the coin. It slipped through his fingers, clattering to the wooden slats of the floor, and Matthew dropped down, slapping his hand on the ground...

But it was too late. The coin had rolled beneath the heavy armoire. Staring at the darkness beneath the large piece of furniture, Matthew felt his breath stutter. He hadn't been separated from his lucky coin since... well, since he'd found it, so many years ago.

What happened?

His mind felt as though it had ground to a halt.

"Reedy!" His voice was high, strangled. "Reedy!"

Surely his valet had not gone far. Did Matthew need to ring for him? Blast... should he ring for him? The urge to flip his coin and find out was so strong he could barely think.

Thankfully, before he had to decide, the door to his bedroom flew open.

"Your Grace? Your Grace, what's wrong?" Reedy came to a halt, frankly staring at Matthew, who was still on all fours in front of the armoire.

"I need you to help me move this!" Matthew could not keep the sheer panic from his voice as he jumped to his feet, bracing his shoulder against the wood, and tried to shove it aside himself. It did not even rock.

"Your Grace!" Reedy's alarm was clear in his voice, but he came forward to stand beside Matthew, trying to push as well.

"My coin." Matthew could barely get the words out. There was no breath in him to speak. "My coin rolled under it."

He felt Reedy pause beside him, then the man pushed hard as well, both moving together. The armoire moved. Sort of. Barely. If it even budged a centimeter, Matthew would be surprised.

An axe. He needed an axe. Then he could chop the damn thing apart.

Was that the right decision?

Hell and damnation… how was he supposed to do this without his coin?

"Your Grace, please breathe," Reedy said, putting his hand on Matthew's shoulder. Only then did Matthew realize he was no longer pushing on the armoire—now he was braced against it in an attempt to remain on his feet. He was lightheaded, and his knees felt like they were going to collapse. "Your Grandmama is waiting downstairs. You need to go to the ball. I will take care of this while you are gone. It will likely take several footmen."

"Right," Matthew said hollowly, pushing himself upright. One night. One ball. Without his coin. God, he wanted to call the whole night off and stay home. But this was Johanna's first ball as his wife; that would not be right, would it? If he had his coin, he could flip to know which was the better option.

It's just one night. I can do this.

"Thank you, Reedy."

"Of course, Your Grace. I'll hand you your coin the moment you arrive home."

Matthew nodded mutely, feeling very strange as he turned and walked away from the armoire. As if he was walking out into the world naked. As though he was missing a part of himself.

He felt unsteady on his feet as he walked down the hallway, heading to the front of the house. Voices drifted up the staircase as he approached, along with laughter. Out of the corner of his eye, he caught a glimpse of white at the end of the hall, but when he turned his head, they were already gone.

Probably Charlotte.

No wonder the staff was unnerved; they must think the house haunted at times.

At some point, he might need to speak with her about it.

He didn't realize he'd reached for his coin until his fingers touched nothing but an empty pocket. The realization that it was empty nearly rocked him back all over again.

Matthew gave himself a shake as he reached the top of the stairs. It was just one night. He could get through one night without his coin. He had lived for years without it before.

And made so many of the wrong decisions.

His shoulders tensed as his father's voice echoed in his ears.

"Where is your common sense, boy? This is not that difficult! Just choose!"

But somehow it was always the wrong choice.

Pausing before the stairs and the crowd at the bottom of it came into view, Matthew leaned against the wall for a long moment, trying to draw a deep breath despite the constricting band that had wrapped around his chest. Reaching into a different pocket, he pulled out his handkerchief and used it to dab at the moisture that had gathered at his hairline.

"Where is that boy?" Grandmama's tones were growing impatient. In a few moments, she'd likely come looking for him herself.

"I am sure he will be down shortly," Johanna replied soothingly. Though her tone was meant for his grandmother, not for him, he found himself being soothed, anyway. His breathing became a little more even, his head less dizzy.

Tonight was her big night. Her entrance to the *ton*. Her presentation as his duchess.

He could do this.

He *would* do this.

For his wife.

JOHANNA

Matthew appeared at the top of the stairs, and Johanna breathed a sigh of relief as Lady Stark relaxed. If Johanna did not know better, she would think that Lady Stark was nervous as well.

Perhaps she was.

None of which helped her nerves.

Thankfully, she had Rose by her side, steady as always, although not entirely pleased about going to a ball. She'd already declared that she would be there as Johanna's companion and *not* as an eligible *parti*. But she looked stunning in a deep-burgundy gown trimmed with ivory lace and gold ribbon, which nicely complemented Johanna's light plum and silver gown with its frothy layers of white lace at the neckline and sleeves.

Now that she could see Matthew, Johanna realized that his cravat matched her gown. A little detail she was certain she could attribute to Lady Stark's keen eye for detail. She and Matthew looked like they belonged together, and Rose would complement them perfectly. Johanna looked over at Lady Stark, who was wearing a silver dress with a deep plum trim that matched Matthew's waistcoat, and her lips twitched.

The older woman thought of everything.

Something that Johanna hoped to emulate in the future.

If it was possible to.

Ruthlessly, Johanna thrust away the thoughts of her mother and their predicament. She could not allow those to cloud her mind tonight. She had to get through this evening and then… she did not know what she was going to do. But she knew the first step was focusing on this evening and acquitting herself well as Matthew's duchess.

Matthew came down the stairs, looking a bit... odd. His usual grin was absent from his lips, his jaw was clenched, and he appeared out of sorts. Johanna's stomach did an odd swooping thing. He had not stopped to check in on her mother, had he?

"I am here," he said to his grandmama, holding out his arm to Johanna. If he had spoken with her mother and was upset, he did not seem angry, at least. What else could make him so off-kilter?

Warily, Johanna took his arm, but he was looking at his grandmother, not at her. Because he was too upset to look at Johanna? Or because he was worried his grandmother was upset with him?

"Then it is time that we go," Lady Stark said with an imperious sweeping motion of her hand.

Johanna's stomach turned over for an entirely different reason.

She was almost accustomed to living with the guilt of keeping such important information from everyone around her. But tonight, she had to be a duchess. In front of the entire *ton*.

And that was something she was not accustomed to at all.

If she was going to keep secrets from her husband, she did not want to keep secrets from him *and* embarrass him in front of Society.

The carriage ride was short and fraught, though if Lady Stark noticed, she did not acknowledge the tension. Johanna was watching Matthew, Rose was watching Johanna, and Matthew was looking out the window of the carriage at the streets of London, seemingly lost in thought. What he was thinking about, Johanna could not tell.

He was certainly not paying attention to his grandmother's monologue on who might be in attendance tonight and who they would need to pay particular attention to if they were. Which meant it was up to Johanna to focus on that, but though she did her best to listen and nod at appropriate times, she could not help but constantly peek at Matthew.

Sitting beside him, she could feel the tension in his body. Saw his hand flexing against his thigh, his fingers opening and closing, tapping against his trousers at odd intervals. Though it was not appropriate for a woman of her station, and though she worried that his distraction was due to her mother, Johanna could not help but slip her fingers through his to hold his hand.

She kept her gaze on Lady Stark, nodding as the older woman explained about the particularities of impressing Lady Jersey, but she was aware of Matthew jerking in the seat beside her. His fingers closed around hers, holding on tightly rather than pushing her away, which eased some of the worry in her heart. Sitting beside Lady Stark, Rose's gaze dropped to where Matthew and Johanna's hands were now intertwined, though his grandmother pretended not to see.

"Now, Lady Cowper and Lady Jersey are great friends, so if you win one over, the other will be soon to follow." From the tone of Lady Stark's voice, one would think she was mustering Johanna to battle.

And perhaps she was.

Taking a deep breath, fingers entwined with her husband's, Johanna focused herself. She was determined not to embarrass Matthew or his grandmother tonight. Their place in Society was riding on it.

CHAPTER THIRTY-THREE

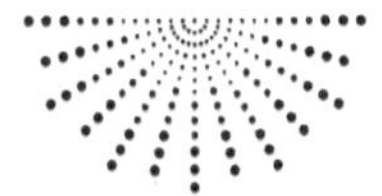

"What is wrong with you?" Sebastian demanded to know, frowning at Matthew.

He jumped at the question. They were up on one of the balconies overlooking the ballroom, and he'd been busy watching Johanna, who was beside Lady Astrid and a stone-faced Rose as they held court for a throng of gentlemen. None of them were particularly objectionable gentlemen, but it still stirred Matthew's ire to watch them conversing with his wife. Making them laugh.

"Other than having to watch those bobbleheads courting my wife?" He was unusually growly; he knew that. It was not just that, of course. Matthew pulled his fingers from his pocket, where they were seeking his coin for the umpteenth time.

Sebastian slanted a look at him. Clinging closely to the shadows of the drapes, his chestnut-brown hair looked darker than normal, and his gaze was nearly black. Very intimidating, when he wanted to be, was Sebastian. Since Gregory was currently down on the floor with Nathanial and Drake, two of the other dukes who were currently off the market, Sebastian had fled to the balcony to get a break. Matthew had already been up here, brooding, which he admitted was not his usual.

But it was easier to stay out of the throng without his coin to help direct him than it was to be among them. Too many choices down there.

Far less up here.

"They are not courting her." His tone was bemused, as if he could not understand why it would bother Matthew even if they were. "They are…"

"Flirting with her. And Lady Astrid." A small smile ticked the corner of his mouth.

"Perhaps not Rose, though."

Not because they would not want to, but because it would take a particularly brave—or foolish—man to attempt such a thing with the way she was looking at all of them right now. He doubted he had to worry about any rakes approaching Johanna either, not with Rose at her side.

"They are flirting with her because she is safe." Sebastian shook his head, his gaze darkening as he cast it over the ballroom at large. "They can speak with her without causing gossip or any expectation on her part *for* courtship."

"I know," Matthew replied irritably. "I still do not like it. I do not understand why we are not supposed to speak to our own wives at these events."

"Of course you can speak to her." Sebastian hesitated. "Just… you cannot monopolize her time. Perhaps you can do more next Season. Once the interest in the two of you has moved on."

"Or I could stop being so damned proper," Matthew muttered. But was it the right thing to do?

He did not want to make the wrong choice, not when it would reflect on Johanna as well as himself. Damn his coin… especially on tonight of all nights. The first time that it had ever slipped through his fingers, and it had to be *now*.

"I thought you wanted tonight to reflect well on her."

"I do."

"Well, then, you cannot hover like a jealous husband who does not trust her." Sebastian cast his gaze around the ballroom again.

Clearly, he did not understand. Matthew did trust Johanna, but he was also a jealous husband. Jealous of her attention. Jealous of the men who could stand beside her and speak to her at the damned ball.

"Besides, she returns home with you."

There was that.

Still.

"I am going to claim a dance," Matthew announced. But he also did not move.

Sebastian eyed him curiously. "Are you?"

"Yes." Still, he did not move.

"Matthew."

"Yes?"

"Where is your coin?"

Matthew took in a deep breath and sighed it out. Gripping the edge of the banister with both hands, he rocked forward slightly on the balls of his feet and lowered back down to his heels as he rolled his head around his neck before answering.

"I lost it." Just saying the words aloud struck him like a lightning bolt to the chest.

He could not look at Sebastian. Did not want to see the mockery in his friend's face or the judgment. Whatever might be there. He rocked back and forth between his toes and his heels, his jaw clenched so hard, he could hear his teeth grinding.

After a long moment of silence, Sebastian's hand landed on Matthew's shoulder, strangely and unexpectedly comforting.

"Where did you lose it?"

Out of all of Matthew's friends, Sebastian was not the one he would have expected sympathy from over the loss of his coin, yet he could hear it in Sebastian's voice.

"Under my blasted armoire. Just before coming here." Matthew shook his head as his throat clogged again. Grief? Panic? Some combination of the two? "I… I do not know what to do without it."

"And yet you got here without it. You came in the door without it.

You acquitted yourself admirably and are currently giving your wife the space Society demands, even though I can see it irks you." Sebastian's voice was gentle. Almost big brotherly. Then again, he had a younger sister. Matthew wondered if this was how he was with Tiffany. "You came up to the balcony without it. And now you know you want to dance with your wife. So go dance with her."

"What if it is the wrong decision?"

"Then you will deal with that when it happens. Just like the rest of us mere mortals. Now you will know what it feels like for everyone else." A bit of gentle teasing had slid into Sebastian's voice, but Matthew did not mind. "Though, even without your coin, you are still the Lord of Luck."

That was… true enough.

Rolling his shoulders back, Matthew straightened and released the banister so he could tug his jacket into place. He *was* the Lord of Luck.

And he had not considered that everyone else did not have the benefit of his luck, nor his coin, to make their own decisions. If they made the wrong one, they had to do exactly what Sebastian said… deal with it when it happened. And only with the consequences because his father was dead and could not dole out anything additional.

"I am going to go dance with my wife." He sounded far surer of himself than he felt, but that would have to do.

"Enjoy your dance." Sebastian smiled at him, then turned back to look out over the assembled guests, his lips turning back to a frown. Probably because he was thinking about his own wifely prospects.

Matthew did not envy him. Nor could he think of any way to assist him at the moment. He clapped Sebastian on the shoulder, in a bolstering manner, then turned away.

He was going to dance with his wife.

JOHANNA

Extremely grateful for Lady Astrid's stalwart friendship and Rose's steady companionship, Johanna did her best not to show the strain as the gentlemen thronged about them flattered and flirted. None of them seemed particularly serious, thankfully, yet she had to be on her toes to give them a good impression, regardless.

Matthew had gone to join the gentlemen almost as soon as they'd entered. Then Lady Stark had joined her own circle of *grande dames*, after giving Johanna over to Lady Astrid's care. Johanna felt rather adrift, but Lady Astrid's *sotto voce* remarks helped.

Apparently, gentlemen could not dance too much attendance on their wives. Even newlyweds. Lady Stark was signaling that she trusted Johanna to acquit herself well without her. But she'd also ensured that Johanna was left with an ally, for which she was grateful.

"I'll show you the ropes," Lady Astrid had murmured, just before the curious gentlemen descended. "Remember, you are a duchess now. There is very little you do that we cannot explain away, one way or another."

Strangely, that reassurance had greatly helped.

But dealing with the gentlemen was still quite draining.

"I say, Your Grace, it is quite unfair of you to grace our ballrooms only after your marriage," Lord Catterly said, giving Johanna a wistful look from the other side of the circle. He was a handsome man, with fair hair and kind hazel eyes, a bit of mischief dancing in them. "The rest of us did not even have a chance to enter the race for your fair hand."

"Oh... well..." Johanna stammered over her words.

"I did not realize you were in the market for a wife this Season, Lord Catterly," Lady Astrid said smoothly, tapping his shoulder with her gold-and-orange-lace fan, which went very nicely with her orange-and-black gown. Orange jewels shimmered against her skin and in her hair as she turned to face him. "I have some young ladies I should introduce you to."

"Oh... well..." Lord Catterly repeated Johanna's stammered words, much to her amusement, as Lady Astrid smiled widely at him. "That is very kind of you, Lady Astrid."

"Yes, I am often described as very kind." Lady Astrid fluttered her fan, smiling like a cat toying with a mouse.

Beside Johanna, Rose coughed. It was not a real cough, though. Johanna could tell Rose was covering for a laugh, and she could not blame her cousin.

Lady Astrid was shameless.

The sound of a violin tuning quavered through the air, and the energy within the circle changed as all the men perked up. Johanna's eyes widened as she found herself, Rose, and Lady Astrid all pinned with eager looks from the gathered gentlemen.

"Your Grace, would you do me the honor of dancing with you?" Lord Boyd quickly said. He'd been standing beside her, rather quietly, for the entirety of the conversation. Now he'd turned to her, bowing, and holding out his hand for her to take.

"Oh…" She managed to keep from casting a frantic look at Rose; such a movement would be impossible to hide, and she did not know how he would take it. Johanna did not particularly want to dance, if she was being truthful. Having to make conversation alone on the dance floor, without Rose or Lady Astrid there to rely on if she floundered? "I—"

"Apologies, Boyd, but this dance belongs to her husband."

Matthew's cool tones, which she had only heard once before in Hyde Park, made Johanna jump. She had not realized her husband was nearby, but she was not at all sad to find him suddenly beside her, winding her arm through his.

"Ah, well then, perhaps Miss Belle." He might be quiet, but Lord Boyd clearly had more mettle than Johanna would have credited him with. Rose's glare did nothing to deter him from continuing to hold his hand out to her. If anything, his smile widened and grew more sincere than it had been for Johanna.

Rose shot Johanna an exasperated look before nodding and taking his hand.

"Thank you, my lord," she said, sounding anything but thankful. If that bothered Boyd, it did not show. He merely chuckled and turned, her gloved hand in his, and led her to the dance floor.

Matthew seemed to relax as Boyd turned away, though he kept Johanna close to him on their way to the dance floor.

She relaxed as she recognized the first notes of the music, and she and Matthew got into position. This was one of the dances she'd practiced and one that did not require the switching of dance partners. Though it did mean that she was faced with her husband. The guilt simmering in her stomach welled up as she looked into his handsome face. It was so difficult as she wanted to cling to him, yet felt horrible about keeping such a monumental secret from him.

"Are you enjoying yourself?" he asked.

Johanna hesitated because although she knew she should say yes, she did not want to lie to him any more than she already was.

"Being with Lady Astrid is very enlightening," she responded after a long moment. "Are you enjoying yourself?"

He hesitated before answering as well.

"I am now."

A smile curved her lips as she looked up at him.

"I was not certain we would dance together tonight."

"It is not the done thing, normally," he agreed. "But I wanted to. Sebastian encouraged me."

It took Johanna a moment to realize what was odd about that statement.

"Sebastian encouraged you? You did not use your coin to decide?"

A shadow moved over his face, and he glanced away before returning his gaze to her. He was practiced enough in the steps that he did not stumble at all, which she envied because she was as focused on her feet and hands as she was on their conversation.

"I lost my coin," he said softly, in such a manner that her heart went out to him. *He* sounded so very lost.

"Where?"

"At home." He sighed. "Hopefully, the footmen will be able to move the armoire and find it for me while we're here. If not, I am taking an axe to the damn thing when we return home."

Though he said it as a jest, there was a grimness to her voice that made Johanna think he would likely do just that. She squeezed the hand she was holding.

"Do you want to go home now?" she asked.

"I do not think we can. Can we?" Uncertainty flickered across his expression. "I do not want to scupper your first evening out in the *ton*."

Johanna considered that for a moment. He knew the vagaries of the *ton* more than she did. Even if he did not like making decisions without his coin.

"How much longer do we need to stay to prevent that?"

Another hesitation, but then he shrugged.

"Likely we could leave now without drawing any ire." He glanced around. "Well, other than Grandmama's." Johanna giggled, and he winked at her, seeming to relax.

"Then," she said, feeling quite daring. "Perhaps we should do what we want? In lieu of having the coin to direct you."

"That is what Sebastian said," he admitted. "To do what I want and deal with the consequences after. Like most people do."

The music drew to a close, and Matthew took Johanna's hand on his arm and began to move them through the crowd. Out of the corner of her eye, Johanna saw Rose's burgundy gown and knew that her cousin was directing her suitor to follow them. Good then. Perhaps they could all leave a little early.

Matthew took her over to where Lady Stark was seated with her friends, including the Duke of Clarence's mother, whom Lady Johanna had already met. She beamed at Johanna in a very friendly manner, which helped relieve some of her nerves about approaching such a formidable group of ladies. The Dowager Duchess of Clarence was a breath of fresh air among the gimlet-eyed dragons of the *ton* and a much-needed tonic for courage.

"Grandmama, Johanna and I have had enough. We are going home," Matthew said, very firmly.

Johanna's eyes widened. When her husband decided to take charge, he decided to take charge.

Lady Stark tilted her head at him, considering. Her eyes glanced to the side as Rose came up, still on the arm of Lord Boyd, who was now grinning widely. Rose appeared as calmly collected as ever—what her emotions were, Johanna could not tell. On the other hand, she did not seem displeased, so maybe she'd enjoyed herself.

"Very well," Lady Stark said with a wave of her hand, glancing at Lady Cowper, who was seated beside her. "I suppose one cannot expect newlyweds to stay for the entirety of their first event, after all." The other women laughed lightly, and Lady Stark returned her attention to Matthew, Johanna, and Rose. "Rose will stay here with me, as my companion."

"Oh…" Johanna started to say but wilted under Lady Stark's raised eyebrow. She could not think of a good reason for Rose to come with them.

Rose sent her a reassuring glance.

"I am happy to stay with Lady Stark," she told Johanna, stepping away from Lord Boyd's arm, to his obvious disappointment. "It will be good to sit for a bit."

"Oh, no," Lady Stark said, getting to her feet and taking Rose's arm, the one opposite Lord Boyd. "I want to take a walkabout. Come, Rose, there are some gentlemen I want to introduce you to."

Lord Boyd's face fell, as did Rose's.

Sorry, Johanna mouthed at her as Lady Stark began to move away, taking a slightly panicked-looking Rose with her.

Matthew was already tugging on Johanna's arm to take her in the opposite direction, clearly willing to sacrifice Rose to distract his grandmother. Johanna did not have much of a choice, either. She wondered if Rose would ever willingly accompany them to a ball again after this.

"Come," Matthew whispered in Johanna's ear. "Before Grandmama changes her mind."

She would have to find a way to make it up to Rose later.

CHAPTER THIRTY-FOUR

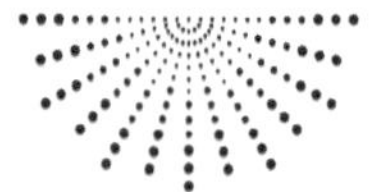

JOHANNA

"I feel terrible," Johanna confessed once they were safely tucked into the carriage, and she was staring at the empty bench across from her and Matthew.

"About what?"

"Abandoning Rose."

Matthew shrugged.

"When it comes to my grandmother, it is every man—or woman—for themselves. Besides, Grandmama was going to get her hooks into Rose one way or another now that I'm married off."

"Rose is illegitimate. I know that some men have been interested in her before, but not for honorable reasons." She shook her head.

"It will not matter to some of the minor gentry. She is acknowledged and educated and is now the cousin of a duchess, as well as of an earl. That social standing will give her protection against most dishonorable offers." His voice hardened. "And anyone who dares to think otherwise will answer to me."

Johanna sat back against the bolster of the seat as she realized that her own increase in status had affected Rose's as well. That was something that had not come up during the suppertime conversation. Now, she had to wonder if Lady Stark had not brought it up on purpose, so as to be able to take Rose off guard, just as she had tonight.

"Is Lord Boyd minor gentry?"

"No, but he might just not care." Matthew grinned. "The Earl of Derby married an actress. She's been the Countess of Derby for decades now. It was a massive scandal at the time, but if a nobleman decides to marry beneath him, then it is not as though anyone can stop him if that's what he truly desires."

Although she did not like hearing Rose described as being beneath anyone, she knew what Matthew meant. Much of the *ton* would already think that about her just because of her parentage. On the other hand, she did have to think better of Lord Boyd that he clearly did not care what the *ton* thought.

Unless, of course, he was angling for some kind of favor from her and Matthew by courting Rose.

Johanna let out a long breath. That would only work if he managed to turn Rose's head, and if there was a more sensible person in the world than Rose, Johanna had not met them. And perhaps he was, as Matthew said, in earnest. Which would give Rose a place in the *ton* on her own rather than having to rely on others, which she knew chafed her cousin.

Still.

"I am not sure that is what Rose wants."

"Well, if anyone can resist my grandmother's manipulations, it's Rose." Matthew chuckled and reached over to take Johanna's hand, giving it a squeeze. His stalwart support made Johanna feel even worse. Here she was, hiding this massive secret from him, and he was ensuring her comfort, dancing attendance on her, and even whisking her away from the ball early.

Making decisions that discomfited him, without the coin that she knew he so heavily relied on.

"I still feel terrible," she said. She did feel bad about Rose, but mostly she felt bad about the things she was keeping from her husband… and from Rose, for that matter. "Perhaps… perhaps you should spank me."

She said it with great daring, almost unable to believe she was making the request, but at the same time, she knew she wanted it. Perhaps it would make her feel better.

"You want me to spank you for leaving Rose at the ball?"

"Yes." It was a good excuse for the punishment she so richly deserved. If he spanked her, even though he did not know the real reason, it might alleviate some of the guilt that kept surging within her. "As a punishment. I cannot ask her to do it."

"Well, no, I suppose that is true," he said slowly. Johanna was aware of his fingers reaching for his pocket before he dropped them down again. "I… well. Very well. If that is what you want."

Taking her hand, he tugged her forward, and Johanna let out a little cry as she found herself being pulled over his lap.

"I meant when we got home!" she squeaked as she felt her skirts lifting. Her face was furiously hot as they rocked along the road, her ears already straining to hear if there were any passersby outside… or for some reaction from the coachman… The drapes were open, though it was unlikely anyone could see inside the carriage, yet it still felt as though the entire world must know that her husband had just put her over his knee.

"Why wait?" he asked. "If you've been naughty, we should attend to your punishment as quickly as possible."

"Oh!" Johanna quickly covered her mouth with her hands as his palm came down on her backside, leaving behind a sharp sting where it landed. She uncovered her mouth enough to whisper, "Someone will hear!"

"Then you had best be quiet." Amusement threaded through his voice.

Johanna realized that *he* did not very much care if someone heard or not. His hand came down again, making her squeak and wriggle on his lap. One arm pressed down across the center of her back, holding her in place over his knee as he began to bring his hand down again and again with sharp, crisp swats.

Johanna had to admit, the actual sound of the spanking was not very loud, so it was up to her to keep her reactions quiet. She pressed her hands to her lips, muffling her gasps and cries as he heated her bottom with the stinging swats. It did hurt, yet her body clenched with every strike, in a manner that was far more related to pleasure than pain.

She felt herself shudder as arousal and need curled within her, stoked by the punishment she was receiving. Which was not the point of being punished at all, yet she could not stop the reaction, even if she wanted to. Her husband was heating her inside and out, and it was mostly the embarrassment of the situation that truly felt like discipline.

MATTHEW

There was something going on with his wife, and Matthew was not certain what, but he was determined to find out. Eventually.

In the meantime, if she wanted a spanking, then she would get a spanking. She was feeling guilty over something, and he thought it had far more to do than with leaving Rose at the ball. Of course, it being Johanna, Matthew could not imagine it being anything too terrible, but clearly, she wanted some kind of punishment for whatever imagined infraction she'd committed.

He did wish he could have flipped his coin to find out if using the carriage ride for her punishment was the right decision, yet Sebastian's words had stuck in his mind.

If there were consequences, he would have to deal with them.

Just like everyone else.

There was a kind of rush in taking action without the surety that it was the right choice. The not knowing. Was this how everyone felt? All the time?

He was almost giddy from taking Johanna over his lap, just because he felt like it. Baring her bottom to the moon as its light filtered in through the carriage window, without knowing if it was the right decision or not.

Those pale cheeks were now glowing a pretty pink, though he was taking care not to spank her too hard. The sound should not be truly audible over the noise of the carriage and the horses' hooves clopping along the ground, much less the others currently on the street. Even if his coachman could hear some of what was going on, how would he even begin to guess at the reality?

They were about halfway home when Matthew decided to stop —*he* decided. In large part because his cock was hard as a rock within his breeches, and there was something he'd always wanted to do in a carriage, but had never been in a position to attempt. The few times he'd been with a lover in a carriage before, the coin flip had always denied him engaging in the fantasy.

But there was nothing to tell him no now.

Even in the dim lighting, Matthew could see the flush in his wife's cheeks when he pulled her back up. Her eyes were wide, her lips slightly parted, and there was an expression of both excitement and shock on her lovely face. She took a moment to focus her gaze on him.

Cupping his hand under her chin, Matthew pulled her to him for a kiss. She kissed him back, passionately, eagerly. Spanking her made her as aroused as it did him. Sliding his hand around to the back of her neck, he used his free hand to undo the front of his breeches, freeing his cock.

Ending the kiss, his fingers pressed her head down to his lap.

Johanna shifted on the seat beside him, getting into a more comfortable position to bend down and take his cock into her mouth. Leaning back against the seat, Matthew groaned as her lips pressed against the tip, then opened to take him into the wet heat, her tongue flicking against the crown as she did so.

He hissed, thrusting his hips up, leaning even farther back and letting his head fall back as well as she slid her lips down the length of him. The carriage rocked, moving them with its motions, even as he guided her head up and down.

The cozy confines around them locked out the rest of the world. He was no longer paying attention to what was outside the carriage window, whether anyone might be able to hear them, or anything other than the way his wife's mouth moved over his shaft. His grip tightened on the back of her neck as she sank down, her tongue working as she sucked hard on the length of him, taking him deeper until his tip bumped up against the back of her throat.

"Bloody hell."

He thrust up into her mouth, his hand firm on the back of her neck, her fingers curled around and digging into his thigh as he used her mouth for his pleasure.

It was every bit as perversely wicked as he'd always imagined it would be, engaging in such intimacies while moving along the streets of London. Knowing there were others outside the carriage who had no idea what was happening within—who would be utterly scandalized if they did.

Johanna hummed around him, and Matthew groaned, doing his best to keep his voice as low as possible. Not truly caring if someone heard him. His excitement was growing with every lick, every suck, and he knew he was not going to last much longer. Indeed, he could *not* last much longer without risking the coachman an eyeful as they were nearly home.

Shuddering, he closed his eyes and gritted his teeth against a shout as Johanna's mouth slid down all the way to the base of his dick, swallowing him completely. Pure pleasure shot through him, pulsing within him, as he began to spurt into her mouth. He could feel her throat working against his fingers as she drank him down, milking every last drop from his aching shaft.

It was sinful heaven.

By the time the coachman opened the door, they were both in their seats, as primly proper as they'd appeared when he'd closed it. If the coachman noticed Johanna's rumpled skirts, flushed face, swollen lips, and slightly disheveled hair, he did not show it as he helped her down out of the carriage. Matthew felt a bit unsteady on his feet as he stretched his legs out a bit, following their carnal activities on the road, but he managed.

Taking his wife's arm and grinning at her hot blush, he led her into their house, a very different kind of eagerness rising within him.

There was something very nice about being able to just do as he wished. Especially when it came to his wife. It had been a lovely interlude. But now that he was home, it was like he could feel how near his coin was to being back in his hands again, and he wanted it. Needed it.

Then he and Johanna would be able to enjoy the rest of their evening together, and he could flip to see whether or not to press her about whatever secret she was keeping from him.

CHAPTER THIRTY-FIVE

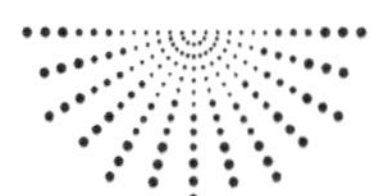

Bottom burning, lips swollen, need throbbing within her, the taste of her husband on her tongue, Johanna did not at all feel proper as Matthew led her into the house. How could she feel proper when they'd engaged in such improper behavior in the carriage? She desperately hoped the coachman had not heard. If he had, he did a remarkable job of pretending and keeping a blank expression. Not that she'd been able to dare more than a quick glance at him as she'd stepped down from the carriage.

It was a relief to have her husband back at her side, leading her up to their home. She was very aware of her skirts brushing against her sore bottom, which made the need between her thighs tingle and throb.

The real punishment might not be the spanking, but the wait for satisfaction.

"Reedy!" Matthew called out to his valet with anticipation and relief threaded through his voice. The man was standing at the top of the stairs, speaking with Nettie, and they both turned to look down at Matthew and Johanna.

From the expressions on their faces, Johanna feared they did not have good news. Reedy was stoic, but Nettie looked sympathetic and a touch worried.

"Your Grace." Reedy hurried down the stairs, leaving Nettie hovering at the top of them, and quickly bowed. "I ah… unfortunately do not have the news you might wish."

Johanna could practically feel her husband's energy fall, from excitement to pure disappointment.

"What? Could the armoire not be moved?" His arm flexed beneath Johanna's hand, and she put her other hand atop his, hoping to assuage some of the emotions she could sense roiling through him.

"No, Your Grace, I mean yes, the armoire could be moved, but…" Reedy lost some of his blankness as he wrung his hands in front of him. "Your coin was not beneath it."

"Not… beneath…" Matthew sucked in a large breath, and Johanna felt him list toward her, so he was now almost leaning against her. Bracing herself against him to help hold him up, she looked up at him, concern threading through her when she saw how very pale his face had gone. "But then, where is it?"

"We do not know, Your Grace. I looked everywhere in your room that I could think of, I swear to you—"

"I need to see for myself." Matthew began to move, and for a moment Johanna was worried that he would tear himself away from her. He came to a halt as her hand tugged on his arm, though, rather than continuing onward, and looked at her with an expression she'd never seen before. A little lost. A little fearful. "Will you come with me?"

"Of course."

How could she not?

Although he'd seemed to be doing well enough without his coin this evening, clearly, he was not ready to be without it at all. She wondered if the expectation of having it again once he returned home had been part of what had helped him so much with its absence. Arm looped through his, she kept up with his rapid pace as he led them to his bedroom, Reedy and Nettie trailing behind them.

The door was open, and there was a small army of footmen inside when they entered. Some of them were crawling along the floor and checking every inch of the rug that covered the room, one with his head in the armoire—the contents of which had been emptied onto the bed—several searching along the baseboards, and one underneath Matthew's bed.

It was clear that they were being excessively thorough. Johanna let out a long, slow breath. Surely, so many of them could not have missed a shiny coin on the floor. It appeared as though they were checking every square inch of it. Her heart sank on her husband's behalf.

To her surprise, he did not seem to sink, though he did put his hand over hers on his arm and press very tightly on it.

Reedy cleared his throat, and everyone in the room looked up, then jumped to their feet, bowing, as they realized the duke and duchess had arrived.

"Any luck?" Reedy asked, sounding as nervous as Matthew was anxious.

All the footmen shook their heads.

"I think it could have fallen through this knothole in the floor, Your Grace," one of the footmen said, gesturing at the section of the floor that the armoire used to cover. It had been moved several feet to the side of that spot. "But we ran downstairs to check and could not find anything, so we came back up to look through the room again."

"Thank you for your diligence." Matthew's voice sounded hollow. He looked at Reedy. "I'll spend the evening in my wife's chambers to give them time to set the room back aright. You may stop looking."

Oh, her poor Matthew.

He sounded so incredibly sad. Resigned. It was like the spark of life had been sucked right out of him, and all Johanna wanted to do was see it returned. This was such a small thing, compared to the burdens she had been through with her family, yet she could see how deeply it affected him. He had not had an easy childhood, despite his wealth and status, and that coin had meant something to him during that time.

If she'd had a talisman she could use to help her make decisions, that led her family out of the dire straits they'd been in, she would have been devastated at its loss as well. Even now, she knew she owed her own current good fortune to that coin. Without it, would Matthew have married her?

She did not know.

But she hurt when he hurt.

She loved being married to him. Seeing his smile. Learning from his passion. The way he interacted with her siblings. His protectiveness. His humor. The way he made her feel.

She…

She could not finish that thought right now.

"Come," she murmured, closing the door to her room behind them and shutting out the noise of the footmen in his. They could still hear bits and pieces as the armoire was being moved back into place. Her room was not as small and cozy as the carriage, but at least it gave them a modicum of privacy. A sense of shutting out the rest of the world, with its weight of decisions, choices, and other people.

She placed her hands on either side of his face, looking up into his eyes.

"It's just us in here," she murmured. "What do you want to do? Whatever you say, it will be the right decision."

Matthew

Looking down into his wife's violet eyes, Matthew's emotions bubbled and popped inside him, a simmering stew of confusion. The pure acceptance he saw staring back at him helped to soothe some of the worst of it.

He could tell Johanna what he wanted to do, and she would not judge him for it. He would not be punished. She had already shown that in the carriage.

So, why was it so difficult?

Taking a deep breath, he closed his eyes for a moment, focusing on the feeling of her hands gently touching his face. The careful way she held him. The scent of her perfume, like a field full of posies, rose to meet his nose. His hands found her hips as he opened his eyes again, looking back down at her. Focusing on her.

"I... want to strip off your dress." He slid his hands up her sides, cupping just underneath her breasts, watching them rise and fall as he did so. "Then I want to brush your hair. While you're completely naked. Then I want to carry you to your bed and put you on your hands and knees, so I can fuck you from behind while seeing the pretty pink of your bottom."

Heat and desire rose in her gaze with every word he spoke. She shivered in place as his hands moved back down her sides and around to her bottom, so he could cup her punished cheeks through her dress on the final word. He pulled her against him, watching as her breath caught in her throat.

Once again, the ability to do what he desired with his wife, without having to flip his coin was... exciting. Distracting enough to almost make him forget his panic. Tomorrow, there would be a myriad of decisions he must make, without knowing if they were the correct ones, but tonight, the only person he had to please was his wife.

And she was pleased to do whatever he wished.

"I want that, too," she whispered.

Lowering his head to her lips, Matthew kissed her. Claimed her with his mouth. His hands massaged her bottom before rising to the buttons on the back of her dress. Slowly, he stripped her out of her clothes, just like he'd said he wanted to. Revealing every inch of her. Giving each inch a kiss as the fabric slipped off her silken skin.

Johanna moaned, nearly making him want to skip over the second part... but he wanted the whole thing.

She sat at her vanity, clothed in nothing but the hair he was brushing, blushing furiously. He was still fully dressed as he attended her. Leaning down, Matthew could not help but take a lock of hair between his fingers and use it to brush over her nipples as he gave her another kiss. Her hand came up to curl around his neck, holding him there as she kissed him back with passionate desperation.

Releasing the lock of hair, he closed his hand around her breast, cupping the soft flesh and pinching her taut nipple between his fingers. She moaned against his lips, her other hand coming up to wrap around his neck as well.

Crouching down, he slid his hands beneath her so he could lift her as he stood back up, holding her tight against him.

These were easy decisions.

They felt right, down to the marrow in his bones.

He could get lost in his wife, without fear, without worry.

Laying her on the bed, she immediately went up onto her knees, her hands going to his cravat and pulling the pin free. It clattered to the floor a moment later, followed by the fluttering fabric of the cravat itself. They kissed. Slowly. Passionately. Deliberately. Her hands moved over him as he stripped off each article of clothing, helping him to divest himself of the coverings until he was completely naked as well.

Matthew climbed onto the bed, running his hands over her bottom, which was barely blushing pink now.

"It appears as though I did not spank you hard enough," he murmured, smiling with the jest as he cupped her cheeks.

"Perhaps you should try again?" The mischief in her eyes as she looked over her shoulder at him made him chuckle. There was something else there, too, though. Something more than a light jest.

Once again, he felt sure that she was hiding something from him, and that the 'punishment' in the carriage had nothing to do with Rose. But this did not seem like the time to question her about it, even if he did not have his coin to tell him not to.

Instead, he lifted his hand and brought it down on her bottom, making her gasp as her head dropped back down in front of her. Braced on her forearms, her bottom high in the air, it was as though she was bent before him in supplication. Matthew pressed his thumb against the slickness of her pussy, coating the digit in her wetness.

"Do you know what truly naughty girls get, kitten?" he asked in a low voice, enjoying her little wriggles as he moved his thumb across her sensitive flesh.

"What?"

He shifted his hand up and pressed the tip of his lubricated thumb against the crinkled blossom of her rear entrance. Johanna gasped, tensing, her head starting to come up as her muscles tried to clench together—but could not fully because her legs were so far apart with him kneeling between them.

"Naughty girls get their bottoms punished with more than a spanking." He pushed his thumb into her bottom at the same time he thrust into her pussy with his cock, making her cry out and rock forward onto her arms. His other hand was curled around her hip, helping to hold her mostly in place as he sank into her with a groan, the warm, wet heat of her body wrapping around his cock.

The tight grip of her bottom squeezed his thumb, and he could feel his cock through the thin lining between her channels.

Gripping her hip tightly with his other hand, he began to ride her, his thumb fully embedded in her bottom all the while.

JOHANNA

The very perversity of her husband's thumb *in her bottom* was enough to make Johanna feel faint. And what did he mean by punishing her with more than a spanking? As shameful as the sensations coursing through her were, there was no more than a slight discomfort at her tiny hole being stretched around his thumb. Not at all like a spanking.

His thumb moved in time with his thrusts, his cock sinking into her again and again, stoking the fires of her arousal, and the most incredibly wicked thought occurred to her. Surely, he could not mean that…

That could not possibly fit…

The slight sting of his thumb pushing into her had not felt at all like punishment, but if something so much larger were to thrust into that narrow space…

Now, Johanna really felt like she might faint, yet her passion was climbing higher and higher with every thrust. Picturing him like this, behind her, pushing his cock into her bottom, made her toes curl as desire coursed through her. That could not possibly be what he meant.

And yet she could not get the image out of her head.

Her body clamped down around his thrusting cock. She was already so primed from the spanking and the way he'd touched her as he'd stripped her down. Every part of her was buzzing, her skin tight on her body, the need inside her pulsing as she soared to her pinnacle.

"Matthew!" She cried out his name, her head dropping down as her body clenched around him. She was so hot. So full. So inundated with pleasure, it felt as though she was about to burst.

And burst she did, in spiraling swirls of ecstasy. Her fingers dug into the sheets beneath her, her toes curling, her head bowing down as the pure sensual rapture went off in a dizzying array of fireworks throughout her body. Matthew's thumb slid away, then his hands were gripping her hips, holding her in place as he moved with hard, rough thrusts that sent her soaring ever higher.

Johanna cried out his name again, the intense pleasure overwhelming her senses, until he groaned and embedded himself fully within her, flooding her with his seed.

Panting, she dropped her head to the bedding beneath her, closing her eyes. She felt… good. Better than she had any right to be. Some of the guilt had been soothed.

But not all of it.

CHAPTER THIRTY-SIX

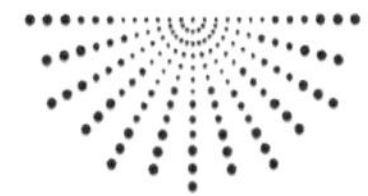

With his wife snuggled against his side, her head pillowed on his shoulder, Matthew stared up into the darkness above them. His finger made idle patterns on her shoulder as he tried to arrange his thoughts.

Tried to decide how he was going to proceed tomorrow without the talisman that had guided so many of his decisions.

He had not done so badly tonight, but there had also been very little for him to do. Social matters were important, of course, but there were easy rules to follow. And, as a duke, very few repercussions when he chose to bend them. Like claiming a dance with his wife or leaving the ball early.

That he'd had Sebastian and Johanna to encourage him, and his grandmother's approval, had helped immensely. But he could not lean on them for everything. Like matters of the estate.

And then there was the murder of his father and his friends' fathers.

How was he supposed to assist them without his luck? They were out of clues. The only way forward that he could think of, without information, was luck. Yes, he'd always been lucky in general, but it was the coin that had guided him.

His deepest fear—the one that hurt to even think about—what if his luck had abandoned him along with his coin?

At some point, he would find a gaming table to test the possibility. Even the thought of it made his stomach turn over, though. That would have to wait until he was sure he could face the answer.

Johanna's hand slid up from his stomach to the center of his chest as she shifted against him, and Matthew reached to hold it.

"What are you thinking about?" she asked softly.

He had thought she'd fallen asleep, due to her even breathing, but apparently not.

"My luck," he admitted. Somehow, it was easier to say under the cover of darkness. He could not see her, and she could not see him. And his coin was not there to tell him not to say what he wanted to. "I… I probably should have told you before, though it's possible it has no bearing on us and our future. But, you know how my father and my friends' fathers were all killed in a tragic accident?"

She went very still beside him.

"Yes."

"It was no accident." The relief that came with being able to finally tell her was strong. "They were murdered, and we are searching for the murderer. In fact, we believe it was a conspiracy, so we are doing it secretly, because we believe that the only threat will come if it's known we suspect the truth."

"I… I know."

Matthew blinked, shifting slightly, but it was far too dark to see her face. Which had made his confession much easier, but now he wished he could see her expression.

"You do? How— Oh." He shook his head, relaxing back against the pillow as the realization struck him. "The other duchesses."

"Yes." She let out a soft exhale that stirred the hair across his chest. "The other duchesses told me. The day after our wedding."

"Oh. Well. Good." He chuckled, feeling much lighter now. "That's a relief."

"They are very put out that they are not able to engage in the search as much as you gentlemen are."

"Ah, well. I am not sure what good they could do right now. The investigation has reached a standstill." He explained to her about Gregory's old steward, the threatening letters Nathanial's father had received, and why he, Christian, and Drake had been in the brothel the fateful evening of her auction. Then he told her about questioning Cornwall and his frustration at the current direction of the investigation. Did it really matter who had suggested Cornwall invite Hereford to the lodge?

To his surprise, he felt his wife growing tenser and tenser against his side as he spoke. He rubbed his hand along her upper arm, trying to reassure her.

"There's no need to worry, kitten. No one outside of our group knows we suspect our fathers were murdered, much less that we're investigating. There should be no danger."

"It is not that." She turned her face into his shoulder, and Matthew felt a spark of alarm at the wetness he felt against his skin. Was she crying?

Turning to her, he released her hand so he could wrap both arms around her, holding her tightly against him. Felt her burrow into him. Felt her start to shake as she began to cry.

"Kitten," he said gently, stroking his hand over her head and down the long length of her hair, "what's wrong?"

"I... I..."

"Tell me."

"I cannot." She shook her head, but he could feel the tension in her body, the conflict within her. She wanted to tell him. She felt she could not.

Matthew kept stroking her, petting her. If he'd had his coin, he would have offered it to her. But he only had himself.

"You can," he said softly. "Whatever it is, it cannot be all that bad."

"It is, though, it is."

JOHANNA

Her husband's gentle reassurance was going to be her undoing. She felt so safe in his arms, so protected, as though nothing could go wrong. The urge to tell him was growing stronger within her. Keeping this secret was tearing her apart, yet the unknown of what would happen once she told him was even more terrifying.

He did not have his coin, though. However he reacted, whatever he did, her mother's fate would not hang on the random flip of luck.

"I promise, whatever it is, you can tell me." His voice was so gentle, so sincere. So coaxing.

Her stomach fluttered, her heart aching within her chest, a physical pulsing ache that made it hard to breathe.

"I…"

She wanted to.

She so badly wanted to. The dark room around them, the cozy snugness of her bed, made it feel like maybe she could tell him. As though if she said it here and now, in the privacy of her room, in the dark, it would still be a secret. Yet she knew that was not true.

"What can I say to make you believe me?" His fingers slid through her hair, the strands slightly tugging on her scalp in a way that was almost hypnotic.

Everything about him, his words, his touch, made her feel safe. Made her want to trust him. Made her want to tell him. What could he say to make her believe she could tell him? What would she need to feel safe to confess?

"I… I need your word that you will protect my mother." The rush of relief that she felt as she made the request confirmed this was what she needed.

His hand on her hair stilled.

"Your mother?"

His confusion would have been comical if the situation were not so dire. She almost laughed, despite herself.

"Yes. Your word that you will protect my mother, no matter what I tell you."

He hugged her close again, stroking her hair the way he had been before.

"Of course I will protect your mother. My word on it as a duke."
He chuckled. "May I never find my lucky coin again should I
break it."

There was no 'of course' about it, but his words did give her some
relief. Even if he did not want to, once he heard what she had to say,
she did believe he would hold to his promise.

Thankfully, it was so dark, she would not have to see his face.
Would not have to see if his expression changed from tenderness to
anger or even hate. If it were not so dark, she did not think she would
be brave enough to say the words.

"I… my mother… the Duke of Clarence's steward bought sleeping
potions from my mother." The words came out in a rush, and even
though she could not see his face, she screwed her eyes shut as tightly
as she could, her shoulders hunching as she waited to see if he would
push her away from him.

Matthew's fingers in her hair slowed but did not stop.

"Alright," he said cautiously.

Obviously, he did not understand the magnitude of what she was
saying. She would have to explain more.

It felt like dying as she forced each word from her mouth.

"He bought them from her mere weeks before your fathers were
murdered." Johanna took a deep breath, feeling as though she had just
run for miles. Weariness, not physical but a kind of soul weariness,
pulled at her. "It is possible, likely even, that they could have been
used to keep the dukes asleep after the explosion. To ensure they
perished in the fire."

There. She had done it. She had said it.

Confession was supposed to be good for the soul, but all she felt
was resigned to whatever happened next.

For better or for worse.

Matthew

His wife's words circled round his head, and it did not make sense to him right away, though he could practically feel the fear emanating from her. Fear that he did not understand.

"Your mother provided Gregory's steward with sleeping potions?" he asked, wanting to be sure that he understood everything she was saying and figure out exactly what she was afraid of. Rather than answering him verbally, she nodded, which he felt as she moved her head against his shoulder. "And you think it's possible that those potions were used to keep my father and the others asleep, to ensure their deaths?"

Another nod he felt against his shoulder. He stroked his fingers through her hair.

Matthew let out a long breath of air, turning it over in his mind.

"What do I need to protect your mother from?" he asked finally. His wife stirred beside him.

"She helped to murder your father. All of your fathers. All dukes."

"Did she know what the potions would be used for?"

"No. She had no idea." Johanna sighed. "She is not even certain they *were* used, but it makes sense. I… I did not know how you would feel once you knew. Or how the others would feel. If they would blame her."

Ah. Well. That did make more sense. Matthew had not considered that aspect.

"I do not blame her," he said immediately. "Even if her potions were used."

Such a plot would be diabolical, but it also made an unfortunate amount of sense. Whoever was behind the murder of his father and the other dukes *was* diabolical. They'd already used Gregory's steward. A man who had a considerable amount of hatred for Gregory's father, but none for the other dukes.

And he'd reached out to Johanna's mother. A woman desperate for money, who would keep quiet, if she even realized what she'd unwittingly become a part of. Perhaps it had not even been his idea. Perhaps he'd been directed.

"Will your friends blame her?"

"I…" Matthew's voice trailed off. He wanted to reassure Johanna and tell her that, of course, none of them would, but he could not be sure. If he had his coin, he would *know* whether or not it was safe to tell them. But he did not. "I do not think so."

He could feel her burrow her face against him.

Matthew slid his hand to cradle her head, pulling it back so he could brush his lips over hers, so she could feel him even though they could not see each other.

"I will protect your mother, kitten," he whispered in the darkness. "My word on it."

"Thank you," she whispered back.

When she kissed him, he could taste the salt of her tears, and he internally vowed to see that she never had cause to shed another over worry for her mother. As long as that was in his control.

As they kissed, she clung to him in the dark, and he felt his cock begin to thicken again. Rolling her onto her back, they moved together as one. It was achingly intimate, almost painful in its intensity, lovemaking that left him gasping in more ways than one.

He did not have his coin to give him a definitive answer, but Matthew was beginning to suspect that he very well may be in love with his wife.

CHAPTER THIRTY-SEVEN

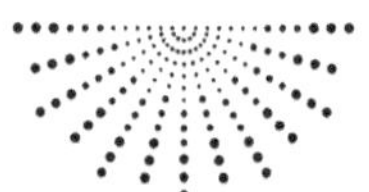

MATTHEW

It was a rather sleepless night, even after his wife fell asleep in his arms, but it was worth the tiredness in the morning because he had come to several decisions. All on his own. It had taken him much longer than he would have with his coin, but he felt fairly confident of them after such a long period of contemplation.

"I need to talk to your mother," he told Johanna after she woke. Because of the light coming in through the cracks in the curtains, he could see her frown, then the fear that lit up her eyes. "That is the best way to protect her. I need to talk to her and ask her some questions, then if she is able to give me anything useful, I can bring the information to my friends, and I do not have to tell them exactly who I got the information from."

"I do not know if she will talk to you," Johanna admitted. She tilted her head back so she could look at him better. Her teeth dragged over her lower lip. "She is very afraid."

So was his wife. But she trusted him. Enough that she'd told him the secret, even though she was frightened of what would happen to her mother.

"You can be there with her. So can Rose if she wants."

"Rose does not know yet," Johanna confessed.

Perhaps it was petty of him to feel good about knowing something that Rose did not. The cousins were so close, he'd assumed Johanna must have told her. He had not minded thinking that Rose knew before him. Still, he could not help but feel chuffed at hearing she did not. Puffed his chest right up.

"Well, she can still be there if you'd like."

Johanna laughed, almost reluctantly, and poked him in the side.

"Do not sound so pleased that she did not know."

"I cannot help it. I am pleased." He slid his hand up to cup her face, running his thumb along her soft cheek. "I am pleased that you trust me, and I will not betray that trust. I will do everything in my power to protect your mother. She has nothing to fear from me and mine. Consider me your Knight of the Round Table. I will fight any other knight, slay any dragon, complete any quest you set before me, for no other reason than to see the fear wiped from your eyes and a smile upon your lips."

Her hand pressed against his chest.

"I do not know what to say to that," she whispered, tears filling her eyes.

These were the kind of tears Matthew did not mind, though.

"You do not have to say anything," he told her. "Except 'yes, Matthew.'"

"Yes, Matthew."

He pressed his lips to hers for a kiss, holding her tight against him. Despite the desire that swelled from holding her naked body, Matthew ruthlessly pushed it away. He did not need a coin to tell him that this was not the time.

Besides, the sooner he talked to her mother, the more time he would have to plan out what to do next. Another decision. Without his coin.

"Before or after breakfast, do you think?" he asked. Not because he wanted to burden Johanna with the decision, but because she knew her mother best, and it seemed wise to be guided by her on such a matter.

"After." She sighed and pressed her forehead against his chest. "For my own sake, if not hers. I am not prepared at the moment."

Which made sense. She had just woken up, and, unlike him, she had slept soundly through the night. Giving her another sound kiss, Matthew reluctantly abandoned the warmth of her bed and returned to his room.

He glanced at the armoire as he rang for Reedy.

The reality of having to live without his coin was starting to hit home. Not in the panicked manner it had struck him the night before, when he'd still thought he would get it back, but a kind of cold, creeping dread that he was barely able to keep at bay.

Sebastian's voice in his head helped to bolster him somewhat.

You'll deal with the consequences, like the rest of us mere mortals.

Other people did this every single day.

He could do it, too.

Getting dressed was easy. Reedy usually chose Matthew's outfits for him, anyway. So not much had changed about getting ready for the day. Obviously, once he was done getting dressed, it was time to go to the dining room.

Matthew had always thought that he flipped his coin for everything, but now he was realizing how many small decisions he made without flipping it. Because, of course, he did not *have* to go to break his fast. But it was what he did, every morning, without flipping his coin to see if he should.

Of course, now that he was married, and he knew Johanna was getting ready for the day, there was the question of whether he should wait for her. But that was an easy decision, too. Last night, Johanna had asked him what he wanted to do, then they did that.

Right now, he wanted to wait for his wife, so they could walk to the dining room together. Easy.

And he could acknowledge that in the past, he might have flipped his coin to make such a decision. Now, he just did it. Because what would the consequences be of not doing so?

He could arrive in the dining room alone, or he could have company along the way. Besides, he did not want Johanna to feel as though he'd left and walked on without her or that he did not want her company.

It was a bit odd, having to think through what might happen depending on what choice he made, when he'd stopped considering such things before. He'd let the coin guide him. Not bad. Just odd.

This was an easy decision, though. Very little bad could come of it either way. He did not think Johanna would be upset if he did not wait for her, but he thought it would make her feel good that he had.

Easy.

Harder choices were still to come.

The door to Johanna's room opened, and she stepped out into the hallway, catching his gaze immediately. Her whole face lit up when she saw him, which was a very nice feeling indeed.

JOHANNA

Despite her nervousness over what was to come after breakfast, Johanna found herself enjoying the meal immensely. Not just because Bridget was peppering her and Rose with questions about the ball or because Charlotte appeared to be having some kind of mute communication with the air in front of her (or was gracefully moving her hands about for some other reason), but because of Matthew's clear delight in his life without his coin.

"Do you know, I cannot remember the last time I flipped my coin on what to eat for breakfast?" he whispered to her, sounding positively gleeful. "I make my decisions for my meals all the time without it."

Johanna's lips twitched, and she nodded seriously, suppressing her smile. She did not point out that he ate the same thing for breakfast every morning, so it did not surprise her that he would have no trouble with that choice. He was so very happy to have discovered it.

His joy was utterly endearing. It was something she'd appreciated about him before—the lightness he had about him. If she had not known about his childhood, she might have thought it was due to his position and privilege, but while he might have been the son of a duke and all that entailed, he had not known the love and care that she'd gotten from her parents.

Now, watching him, seeing his appreciation for realizing how many choices he'd made on his own, without his coin, she felt emotion well up in her breast. The same emotion she had not wanted to admit to before.

She was happy that he was happy.

Because she loved him.

Just as she wanted her siblings and Rose to be happy because she loved them.

Although it was a very different kind of love, to be sure.

But there was no longer any escaping how she felt about him.

"What are we doing today?" Bridget asked, finally leaving Rose alone.

"Lessons," Lady Stark replied, without glancing up from her plate. "Micah's new tutor will be arriving shortly, and Miss Swift is going to give you and Charlotte singing lessons."

"Why do we need to learn how to sing?" Bridget asked, getting that particularly mulish expression on her face that often preceded a fight.

"Because if you want to have your pick of the gentlemen, you need all the attributes that a proper young lady should have." Lady Stark took a sip of her tea. "Those ladies who have mastered all the expected skills for the marriage mart are the ones who can choose who they marry. Those who are not skilled must take what they can get."

Which made Johanna very glad she'd not had to be a debutante. She had certainly not mastered the skills required.

"Johanna does not know how to sing, and she landed a duke," Bridget said, frowning.

"So, she did. It was very lucky for her that matters worked out that way. Would you like to rely on luck, or would you prefer to control your own destiny as much as possible?" Lady Stark said, finally raising her gaze to look directly at Bridget.

Bridget's frown deepened.

"I am going to control my destiny," Charlotte announced. "I will choose the best husband."

"What if you marry him and it turns out he's terrible?" Micah asked, teasing.

Charlotte shrugged. "Then I will get a new one."

"He would have to die for that to happen, you know."

Charlotte shrugged again, and Micah eyed her with growing consternation. As did everyone else.

Perhaps Johanna would need to pay closer attention to her youngest sister.

"Well, I am sure you will make a good choice the first time," Lady Stark said lightly. Then she muttered under her breath as her gaze dropped down again. "I hope so for his sake."

Charlotte smiled beatifically

Matthew leaned over, and Johanna tensed. Was he worried that her sister might actually kill her future husband? Would he think she got that from their mother?

"I just realized, I never flip to decide to leave the breakfast table either," Matthew whispered gleefully.

"There are certainly a lot of things you do not use your coin for," she agreed, suppressing her laughter, though she could not suppress the smile he brought to her lips.

Soon enough, breakfast was over, and it was time to make their way to her mother's room. Johanna breathed a sigh of relief as her brother and sisters went to their respective lessons, Lady Stark escorting Micah in order to introduce him to his tutor.

She and her family owed Matthew and his grandmother so much.

Letting him talk to her mother was the very least she could do. Especially after he'd promised to protect her.

"Rose," she said, as she got to her feet. "Will you help me with Mother? We need to get her dressed today. She's going to meet Matthew. In the sunroom." Which was closer to her bedroom than any of the other public rooms. Johanna glanced at Matthew, who nodded, the smile fading from his lips.

"I will meet you there."

Nodding, Johanna felt her mouth grow dry as she turned away. Rose was frowning at her as she came around the side of the table and looped her arm through Johanna's.

"What is going on?" she asked in a low voice as they exited the dining room.

"You will see," Johanna told her. Inside her chest, it felt as though her heart was constricting, despite Matthew's promise. He already knew the worst of it, surely. Johanna had questioned her mother, after all. There was nothing more than Johanna had been able to tell him, but she understood why he wanted to question her mother himself. "You will know everything after this, I promise."

"Very well." Rose skewered her with a look. "I do not like it when you keep secrets from me."

That brought Johanna's smile back.

"I do not like keeping secrets from you. Nor am I very good at it. I am sorry I have been avoiding you."

"I thought this might just be what it is like now that you are married and I am not." Rose shrugged, but she looked away, and Johanna knew it was because she was hiding her hurt. Because that was what Rose did.

"No. You will always be the sister of my heart. I have been trying to protect you." Johanna sighed, shaking her head. "You will understand after Mother and Matthew's conversation."

"We shall see."

Johanna did not blame Rose for her skepticism.

Of course, it was not as easy as all that. Johanna's mother was not exactly leaping to get out of bed and meet her husband.

"You are going to be the death of us all," she said, wringing her hands, even as Johanna and Rose pulled her from the bed.

Rose's look of alarm did much to help Johanna feel like sticking out her tongue at her cousin. *See? I was not exaggerating.*

"Matthew has promised me that he will protect you, Mother," Johanna said gently but firmly. "And I believe him."

Even so, her mother stood uselessly, tears rolling down her cheeks. She was like a doll Rose and Johanna had to dress. The silent weeping nearly broke Johanna, but she knew this was for the best. Matthew was providing for her whole family. He had promised to protect her mother.

The only thing he had asked for was to be allowed to meet with and question her mother personally. How could she possibly reasonably deny him that?

She could not.

Johanna was putting her faith in her husband. The man who had rescued her. The man who had taken her family in. The man who had made her his duchess and given her the keys to a future she could have never imagined, even a month ago.

The man she had fallen in love with.

All she could do now was hope that he would not betray that faith.

CHAPTER THIRTY-EIGHT

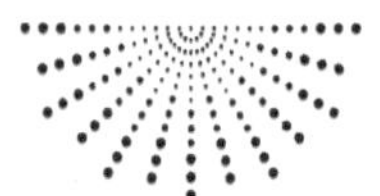

Matthew

While Matthew was waiting for Johanna and her mother to come to the sunroom, he had even more time to think. He went to his study to write a quick list of the questions that he'd been formulating in his head, not wanting to forget any of them in the moment.

As he was leaving his study, he paused, then summoned some of his footmen to bring a small table and chair into the sunroom, along with his blotter and ink, so that he could take notes. He did not know what would be important, so he wanted to make sure he got every-thing down.

Once things were arranged to his liking in the sunroom, he dismissed the footmen and sat down on the chair. It was a good room, he felt. Not only because it was close to the countess' bedroom, but also because it was bright and sunny. Even the wallpaper, which was yellow and decorated with purple flowers and green stripes, was nicely cheerful.

The kind of room that should be unthreatening. Hopefully, it would make his mother-in-law feel more comfortable.

Matthew had set up the room so the table was across from the couch, so Johanna's mother could sit there with her. He would not be directly across from them, but a little to the side, so it would hopefully feel less like an interrogation. It seemed right.

He hoped it was right.

Once again, his hand brushed over his empty pocket. The only reason he even noticed was when his fingertips found nothing, and he was reminded, once again, that he did not have his coin. Although he'd enjoyed breaking his fast and realizing how often he did not use his coin to make some decisions, the number of times he reached for it only to come up empty made him realize how often he did.

Sighing, he sat down, then was immediately forced to jump to his feet again as the door opened, and Johanna came into the room with an older woman on her arm. Rose came in behind them, a very strange expression on her face. Matthew wondered if Johanna had told her everything already.

Johanna and her mother were very similar in facial features, but she, Micah, and Charlotte must have gotten their coloring from their father. Their mother's honey-wheat hair was more akin to Bridget's dark blonde, and she had very blue eyes rather than the violet of three out of four of her children. Her hair was pulled back into a neat chignon, showing off the angular lines of her face.

If he had not known she'd been starving herself, he would have been able to guess by her appearance. Her dress hung loosely on her frame, and there was still a tight gauntness to her mouth—though that might have as much to do with the obvious fear in her eyes as she looked at him as anything else.

"Matthew, this is my mother, the Countess Falmouth. Mother, this is my husband, the Duke of St. Albans." Johanna shook her mother's arm gently as Matthew bowed, and she dropped into a rather awkward curtsy before straightening again.

"It is a pleasure to meet you," he said, coming forward to take her hand. "Please, come and sit. Would you like me to ring for some tea? Or something to eat?"

Some of the fear in her expression receded, and she glanced at Johanna, who nodded eagerly.

"I have already broken my fast, thank you," she said faintly as

Matthew escorted her over to the couch and helped her to sit in the middle. Johanna was there a moment later, seating herself on one side, leaving the other open for Rose to take her place. Johanna's mother glanced at her daughter as Johanna took her hand, as if she was unsure of what was happening.

Matthew had given a great deal of thought about how not to frighten the poor woman. After all, she was his wife's mother. He certainly did not want her frightened of him.

"Thank you for agreeing to assist me with the investigation," he said, taking his seat at the table. He glanced up to see Rose mouthing the word 'investigation' as her brow furrowed, and she glanced at her aunt, who was now holding both her daughter and her niece's hands in her lap. The three women had managed to hold together an entire family and estate while the man who was supposed to have taken care of them stole their funds.

"I... yes." The countess glanced at Johanna, who smiled encouragingly at her, then positively beamed at Matthew.

Warmth filled his chest, and he sat up a little straighter.

"I hope you do not mind me taking notes. I do not want to forget anything important."

"Of course." Appearing confused but much less frightened, the countess straightened in her seat. "I did not mean harm to anyone, ever. I thought I was helping. All I have ever wanted to do is help. That's why I learned about herbs and healing."

Rose pressed her lips together, obviously wanting to ask questions but keeping them to herself for the moment.

"You were taken advantage of. You could not have known." At that moment, Matthew knew his statement to be utterly true. The woman in front of him would not have harmed anyone, not for any amount of money. Not even to save her family. "And you are not the only one. We know the Duke of Clarence's steward was involved in the plot to murder our fathers, but we are convinced he did not know the full breadth of the conspiracy or how many of them would be killed."

He explained it that way for Rose's benefit, and her eyes went wider and wider with every word until her lips popped open in shock.

By the time he finished, her head swiveled around to try to pin Johanna with a look, but the countess was between them, and Johanna was looking at him.

Obviously, Rose was less than pleased about being kept in the dark, but she was going to have to hold it together for the moment for the countess' sake. She fumed silently, forced to hold her tongue by the circumstances that her cousin had arranged.

Matthew made a mental note that his wife was perhaps more diabolical than he had realized.

"I did not know. I promise," the countess replied, tears filling her blue eyes. "I thought perhaps the duchess needed something to help her sleep. Or even the steward himself. He did not seem well."

Matthew made a note. He wondered if Gregory had noticed anything about his steward seeming unwell in the weeks before his father's death. If he had, he had not mentioned it before. It was worth asking.

JOHANNA

If she had not fallen in love with her husband before, seeing how gentle he was with her mother would have done it. She could not even be worried about Rose's reaction to everything Johanna had been keeping from her because she was so overcome with absolute adoration and relief. It felt like being rescued all over again.

He was very serious, taking notes as he went through everything with her mother that Johanna had. Everything she had already told him. Johanna wished there was more for him than she had been able to give. It did not seem very helpful.

"So, the steward collected five potions from you, then sent a man to collect the rest of the order a few days later?" Matthew asked, repeating what her mother had said. She nodded.

"Yes, five more potions."

Which was more than he could have needed for eight dukes. Had more been prepared in case more dukes arrived? Had there been other targets at the lodge that had managed to escape the dukes' fate? Or had the murderers just wanted to be prepared? Johanna felt sick to her stomach at the ruthlessness of it all.

Perhaps, she reasoned, the steward had wanted a few for himself, to help him sleep at night, either before or after. He must have known some of what was going to happen, from what Matthew said.

"The steward, what did he look like?" Matthew asked, which made Johanna blink. That was not a question she'd asked her mother. She'd assumed when her mother said that the man who bought the potions from her was the Duke of Clarence's steward, that he was. Especially after she'd found out that Clarence's steward had been involved in the plot.

It had never occurred to her to double-check what the man looked like.

Matthew nodded as he wrote down the description her mother gave.

"And the man who came for the rest of the order? Did he give you his name? What did he look like?"

"No name," her mother said, squeezing Johanna's hand as she sighed and looked down into her lap. The shame she clearly felt, even though it was not her fault, broke Johanna's heart. "I barely remember him. I only saw him for a very brief moment. He had dark hair and a beard, and I only remember that because of his scar."

"His scar?" Matthew's head came up.

Johanna's mother nodded, releasing Rose's hand so she could use her own to draw a line across her face, from beside her nose down to her chin.

"Right through his beard. Looked ill-healed, and I remember thinking it likely should have been stitched and was not." She shook her head, reaching for Rose's hand again. "I only noticed because it was so striking. I could have done a better job of it, and I remember wishing I'd seen him when he'd first gotten it."

"Was he very thin or more broad-shouldered?" There was something in her husband's voice, the tiniest change, that had Johanna's focus sharpening.

"Broad-shouldered." Her mother hesitated. "Why? Is he important?"

"Perhaps." Matthew looked down at his notes and took a deep breath. His voice was tight as he spoke, with controlled emotion that made Johanna's heart ache for him. "It's the scar, you see. There was a tenant my father threw off our land—Aaron Heywood. He was a tall, broad-shouldered man with a beard, and about five years ago, he was gravely injured by a bull that had gotten loose. When he could not pay his rent, my father threw him and his wife out of the home his family had lived in for five generations."

Closing his eyes, Matthew swallowed hard.

Releasing her mother's hand, leaving her to Rose, Johanna got to her feet and went to him. Tears had welled in her eyes in sympathy for the repressed emotion emanating from him.

"What happened to them?" she asked in a low murmur, giving his shoulder a gentle squeeze.

Matthew reached up to put his fingers over hers, and she felt the sigh ease out of him.

"I do not know," he said quietly. "By the time I found out, they were long gone. I looked for them, briefly, once my father died, but…" He shook his head. "There was so much to do, and it had been so long. Perhaps I should have looked harder."

"Perhaps not, if he had something to do with the plot. He might not have wanted to be found by then. And there was naught you could have done for them before your father died."

"No. Perhaps. I could have given him some coin, at least." Matthew squeezed her fingers. "Well. What's done is done. It might not even be the same man."

Though it was clear from his tone, he did not believe his words for even a moment. Neither did Johanna. The coincidence was far too great.

A knock on the door made all of them jump, and out of the corner of her eye, Johanna saw her mother clutch Rose's hand with both of hers. Even though she seemed relieved at having unburdened herself to Matthew, the general fear still remained.

Holt opened the door, stiffly upright as ever, his gaze quickly scanning the room and finding Matthew with Johanna standing behind him.

"Your Graces," he said, bowing. "I apologize for the interruption, but the Duke of Ormonde has called and is most insistent that he speak to the duke and Lord Falmouth immediately."

"My brother?" Johanna asked, bewildered. "But why— Oh." It suddenly struck her that this must have something to do with Mr. Blash. With everything going on with her mother, she had almost forgotten about her brother's former guardian, especially since Micah's guardianship had officially been turned over to her husband.

"Put Ormonde in the library and fetch Lord Falmouth, please, Holt," Matthew told the butler. "I think we are finished here, anyway."

"I would like to come with you," Johanna said quickly, and relief rushed through her when Matthew nodded his agreement. He rolled up the paper he'd been writing his notes on and held it in one hand while holding out his other for her to take. She glanced over at Rose and her mother. "I will come join you shortly, I promise."

"Not to worry, dear. Rose can keep me company." Her mother looked around the room. She appeared almost ten years younger than she had when Johanna had entered her bedroom this morning, such was the weight that had been lifted from her shoulders. There was a lightness to her expression that did Johanna's heart good to see. "I think I want to stay in this room for now. It's very nice."

"I am glad you like it," Matthew said, his lips curving up in a genuine smile. "Please feel free to make as much use of it as you like. It does not get used often enough."

"Thank you." Her mother's smile was as genuine as Matthew's.

They liked each other, then. After such a fraught conversation, Johanna had not known what to expect, but Matthew had handled things perfectly—and without the use of his coin.

"We will speak when you return," Rose said, giving Johanna a look.

She smiled sheepishly back at her cousin. Whatever tongue-lashing Rose wanted to give her, Rose would feel Johanna deserved for keeping her in the dark, and Johanna rather felt she deserved it, too, even if she would not do anything differently given the chance. Rose tended to play the protector in their relationship, but Johanna could not regret her decisions. Neither would she try to escape the scolding Rose was no doubt already preparing in her mind.

"We will."

With that, they swept from the room. Johanna might have been grateful for the short reprieve, but anything to do with Mr. Blash was going to get her ire up. The man had stolen from them. Lied to her. Even when she'd told him that her mother was starving, he had not confessed to his crime nor provided the funds to feed the family, convincing Johanna to sell herself instead. If not for Matthew, she could not imagine what straits she and her family might be in now.

She was not certain he would have even given her the money he'd promised from Mr. O'Connell's payout.

Whatever news the Duke of Ormonde had brought of Mr. Blash, she wanted to know.

CHAPTER THIRTY-NINE

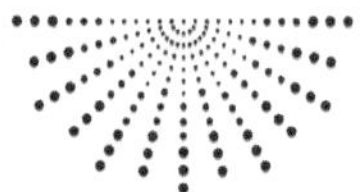

The surprise that flitted over Drake's face when he saw Johanna on Matthew's arm was highly amusing. Matthew was all too aware of the notes clutched in his hand, but one matter at a time. He did not want to derail Drake from whatever news he'd brought about Mr. Blash.

"Duchess." Drake bowed, glancing at Matthew with a reproving look. Matthew shrugged. Johanna was the one most personally affected by Blash's deception, and he was going to tell her whatever Drake told him, anyway. This bypassed one step.

Besides, it would not be the first time one of the wives had been included in conversations that Drake thought them best left out of. The ladies had already proven helpful in the investigation into the dukes' deaths. Although he noticed Drake still endeavored to keep them at arm's length.

"Your Grace. Would you care for some refreshment?" she asked as Matthew escorted her to one of the wingback chairs.

Drake shook his head, shifting his weight back and forth on his feet, likely wishing to resume the pacing he'd been doing when they'd entered the room. Whatever news he had, he was in a bit of a state about it.

"No, thank you. We will not be here long."

"We will not?" Matthew asked, as the door opened again, to reveal Holt and Micah with a curious expression on his face. The young man hurried in, and the butler shut the door behind him, giving Drake an abbreviated bow as he looked between all of them.

"Your Grace," Micah said to Drake, his voice cracking on the last word. He winced but forged ahead. "What has happened?"

Drake cleared his throat, moving over to stand behind the chair opposite Johanna, gripping the top of its back as he gave himself a little shake.

"I am pleased to inform you that Blash did not actually go to America." A small smile curved his lips. "Though he laid a very good false trail, he actually never left England. Never left London, in fact."

Johanna gasped, her hand rising to her lips.

"He's *here?*"

"Well, he is in Newgate now." Drake's smile made more sense as he delivered that news with relish.

Now it was Matthew's turn to put his hand on Johanna's shoulder, the way she had for him when he'd realized her mother might be describing Heywood. Trying to give what reassurance he could. Not that he thought she was upset to hear that Blash was in prison, but perhaps at just realizing he'd been so close by all this time.

"Newgate," she said faintly, her fingertips rising to her lips.

"Good," Micah said furiously. "I am glad he is in prison. He can rot there for all I care."

"My sentiment as well," Drake said. "However, I wished to come by and see if there is anything you would like me to ask him. I am on my way to visit him now for some questions on a separate matter, and I already planned to wring him for information about where the money he stole from you went, but I thought I should ask if there was anything specific you wished to ask about."

"I wish to see him," Micah said immediately, fisting his hands at his side, his small chin lifting defiantly. Johanna's own fingers gripped Matthew's hand tighter at her brother's declaration. "I wish to see him myself and tell him what a vile worm he is."

"No." Three voices spoke at once, and Drake shot Matthew a look of bemusement. Obviously, since Matthew agreed with him, Drake wanted Matthew to take the lead on denying the young earl.

"Newgate is no place for a youth nor a lady," Matthew said, shaking his head. Not that Johanna had asked to go, but just in case.

He had not needed to flip his coin for that answer. It had been instinctive. Should he go? His fingers brushed his pocket. There did not seem to be any great reason to. Though Matthew would certainly like to see Mr. Blash have his day in court when that came to pass, and that was something he could take both Micah and Johanna to.

"I am very happy to pass on the message about what a vile worm he is," Drake offered when Micah deflated. "Matthew is correct, though. Newgate is… well, it is a fitting place for a man who would prey on others and maximize his own benefits at their expense. Especially those whose care he was entrusted with, and who he should have honorably guided. Only the worst kind of people use children and the innocent for their own ends."

The sheer contempt and repugnance in Drake's voice were more than Matthew would have thought possible, considering how removed he was from the situation. Drake sounded almost as though he was taking Mr. Blash's crimes as personally as if they were against him and his. Then again, Drake could be very black and white in his thinking, with very little room for compromise.

"Very well." Micah sighed, scrubbing his hand over his face. "I cannot think of any questions. I just want to know that he is aware of what an utter cad he is."

"If he is not already aware, I will be sure to tell him," Drake promised. "I will also take great pleasure in telling him that we are in the process of recovering *all* the funds he stole from you, that there are several moneylenders who would now like a word with him, and that your brother-in-law, the Duke of St. Albans, will certainly be paying close attention to his trial."

"Very close," Matthew said, nodding. There were enough among the aristocracy who bent the law to favor themselves, even when they were not innocent; it was only fair that it should be bent to condemn a man who was truly guilty. Especially after meeting Johanna's family.

How could a man, a relation no less, condemn actual children to starvation or worse? He'd met with them, broken bread with them, and still been ready to sell Johanna to the highest bidder. Matthew shuddered to think what his plans for Bridget and Charlotte might have been.

Or perhaps he'd had no plans at all but had only thought of it when Johanna appeared on his doorstep. Matthew would not have put it past him to start making plans, though.

"I need to speak with you and the others. Today, if possible," he told Drake, squeezing his hand around the paper rolled within it.

Drake nodded, though he was obviously distracted as he took out his pocket watch to check the time.

"It should not take me too long. I sincerely doubt Blash is the type to hold his cards close to his vest, especially if he is hoping for any kind of leniency."

"Are you going to help him get that?" Micah asked, obviously worried.

"Absolutely not." Drake grinned, and there was absolutely no humor in his expression, only the vengeful light of a man on a mission. "Trust me. Blash will receive exactly what he deserves. But desperate men have nothing left to hold on to but hope, and I will be very surprised if that does not loosen his tongue."

"This afternoon, then," Matthew said, drawing Drake's attention back to him.

Drake nodded. "We can gather at White's." His gaze alighted for the briefest moment on Johanna. Once again, Drake was trying to keep the ladies out of things.

Matthew was not surprised, but he also was not going to object. His fingers slid over his empty pocket. Drake seemed determined, and in this case, it seemed easiest to just go along.

Johanna was already nervy enough. Besides, she was attending tea with his grandmother and Rose at Lady Chesterham's. If she was not there, his friends would only be able to pepper him with questions, not her, and he had promised to protect her and her mother.

JOHANNA

"Mr. Blash has been found and is now in Newgate prison," Johanna announced as soon as she returned to the sunroom, then immediately came to a halt as she realized Lady Stark had joined her mother and Rose. As far as she knew, this was the first time Matthew's grandmother had met her mother, and the sight of them together made her heart stutter.

Everyone was smiling—at least they had been before her announcement—though, so hopefully it was going well. She already felt so much lighter, having finally unburdened herself to her husband. It was though she was floating on air. Even thinking about Mr. Blash could not bring her down.

"That is too good a place for the likes of him," Rose said, a scowl furrowing her brow. "Though how can he possibly be there? I thought he had fled to America."

"Apparently, that was a false trail, well laid." Johanna shook her head at the sheer audacity of the man. Though it had worked well enough at first, the arrogance to think it would last forever was astounding. Especially since he had stayed in London. What if she had seen him on the street? Had he not thought that possible? Then again, trying to understand his mind was not at all something Johanna thought she would ever be able to fathom.

And she did not want to.

She did not want to be able to understand such cruelty.

Explaining to the ladies everything the Duke of Ormonde had said, little though it was, made for entertaining conversation. All of them were appalled at the idea of Micah going to Newgate with Ormonde and relieved that the dukes had rejected the notion immediately. Though Micah was growing up far too fast, he was still not yet a man, and the idea of him visiting a prison...

Johanna shuddered to think of it. Her mother was also clearly relieved that he'd been denied, and Johanna was sure Mother would seek out her only son later to speak to him. Now that she was out of bed and out of her room, and she and Lady Stark seemed to be getting on famously, despite their very different demeanors.

She did not bring up the fact that the dukes would be meeting later today to discuss the investigation into their fathers' deaths. That was what she knew Matthew wanted to talk to his friends about, and she'd been very relieved when Drake had suggested White's, which would prevent her from attending. Not that she could, anyway; Lady Stark was very much looking forward to showing her off at tea this afternoon.

The morning slipped by quickly, as one conversation led to another. Even though Rose must be chafing at the bit at her inability to question Johanna about the dukes' fathers and their murders and Johanna hiding her mother's involvement, she did not show it. After denouncing Mr. Blash, the topic quickly changed to the current Season and fashions. Johanna had not realized that, at one time, her mother had quite a few friends and acquaintances among the *ton*, although she probably should have.

Listening to her mother's delight in being updated by Lady Stark on their comings and goings, she realized her mother must have let those relationships fall by the wayside after the death of Johanna's father. Which made her feel terrible. They'd had each other to lean on, as much as possible, but it was not the same as having a friend. She'd had Rose, all these years, while her mother had had no one of her own age and experience to bolster her.

She positively lit up, hearing about the scandals she'd missed, the marriages, the government appointments, the children.

"Would you like to come to tea with us?" Lady Stark offered. "Lady Chesterham will certainly not mind. She is in *alt* since her granddaughter secured an offer from a marquess earlier this week."

"Oh, no, but thank you." Some of the light dimmed from mother's face, and she sat back, delicately folding her hands on her lap. "I do not think I am quite ready to face Society yet. And… I have nothing to wear."

"Well, that we can fix quickly enough," Lady Stark said with a gleam in her eye that Johanna immediately recognized. She wondered if her mother realized that she had just appointed herself Lady Stark's newest project, now that Johanna, Rose, and her sisters had been taken care of. Though she was fairly certain Lady Stark was not fully done with Rose. "Tea this afternoon. Tomorrow we will go shopping."

Johanna could not blame her mother for the look of alarm on her face.

CHAPTER FORTY

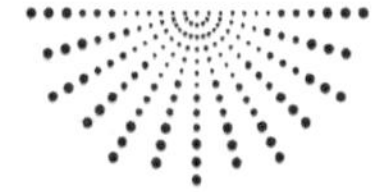

When Matthew arrived at White's early that afternoon, Gregory and Sebastian were already there, seated and speaking with a weary-looking Zachary. They'd already had the chairs in the room arranged in a circle, with small tables set between them to rest any food, drink, or pipes on. Monkey Sinclair was perched on the top of Zachary's wingback chair, looking around with an alertness that made it appear as if he was watching over Zachary.

"Good afternoon," Matthew said, going to the drink cart to pour himself a snifter of brandy before seating himself beside Gregory.

"I take it you have some news for us," Gregory said, smiling genially.

"I do indeed, but let us wait for everyone to gather." Matthew did not want to have to go over everything more than once. He cocked his head at Zachary. "You appear done in."

"We had a small fire in the kitchen last night," Zachary explained, rubbing his hand over his face. "There was not much damage to the house, thankfully, but mother panicked, of course. I cannot blame her. It brought up all sorts of thoughts for me as well."

All the gentlemen grimaced. Matthew could not imagine how

difficult that must have been, especially since it was Zachary's mother in the household. She had truly loved her husband to the point of defying Society's dictates and continuing to wear her widow's weeds long after the official end of her mourning period. It was only the hunt for Zachary's bride and the possibility of marrying her son off to her best friend's daughter that had brought her out of her deep grief.

Being reminded of her husband's death in such a manner would have been… fraught.

"How is she this morning?" Matthew asked sympathetically.

"Still sleeping when I left, thankfully. We had to dose her to calm her." Zachary shook his head. "I had to sit in a chair beside her, holding her hand, until she fell asleep last night. She cried until she finally dropped off."

There was a bone-deep tiredness in his voice, the kind that came from far more than a single night of ill rest. Matthew did not envy him at all. He might have secured a fiancée and a future that was helping his mother with her grief, at least most of the time, but he had done it at the expense of his own happiness. And now his mother was struggling again, anyway.

The door to their room opened, and Christian and Nathanial came in, smiling and laughing together. It was very nice to see Nathanial so happy now, rather than being part of the dour club with Zachary. Not that Matthew blamed Zachary for being depressed; it was just nice that Nathanial no longer was.

If he still had his coin, he might offer to flip it for Zachary. It had worked out very well for Nathanial, by all appearances.

His fingers ran over his pocket, and he sighed internally when they came up empty, but at the same time, there was a kind of resigned acknowledgment that, of course, they had. Matthew was finally becoming used to the lack. Somehow, he felt like it should take longer for the change, but he was also grateful for it. He did not like feeling panicked every time he reached for his coin and found his pocket empty.

"Well met, fellow dukes," Christian said, clapping his hands together. "I have just come from giving my mistress her *congé*."

Matthew snorted as the others all stared blankly at him.

"Are we supposed to celebrate that for you?" Sebastian asked blandly, shooting a worried look at Zachary. Who, of course, had broken things off with Delilah before embarking on the search for a wife. Although Christian's mistress had been an actress, not a widow of the *ton*, so it was not as if she could have any expectations of becoming a wife.

Not like Delilah had.

"Absolutely." Christian nodded, rubbing his hands together. Like Matthew, he and Nathanial stopped by the drink cart. Nathanial handed him a glass, allowing him to make his way into the circle to sit beside Zachary. "My time is now completely freed to focus on the next step in our mystery. I am delighted to discover that there is a next step to take."

"Should you not be focused on finding a wife now that you no longer have a mistress?" Zachary asked, turning his head to frown at Christian.

With an exasperated sigh, Christian shook his head.

"I told you, having a mistress was no impediment to finding myself a bride. It is not as though I announced it at every ball I attend. However, it was becoming difficult to pay proper attention to Susette, look for a bride, *and* assist with the investigation. This way, I only have two things to do." He grinned. "It works out well for Susette, too; she's been offered a part in a traveling company, so she's off to France next week with some pretty new jewels to remember me by."

"What he means is that she was going to leave him anyway, so he might as well break it off with her now," Nathanial joked, coming to sit by Matthew, leaving the chair between him and Christian for Drake.

Christian shrugged and took a sip of his brandy. "Does it really matter the order of things?"

"Not in the slightest." Sebastian shook his head, a bemused expression on his face. Of their whole group, he and Zachary were the most likely to do things the 'proper' way. Unfortunately for Sebastian, his mother had turned out to be quite vicious to his sister, and Sebastian had banished her to the countryside, so he did not have a mother or even a grandmother to assist him in finding a bride. Lady Astrid had suggested several times that he use Lady Hu, the matchmaker, but so far, he was proving to be very resistant to the idea.

The door opened again, admitting the final member of their group. Drake had a rather vicious smile on his face as he strode in, one that made Matthew wonder about what condition he'd left Mr. Blash in at Newgate. He appeared very pleased with himself as he shut the door behind him and locked it, so they would not be disturbed.

"Gentlemen," he said with a nod, and like the others before him, headed for the drink cart.

"Where have you been?" Nathanial asked, raising one eyebrow.

"I had some matters to attend to. Nothing to do with this," Drake replied, taking a sip from his snifter as he moved to claim the seat left open for him. "Have we started yet?"

"Not at all," Gregory replied. "There was a small fire in Zachary's kitchen last night; his mother was very distressed by it. Christian has given his mistress her congé. And, as usual, Sebastian still has no marital prospects." He chuckled as Sebastian reached over to punch him in the shoulder.

Even before Gregory had married Sebastian's sister, the two had been close and treated each other more like brothers than friends. Hence the teasing.

"I am a duke. I have *all* the marital prospects; it is just a matter of picking which woman." Sebastian huffed. "Just because you accidentally fell into a happy marriage does not mean it will be so easy for the rest of us."

"Go to more house parties," Nathanial suggested. "Perhaps you will be trapped in a happy marriage." He chuckled when Sebastian glared at him.

"I want to hear what Matthew has to say," Drake said, cutting off the inevitable deterioration of the discussion. Matthew sat up straight in his chair as everyone looked at him. "Since you were the one who wanted to call the meeting."

"Yes." He cleared his throat. "I ah… I have some new information that has been brought to me. An unexpected clue." Everyone's expression changed, becoming much more serious. They had all known why, but saying it aloud dampened whatever lightheartedness the jokes about the marriage mart had managed to inspire. "I was approached by a person—"

"Who?" Drake asked immediately, interrupting him.

Matthew shook his head. "It does not matter who. Their identity is not important to the information." And he had promised Johanna he would protect her mother. The best way to do that was to keep where he'd gotten the information from a secret, even from his friends. That way, they could not slip up and accidentally reveal her identity to the wrong person.

"How can that be?" Nathanial asked, frowning.

"Just let me finish. They told me that they were approached by Gregory's steward for some sleeping potions, a few weeks before the hunting lodge—"

"Sleeping potions?" Christian asked sharply.

"To ensure they slept through everything," Drake murmured, leaning back and sliding his brandy onto the table beside him as he closed his eyes. He swallowed hard, tipping his head back to rest against the back of the chair. "So that even if they were not immediately killed in the explosion..."

"They'd sleep long enough or be drowsy enough to be incapable of escape," Zachary finished. Unlike Drake, he was now leaning forward, his weariness erased, and his dark eyes burning with anger. "Who is it? Why are you protecting them?"

His voice went higher.

"Obviously, it's his wife," Nathanial said, turning to look at Gregory. "Who else would he be protecting?"

"It's not important who it was—"

"How can you say that?" Zachary slammed his fist down on the arm of the chair, making Matthew jerk in surprise. His fingers grazed over his pocket as his heart began to beat faster under the weight of Zachary's furious glare. "Of course it is important! Whoever it was must be punished!"

Matthew immediately shook his head, his heart sinking in his chest. He was doing a bad job of this. Somehow. He'd chosen the wrong words. Or maybe he should not have promised Johanna that he would protect her mother?

Or perhaps he should tell them that it *was* Johanna's mother?

But how could he do that when Zachary was calling for punishment?

And he kept getting interrupted before he could get to the truly *important* part.

"I have taken them under my protection," he said firmly.

Zachary got to his feet, slapping his hand against his thigh.

"Give me their name."

"Zachary," Drake murmured, not moving, but Zachary ignored him.

Matthew shook his head.

"Then it shall be pistols at dawn."

Matthew sucked in a breath, his heart feeling like lead in his chest as Zachary challenged him to the duel. They were illegal, but they still happened often enough that there was no mistaking what he was saying. His stomach turned over.

He did not want to duel Zachery.

One of them could easily be killed.

Surely, there had already been enough death and loss.

But looking into Zachary's red-rimmed eyes, his emotions burning in his gaze, Matthew could see that his friend did not feel the same.

Brushing his fingers over his pocket, he found it empty. He felt frozen in place, unsure of what to do. Sebastian had said he must make decisions, then deal with the consequences, just like everyone else, but this… what was he supposed to make of this?

He did not want a duel. He had promised Johanna he would protect her mother.

And it seemed like that oath of protection was going to include protecting her against his very own friends.

"Zachary," Nathanial chided, aghast.

"What?" Zachary turned in place, his fists clenched at his side. "He is *protecting* a murderer."

"No, he is protecting someone who sold sleeping potions to a murderer," Gregory corrected, rubbing his fingers across his brow. His usual smile had been wiped from his lips. "It is not the same thing."

"They still need to be punished." Zachary slammed his fist into his palm, looking around the circle at the rest of them in disbelief that no one was jumping to agree with him. He looked at Drake, who was still sitting back in his chair with his eyes closed, the rise and fall of his chest so even with long, deep breaths that he might have been sleeping, but they all knew he was not. "Drake... you loved your father..."

"I did," Drake confirmed.

"You cannot just arbitrarily punish everyone," Christian interrupted, with surprising heat. He glared at Zachary. "This plot seems to go wider and deeper than we realized, and—"

"Easy for you to say. Everyone knows your father thought you were a disappointment and your mother is dead, so you do not have to explain to her why you're unwilling to punish those involved." Zachary snapped out the words.

Everyone leaned back in their seats, and Drake's eyes flew open. Gregory hissed under his breath as Christian's face went stark white.

Zachary closed his eyes and shook his head. "I'm sorry... I... I'm sorry. I did not mean... but I stand by what I said. Someone needs to pay for what was done to our fathers."

"The right people need to pay," Drake said firmly, staring at Zachary. His expression had hardened to stone. "I do not want dupes and scapegoats; I want the person behind it all."

Zachary looked down at the floor, his shoulders tight with tension. He did not respond to Drake's remark as he sank back into his chair. Matthew got the feeling that Zachary would happily have everyone hang, even those who did not know what they had gotten themselves into. Johanna had been right to be fearful.

He brushed his fingers over his pocket again.

He did not know if he should keep going.

But he did not know if he could just stop now, either. He had already started to tell them.

"Someone has to pay," Zachary repeated, but now he sounded more forlorn than angry.

Sebastian leaned over and put his hand on Zachary's shoulder.

"They will," Sebastian said gently. He was pale, too. Like Zachary, he'd had a good relationship with his father. Matthew was thankful that he was not rushing into anger in the same way. "But Drake is right, we want the person behind the plot." He looked up at Matthew. "This person, did they know what the sleeping potions were to be used for?"

"No, of course not."

"They should have asked," Zachary replied bitterly, sitting up and shaking Sebastian's hand off his shoulder.

"Ah, yes," Christian quipped dryly. He was still pale but had rallied. What Zachary had said to him was cruel. "I'm sure that if they had asked Montblanc, he would have told them it was to assist him in murdering a bunch of nobility. He certainly would not have lied about that."

Zachary looked down at the floor again, shaking his head, but he did not say anything. He likely did not want to say anything else so harsh to Christian, not after his first outburst.

"We do not even know if *he* knew how many of our fathers were targeted," Gregory said. "Since the note he left said that he did not realize what he'd gotten himself into. How can a... well, anyone, selling sleeping potions think that they would be used in such an outrageous manner?"

"That is also not the important part," Matthew interjected. His fingers came up empty again, but it did not matter. Regardless of what Zachary, or any of the others, thought about him protecting Johanna's mother, he was going to do it, and he was going to focus them on the most important part. The actual new clue. Hopefully, it would be enough to divert Zachary's attention, though he would have to tell Johanna not to trust Zachary in the future. The thought made his chest ache, but Zachary's rage was too hot to be logical. "The important part is that the steward sent a man to pick up some of the potions, and I recognized his description."

"Another dupe?" Zachary asked sarcastically. "And what does that matter that there is now another person we have to chase down, who was not directly connected to our fathers' deaths? Or are you saying that you believe this man might be the leader of the plot?" His voice dripped with disdain, obviously still unhappy that he was not getting what he wanted.

Matthew shook his head and leaned forward.

"Because, unlike the person who came to me with the information, who had no connection to any of our fathers, this man had good reason to want my father dead."

CHAPTER FORTY-ONE

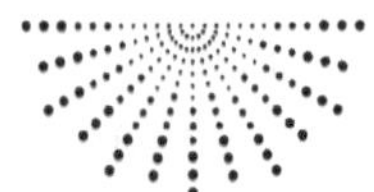

Lady Chesterham greeted Lady Stark, Johanna, and Rose with warmth and a wide smile as they congratulated her on her granddaughter's marital match.

"We owe it all to Lady Hu," Lady Chesterham enthused. "It was her keen insights that made my daughter aware of the marquess' interest in my granddaughter. He was too shy to put himself forward, but once they were formally introduced... well, they've been nigh inseparable ever since. It looks to be a very happy union."

"How lovely," Lady Stark said, patting Lady Chesterham's hand. "I am so glad to hear Lady Hu was able to help."

"Oh, yes, and she is here today with her granddaughter." Lady Chesterham beamed. "Do go on and say hello, they're a bit further into the garden. We are being a tad informal today. There are tables and sitting areas set out all throughout the space. I wanted to be a bit frivolous." She giggled, blushing, looking quite girlish despite her years, as the joy for her granddaughter filled her face.

They thanked her and went onward, down the stairs from the porch where she had met them and into the gardens.

"Ah, I see some of my friends over there. You two go on and find yours," Lady Stark said, nodding her head in the direction of a group of older ladies seated around a small table, which was piled high with various nibbles. She waved her hand at Johanna and Rose. "Enjoy yourselves."

"Thank you, Lady Stark," they chorused, grinning at each other. Rose linked her arm through Johanna's as they began walking down the pathway, heading deeper into the gardens, looking for ladies of the younger set.

"So." Rose eyed Johanna.

She sighed.

"I did not know how Matthew would take Mother's actions," Johanna explained, keeping her voice low even though they were on the move and she could not see anyone. The hedges made their conversation feel private, but it did not actually ensure such. "It was all too possible that he might blame her for his father's death and me for keeping it from him."

"You did not need to protect me." Rose shook her head.

"But I did. Because if something happened to Mother and me..." She let her voice trail off. Rose would be the one to take care of Micah, Bridget, and Charlotte, and she knew it. "I knew I could trust you to keep them safe but only if you were kept out of it."

Rose made a derogatory noise, though she did not answer right away, obviously thinking about Johanna's point. After a moment, she gave herself a little shake.

"Well. Do not do it again."

"Hopefully, I will never have cause to. I do not think it is very often that someone will approach anyone in our family with an offer that will make them an accessory to... something like that." At least she certainly hoped not. Once was more than enough.

A rustle of leaves was the only warning they got before Tiffany came through an opening in the bushes that Johanna had not immediately noticed, making both her and Rose jump.

"There you two are!" Tiffany beamed at them. "We saw you arrive, and I came to fetch you, as you would not likely find the way otherwise."

"We would not have," Johanna admitted as Tiffany turned, leading them through the cleverly hidden opening. There was more than enough space to walk through, but it was set at a diagonal to the pathways, so that it was very difficult to see while walking along. If Tiffany had not come out of it, Johanna would not have seen it at all.

"How did you see us?" Rose inquired.

"Oh, we have the perfect view of every arrival," Tiffany said cheerfully. "And you two do stand out in your purple and red today. Johanna is like a lily, and Rose is… well, like a rose."

"Too true," Johanna replied, glancing down at her lavender-and-white-striped dress. Rose's gown was a deep red, though a brighter hue than she had been wearing before Lady Stark helped revamp her wardrobe. "Does that make you a bluebell?"

As usual, Tiffany was garbed in a pretty shade of blue, which brought out the highlights in her hair and the color in her cheeks. She laughed as they broke through to the next opening in the hedges, and Johanna marveled at the surrounds. It was a square space, between all the bushes, and it did indeed have a splendid view of Lady Chesterham greeting her guests if one looked up in that direction.

Rather than a table, there was an array of blankets and cushions set out for a picnic, complete with baskets of refreshments.

Lady Astrid sat in the middle, Mei on one side of her and Delilah on the other, while Kalina waited opposite them. If they were describing the ladies by flowers, Lady Astrid was a bright orange tulip with red tips, Delilah a stunning sunflower, and Kalina a pink rose. Johanna could not think of a flower that was the shade of green as Mei's outfit, but she was put in mind of a holly bush, as there were tiny red embroidered accents dotted over the fabric.

"Ladies, welcome to the cabal," Lady Astrid said, lifting a champagne flute. Her eyes sparkled with mischief. "We have escaped the constraints of Society and are doing as we please."

"How have we escaped when we are still at the tea party?" Rose asked, amused, as she and Johanna joined the group. The cushions were very comfortable, though it was a bit odd to be sitting on the ground. It reminded Johanna of the happier times in her childhood, which felt so very far away now.

"According to Lady Astrid, no one knows we are here, and it is very difficult to be overheard from this particular spot if we keep our voices low," Kalina explained with a smile. "Indeed, any conversations *we* have heard from passersby have been very muffled."

"Which means we can talk about whatever we wish," Lady Astrid said wickedly. "As I am soon to be a married woman, I am endeavoring for Tiffany, Kalina, and Delilah to explain the delights of the marital bedroom." She waved the champagne flute in the air as Delilah shook her head.

"You are terrible," Delilah said to Lady Astrid with a throaty laugh. She had the most amazing voice, sultry and beguiling even when she was scolding her friend. As the eldest of them, and the only widow, she was likely the only one who would dare say such a thing to Lady Astrid. "As if you do not know enough already."

Lady Astrid smiled and took a sip of her champagne. "Well, what is good for the gander is good for the goose."

"I believe it is the other way round," Delilah murmured.

"But what do you mean?" Tiffany paused as she reached for a crumpet, her hand hovering in midair as her attention was arrested by Lady Astrid's statement.

"Oh, do not look at me like that." Lady Astrid threw a napkin at Tiffany, though the air caught the thin linen, and it did not make it even halfway, falling atop a plate of scones instead. "My all-important virginity is still intact. I am just saying, there are ways to enjoy oneself that do not require the loss of it."

"There are, but I think you are still not supposed to be indulging in them," Kalina replied, clearly amused and not quite as scandalized as Tiffany. She glanced over at Rose and Mei. "Besides, I believe this topic is not at all appropriate for *everyone* here."

"I do not mind," Rose said immediately, taking the glass of tea that Tiffany offered her. "I know far more about the pitfalls than the pleasures of such engagements, I will admit."

"Who are you indulging with?" Delilah asked Lady Astrid, but she just smiled enigmatically.

"Drake is sowing his wild oats," she replied, bypassing the question entirely. "Why should I not? I have to know about his exploits, and what he does not know will not hurt him."

"I am not certain of that," Delilah muttered, shaking her head. She turned to Johanna and Rose. "How go things with St. Albans? I always thought he was the sweetest of the group. Good husband material, if you can tolerate his need to flip that blasted coin for everything."

"He really flips it for *everything?*" Mei asked, appearing intrigued, before Johanna could answer. "I thought it was a gimmick."

"No gimmick," Johanna said, shaking her head. "There are some small decisions he makes, but for most things… yes, he did."

"Did?" Tiffany asked, her hazel eyes widening.

"Did. He lost it the other day."

Delilah and Lady Astrid both sat up with gasps, which made Mei's interest even more acute. She was the only one still smiling; even Kalina looked somewhat alarmed, and she did not know Matthew very well at all.

"Lost it?" Delilah said, clearly aghast. "My goodness… is he well?"

"Is he shut up in the house and refusing to come out?" Lady Astrid asked.

"No, he is dealing with it remarkably well, I think," Johanna said, immediately feeling defensive of her husband, though she internally acknowledged that their reactions were not unwarranted. "In fact, he called a meeting with the other dukes today."

"He did? Without flipping his coin for it?" Delilah's usually low voice had gone rather higher than usual with her surprise.

"He did," Johanna said firmly, then took a deep breath. "My mother was able to give him a clue in regard to their investigation."

There was no need to say exactly which investigation; all the ladies immediately knew what she was talking about, of course.

Tiffany scowled.

"Oh, so that was the message that came in. Gregory said he was going to White's while I am at tea." She huffed. "I wish they would stop leaving us out of things."

"Drake's doing, I'll warrant." Lady Astrid sniffed. "Lucifer does not want us involved. It's not ladylike."

"Well, I have no reason to be involved, but I find I am too curious about what your mother told Matthew to not ask," Delilah said. "Whatever it was, it must have been quite important for him to decide to call a meeting, especially without his coin."

"It is." Johanna took a deep breath and deliberately did not look at Tiffany as she relayed her mother's possible part in the death of Tiffany's father. Out of the corner of her eye, she saw Kalina reach over to hold Tiffany's hand as she spoke, but she did not dare look up to see the duchess' expression. If she did, she might never be able to get through it. She told them about her mother's part, about Matthew questioning her this morning, and the revelation that he recognized the description her mother gave.

"Wait." Tiffany's voice was sorrowful but did not hold the anger Johanna had feared. "A scar through his beard? Here?"

Johanna had to face her now to see where Tiffany was indicating. But, like her voice, there was no anger in Tiffany's expression. Grief, yes, but nothing of blame or vengefulness.

"Yes, I believe so." Johanna glanced at Rose, who nodded. "We have only what Matthew had to say about it."

"You recognize the description as well?" Lady Astrid asked sharply. She had put down her champagne glass, and all the easygoing mischief was gone from her demeanor, her focus entirely on Johanna's story.

"I believe so. It might not be the same man, but... there is *a* man who now works in the stables on the estate who does fit that description. My father hired him the year before... the year before. I do not know if I ever got his name; we were not introduced or any such thing." Tiffany scraped her teeth across her lower lip. "You said the old St. Albans threw him and his wife out of their home?"

"Yes. That is what Matthew said."

Tiffany shook her head, her eyes filling with tears as her face paled. "The man we have does not have a wife. He is a widower."

"Which would give him even more of a reason to hate Matthew's father and be willing to act in revenge," Lady Astrid murmured. "Bold to find employment and assist in murdering your new employer, though."

"Unless he did not know what he was getting into," Kalina pointed out. She looked at Tiffany. "That is what happened with Gregory's steward, is it not? He said he did not know the full breadth of what he had become involved in."

"That is true." Tiffany took a deep breath and shook her head. "I do not know very much about him. It might not be the same man."

But what a coincidence if it was not.

"We need to tell our husbands," Kalina said.

"Why?" Lady Astrid asked. "They are leaving us out of everything."

"Drake might be leaving you out, but Nathanial tells me everything afterward, even when we are not invited to the discussion." Kalina glanced at Tiffany, who nodded.

"As does Gregory," Tiffany added. "Besides, at the very least, we'll need to tell my brother. He's the best one to go and question the man. It is not as though any of us can just hie off to Bolton Manor and question the staff."

Lady Astrid sighed. "There is that, I suppose. But I think we should come up with some kind of plan to ensure they cannot continue to cut us out of the investigation."

The discussion continued, though Johanna stayed quiet for most of it. Her only concern had been whether Tiffany would be upset with her mother, but it did not seem to have even crossed the other duchess' mind. Which was a huge relief.

They kept having to lower their voices as they heard passersby coming along the paths beside their hidden spot to ensure privacy. Eventually, Kalina suggested they decamp to the home Nathanial had rented for the Season to continue their discussion, but Tiffany pointed out that she had too many nosy sisters-in-law and suggested they come to Clarence House instead.

Lady Stark seemed pleased that Johanna had become friends with the other duchesses and immediately waved her and Rose off, while she remained with her friends.

Despite protesting that they needed no such involvement in the investigation, Lady Astrid persuaded Delilah and Mei to come as well, pointing out that an outside perspective could be handy, as well as their keen minds.

All in all, Johanna's confession had gone rather well. The rush of relief she felt as she sat in the Duchess of Clarence's carriage, Tiffany as friendly as ever to her, was acute.

She had been worried over nothing.

CHAPTER FORTY-TWO

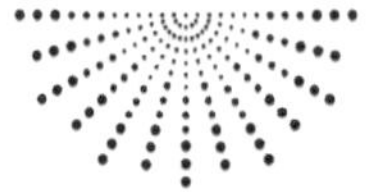

"Who wanted your father dead?" Drake asked, immediately intent on Matthew's statement, which Matthew was grateful for. If he could focus the others on the man with the grudge against his father, rather than Johanna's mother, that was for the best.

Zachary still appeared sullen, though his ire had been dampened by cooler heads. Even so, Drake also appeared to be struggling, but he was doing a better job of hiding it. Sebastian was silent, staring at a painting on the wall of a huntsman atop a horse with a dog beside him.

Those three had had good relationships with their fathers, unlike the rest of them.

"His name was Aaron Heywood, and he was a tenant on our estate. His family had been on that land and in their cottage for generations, but there was a year when he was unable to tithe the required amount, and…" Matthew clenched his jaw, turning his head aside. "You know what my father was like. Threw him and his wife out. I did look for him, for a bit, but not very hard. I had not thought about him until I heard the description of the messenger who collected the second delivery of potions."

"Well." Christian cleared his throat, rubbing his hands over his thighs and pointedly *not* looking at Zachary. "He sounds like a far more likely suspect who might actually know something than some poor person who merely sold the potions with the best of intentions."

Even though he snorted in derision, Zachary did not look at Christian, either.

"Speaking of suspects, Zachary, did you ever ask your uncle about whether he was the one who suggested that Cornwall invite Nathanial's father to the hunting lodge?" Christian asked airily, as if it were not a particularly pointed question, especially at this juncture in the conversation.

Unsurprisingly, Zachary bristled in response, sitting up straight as a poker.

"I did. He thinks he might have been, though he admitted it was so long ago he could not remember to be sure, but he knew there was some conversation about it. Apparently, Hereford had boasted of his win, so it was not uncommon knowledge." Zachary sniffed. "And my uncle had no reason to want Hereford dead."

"No more than a common potion maker would have to want any of our fathers dead," Christian pointed out. "Your uncle is far closer to our father's deaths by comparison."

Now, Zachary did turn to glower directly at Christian, who was still not looking at him.

"I, for one, am not going to blame Matthew for wanting to protect his wife or anyone else who has joined his household," Gregory said stoutly. "Especially since, as he said, they had no motive to harm any of our fathers and certainly could not have guessed what a sleeping potion might have been used for. And while I might not have cared very much for the demise of my own father, you can be sure that I still want justice for *my* wife's father."

"Indeed," Nathanial murmured. "It is hardly any secret that my father's death was not a hardship on my behalf, but I still want justice for those of you who did grieve. Not to mention, I would like the security of knowing that nothing more will be coming for me and mine, and until we know who was behind the dastardly plot and why, there is no such assurance."

The sound of exhalations echoed around the room as more than one of them sighed. Matthew included. He wanted the assurance for Johanna and any children she might bear as well.

"I am not blaming him for wanting to protect his wife," Zachary snapped. "Though, in the interest of justice, I might make a different decision."

"Even if Delilah was your wife and not Lady Annabelle?" Christian retorted, making everyone suck in a breath very much the same way as they had when Zachary had brought up Christian's father.

Zachary actually rocked back in his chair as if Christian had struck him. Sinclair chittered above his head, the first sound the little monkey had made since the conversation started, and climbed atop it, stroking Zachary's hair.

Christian closed his eyes and swallowed hard. "I..." His voice trailed off, as if he could not bring himself to actually say anything. Which was quite normal for Christian. Apologies, arguments in general, were not something he usually engaged in.

"We are square," Zachary muttered, waving his hand at Christian to dismiss the need for any apology, then running it over his face before reaching up to let Sinclair climb onto it. He brought the monkey to his chest, which now seemed quite sunken in, as he hunched over it, leaning against the wide back of his chair.

"We need to work together," Drake said firmly, his jaw working with emotion. "Of course, Matthew cannot tarnish his honor by allowing any of his household to come under suspicion. Nor would it be right or fair to punish anyone for ignorance. We should be grateful we have a new clue. A new name to pursue."

"That is something at least," Gregory said, nodding. "I will ask my current steward about this Aaron Heywood. Since he assisted Mont-blanc in procuring the potions, Montblanc must have known him somehow."

"Now?" Zachary asked, lifting his head.

"Well... I do not see any reason to wait. Perhaps we could all return to Clarence House," Gregory suggested. "That way you can hear whatever it is my steward has to say, and if there is any information on Heywood, we can take immediate action."

Which would be good if there; Zachary was clearly chafing at the bit to find something to do—and someone to blame. Matthew wished he had his coin. Wished he had some sort of guidance in what to do or what to say that would help.

If Zachary persisted in his tack against Johanna, it would not only break apart their friendship, if the others took sides it might very well be the end of their entire cadre.

JOHANNA

The ladies had just sat down in the drawing room of Clarence House when the front door opened again, and masculine voices filled the front hall, making all of them look up. The door between the two areas was open, so they could see the entire group of dukes that had just walked through the door.

"Blast," Lady Astrid murmured from where she was seated beside Johanna. "So much for privacy."

As if aware of so many eyes on them, the Duke of Ormonde turned and looked through the door, causing Lady Astrid to bristle in her seat as their gazes clashed before he turned away to let the other dukes know they were not alone. Now all the dukes turned to look into the drawing room.

Johanna immediately sought out Matthew's face and relaxed when she saw him. It took her a moment, as he came hurrying into the room to come stand behind the couch where she was sitting, putting his hand on her shoulder, to realize his expression was more strained than joyful. A frisson of alarm went through her; she had hoped he would be more cheerful.

The other dukes followed him in.

Like Matthew, Nathanial and Gregory immediately made for where their wives were seated. Sebastian followed Gregory, moving to stand near his friend and sister. Drake stalked to lean against the fireplace, in a position where he could easily glare at Lady Astrid and she at him. Christian moved to stand beside Nathanial, between the chairs where Kalina and Rose were seated.

Only the Duke of Grafton hung back, his face like a storm cloud when his dark eyes met hers from across the room. He hovered by the door, stony-faced and emanating menace despite the tiny monkey seated on his shoulder, clinging to his hair. Johanna shrank back from his gaze, her heart beginning to pound wildly in her chest at the anger she saw there.

She could see Delilah, sitting poker-straight in the chair to the right of the couch, frowning at the duke in the doorway.

"Cut it out, Zachary," Matthew snapped, his fingers tightening on Johanna's shoulders.

"What are you all doing here?" Kalina asked, her voice cool and calm. "Not that we are unhappy to see you. And why is Zachary glaring at Johanna?"

Lady Astrid leaned forward on the couch, so Johanna could only see the back of her red hair, putting herself bodily between the Duke of Grafton and Johanna.

"Well…" Gregory started to say, then coughed, looking over at Matthew and Johanna. "We were meeting to discuss the matter of our fathers—"

"And leaving us out of it again," Lady Astrid snapped. Her head whipped around to pin Drake with a glare, though she kept her body where it was, so the Duke of Grafton's gaze was still obscured if he was trying to look at Johanna. "I can only imagine whose idea that was. But Johanna has already told us everything."

Mei patted Johanna's hand reassuringly as Johanna let out a long, slow breath.

She knew why the Duke of Grafton was glaring at her. Matthew had told *them* everything as well. And, unlike Matthew, Grafton obviously blamed her and her mother. Tears sparked in her eyes as her throat clogged. She had not meant to cause a division among the group of friends.

Yet what else could she have done?

She'd had to confess.

"Of course she has." Drake sounded more resigned than anything else. He shook his head. "Well, do not worry, we are handling it."

"How?" Lady Astrid asked, smiling sweetly. "Where are you beginning your search for Aaron Heywood?"

Something in her voice made all the men look at her, and Drake straightened, his brow furrowing.

"What do you know?" he asked, though it was really more of a demand.

"Know? What could we possibly know?" Lady Astrid looked around at the other ladies, her eyes wide. "We are but mere women. Surely, we could not have anything useful for such all-knowing and powerful men. You do not need us at all."

Tiffany covered her lips with her hands, but a giggle still escaped her mouth. Drake looked as though he wanted to throw himself across the room and throttle his betrothed, who smiled sweetly at him.

"Ladies." Christian smiled, his most charming smile, and Johanna felt her own tension ease as he swept his gaze around the room to include everyone… well, everyone except Rose, who refused to turn to look up at him. No wonder he was known as the Adonis of the *ton*. When he flashed that smile, he must send ladies' hearts fluttering. Even she was not entirely unaffected, despite her preference for Matthew's joyful grin. "Please, we would be in your debt if you have any information you can share with us."

"Yes, you will," Lady Astrid replied tartly, though her words and the tartness were directed at Drake. He crossed his arms over his chest as he continued to glare at his betrothed. "Tiffany?"

"I think I recognize the description of Mr. Heywood," Tiffany said hesitantly. "There is a man in the stables, at home, who matches it, down to the scar on his face."

"Our home?"

"Which home?"

Gregory and Sebastian spoke at the same time and then glanced at each other. Tiffany twisted around in her seat to look up at her brother.

"At Somersham Hall." She looked apologetically at Gregory. "My old home. Father hired him."

"I… do not know if I have seen him," Sebastian said, shaking his head.

"Well, you were in London at the time, I believe." Tiffany faced front again. "And you did not spend as much time on the estate as I did. As far as I know, he is still there. I only noticed him because of the scar on his beard and because he works well with the animals."

"Well. That is good news," Sebastian said. "That means we have a place to start. I will leave for the Hall immediately."

"You cannot. You will miss the Manchester Ball tomorrow," Tiffany said immediately. "You cannot miss such an important event —and it will cause a great deal of talk if you rush back to the estate for no good reason, especially after… after sending Mother to the countryside."

"She is right," Delilah said, breaking into the conversation with her throaty voice. "There has already been some talk among the ladies about your mother leaving the Season so soon and so suddenly. No one believes it is for her health, by the by. If you do not wish to focus attention on her absence, you cannot miss major events that you were already planning to attend."

"Could you send for him to come to London?" Kalina asked, looking around.

"No." Nathanial shook his head. "We are trying not to draw attention to our investigation. If Sebastian sends for him, it would be completely out of character, and it might even cause him to flee. The same with leaving abruptly. He has already been working in your stables for years. He will keep for a while longer until you can leave for a few days without suspicion."

"Not just you," Drake said. "One of us should go with you. Zachary, perhaps."

"You are just trying to get me out of London." The Duke of Grafton's voice was harsher than Johanna had ever heard before, without any of its usual elegance.

"If that is what you need to cool your temper, yes."

"Yes, of course, *I* am the problem. Not the person who was *actually* involved in our fathers' murders. Not the person who provided the murderers with the means to ensure our fathers burned to death."

Johanna shrank back in her seat as Lady Astrid stood up in front of her, blocking Johanna from Grafton's view with her skirts. Matthew came round the couch as well, to stand at its side where he could hold Johanna's hand, glaring at Grafton from over Lady Astrid's shoulder.

"You are not seriously blaming Johanna," Rose said, obviously aghast.

"Why? Was it you who provided the sleeping potions?" The sharpness in Grafton's voice was quick and cutting.

Frozen in her seat, unsure of what to do or say, heart pounding in her chest, Johanna was relieved to see Christian step forward, blocking Rose from Grafton's view the same way Lady Astrid and Matthew were guarding her.

"You are bang out of line, Zachary," Christian said sharply. "Again."

She could hear the soft chitter of the monkey on the man's shoulder, almost like it was trying to soothe the irate duke.

"I… apologize." The strain in his voice made Johanna's heart go out to him. "I am not myself. I need… I need to go. I cannot be here right now. I need to go."

The pain he felt was clear in his words, and more tears sprang up in Johanna's eyes in sympathy.

The sound of his footsteps on the marble floor of the hall echoed in the silence of the room. The front door opened and closed. Johanna looked away and caught a glimpse of Delilah's face, agony in every line of her expression, as she watched her former lover go.

Then the other woman blinked, and her polite social mask descended once again.

CHAPTER FORTY-THREE

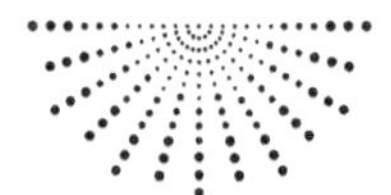

The day had been exhausting, and Matthew was very happy to be home with his grandmother and Johanna's family for supper rather than out with his friends. The impromptu gathering had dispersed not long after Zachary's dramatic exit. Matthew had wanted to go after him, but he had not wanted to leave Johanna, and without his coin to help him, he'd decided that his wife had to take precedence.

Thankfully, unlike his friends, none of the ladies seemed upset with Johanna. Including Tiffany.

He'd noticed that Drake and Sebastian had hung back from her, but that could have been for other reasons, even if it was partly due to their grief. Matthew would not push them.

Hopefully, things would soon return to normal. Emotions had been heightened today. He hoped Zachary would calm down.

Regardless of whether he did or not, Matthew would be there to protect Johanna and her family. He did not believe Zachary would truly send the authorities after her mother… he was angry and lashing out, but he was not that far gone.

In the meantime, Matthew would do whatever he needed to ensure his wife's happiness. He glanced at her beside him at the dinner table and could not help but smile as she listened to Micah enthusiastically expounding about the book his tutor had assigned him today. Apparently, Micah had a great love for the stoics.

Rose was listening to Charlotte and Bridget take turns describing their lessons—Bridget was far more enthusiastic about them now that they'd started. And his grandmother and Johanna's mother sat beside each other, discussing the latest fashions and his grandmother's opinions on how they should outfit Lady Ashmore tomorrow. She seemed to have accepted her fate as his grandmother's latest project.

Johanna's hand touched his, and Matthew blinked out of his observation of the table at large.

"Is everything all right?" she asked softly, leaning toward him. He caught her fingers in his.

"Everything is perfect." He squeezed her fingers. "I was just thinking how happy I am with our supper table. I would much rather be here than at any ball... or anywhere else, really."

Tomorrow, they would have to attend the Manchester Ball, of course. The social whirl was a demanding mistress. But right now, he was so very content just like this.

Johanna's smile in return was brilliant.

"As would I," she murmured back before Micah said something to garner her attention again.

After supper, they all retired to the drawing room for a rousing game of charades. Charlotte was easily the most dramatic of the group, though Bridget ran a close second. Johanna was terrible, to everyone's amusement and gentle teasing. His grandmother and mother-in-law did not join in, but they did thoroughly enjoy themselves laughing at the antics of the younger generations.

The evening was over far too quickly, with Miss Swift escorting Charlotte and Bridget up to bed, while Micah trotted dutifully after them. Lady Ashmore walked more slowly, with Rose and Johanna by her side.

Leaning against his chair, Matthew sipped his brandy as the room emptied out. Once the ladies were gone, he was going to sit down and enjoy a few moments of peace and quiet before he followed his wife upstairs.

His grandmother paused beside him. She shook her head.

"You do have the devil's own luck, I swear," she said.

Raising his eyebrow, Matthew looked down at her.

"What do you mean?"

"Well, I truly did not think you could flip a coin for love, but here you are," she replied, chuckling as she reached up to pat his cheek. "Married and in love. Johanna is a true delight, but I cannot countenance what massive luck you had to have things all fall out this way. I suppose there is no end to it."

With that, she left him there, standing and blinking.

Married and in love.

He'd had the thought, of course, multiple times.

Even tried to flip his coin over it.

But to have his grandmother confirm it.

It was not just him. Not just in his head. She would not say it unless she also saw what was truly between him and Johanna.

Love.

He was in love with his wife.

Yes. Yes, he was. And he did not need his coin to tell him so.

Matthew lifted his glass to his lips and took a long draw as another thought occurred to him.

He had not reached for his coin all night. Had he? He could not remember. Which was a kind of shocking discovery in and of itself. He must not have, because if he had, surely he would have noticed its absence. As he had done previously.

But once he was home, with his wife and his family, he must not have felt the need for it.

How very curious.

So.

What did he want to do now?

I want my wife.

Matthew threw back the rest of his drink and set it down on the drink tray. He wanted his wife; therefore, he should have his wife.

Grinning, he headed for the stairs.

JOHANNA

After seeing her mother to her room, she and Rose hugged and said goodnight as well. It had been quite a day, and Johanna could feel herself flagging. All she wanted to do right now was curl up with her husband. To feel him against her. The safety and security of him wrapped around her.

There was a sense of relief in having everything out in the open, even though the Duke of Grafton had taken it poorly. She had noticed that Ormonde and Bolton were more distant with her as well. Johanna did not blame any of them. Matthew had explained on the way home from Clarence House that he had not told them where his information came from, though they had guessed it must be her or one of her family members.

Which explained why Grafton's anger had been focused on her. He wanted someone, anyone, to focus his emotions on.

Understanding made it only marginally easier to bear.

She clung to the knowledge that Tiffany had not changed in her behavior toward Johanna at all. Neither had any of the other ladies. They were her friends in the truest sense of the word.

Her husband, rather than Nettie, was waiting for her in her room, wearing a dressing gown. Somehow, he had beaten her up here and gotten undressed. Johanna's lips curved into a smile when she saw him standing by her vanity, and she closed her bedroom door behind her, locking it.

"Are you my ladies' maid this evening?" she asked teasingly, her skirts swishing as she walked toward him.

His eyes sparked with warmth and hungry interest.

"Yes, my lady," he murmured, reaching for her. Johanna sank into his embrace, tilting her head back to receive his kiss. Pressing her hands against his chest, she let herself fall into the heady embrace. Heat flared within her as his hands moved over her.

Her husband. Her knight-in-shining armor. Her protector.

Despite the bonds between him and his friends, he'd kept his promise of protection today. Put himself between her and the Duke of Grafton's anger.

When his lips raised from hers, tenderness in his eyes, Johanna stared up at him and gathered her own courage.

"I love you," she whispered. His eyes widened in surprise, and she lifted her fingers to his lips before he could reply. "I do not expect you to return my feelings nor need you feel compelled to respond, but I… I had to tell you. It is not only because you rescued me, but because of your kindness. Your warmth. The way you make me laugh. The very essence of who you are. I do not care that your coin chose me; I only care that we are together."

Grabbing hold of her wrist so she could not move her hand, Matthew kissed the tips of her fingers. His gaze bore into hers as he pulled them away from his mouth.

"I love you," he said.

Johanna frowned at him even as her heart did a little skip inside her chest, wishing it was true.

"You need not say it just because I did."

"I know. But it is the truth. Even my grandmother recognizes it. I love you."

"You cannot."

Tilting his head to the side, he lifted one eyebrow at her.

"Why not?"

"Because I have not done anything for you."

A deep chuckle rumbled through his chest. "Did you not just finish telling me that you love me for reasons besides what I have done for you?"

"I…" Johanna's chest tightened, and she blinked, rapidly trying to sort through her thoughts. Yes, she had just said that. And meant it. But that was about him, not about her.

"I love you for your sweetness." He kissed her fingertips again. "The way you are always watching over your siblings." He kissed the palm of her hand, and Johanna sucked in a breath. "Your courage." He pulled her arm higher, so his lips could reach her wrist. "Your acceptance of me… not many people can accept me the way I am, but you see straight through me." His lips moved back to hers. "When I flipped my coin at the auction house, I did not ask it if I should rescue you… My thought was whether or not I should marry you."

Johanna closed her eyes as his lips brushed over hers.

"Even then, that was what I wished."

"I am glad of it," she whispered back. Warmth filled her chest—a happy, joyful feeling that made her feel both weaker and stronger all at once. "I love you."

It felt so easy, so natural to say now.

She wanted to hear him say it back. Again.

Now, when she would be able to believe him.

"I love you," he murmured. "My good girl. My sweet kitten."

The emotion in Johanna's heart swelled, her insides turning to melted butter at his endearments.

Their lips met.

Clothing began to fall to the floor.

"I love you." He said the words over and over again, dropping kisses along her body as it was bared to him, whispering the words against her skin. Heat sizzled everywhere he touched her. Caressed her. Kissed her.

When they finally made it to the bed, she was whimpering from the desire that tightened her insides. She wanted to feel him within her, to be as close to him as possible. Matthew rolled onto his back, setting her atop him.

Blushing furiously, Johanna had to impale herself on his shaft, his hands full of her breasts, as he stared up at her, watching her move. It felt shocking… and at the same time, watching his expression as he strained and groaned beneath her, feeling him thrust up inside her, being able to control their movements… Johanna found herself reaching her pinnacle faster than she ever had before.

But he did not let her stop. His hands gripped her hips, moving her when she was already breathless and gasping from the flare of passion, sending crackling bolts of pleasure shooting through her.

"Matthew!" She did not know if she cried out in ecstasy or protest as the sensations became too intense to bear. Her nails raked over his chest, and he let out a sound somewhere between a groan and a growl before flipping her onto her back. His body was still between her thighs, his cock still hard inside her. She wrapped her arms and legs around him as he took control and thrust hard and fast into her slick heat.

Exquisite agony spiraled inside her as the onslaught of pleasure rode the fine edge of pain, leaving her caught between them in a tug-of-war on her senses until he finally buried himself inside her. He gasped against her neck as he rocked forward, rubbing his hard body against her sensitive flesh, throbbing as he emptied his pleasure within her.

Johanna shuddered beneath him, gasping for breath. His heavy weight pressed down on her, pinning her to the bed. Even though it made it a little harder to breathe, Johanna did not mind at all. She closed her eyes, turning her head toward him as she ran her hand down the center of his back.

There was no place she felt safer than in his arms, his body making a haven around her.

She wished they could stay like this forever.

CHAPTER FORTY-FOUR

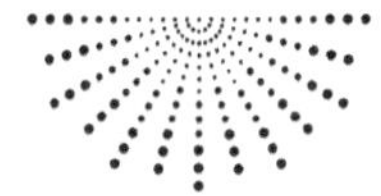

MATTHEW

There was a small crowd of ladies around his mother-in-law. She'd begged off attending the Manchester Ball, but once she received her first round of new dresses, Grandmama had insisted she return to Society with them. So far, her appearance at Lady Jersey's rout was a massive success. Lady Jersey and Lady Cowper had both remembered her and been thrilled to see her return to Society—Lady Jersey, particularly, chuffed that her event had been chosen for the honor.

Johanna was with her friends, only a small group of gentlemen willing to dare the group of young but powerful ladies. Lord Boyd was there, standing next to Rose and endeavoring her to talk. Across the room, Christian was glaring at Lord Boyd, but he was surrounded by a gaggle of young, pretty things all hoping to catch a duke. Matthew wondered if he was ever going to admit that he was far more interested in Johanna's cousin than in the debutantes who were vying for his attention.

Of course, it would be a difficult road, even for a duke, to push Society to accept an illegitimate wife. On the other hand, Rose certainly had many connections that would assist in establishing her.

Christian tended to take the easy road, though. Perhaps, despite his obvious attraction to Rose, he thought the path too difficult.

Scanning the crowd, Matthew felt a spot between his shoulder blades itch. He turned and looked up. Sebastian had been hiding on the balcony last time… tonight, apparently, it was Zachary's turn.

His fingers brushed over his empty pocket.

It still happened once or twice a day.

Should he go speak with Zachary?

They had not talked since the day Zachary had stalked out of Clarence House. He'd been at the Manchester Ball with his fiancée, but he'd avoided all his friends while there and remained glued to Lady Annabelle's side with a blank expression on his face.

Matthew wanted to know what Zachary was going to do. Therefore, he needed to go speak with Zachary. Sitting back and waiting to find out did not suit him.

Sighing, Matthew made his way up to the balcony.

Zachary was there, Monkey Sinclair perched on his shoulder. His hand stroked over the monkey's back, from the tiny creature's head to the tip of his tail, as he stared down at the ballroom below them. The monkey saw Matthew coming and chittered, drawing Zachary's attention away from his observation.

He turned his head. Saw Matthew. Sighed. Returned to his study of the ballroom.

Matthew walked up to stand beside him, looking down at the pretty swirling patterns the dancers made on the floor. Bright clumps of ladies' dresses dotted the edges of the room, interspersed with the gentlemen's more sober clothing. Well, other than a few of the dandies, who were just as brightly and dramatically attired as some of the ladies.

They stood there in silence for a long moment.

"No Lady Annabelle this evening?" Matthew asked. He tried to track where Zachary was looking, assuming that he would see Delilah… but she was nowhere in sight. The canary-yellow gown she'd donned for the rout was very easy to spot.

Instead, it appeared that Zachary was focused on the group of ladies around Matthew's mother-in-law.

Damn.

"She is coming from a supper party at the Hoods." Zachary dropped his hand away from Monkey Sinclair, bracing both of them on the balcony just as Matthew was. "It was Johanna's mother, wasn't it?"

Though it was phrased as a question, it was a statement.

This time, Matthew did not reach for his coin, but he felt the impulse to. He did not know what to say. Zachary seemed sad, not angry, but that could turn on a dime. He'd seen it. Yet at the same time, he did want to mend the friendship. Zachary was hurting, perhaps the most out of all of them.

"My mother is not here tonight," Zachary said quietly, still watching Johanna's mother. "She is unwell." There was something about the way he said it that made the word 'unwell' sound very weighty. As if he was trying to say something altogether different.

"She is sick?"

"She is unwell," Zachary repeated. Sighed. "Some days are better than others. Today was… very bad." His voice was soft. Low. The words even and without any emotion. As though if he showed even the smallest hint of feeling, it would break him wide open. "I am doing everything I can to keep my own mother alive. I have given up Delilah. I am marrying Lady Annabelle. I have sacrificed everything I wanted to hold on to the one parent I have left. I will not take anyone else's mother from them. You and Johanna, her mother, have nothing to fear from me."

Matthew's chest ached in sympathy. He could not remember his mother. Was it better that way, or would it be worse to know his mother and love her and have her in such a state that he had to upend his own life for the sake of her happiness? Because she so greatly desired to follow his father into death that she might take matters into her own hands?

He could not imagine what Zachary was going through.

Reaching out his hand, he put it on Zachary's back, just below where Monkey Sinclair sat on his shoulder. The monkey cocked its head at Matthew and chittered again. Maybe it was his imagination, but even its chitter sounded sad. He wondered if perhaps naming the monkey after Sinclair—Zachary's closest friend among the dukes whose unexpected and tragic death had spurred them to quicken their haste to find brides—had backfired on Zachary. Being the duke meant that he had a daily reminder that his father was gone—had the monkey become a daily reminder of the other great loss in Zachary's life?

"We are all doing the best we can," he said softly. "If there is anything I can do for you…"

"Flip your coin to know if I have made the right decision or made a right mess?" Zachary managed the curve up one side of his mouth in the facsimile of a small smile. "Although I know you claim it does not work for others, it did predict Nathanial and Kalina."

"I have lost it."

"Lost it?" Zachary's almost-smile dropped, and he studied Matthew for a long moment. There was sympathy in his dark eyes. "I am sorry to hear that."

"Thank you." Matthew looked out over the ballroom. "I seem to be managing well enough now. I make a choice. I live with the consequences. Just like the rest of you mere mortals."

That actually managed to get a chuckle out of Zachary, which eased some of the tension in Matthew. He hated to see his friend so distressed.

"Yes, yes, we do." Zachary sighed and waved his hand. "Go. Lady Annabelle will be here soon, and I need to gather myself before my fiancée arrives."

He said 'my fiancée' the same way another man might say 'my executioner.'

Matthew patted the back of his shoulder and turned away, but not before he saw Zachary's gaze lock in on a splash of bright canary yellow that had just rejoined the others in the ballroom.

JOHANNA

The evening had been a roaring success, much to Johanna's relief and her mother's delight. Being back in Society, reconnecting with her old acquaintances, had allowed Johanna to see a side of her mother that she was not sure she'd ever known. While her memories were full of love from both her parents, that was different from seeing her mother in the social whirl.

It was good to see her smiling again, laughing again.

She leaned against Matthew's shoulder on the way home, while her mother and Lady Stark compared notes from the evening, the carriage rocking her between Matthew and Rose. Poor Rose, who was doing her best to set herself up as Johanna's companion and firmly on the shelf, again, yet found herself being pursued by more than one gentleman. Lord Boyd had even managed to coax her into a dance at one point before the Duke of Montagu had joined their circle, bringing with him a bevy of young ladies and forcing all the present gentlemen to divide their attentions.

It had been rather amusing to watch, although Rose was exasperated. She was probably even happier to be going home than Johanna was.

"We are here," Matthew murmured.

Johanna lifted her head from his shoulder as the carriage rocked to a stop. She covered her yawn with her hand.

A few minutes later, Matthew was brushing his lips over hers as he left her at her bedroom door, his voice a low murmur. "Come to my room once your dress is off."

Nodding, Johanna stifled another yawn as she let herself into her room. Nettie was not there, but she was likely already on her way. The soft flickering light made for deep shadows in the recesses of the room, and Johanna nearly screamed as a white specter unfurled from her window seat and glided toward her. Her heart pounded madly in her chest as the instinct to flee gripped her before her mind caught up and realized what was happening.

That was no spirit, only her youngest sister.

"Charlotte! What are you doing up here? You are supposed to be in bed." Johanna did her best to sound normal, but she could hear the breathiness in her voice from the fright her sister had given her.

Charlotte's pale eyes seemed to glow from within as she glided up to Johanna in her stark white nightgown that went down to the floor. The blonde braid resting against the fabric was only a shade or two darker than it. Charlotte smiled dreamily and held out her hand, closed into a fist, like she was holding something that she wanted to give to Johanna.

Johanna reached for her sister's hand, her palm and fingers cupped to receive it.

The cool weight hit her palm, and she closed her fingers around it to stop it from falling to the ground.

Without a word, her sister glided around her—she'd barely paused to drop the thing in Johanna's hand—and went for the door. It opened just before she reached it, and Nettie shrieked loud enough to wake the house, jumping back and slapping her hand against her heart.

"Miss Charlotte!" She gasped out the words, shaking her head. "I wish you would not do that."

"Sorry, Nettie." Charlotte's voice was floaty, just as eerie as the rest of her, as she glided forward. With how long her nightgown was, her feet were invisible, and it looked like she was floating off into the darkness of the hall. Nattie paused, looking torn.

"She does not have far to go; she will be fine," Johanna reassured Nettie and shook her head. "We should worry more about those who might run into her at this hour and the fright they will take."

"That is the God's honest truth," Nettie said, crossing herself and shaking her head. "That child is as sweet as can be, other than how much she enjoys scaring us out of our wits."

"You get used to her eventually," Johanna promised. Though it was a difficult promise to make when Charlotte had just scared her out of her own wits as well. She sighed. "It might be that our family got a little too used to her, and she is enjoying having fresh victims."

Smiling ruefully, Johanna turned so Nettie could undo the laces on the back of her dress.

"That girl." Nettie sighed, but her tone of voice was fond if exasperated. Charlotte had that effect on people. So did Bridget, though for entirely different reasons.

As Nettie undid her laces, Johanna looked down at the item Charlotte had dropped into her hand. It was a silver circle, the same size as a silver crown, but shiny and flat. No, not entirely flat. After Nettie had helped Johanna out of her dress, she lifted it closer to her face, and she could see the extremely faint edges of what used to be on it. It had been rubbed nearly flat, to the point where the images were indecipherable.

"What on earth..." she murmured, then paused as the strangest thought occurred to her.

But that made no sense.

How would Matthew even make use of such a thing? Which side was which was indefinable.

How would Charlotte have gotten it?

"Anything else, Your Grace?" Nettie asked.

Johanna realized with a start that her maid had finished the usual procedure of getting her to bed. She was more tired than she'd realized.

"No, thank you, Nettie. I will ring for you in the morning."

"Yes, Your Grace."

As Nettie left the room, Johanna flipped the silver circle over and over again, examining both sides closely. She could not tell the difference between the sides.

Is it possible...

The door between her and Matthew's room opened, making her start as he came into the room, grinning. He was wearing his dressing gown, which gaped open at the chest as it had been tied too loosely, revealing that he was wearing nothing underneath it.

"You were taking too long," he said with a wink, coming toward her.

"Charlotte was waiting for me," she replied, holding out her hand with the circle of silver flat on her fingers. "She gave me this."

It only took him a moment to glimpse the circle, then he let out a cry of joy as he rushed the last few steps to meet her, taking hold of her hand with one of his and picking up the silver from her palm.

"My coin!"

Johanna stared at him in disbelief.

CHAPTER FORTY-FIVE

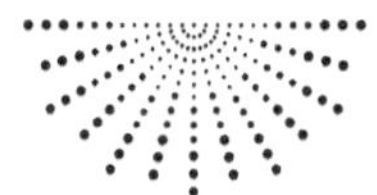

The rush of relief Matthew felt as his fingers closed around his coin was full of joy, but it did not last very long. As soon as he held it in his hand, his thoughts pushed past the initial emotion reaction as he realized he had not needed it to make his decisions. His world had not fallen apart without it. In fact, there had been a kind of freedom in doing what he wanted, even making it through some of the hardest decisions he'd ever had to make.

"Matthew." Johanna's voice was odd. "That is your lucky coin?"

"Yes." He rubbed his thumb across its surface. Even though he was now uncertain as to how he truly felt about its return, he had to admit that he still liked having it in his hand. Feeling it.

"Matthew. How can you tell which side is which?"

"What do you mean?" He met his wife's troubled violet gaze. Her peignoir was open, revealing the filmy lilac silk nightrail underneath, cream lace edging the neckline. The view was decidedly distracting, but her expression was more worried than anything else.

"Matthew." Her voice was gentle as she reached out to cup his hand holding the coin with both of hers. "Look at the coin. Really look at it." She pushed his hand a little higher, and Matthew looked down at it. "You have rubbed it nearly flat on both sides. How can you tell which side is which?"

"I..." He stared at the coin. Used his thumb to flip it over on his palm. The other side looked exactly the same. Just as she said. He'd noticed the sides wearing down over the years, but he'd always been able to tell which was which at a glance.

Now that he was staring straight at it, he could not decipher the difference.

Perhaps it was not the right coin?

But he knew it was. He'd recognized it the moment that she'd held it out to him. Matthew slowly used his thumb to flip it over again.

Flat. Both sides were almost completely flat with no discernible difference between them.

"I..." He could not find the words to explain how he'd always known. "I just knew, I suppose. I would just look at it, and I would know."

How long had his coin been like this? How could he possibly have known what the decision was? Yet somehow, he always had.

Johanna still held his hand cupped in hers, her gentle touch keeping him anchored through the storm of emotions sweeping through him as the questions, the confusion, cascaded over him.

"I do not know." He shook his head, suddenly wishing he could drop the coin, so he did not have to look at it. Did not have to think about it again. "I do not know how I knew. I..." The strangest thought occurred to him. "What if I just saw what I wanted to see?"

"Perhaps you did." His wife smiled at him, her fingers curling around his, closing his fist around the coin. "Perhaps you were making the decisions all along without realizing it."

"Not all along. It did not use to look like that." Matthew shook his head. "I do not know when it might have changed. It must have done so slowly enough that I did not really notice."

"Which means you chose to marry me." Her smile had turned rather brilliant. "Not the coin."

"Yes... I... yes, I did." That was what that meant. He'd seen her on that stage, and his first thought had not been to purchase her to rescue her, but to marry her. Which was exactly what he'd done because he'd wanted to… It was not so long ago that his coin would have had its sides.

How very odd to discover that *now*.

Stepping into him, Johanna went up on her tiptoes, pressing her lips to his. Their arms bent, hands still together between their bodies, the coin trapped in his fist. Matthew moved his other arm to hold her, keeping her from stepping away as he kissed her back, his tongue sliding into her mouth to deepen the kiss.

When he lifted his head again, she was smiling up at him, her eyes sparkling like the amethyst jewels she'd worn tonight.

"Are there any other important decisions you would like to make this evening?" she asked, teasingly.

"Actually… yes." Matthew glanced over to her vanity, where the jewels were sitting. "There is something I have fantasized ever since I brought you home."

"Oh?"

✦

JOHANNA

Bedecked in a tiara, necklace, earrings, and bracelet, but nothing else, Johanna could not help but blush as Matthew stared at her. She was now standing in front of his bed, entirely naked to his gaze, other than the jewelry, and the way he was looking at her made her feel utterly wicked. The metal was cool against her skin, but the heat of desire coiling inside her kept her warm.

"You are so beautiful," he murmured, smoothing his hand over his dressing gown.

Johanna did not entirely know how to respond to that.

"Thank you, Your Grace," she said, blushing furiously and trying to tease him rather than give in to the embarrassment. His eyes flashed.

"Oh. I do like hearing you call me that, kitten," he said, walking toward her. Johanna's head tilted back as he came closer, her gaze holding his. His dressing gown was soft against her skin as he trapped her between his body and the bed, making her nipples pucker against the soft velvet. Her insides throbbed in response.

Bending down, his lips brushed over hers, and she hummed low in her throat as an anticipatory shiver went down her spine.

"Are the jewels the only part of your fantasy?" she asked.

"Oh, no." He grinned wickedly, pressing his lips more firmly against hers for a kiss. "They are just the beginning."

Johanna squeaked as he stepped back while keeping his hold on her, just enough so he could bodily lift her and settle her onto the bed with her back against the pillows. His gaze was hot with desire as he stripped off his dressing gown, leaving himself bare. Crawling onto the bed, he lowered his upper body between her legs, his shoulders pushing her thighs wider as she watched him.

Their gazes caught and held as he lowered his mouth to her pussy, watching her as his tongue slid between her nether lips. Johanna moaned, her eyelashes fluttering at the touch of his tongue on her heated flesh. His hands slid under her thighs and up to caress her sides, then moved up to cup her breasts as he began to feast.

Gasping at the sensations as his hands cradled her breasts, squeezing and kneading the soft flesh, his tongue going to work on her sensitive folds and pearl, Johanna clutched at the bedsheet beneath her. Her heels pressed into his upper back as she whimpered from the sensations now coursing through her.

Matthew's head lifted for just a moment, his eyes flashing.

"Hands up, kitten. Hold on to the headboard. I want you completely open to me."

The order made her insides clench, and she lifted her arms above her head, reaching for the headboard. With the pillows behind her, she had to stretch to grasp the spindles, pushing her breasts up into his hands. He pinched her taut nipples, and her grip tightened on the hard wood as she jolted in reaction. It hurt, but it felt so good.

His tongue delved between her folds, teasing her, tasting her.

Johanna moaned, moving her hips up and down, pressing her pussy against his mouth as pleasure ignited through her body.

One hand left her breasts, and he shifted, suckling on her clit for a moment before letting it go. She cried out at the sensation, her body pulsing in reaction.

"I want you to do something for me, kitten," he murmured.

Johanna moaned as she felt his fingers press against the opening of her pussy.

"Yes, Your Grace?" Again, she tried to be teasing, especially after his previous reaction, but she sounded more breathless than mischievous.

Matthew chuckled and began to slide his long fingers into her wet heat, stroking her insides and making her gasp and arch again.

"Do not climax until I give you permission."

Johanna's pussy clamped down around his invading fingers, the growing pleasure distracting her, and it took her a moment to fully comprehend his words.

"What?"

His fingers pumped, stroking her insides.

"Do not climax until I give you permission," he repeated. "You are my good girl, yes?"

"Yes..." She moaned, tightening, as his thumb brushed over the sensitive nub, sending a shock of pleasure through her.

"I want you to do your best to hold off your climax until I give you permission. Do you think you can do that for me?"

"I... do not know," she admitted, flexing her fingers around the spindles of the headboard again. She was already so close to her pinnacle, and he wanted her to hold it off? Was such a thing even possible?

His deep chuckle was full of sinful promise.

"Let us find out."

Johanna opened her mouth to protest, but his fingers thrust again, his mouth descending on her pussy, and all that came out as a moan as her lower body tightened. Somehow, some way, she had to stave off the growing ecstasy. She tried to squirm away, but the hand still on her breast now left and wrapped over her hips, holding her in place for his mouth.

She cried out as his fingers thrust again, stroking inside her, hitting a spot that made her entire body jerk against his hold. Her head fell back, thighs trying to tighten around him, to no avail, as the sensations rippled through her. Whimpering, she closed her eyes, trying to fight back against the rising tide of passion.

Matthew

His wife's body, bedecked in jewels, while she held onto the headboard, was everything Matthew had wanted to see. The taste of her on his tongue, the way her body clenched around his fingers, her moans of pleasure, were utter perfection. She wore the jewels of a princess while he made depraved plans for her body.

Because he already knew she was not going to be able to keep from climaxing. That was just part of the game. Part of the fantasy that had been building in his mind since their marriage. He wanted her to fight it and fail... then he could spank her and claim her completely.

His fingers curled inside her, stroking that sensitive spot, as he licked all around her clit. The salty sweetness of her cream was pure aphrodisiac, and his cock throbbed in response.

"Matthew!" She cried out his name as he sucked her clit into his mouth. "I cannot... I cannot... Please..."

Her begging was sweet music to his ears. He felt her insides clamp down on his fingers as her body arched.

Releasing her clit, he went back to licking around it as she whimpered and strained. Holding her in place as she attempted to writhe, he twisted his arm so he could rub his thumb over the tiny crinkled hole he planned to plunder before the night was over. It was already slick from the sweet cream spreading from her pussy, and she gasped, hips jerking in reaction to his touch.

"Please, Matthew, I need permission," she begged, and the headboard creaked, emphasizing her plea. "I cannot... I cannot..."

Her body bowed.

"No."

Matthew denied her request, then moved his mouth back to her clitoris, sucking the pleasure nubbin between his lips and sliding his tongue across it. His wife screamed as forbidden ecstasy exploded inside her. Matthew held her down in place as he sucked and sucked, sending her on wave after wave of wicked erotic bliss.

Only when she was limp and panting did he release her from his grip, pushing himself up and grinning as he looked down at her forlorn expression.

"Oh, dear, kitten," he purred. "You've been a very naughty girl. Whatever shall I do with you?"

CHAPTER FORTY-SIX

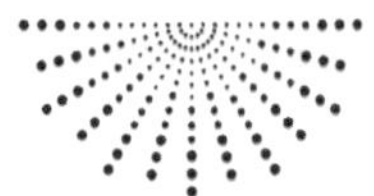

"That was not fair!" Johanna felt her face flush as she stared up at her husband. She'd tried so hard to obey and fight against the pleasure, but he'd tricked her! And she had felt bad about not being able to obey!

Matthew chuckled as he put his fingers in his mouth, cleaning her juices from them.

"What was not fair, kitten?" he asked, bending over her to kiss one of her nipples. The little nub had started to soften but quickly budded as he sucked it between his lips. Johanna gasped, her body extra sensitive after the rush of pleasure from her climax, and let go of the headboard to grab at his head.

Immediately, Matthew released her nipple and took hold of her wrists, pulling them together so he could hold them with one hand. Shaking his head, he made a clucking sound.

"I did not tell you that you could let go of the headboard," he said in a light, scolding tone. "My, my, you are being a very naughty kitten tonight."

Heat and cold rushed through her body, at both the unfairness, yet the thrill she got from being called a naughty kitten. She'd meant to be his good girl, but now that was impossible… and the fact he obviously was enjoying her being his naughty kitten instead did all sorts of interesting things inside her body. It did not matter that she'd just climaxed; there was still a deep need aching inside her, and his words only amplified it.

"I did not know," she whined, but it did not matter. He was already repositioning himself, using his hold on her wrists to pull her over his lap. She caught a glimpse of his hard cock before she was in position and felt it digging into her side. The tiara tilted on her head, reminding her that she was wearing it, and something about that made her blush even harder.

She was wearing jewels fit for a queen, but she was Matthew's naughty little kitten, and he was going to spank her for it. The juxtaposition was very arousing for some reason.

"Let's see… climaxing without permission, letting go of the headboard without permission, and sassing a duke." Matthew put one hand on the middle of her back while the other caressed her bottom. "That's quite a punishment you've racked up there, kitten."

"But—"

Before she could protest, his hand had lifted and come down on her upturned bottom, making her shriek.

The sensitivity of her body post-climax remained, and the stinging burn from the swat went straight through her to her core. Gasping, Johanna rocked forward, but his hand on her back held her in place, and his palm came cracking down on her other cheek.

It hurt, yet it made her insides clench at the same time, the same way they'd clenched around his fingers while his tongue worked her over. Again and again, his hand came down, peppering her bottom, heating her skin and her insides. Johanna squirmed on his lap as heat and need began to curl inside her, offsetting the stinging pain from the swats.

"Ow!" She tried to buck against his hand.

The heat was growing, and since she could not get away, the only thing she could try to do was put her hands back over to cover her bottom. Even as she moved, deep down, she knew the attempt would be useless, but she could not stop herself from trying.

Matthew just chuckled again, catching her wrists and pinning them with the hand that had been pressing down on the middle of her back.

"Very naughty kitten," he scolded. "Trying to get out of your punishment."

"It hurts!" She squirmed, but it did no good, which just excited her more.

"If it hurts so much, why are you so aroused?" he asked, dipping his fingers into her pussy.

Johanna would have liked to say that it was left over from before, but what came out of her lips was a heated moan. There was a part of her that very much enjoyed being over his knee, with his hand coming down on her bottom. There was a part of her that felt the stinging swats, felt the burn, yet somehow derived pleasure from it.

MATTHEW

His poor, confused kitten.

Matthew's cock throbbed against her soft side as he watched her struggling with her desires. She was so sweetly submissive and so shocked by how he could play her body like a fiddle. Pulling his fingers from her, he stuck them in his mouth, cleaning them off with his tongue for the second time that night.

Delicious.

The pink of her bottom was bright against the pale translucence of her skin, splotchy in places where his hand had landed multiple times. Now, with her hands pinned to the center of her back, he could enjoy the view of her amethyst bracelet shimmering on her wrist while he spanked her. The only downside to having her over his lap like this was the inability to see the regal jewelry adorning her while he debased her.

"Ten more," he declared. "For trying to cover yourself during your punishment."

"Oh, please—"

Her little shriek as his hand came down on the sit spot between the curve of her bottom and her thighs was delightful. That sensitive area had so far gone unmarked, and Matthew decided to attend to it now. Back and forth, her right leg, then her left leg, again and again, until he'd delivered five to each, and her cries were becoming tearful.

There now. That was a very nice hot bottom.

"Good girl," he said soothingly, smoothing his hand over her hot skin, feeling the heat against his palm. She panted for breath, shuddering as he caressed her. "Good girl for taking your punishment so well."

"It still was not fair," his stubborn kitten muttered.

Matthew grinned. "Ah, well, still feeling sassy, sweetness? Perhaps you need more."

"No!" She squeaked out the word. "I do not!"

"Hmm." A glint of silver from the nightstand, where he'd put his coin before decking his wife out in her jewels, caught his eye, and he grinned. "Well, we shall let the coin decide."

"But you cannot tell which side is which!" she protested, squirming as he leaned over to pick up the coin.

Matthew shrugged, even though she could not see the movement. "That is what you say, but I have been using it to make all my decisions, remember?"

The little growling noise she made was truly adorable. He chuckled and flipped the coin, slapping it down against her hot bottom. Which was truly becoming his favorite way to do a coin flip. He had assumed he would never have his coin in the future to use for his decisions, accepted that it was lost, and now that he had it back, he knew he did not need it… but he anticipated there would be 'decisions' he would use it for in exactly this manner of flip in the future.

"You are just choosing what it says!" Johanna squirmed again as he lifted his hand from her hot buttocks.

"Ah, yes. The coin says you need more punishment. Naughty girl sex should do it."

His wife froze over his lap. Twisted her head around. Her face was flushed, tiara askew, hair mussed.

"What is naughty girl sex?" she asked, a slight tremor in her voice, but she could not hide her curious interest.

Matthew chuckled as he drew her up against him.

***

JOHANNA

Once more, Johanna found herself gripping the headboard with her back against the pillows, though now she had a burning bottom, her tiara felt permanently askew, and she was flushed from being over Matthew's lap. With her legs wide open and draped over his forearms while he kneeled between them, she squealed against his lips as his oiled finger pushed into the narrow aperture of her bottom.

Rather than answering her question about naughty girl sex, he'd gotten her into position and ordered her to remain holding onto the headboard while he opened the nightstand and got out a small bottle. The oil inside gleamed on his fingers.

Johanna had not understood what it was for until this moment.

Her cheeks flushed hotter than ever as he wickedly thrust his fingers deeper into the tight hole, his gaze boring into hers, making the sinful act almost unbearably intimate. Because he'd told her to hold on to the headboard, she could not even cover her face with her hands.

"Look at me, kitten," he murmured, twisting his fingers inside her, making her squeak as her eyes flew open at the odd sensation.

It did not hurt, exactly, especially in comparison to the way her bottom cheeks were burning from the spanking, but it was hardly comfortable, either. Yet having him touch her in such a base, perverse manner also aroused her to the point where she could feel her pussy fluttering, as if she had not recently been worked to the point of climax.

Looking at her husband, watching him watch her as his fingers invaded her so horribly intimate was both awful and wonderful. Johanna whimpered as he moved his fingers inside her bottom, staring back at him as heat crawled over her body, blooming in her face. The sting of the spanking was fading under the embarrassment of what he was doing to her.

How it was making her feel.

When he withdrew his fingers, wiping them on a nearby cloth he'd procured—she'd wondered why he'd brought that to the bed—he fisted his cock and pressed the oiled tip to her bottom.

"Oh!" Johanna gasped, arching and her fingers tightening around the spindles of the headboard as her tiny hole was stretched to receive him. His cock was much thicker than his fingers, the discomfort increasing as he slowly pushed inside her tight channel, the burn making her want to writhe… but she could not because of the way her legs were draped over him. "It's too much!"

"No, it's not," he murmured, slowly continuing to slide into her bottom. "You can take it for me, kitten. You feel so good around my cock. So hot and tight. You want to please me, don't you, naughty girl?"

"Yes!" A little sob caught in her throat as the assault on her senses increased when he retreated slightly, only to thrust forward again, going deeper this time, opening her farther. He felt impossibly large, filling her in a manner she'd never imagined.

He was using her bottom because she was a naughty girl.

This was what naughty girls got.

And she did want to take it for him. To please him.

"That's it, good girl," he murmured as he thrust in deeper. His hands slid up to her breasts, bending her body in half because of her legs draped over his arms, squeezing the soft flesh. Johanna moaned as he pinched her nipples, pulling back and thrusting in, opening her inch by inch.

She was being his good girl by letting him use her in such a perverse manner for his own pleasure.

Taking the discomfort, the burn, and pushing past it for him.

"Look at me, kitten," he commanded.

Johanna's gaze clashed with his again, just as his body pressed up against hers, his cock fully embedded inside her. It felt like the very breath had been driven from her body; she was too full of him to have room for anything else.

"Good girl." He pinched her nipples again.

She moaned, her muscles clenching around him, squeezing his cock within her. Despite the discomfort, despite the pain—or maybe because of it—her arousal was growing all over again. Johanna whimpered, then gasped, as he began to withdraw.

The sensation was unnerving, like a pulling deep within her, so it was almost a relief when he reversed directions halfway and thrust back into her. The thrust burned, her body throbbing in response as he filled her again, and she arched up against his hands on her breasts.

"Matthew!" she cried his name as he began to move, sliding halfway out of her slickened channel and pushing back in with slow, firm thrusts that set her body afire.

He was gentler, slower—at least at first.

As his passion rose, so did his pace, and Johanna found herself straining, clenching around him as though her body was trying to slow his thrusts. The sensations were too intense, yet she had no choice but to bear them.

She could feel the necklace around her throat bouncing on her chest as he moved harder, faster, rocking her body with every thrust. His low groan filled the air as his hands shifted to slide away from her breasts, curving under her and holding her in place for him to pound into. It hurt, but it felt so good at the same time, and Johanna was shocked when she realized another climax was building within her.

As if sensing her growing ecstasy, Matthew's hand slipped out from under her, moving down to press over her mound, his thumb sliding between them to rub against her pleasure nub. Johanna's mouth opened in a silent scream as he rubbed over the tiny bud, sending shocking waves of pleasure rippling through her with every thrust of his cock.

It should not feel so good.

She truly was a naughty girl for enjoying this, but she could not stop the rush of ecstasy that crashed through her, his thumb working on her pleasure as he moved within her. Johanna's head thrashed back and forth as she found her voice again, crying out his name as another climax crashed over her, racking her senses and sending her reeling.

MATTHEW

The sight of his wife creaming herself while he used her arse, looking like a fairy princess in amethysts that he was using for base pleasure, was Matthew's undoing. His own pleasure bubbled up and burst, and he buried himself in her tight, clenching hole as she sobbed his name. The rippling muscles within her milked him as he spurted his seed, sucking every last drop from him as he gasped and shuddered against her.

Groaning, he lowered his forehead to hers, still fully embedded within her, as he let her legs slip down on either side of him. Their hot breath mingled, and he ran his hands up and down her sides, enjoying her little whimpers as he touched her.

"That's my good girl," he murmured, and felt her clench around him all over again. "See? The coin is always right."

A reluctant laugh huffed from between her lips, and Matthew grinned as he pressed his mouth to hers, stealing another kiss.

"You are incorrigible," she whispered to him.

"Mmm. You can let go of the headboard now, kitten. I want to feel you touch me." That was all he needed to say. She immediately wrapped her arms around his neck. He was still embedded in her bottom, half-hard and reluctant to leave the tight, slippery warmth. The feel of her hands on him stirred his senses. "Good girl."

The smile that lit up her expression was almost shy.

"I like being your good girl," she admitted.

Matthew chuckled, angling a kiss over her chin and down her throat.

"Do you like being my naughty girl, too?"

She giggled as his face brushed against a ticklish spot on her throat.

"I do."

"And do you like being my sweet kitten?"

"Meow."

Matthew chuckled, bending his head to press a kiss to her breast, working his way to her nipple. She gasped as he sucked the little bud into his mouth, suckling it back to hardness, and his cock twitched within her. Her arms and legs tightened around him.

"Oh… Matthew…"

He lifted his head.

"I love you, kitten." He bent to take her other nipple in his mouth, and she whimpered again, squirming in his arms.

"I love you, Matthew." She slid her fingers into his hair as he bit down gently on the turgid bud. "Oh… but I cannot possibly…"

"Cannot possibly what?" he asked, lifting his head again and rocking slightly within her. His cock was already hardening again, thickening within her tight channel.

"Is it possible to have too much pleasure?" she asked, then moaned as he rocked again, his cock lengthening, using the slick mix of oil and his seed to ease its passage. "Oh God… Matthew…"

"Let us find out," he whispered against her breast, as he began to move again.

Much, much later, freshly cleaned and sated, he curled up around his exhausted wife and pressed a kiss to the back of her neck, his softened cock limp between her abused cheeks. Whether or not his grandmother had been right, and he had flipped a coin for love, he knew one thing was true…

The day he'd purchased his bride had been the luckiest day of his life.

EPILOGUE

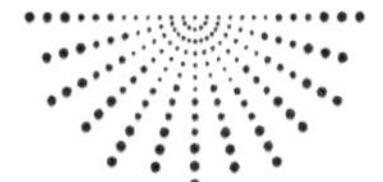

Having to eat one's own words was a difficult thing, but sometimes it must be done. Sebastian braced himself when his butler, Riggs, appeared in the doorway of his study.

"Miss Hu is here, Your Grace," he said, blank-faced in that manner that he often was, making it impossible to tell whether he approved. If he knew who Miss Hu was, he might not.

Sebastian frowned.

"Not Lady Hu?" he asked.

He'd contacted Lady Hu, the matchmaker, not her granddaughter. Miss Hu was...

"No, just Miss Hu, Your Grace." Riggs' expression did not change, but Sebastian felt somehow sure there was disapproval there. Or perhaps it was his own emotions he was feeling.

"Yes. Well." Sebastian cleared his throat. "Send her in." He could not, in good conscience, send her away without at least greeting her. If she were not friends with his sister and the wives of several of his friends, it might be different, but he would hear about it for days if he did not meet with her.

He would likely hear about it for days over using a matchmaker, regardless, but it would be far worse if he made an appointment, then sent her away. Even if he had made the appointment with Lady Hu and not her granddaughter.

Riggs returned a moment later with Miss Hu.

At least Sebastian was braced for seeing her again.

She was, in a word, stunning.

It was not just the wealth of her long ebony hair, the velvet of her dark brown eyes, or the pink rosebud of her perfectly formed lips… It was also the way she held herself. With confidence. With self-assurance. With a kind of calm that emanated from her, regardless of what was happening around her. Considering she'd been swimming through the upper echelons of British Society for several months now, those were admirable traits to have. Especially in comparison to the near-frenetic energy of most debutantes.

Every time he encountered her, he was struck with a completely unfathomable desire to be near her. Closer to her. Which, of course, was ridiculous.

Dukes did not mingle with matchmakers.

It was all well and good for the ladies and his married friends, but he was not looking to have a matchmaker decide his future for him.

Well.

He had not been.

The situation had changed. Because he needed a wife and heir, but he also needed to be free to leave London and return to his estate. He and his friends had finally identified a new thread to pull in the investigation into who had murdered their fathers, and that thread required he return home.

Sebastian was itching to do so and to discover whether Aaron Heywood was indeed currently employed by him, and if the man had anything to do with the death of his father and the other dukes. It was possible the man Tiffany remembered was not Aaron Heywood, but Sebastian did not believe in such coincidences.

Right now, he needed to be both in London and at his estate, at the same time. Such a thing was impossible, and it had become too difficult to try to choose a bride in haste when there were so many options. Sebastian hoped Lady Hu would be able to help him narrow down his options and perhaps even help him choose the perfect one.

He had hoped to have as little to do with her granddaughter as possible.

"Miss Hu," Riggs announced, appearing in Sebastian's doorway again, then stepping aside to admit the young lady as Sebastian got to his feet.

Bracing himself for the effect she always had on him, Sebastian did his best not to notice how very charming her emerald-green-and-black outfit was. She often wore traditional Chinese garments, though he had seen her occasionally don a more English style of dress. Today, she had opted for the former, her hair up in a complicated-looking knot with sticks pinning it in place, small charms hanging from the ends.

"Miss Hu," he said, bowing in greeting and gesturing to one of the chairs across from his desk. "Please, have a seat. I take it your grandmother is not joining us today?"

If she heard the censure in his voice, she did not show it. Gliding forward, Miss Hu smiled at him. A small social smile, the kind she usually wore when dealing with Society. Sebastian had seen her real smile, the one she used with her friends, and this was not it.

To be disappointed that she used her social smile with him instead was ridiculous.

"Your Grace." She curtsied before seating herself and folding her hands neatly on her lap as she studied him. Cool, calm, collected, and with a gaze that seemed to pierce right through him. Sometimes, he wondered exactly what it was she saw as an outsider looking into the intricacies and foibles of upper-crust English Society. As ever, her face was a mask, hiding her opinions. "Unfortunately, my grandmother is not feeling well today. I assure you, everything we discuss will be passed on from me to her but otherwise held in confidence."

"Right." Sebastian smoothed his hand over his waistcoat as he sat down. "I suppose you mean that you will not discuss my request for your grandmother's services with my sister and the others?" He raised his eyebrow, but Miss Hu nodded serenely.

"That is exactly what I mean. Of course, if you are pleased with the match, it would be lovely if you would pass on a recommendation to others, but it is not a requirement."

If she remembered his statements about dukes not needing matchmakers, she did not indicate it, by word or look. Whatever her thoughts about him, they were carefully tucked away in her mind.

Strangely, he believed she would not tell Tiffany or her other friends that he was acquiring her grandmother's services. He did not have to eat crow unless he chose to. Though it hardly seemed honorable to reap a benefit without acknowledgment where acknowledgment was due.

He would cross that bridge when he came to it.

"Yes. Well." Sebastian studied her. Facing her instead of her grandmother was making him feel rather unbalanced.

If she was at all discomfited, it did not show.

"Perhaps we should start with your requirements," she suggested. "What attributes would you like your wife to have?"

That did seem the proper place to start, yet it felt very odd to be discussing such things with a woman. A young woman, at that, of the same age as the ladies he would be courting. Part of the appeal of using her grandmother was that the matrons of the *ton* tended to assist their sons and grandsons with matrimonial matters.

His mother, unfortunately, could not be trusted.

Not after he'd seen the way she was with Tiffany. Not after he'd realized there was an entire side of her that he had never known existed and that she could be so awful to his sister. There was still a part of him that could not believe it, but he had seen it with his own eyes, heard her cruel words with his own ears. She'd insisted he did not understand, but he'd still exiled her to the countryside to rusticate for the rest of this Season.

Sebastian cleared his throat. Miss Hu would be passing the information along to her grandmother. Perhaps he could pretend she *was* her grandmother. His gaze dropped to the desk in front of him, as looking at her did not help with the pretense.

"The ability to run my household," he said. "So, she must be intelligent. Beautiful. Kind. Able to hold a conversation."

"What would you like to be able to converse with her about?" Miss Hu asked.

Was there a hint of amusement in her voice? Sebastian glanced up at her. If there was, it did not show in her expression.

"Art? Music? History? Current events? Politics?"

Sebastian stared at her. Was she jesting? Most debutantes he met could scarcely talk about the first two topics. His sister was a bit of a bluestocking, and even she eschewed history and politics, and her interest in current events was focused on whatever musical talent was being featured at the opera.

"Whatever interests her," he finally said. Which got his first response from Miss Hu as her delicate eyebrows rose for just a moment before returning to her blank expression.

"Interesting," she said after a moment. "No preferred subjects at all?"

"Truly engaging conversation happens when at least one of the participants is enthusiastic about the topic," he said, fighting the urge to twitch. Part of him wanted to ask if she should be writing some of this down for her grandmother, but the intense scrutiny of her gaze convinced him it was unnecessary. He only wanted to ask because her intent contemplation of him was so unnerving, and he knew it. "If it is something that she is passionate about, the conversation will be far superior. Hopefully, she will also enjoy listening to my interests, but I do not expect her to cater to them exclusively."

There was another long moment, and he swore he felt like Miss Hu was studying him even harder. As if that were possible.

"What interests would you say you have?" she asked when the silence stretched.

Before he could answer, there was the sudden sound of a commotion down the hall—quite a commotion since anything happening in the foyer that was loud enough to be heard in his study was *very* loud. And it did not immediately quiet. There were quite a few raised voices, as well as what sounded like the banging of very heavy objects being put down on the floor.

Frowning, Sebastian got to his feet.

"Excuse me, Miss Hu," he said. "I should see what is going on. Please wait here."

He had just rounded the desk, Miss Hu's alert gaze following him, when Riggs came running into the room. Sebastian gaped at him. Riggs *never* ran.

"Your Grace... Her Grace..." The man was positively puffing, looking as though he was about to have an apoplexy, even though it was a very short distance to run.

"Which her Grace?" Sebastian asked immediately, a sick feeling stirring in his stomach. But no. Surely not. He'd made himself completely clear—

"Your lady mother—" Riggs was cut off as the woman in question appeared in the doorway to Sebastian's study.

Dressed in a dramatic gown of chartreuse and ivory, her Grace, the Duchess of Bolton, came to a halt and beamed at Sebastian as if her presence in the London house was not against his express orders.

"There's my darling boy!" It was the same way she always greeted him when they'd been apart for any length of time, and Sebastian felt the tug in his chest. The boy, the young man, who wanted his mother's attention and affection, who was so happy to see her.

Right now, looking at her bright smile, it was hard to remember how she'd spoken to Tiffany. Hard to believe she'd shrieked at him like a harpy the last time they'd spoken and told him that he was breaking her heart and that she would likely die from it before he laid eyes on her again.

Seeing her now, looking at him with the warmth and love she always did, it felt like maybe he'd dreamed that last conversation. That perhaps he was somehow misremembering it. Because surely, she would not be smiling like this now if it had truly been that bad. Yet he knew it had been, so he could not align what had happened with her smiling joy now.

"Mother," he said, after a beat. "What are you doing here?"

She trilled a laugh.

"What am I doing here? Why I am here to help you find a bride, of course!"

The blood in Sebastian's veins froze. He looked from his mother to the stoic Miss Hu, then back to his mother.

Bloody hell.

SEBASTIAN, HIS MATCHMAKER, AND HIS MOTHER RETURN IN THE DUKE'S Indecent Desires.

ISABELLA'S DIARY - ENTRY 3

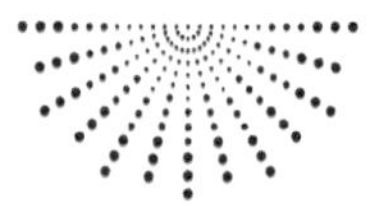

News of another marriage among Sinclair's friends has come. I was not invited to this wedding, because it happened so hastily.

Matthew is married.

I can only imagine how Sinclair would laugh...

We always joked that Matthew might never marry if his coin did tell him to. Perhaps it did.

Eventually I will find out.

I have come to accept that my mourning must come to an end eventually.

Most days, Sinclair is no longer at the forefront of my thoughts anymore. He slips in there from time to time, but sometimes hours go on before I remember now. I miss him with an ache that is ever present, but also beginning to fade into acceptance.

Life goes on.

Our friends get married.

William has begun to hint that he would like to marry me.

He does not say so outright, of course, but when he talks of the estate, he speaks of how I was always meant to be its lady. How Sinclair had chosen aright in his duchess. That, as Sinclair's best man and heir, it is his duty to take care of me.

I have no indicated that I understand his hints, as yet. Part of me wonders if I should even consider becoming William's duchess, because how can I live at Northumberland without Sinclair? How can I have the life we were meant to have together with someone else?

And yet it feels equally wrong to consider marrying anyone else.

I know I must marry eventually.

My parents have begun to make stronger hints about ending my mourning and moving back into Society. They're delighted to welcome William to the house and I believe he must have spoken to my father about his intentions, even though he has not said them outright to me.

Eventually, I know they will force the issue.

Is it not better to be able to choose my own husband, rather than allowing them to do so for me?

Mother is doing her best, but father is growing impatient. They are not a love match. They do not understand.

I do not think he will force the issue with William, if I am against it, but he will find some man. Then I will be married, possibly to a stranger, someone who might take me far away from Sinclair.

If I marry William and become the Duchess of Northumberland, I will still be close to Sinclair. In a way. As close as I possibly can be in this life, under these circumstances.

I could return to Society. See his friends. Meet their wives.

I will do that eventually anyway, married to William or not. I do not miss the social whirl but... I would like to meet their new duchesses. See Lady Astrid and Delilah and perhaps ask their opinions on marrying William. I have no one to talk to about such things here.

Speaking of Delilah, I would also very much like to smack Zachary over the head. News of his engagement has reached me as well, and he is not engaged to Delilah, the utter bufflehead. I can only imagine the words Sinclair would have for him. I feel as though I should say some of them in Sinclair's place.

I have not been able to write him about it yet, because I do now know why he would propose to Lady Annabelle Walsh, rather than Delilah. Sinclair and I always assumed they would marry and that Zachary was just taking his time about it. I do not know what changed. Speaking to him in person would be best...

But I am not quite ready to leave the house.

Not yet.

Perhaps I could issue some invitations though... Perhaps I could have them come visit me.

I will have to think on it.

ACKNOWLEDGMENTS

I have a lot of people to thank for helping me with this book.

My amazing beta readers, who are invaluable in helping me catch mistakes, doing the initial grammar and word checks, identifying continuity issues, and working through problems with me. Marie, Candida, Marta, Rara, and Katherine – you all make these books so much better!

My Patreon readers who not only read ahead but are kind enough to give me invaluable feedback as they're reading.

Another extra special thank you to Katherine, who got me started down this career path and has been by my metaphorical side ever since.

And, as always, a big thank you to all of you for buying and reading my work… if you love it, please leave a review!

ABOUT THE AUTHOR

Golden Angel is a USA Today best-selling author of heart and bottom warming romance.

She is a big fan of happily-ever-afters, strong heroes and heroines, and sizzling chemistry.

When she's not writing, she can often be found on the couch reading, in front of her sewing machine making a new cosplay, hanging out with her friends, or wandering the Maryland Renaissance Fair.

www.goldenangelromance.com

BB bookbub.com/authors/golden-angel
g goodreads.com/goldeniangel
f facebook.com/GoldenAngelAuthor
o instagram.com/goldeniangel

OTHER TITLES BY GOLDEN ANGEL

HISTORICAL SPANKING ROMANCE

Domestic Discipline Quartet

Birching His Bride

Dealing With Discipline

Punishing His Ward

Claiming His Wife

The Domestic Discipline Quartet Box Set

Bridal Discipline Series

Philip's Rules

Gabrielle's Discipline

Lydia's Penance

Benedict's Commands

Arabella's Taming

Pride and Punishment Box Set

Commands and Consequences Box Set

Deception and Discipline

A Season for Treason

A Season for Scandal

A Season for Smugglers

A Season for Spies

Deception & Discipline boxset

Desire and Discipline

A Season for Bliss

A Season for Desire

A Season for Christmas

Indecent Dukes

The Duke's Indecent Scandal

The Duke's Indecent Match

The Duke's Indecent Purchase

The Duke's Indecent Desire

The Duke's Indecent Proposal

The Duke's Indecent Secret

The Duke's Indecent Courtship

Standalone

Marriage Training

The Duke's Pursuit

Rogue Booty

CONTEMPORARY BDSM ROMANCE

Venus Rising Series (MFM Romance)

The Venus School

Venus Aspiring

Venus Desiring

Venus Transcendent

Venus Wedding

Venus Rising Box Set

Stronghold Doms Series

The Sassy Submissive

Taming the Tease

Mastering Lexie

Pieces of Stronghold

Breaking the Chain

Bound to the Past

Stripping the Sub

Tempting the Domme

Hardcore Vanilla

Steamy Stocking Stuffers

A Sassy Christmas

Entering Stronghold Box Set

Nights at Stronghold Box Set

Stronghold: Closing Time Box Set

Masters of Marquis Series

Bondage Buddies

Master Chef

Law & Disorder

Switch Play

Legally Bound

Shallow Submission

Hidden Away

Secret Submission

Third Wheel

Masters of Pleasure Boxset

Masters of Control Boxset

Masters of Secrets Boxset

Black Fox Security Doms

Danger and Dominance

Cuffs and Cupcakes

Security and Submission

Whips and Weddings

Rescue and Ropes

Bondage and Bad Guys

Dungeons & Doms Series

Dungeon Master

Dungeon Daddy

Dungeon Showdown

Dungeons & Doms Boxset

Daddies Everywhere

Chef Daddy

Foosball Daddies

Taco Daddy

Cheese Daddy

Garden Daddy

Daddies Everywhere Boxset

Cherry Popping Daddies

Emily by Golden Angel

Lottie by Stella Moore

Titania by Raisa Greenwood

Standalone Daddy Dom

Little Villain

SCI-FI ROMANCE

Tsenturion Masters Series with Lee Savino

Alien Captive

Alien Tribute

Alien Abduction

Standalone

Mated on Hades

SHIFTER ROMANCE

Big Bad Bunnies Series

Chasing His Bunny

Chasing His Squirrel

Chasing His Puma

Chasing His Polar Bear

Chasing His Honey Badger

Chasing Her Lion

Night of the Wild Stags

Chasing Tail Box Set

Chasing Tail… Again Box Set